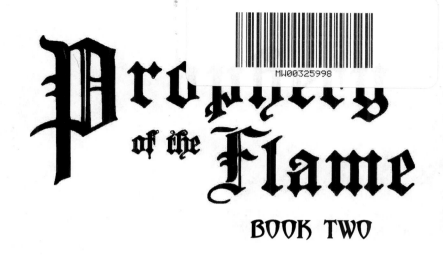

Prophecy of the Flame

BOOK TWO

LYNN HARDY

First Paperback Edition 2010 by
Resilient Publishing
P.O. Box 16043
Boise, Idaho

Resilient Publishing is an imprint of
Borderline Publishing
404 Broad
Boise, ID 83705

ISBN 978-0-165-36627-2

Edited by Andrea Howe at Blue Falcon Editing

Cover by Yivgeni Matoussov
Interior Illustrations by Yivgeni Matoussov

To my loving husband, who has graciously supported me in chasing my dreams.

BOOK TWO

Love's Price

Chapter One

I snuggle down into the feather bed, luxuriating in the downy softness, knowing I am awake but unwilling to leave. My mind recalls where I was last; the feel of strong arms surrounding me makes me tingle in anticipation. Scenes flash through my mind.

Jarovegi, wyverns, and ogres appear in terrifying detail. A leather-clad soldier slices into the neck of a four-legged monstrosity, only to forfeit his life as the acidic blood of the beast saturates his face, eventually penetrating the protection of the paladin stone to dissolve the flesh beneath.

"'Ware, behind you!" Sheridan's warning comes from my left.

Pivoting in her direction, I bring up my hand, ready for danger, but Sheridan's sprint to the charging monster with deadly claws puts her between the demon and me. She draws back to swing a mighty blow at the gremlin, separating its head from its shoulders. Time slows as the horror unfolds.

"No-o-o!" I roar.

Sheridan glances over her shoulder at me but continues to bend down: intent on retrieving the glowing red sphere the creature carried like a football. When the warrior's hand touches the ball of demon energy, her mouth contorts in pain. Black tendrils intertwine with the blue magical energy in her aura. The oozing strands brighten, glowing with a fierce, ruby light as the demonic spell is triggered.

My ears ring as an explosion sends every man within ten feet of the woman hurtling outward. Those that were closest to the royal guard lay in crumpled heaps. The swirling dust parts. There is no trace of Sheridan. Splattered gore and a ten-foot hole are all that remain of my brave defender.

That globe was meant for me. Her life for mine. If I had touched that glowing orb with as much power as I hold in my aura, a third of the town would have been decimated. It is a small comfort. I shrug off the vague and even more terrifying memory rising to the surface. Wiping my eyes, I throw back the covers, no longer having any desire to lounge in warm luxury.

"Milady, shall I have your bath prepared?" Crystal is instantly at my side. The buxom blonde who has become one of my closest friends brings a spark of warmth back into my soul.

I nod.

With a motion, Crystal dismisses Phedra to see to the tasks. The bouncing form of the preteen is another dismal reminder of the chaos my life has become. I was on this planet less than twenty-four hours, and I managed to orphan Phedra and her brother, Keth. *I didn't wield the weapon that killed their family, but I erected a force field around this city, a force field I didn't think through entirely. When the demons broke through, Phedra's family paid the ultimate price for my lack of forethought.*

My mind wanders to the guys who were strangers, mere days ago. Together, we were snatched from Earth and thrust into this magical world. Since our arrival in the kingdom of Cuthburan, some have become close friends; others I have learned to tolerate. We've all come a long way from that first day. . .

Has it really been only a week? Materializing as the characters we were playing in Merithin's tower was like a dream come true. Being endowed with the powers of our gaming characters took some getting used to; we are all still learning the limits to our abilities. Since being stranded in this magical world, we've bonded together like members of an army platoon. Now we truly are the Crusaders of the Light, fighting back the darkness threatening this world. Every day I spend here, Earth seems more and more like a dream.

The fair-haired maid approaches with a tray holding a pitcher of water and a glass. My mouth feels like I have spent a week in the Sahara. Seeing the shimmering liquid, I realize the cottonmouth and swollen tongue probably wouldn't have let me speak, had I tried.

I drain the glass three times. "Thank you, Crystal." With my tongue loosened, I ask the question that has plagued me since waking. "How did the Crusaders of the Light fare in the battle? I know Allinon survived, but I lost sight of the others after I took out that demon."

"All are well. Would you like me to summon them?" she queries.

"Let them rest. After what we've been through, they deserve it." A loud gurgling from my middle brings my speech to a halt. My cheeks redden.

"I was told food and water should be given when you awoke." Crystal tilts her head to one side. "You have recovered much quicker than expected. I apologize for my lapse."

"The fault isn't yours." I pause, taking a sip of water. "Merithin wasn't informed that I changed my bed into a regeneration chamber."

"Re-gin—what kind of chamber?" She is baffled by the long English word I use when I fail to find a Cuthburish term for *regenerate*.

"I enchanted the bed so I will heal faster," I expound.

She nods, shrugging off the talk of magic. Crystal continues as if just a few hours ago I hadn't been fighting creatures more horrifying than anything Stephen King ever dreamed of. "Since you recovered marks before they expected, milady, would you like me to fetch the correspondences that arrived this morning?"

I accept her offer to bring the work to me. *My limbs feel like I'm trying to move underwater. It's probably a side effect from the complete drain of magic from my system. Reclining in the enchanted bed for another mark should stabilize my aura and reenergize my body. Nature can take it from there after a few more hours of magical help.*

"My God, Crystal, what are those?" Tired enough not to censor my reaction, I gape at a tray loaded down with packages of all sizes. Satin ribbons are wrapped around cloth bundles like a rainbow puddle on the tray. Taking up almost half the surface, a massive blue package tied with a silver ribbon draws my attention.

"These, are tokens of appreciation milady." Setting the tray down on my lap, she goes to retrieve the writing utensils and a lap desk from the next room.

"Propriety dictates that gifts given for reasons other than amorous affection should be sent a brief reply in return,"

Crystal informs me as she deposits the writing tray on the stand next to the bed. "The one whose gift you choose to display as an adornment at the victory ball tonight need not be replied to. By wearing it, you state your favor rests with the giver."

"A ball? You must be joking! We leave for a campaign tomorrow at first light and they want to throw a party?" I snort. "Well, I will just reply to all of them. I have no intention of attending. Do I still need to show favor to one of the givers?"

Crystal's brow crinkles in puzzlement, but dutifully she answers. "Milady, wearing one of the gifts at the next opportunity would be adequate."

I dip my head, dismissing her to her other duties. I start with the smallest. *I'll work my way up to that big, blue one.* Undoing the ribbon, I open the cloth. Nestled in the center of olive-colored satin are three diamonds the size of my pinky. The austere note accompanying it reads, *With thanks and appreciation for the work of your hands.* It is signed, *Duke Rokroa of Kempmore.*

I work my way through the mound of gifts, revealing gems and jewelry of all kinds. I have finished my breakfast and replied to all but the largest package when a knock sounds on the outer door. I know Crystal will get it, so I continue my task. My hands tremble. I slide off the wide, silver ribbon that binds the blue silk. Inside, five smaller bundles of silver satin are tied with blue bands.

Crystal reappears in the doorway. "Princess Szeanne Rose to see you, milady." I instruct Crystal to show my guest in, putting aside the last gifts to don a robe.

"Reba, I am pleased to hear of your swift recovery. I was afraid you would be unable to attend the ball at which you are to be the guest of honor." Her warm smile reminds me why we have become close friends. The empathetic abilities granted me in the transdimensional trip to this world makes her genuine concern a sheltering haven, as it has been for me since Merithin snatched me from my home a week ago.

"Thank you for your concern, Rose, but I won't be attending tonight's gathering." Feeling clever, I retort, "I really haven't a thing to wear."

With a nod to Crystal, she smiles. "Then my victory gift is fortunate. I had a feeling my father would overlook the fact that you are a woman as well as a fighter. I arranged for Edward to make this."

My servant makes a timely entry. She carries before her the most elaborate dress I have ever laid eyes on. Southern belle styled, it has a wide neck stretching almost to the shoulders as well as a plunging neckline. *Am I going to have to use an enchantment to keep this dress from dropping to my knees?* Deep auburn on the bottom with shining gold partitions streaking into the blazing hemline, aureate thread embroiders gilded highlights to the bust. The dress is a masterpiece. Phedra holds a pair of burgundy lace-up boots that have two-inch heels.

"Ah, Rose! That is the most beautiful gown I have ever seen. How can I refuse to attend?" I sigh, resigned to my fate. "Not taking this opportunity to show off Edward's work would be criminal."

"Come now. You must tell me what it is about this affair that vexes you so?" The look of kindness accompanying her question is too much for me.

"It seems like a useless waste of time, celebrating before the last battle has even been fought!" I soften the criticism by noting, "Besides, I am inept at dancing to courtly tunes. All I need is to reveal the famous archmage for the klutz she really is!"

"Reba, I cherish your honesty." I feel Rose's surprise at my directness. My lips curve, despite the awkward situation. "I hope I can help ease your concerns. Our ways are foreign to you. I understand your reaction to what must seem to you a triviality." The princess gestures to the couch suggesting we should make ourselves comfortable before continuing. "This siege with the demons has been a lengthy ordeal. Before your arrival, this city was terrified by the coming of every night. The populace has hovered under the gloom of depression for far too long. Your presence has been like the dawning of a new day." Rose pauses thoughtfully.

"This is not a whimsical festival. It is a celebration of the life we did not expect to live. When the populace sees the nobility rejoicing, it will give them the fortitude to endure until the last battle has been won. The men who give their lives to protect us will know we have the utmost confidence in them, that we will be victorious."

"I never thought of it that way." Feeling like a country bumpkin, I stare at the floor. "I guess I have a lot to learn about politics and morale."

"Perhaps. . . but you can count on me to ease your passage. It is the least I can do." Rose's ready smile comes back as she continues. "I happen to be on very good terms with the best instructor in the kingdom. If he could teach me, he will have you gliding across the floor in no time. I will let you get to your preparations and send him by a couple of marks before the ball." Without giving me a chance to refuse, the princess takes her leave.

"Well, Crystal, it looks like I'm going to the dance after all." I sigh and turn my attention back to what was in the big, blue bundle.

I unwrap the remaining presents, that laid hidden within. I arrange them on the bed as the maid comes up beside me. "Milady, those are worth a fortune."

"Yes, but what are they?" The stones set in each piece: a ring, a necklace, a bracelet, earrings, and a tiara are yellow with burgundy lines fanning out from a dark slit in the center, a mirror image of a red-tinted cat's-eye stone on Earth. Even in the dim light, the stones seem to glow with an internal fire. The gems are set on a wire-thin perinthess chain, the burnt-gold metal providing the perfect accent for the lightened edges of the stones.

"They are called molten amber. The smallest stone will bring many gold pieces," my maid mumbles in awe.

The note reads, *Archmage Reba, please accept this token of my gratitude for the guidance your light has shown in these dark times, King Arturo.*

"I think I have found the perfect accessory for Rose's gift," I whisper as Crystal leads the way to the bathroom. "Honoring the king will be most appropriate."

After a relaxing soak, we saunter back to the bedroom. "Milady, we will have several marks until your hair dries enough for the irons. Time will be short. I'm not sure how much will be left to practice dancing."

Several marks, that's like four hours! I've built up my reserves enough for a minor enchantment like this. "Prepare the curling irons. My hair will be dry in a few moments." Without hesitation, I begin a spell.

"Getting late and in a hurry I am,
Dry with gel to get me out of this jam."

An inner push releases the energy stored in my aura. A gentle caress, more intimate than a lover's, brings a smile to my lips. By the time Crystal finishes issuing the orders, I stand before her with my sopping-wet curls encircled by azure radiance. Before Phedra has the necessary undergarment before us to begin the chore of dressing me in the archaic clothes, my hair is dry. The young protégé puts the irons on the metal bars over the fire as Crystal brings a large platter from her bedroom.

Glancing at the contents, I shake my head. She was great with lip-gloss and a comb, but this is too much. "No offense, but I prefer to do my own face. If you don't mind, I will call up some supplies from my world while you take care of the irons."

"Certainly, milady. Shall I bring you a hand mirror?" she offers.

While she fetches the looking glass, I recall my supply of top-of-the-line makeup back home. I picture each piece exactly as I remember it so that the magic here can recreate what I need.

"Estée Lauder and Lancôme are what I seek
To add some color to these fair cheeks.
Base, lipstick, eye shadow, and rouge,
Mascara and liner and accessories too."

Euphoria caresses my body followed by grating pain. The second discharge of energy in so short a time from senses still raw and tender brings spots to my vision. A throb begins behind my eyes. The fountain of youth spell kicks in. The inflamed membranes are soothed before the blue fog rolls out over the table. Powerful, unrelenting magic pulls the items in my mind into the real world. The mist lifts, revealing the items I requested scattered across the table.

Crystal and several other maids work on my hair. I apply the makeup with the expert precision I have worked years to refine. Even taking extreme care, I am finished in less than a mark. Unfortunately using the round, metal rods with wooden handles—medieval curling irons—Crystal takes twice as long to finish my hair.

My head chambermaid ushers me to the full-length mirror. In the transfer from Earth, my auburn hair was replaced. The wavy locks that are deep auburn at the roots, gradually lightening to blonde at the tips mark me as "the Flamed-haired One," the prophesied savior. But this makeover is ever harder to handle.

Flaming masses of orderly curls are piled on top of my head with a few ringlets trailing down each side. The tiara rests on the front, the dark auburn hair a beautiful contrast to the golden stones with the burgundy centers. The choker necklace highlights the graceful length of the neckline, while the cut of the bodice with the skirts flaring out under it makes me look as if I have a tiny waist and a full bust, an hourglass figure.

"I look like a fairy-tale princess." I gape at my reflection.

"What's a fairy?" asks Phedra.

"Now that's a long story." A knock sounds on the outer door. "And if that is my dance instructor, one that will have to wait until later."

Layers of skirts whisper as I follow Crystal to the reception chamber. I smile, trying not to giggle at the dumbstruck look on my visitor's face.

"Trying to catch flies?" I jest to cover my embarrassment.

"My lady, when I first met you, I believed nothing could surpass your beauty. I know now I was mistaken." Prince Szames, a handsome prince from head to toe, gives an elegant bow. His wavy, blond hair is parted to one side, thick and sexy. The Three Musketeers–type clothing accents his broad shoulders and muscular legs, showing the total hunk that lies beneath the mail.

I blush furiously. "If you don't stop talking like that, I'll think someone has swapped my cherished friend for his scoundrel of a brother."

"We cannot have that." Szames grins as he changes the subject. "I hear someone is in need of instruction?"

"I am expecting my tutor anytime now. Rose said she knew a 'Master of the Ball.'"

His eyebrows lift. "I am unsure if I am quite that good, but I am at your service."

"You? You dance?" I sputter, taking no offense when he laughs at my open mouth.

"Shall I send for a musician?" Szames inquires.

I examine his aura. A quick spell will save mega time. I'll only have to use a fraction of my energy to guide his flow. "I have a better idea if you're game."

"With you, milady, I am always prepared to be the game."

Recalling the other instances where I've used that phrase, a flight spell and a knife throwing experience, I chuckle at his misconception of the English slang. My lips curve as I mutter,

> "Learning to dance is what we must do.
> Ask aloud and it is played for you."

Tickling energy gives me goose bumps. Although most of the energy comes from the prince, my reserves are so low that I feel the drain. In the blink of an eye, the radiant blue light of corporeal energy fades from my sight. *The spell should take on more life than just the spoken riddle. It will also take the ideas I had my thoughts resting on when I cast it.*

I give Szames some directions. "All you have to do is name the song or sing a verse from one while you think of hearing it aloud. Magic will be pulled in from around the room, taking the needed information from your memory."

"This time, instead of soaring like a hawk, I will invoke singing such as a nightingale. I am unsure which game I prefer being." He smiles, ribbing me before stating boldly, "It has been years, but I believe this is one of the basic tunes: 'Moonlit Night.'"

The music burst into the room as if a five-piece orchestra is sitting in the corner. Szames glances around like a startled deer.

"Reba, your magic is amazing. It is the best the court musicians have ever sounded."

"I'm glad you remembered their best performance and not their worst!" Our laughter sprinkles in with the tune, giving it even more life.

The prince extends his arm and my lessons begin. I smile, giving a brief curtsey. A little more than a mark later, I am able to sashay around the reception chamber to the most popular dances: a stroll, a minuet, and a waltzlike number that has five beats instead of three with a solitary rest separating two parts.

"You are a quick study. You have mastered the basic technique." He tests my control, addressing me as we waltz.

"I suppose I just needed a good teacher." *Not to mention magically enhanced rhythm and memory.*

Our lessons halt when a knock sounds on the outer door. To my surprise, Szames reaches for the door instead of waiting for a servant to answer it. Prince Alexandros's page bows to me first then to Szames. "Milady, Prince Alexandros relays his wish to offer himself as an escort to the gala this evening."

"A moment please." I turn to Szames. "I see no need to trouble your brother since you are already here."

"Reba, it will be an honor." He bows.

"Please relay to Prince Alexandros my sincere gratitude for his offer. However, his assistance is not required at this time." The page turns smartly on his heel as I finish the dismissal.

"I feel guilty for monopolizing you like this."

The warrior shrugs. "As I recall, we had a deal, you and I. The information exchange: my world for yours. You mentioned you have a dance similar to the fimm-step?"

"We call it a waltz." Quickly I explain the basic differences. Szames bows, extending his hand. I say, "'I See it Now,' Tracy Lawrence." A familiar tune echoes into the chamber.

We glide across the floor. I spin and turn in the harness of massive arms. Relaxing with the familiar ambiance, I whisper, "When I first learned partner dances, all I knew for years was the traditional slow dance."

"You are no longer a beginner." *I sense admiration making it a compliment of the highest order.*

Coloring at his words, I miss a step.

"Your music is quite interesting. That was a simple, yet elegant dance," my tutor says as the song ends. "My fondness for the elegance of a musical promenade is reinvigorated."

"Mine too. I haven't been dancing in ages." I smile at my escort.

With another elegant bow, Szames inquires, "Will we try this 'slow dance' next?"

"There is not much to it, really. You just place your hands at my waist. I place mine on your shoulders. We move back and forth to the beat."

Szames advances to follow my instruction.

Memories of my high school crush flow though me. My heart thumps wildly. *He really wants to slow dance? What song? I haven't slow danced in years!* With a sigh I pull out an oldie: a favorite from my parents' collection of forty-fives. "'Can't Help Falling in Love,' the King."

Szames is as stiff as a teen at his first party. I am not faring much better. *Don't be stupid; it is just Szames. He's become the best friend I've ever known in seven short days.* "For this dance, we just relax," I mumble, covering my unexpected nervousness. "We don't need to hold the space."

Surrounded in Szames's large, strong arms, with the familiarity of my music and my dance, I begin to decompress from the trauma of the nightmarish battle. As the song winds down, his stance finally starts to relax, so I whisper, "'Anymore,' Travis Tritt," as the Elvis song ends. Slowly, gradually, one step at a time, our bodies edge closer together until I am resting my head on his shoulder.

The chorus rings out, "And I'm tired of pretending I don't love you. . . anymore."

He's so big, so tall. I can literally lay my head on a man's shoulder for the first time. I give in. Letting go of all the responsibilities hounding me since my arrival, I luxuriate in the moment. *But even with all his strength, he holds me so softly, gently. . . tenderly.*

To the rhythm of an acoustic guitar, Tritt croons, "My resistance ain't that strong, but my mind keeps re-creating a life with you alone." The words strike a chord in my heart.

I lace my fingers behind his neck. My hands rest in the silkiness of his flaxen hair. My empathy, usually blank with Szames, senses something. *Desire? Not lust but something soft, tender. . . warm.* Instead of irritating me, this softer feeling ignites something deep within my soul. The last measure of the ballad whispers into the still air. I lean back, tilting my head upward. Szames gazes into my eyes. Ever so slowly he begins to lean down. My thoughts scatter. My lips tingle in anticipation. Time stands still.

Ka-click. The sound of the doorknob turning resounds into the silence of the room. We spring apart, widening the one-inch gap between our noses.

"Milady, if you aren't going to be unseemly late, we will need to freshen you up." The look in Crystal's eyes is the same one my mom gives when I screw up—big time. It makes me feel just as guilty.

"Thank you, Crystal." Like a scolded teen, obediently I follow her into the next room.

Milliseconds after the door closes, words rush forth. "You are a life saver. I don't know what came over me." *It must be posttraumatic stress syndrome.*

Crystal stands stiffly, giving me that "I told you so" stare.

When she begins on my curls, I continue, "I need you to do me a favor. From now on, don't leave us alone, me and Szames, that is. I don't know why I'm having such difficulty. I never have in the past. But it's obvious I can't be spending any more time alone with him, or Alex either for that matter." I force my whirling thoughts to focus on memories of my marriage. *Kyle, I am so, so sorry.* "Back home, my husband and I agreed not to have close friendships with people of the opposite sex. I'm beginning to remember why!"

"Milady, obviously love has dawned for the two of you. Are you sure you want me to cloud the sun?" my personal maid queries as I add some lipstick.

"If I had a choice, I would discontinue the relationship with Szames, no matter how much I enjoy it. But that is an option I don't have. I must remain on good terms with him. Crystal, you are my only hope. I beg you. Please don't let me destroy my marriage because I got 'lost in the moment.' I've gotten far too comfortable with Szames."

"Milady, I understand your desire to hold to your vows, but why would one romp, worlds away, destroy what you have? After all, your husband won't know if you don't tell him." Crystal finishes with my hair.

I step to the mirror for a look while I explain. "I would know." *How do I explain my morals to a world that doesn't believe in monogamy?* "Guilt would tear me apart. I would probably take out my frustrations on Kyle. Eventually it could lead to be the end of our relationship."

"Hmm, considering your world's rigid rules about sexual relationships, it seems a reasonable outcome. Thank you, milady. I believe I understand your predicament. For the first time, the strength of your vows is truly tested. I will be happy to assist in any way I can."

With one last look in the mirror, I hustle into the next room, where my royal escort awaits.

Chapter Two

"Milady." Szames bows, seemingly unaffected by our near moral lapse.

The evening bells toll, stating full dark has arrived. We proceed down the hall, arm in arm. I shrug aside the discomfort of physical contact so soon after our near miss. The firm hold of Szames's hand becomes reassuring as we approach the graceful stairway that broadens to embrace the immense plateau of the foyer. Applause rings out from the few hundred nobles gathered. I lock my knees to keep my legs from buckling. Waves of shock and awe mixed with fear resonate from the gathered assemblage. I snap my empathy shield into place.

"We should bow and curtsy at the bottom," Szames mumbles.

Thanks to his warning and the slight squeeze he gives my arm, we make a graceful display. The rest of the royal family waits mere yards away. The king and queen are attired patriotically in the colors of the kingdom: royal blue and silver.

King Arturo reminds me of the old English kings with his cape slung over one shoulder, the outer fabric matching his dark blue breeches and the inner silver lining matching the embroidered doublet. Queen Szacquelyn is regal in her low, rounded neckline. A small ruff, paired with a winged collar, accent her graceful neck while the tight sleeves with pronounced shoulder wings and deep, lace cuffs make her seem lean and elegant. The sapphires sprinkled about her accentuate both her eyes and attire.

Musicians set up at the foot of the stairway down which we have just come. Arturo bows and Szacquelyn curtsies as Szames presents me to them. I am stunned by the gesture, it is the highest of compliments they can publically bestow. I curtsy low in return. The musicians begin to play seconds after we finish the formal greeting.

"My Lady Reba, may I have the honor of your accompaniment for the opening melody?" I blush as Prince Alexandros extends his hand. Though keeping my lips from meeting his has been a continued nuisance since our arrival in this world, the puppy-dog eyes of love are not something I expect to see when he looks in my direction.

I place my hand over his. The crowd parts as the raven-haired hunk guides me toward the floor. The long, jade jacket, accented with a silver embroidered pattern, brings out the color in his eyes while accentuating his broad shoulders. The snug slacks cling to his lower half, revealing a nice butt and hinting at his well-endowed stature—unless he stuffs his breeches. The pants are tucked into tall boots with turned-down tops. I hold in a sigh, pushing the dim memory of my last premonition out of my mind.

The band begins a quin-step waltz as we arrive in the center of the room. With an elegant bow, Alex captures me within his arms. His steps are decisive and strong in a complex pattern.

"Without reservation I believe you are the most beautiful woman I have ever seen. Your blossoming fire sears my heart, nay, my very soul." Absorbed in my attempt to follow his fancy footwork, endeavoring not to wind up on my backside, I almost miss his opening flattery.

My lips twist wryly at the thought of this ridiculous duel I am forced to endure. "Your mastery of the spoken word continues to astound me."

"I see you believe this to be more insincere adulation." Alex's shapely brows draw down as he frowns. "I feel I owe you an apology. Raised as crown prince, I have dutifully learned to inveigle others to my cause. Perhaps I have learned, too late, that you are not a typical woman, wooed by an insincere turn of words. If you will allow it, I would like to begin anew. It is my wish that we may yet become. . . friends."

Mesmerized by the intense emerald of his eyes and the heartbreakingly handsome smile, not quite daring to release my empathy shield to judge the sincerity of what he has said, my lips curve. "I believe everyone deserves a second chance, even a crown prince. If it is my friendship you desire, I expect just one thing: honesty—nothing more and nothing less."

"My lady, for you I will put aside my political upbringing. I will strive to give exactly that." Alex delivers the acceptance with a smile that takes my breath away even though I don't sense any telltale signs that his telepathic charisma is working to persuade me to him. *I have learned how to shield my empathy to protect against his magical persuasion, but how do I keep from falling into the arms of Tall, Dark, and Handsome if he proves true to his word?*

Conversation ceases as he leads me in a turn, turn, reverse, and another turn. Our dance-floor wanderings resemble a tug-of-war as the prince shows off moves that keep me on the verge of introducing my bottom to the tiled flowers beneath our feet. At last the musical number comes to an end. Alex ushers me back to the royal section of the gathering. Almost a mark later, his brother rejoins our group, inviting me to take a spin around the floor.

Stunned, I recognize the music as a waltz: a true waltz. I smile, arching my brows at him. My escort shrugs. "I thought you could use a breather from all the foreignness."

"Szames, I appreciate it more than you know." Secure in the familiar arms, some of the tension drains away as we glide in a spiraling pattern across the floor. My hand feels the warmth of his biceps, gentle yet iron hard. Rose tinges my cheeks. My heart hammers in my chest. Gazing into his eyes, I lose sight of the crowded ballroom; we are alone, back in my reception chamber. I fight the urge to lean into him, keeping my back rigid and arms squared. Comfort, confidence, and contentment swell within me. The round of acclaim we receive as Szames leads me back doesn't shake the center of calm I have formed through the musical reprieve.

The night drags on and on. The nobility promenades before me, as diverse as a bouquet of wildflowers. Even with my improved memory, the names and faces start to blur together as my cheeks begin to ache with the continual grinning.

A small, round woman, layered in orange and chartreuse that only puts on additional pounds, stops before me. Though she must look up to meet my eyes, something tells me that her nose is usually held as high. "Archmage Reba, you seem to be a woman of many talents." Instincts spring into action as a brilliant white sears my vision. High intuition points on my character stat sheet back home granted me a gift of foresight on this world. The future plays out before me:

The Marchioness Asdis of Rhymon stands before her daughter, the dark-haired girl from the noble's class.

"But, Mother. . ." the girl pleads.

In a swift, sure swing, Asdis smashes the guitar I gave to the child into an unrecognizable mass.

Light flashes, the white blinding me once more, as I am thrust further into the future. The spots begin to clear from my vision. Before me sit several mature women who must be pushing thirty. Their heads are bent diligently over their needlepoint.

"You know, Sister, there is still time for you to marry. Jack's uncle is looking for a new bride; his last failed to provide an heir."

"Thank you for your consideration, but my life must hold more than seeing to the wifely duties of. . ." Still as prim and as graceful as the girl who sat before me in the class a few days ago, she holds her disgust in check. "Besides, Jack's uncle is rotund and wrinkled."

The youngest of those gathered shakes her head, smirking with superiority. "I'm so glad Mother kept me from any more contamination. Had I not been removed from that 'nobility class,' I might have wound up an old maid just like you."

The world flashes white once more. I hear the familiar sounds of the gathering before my eyes have cleared. A sense of purpose crystallizes into being.

"I thank you but dancing takes an infinitesimal amount of talent. I believe it is more a matter of finding the proper teacher." I share a smile with Szames, waiting for the change of direction I know the conversation must take.

"Do those beliefs extend to the realm of music as well?" Her lips compress, nearly disappearing.

"Music is an entirely different matter: one-third talent, one-third teaching, and one-third desire." I compose my reply carefully. "Without all three, mediocrity is all one can aspire to."

"An interesting point of view for one reported to have a wondrous ability. It is all my child talks of, the musical demonstration of the great sorceress. Kantri now petitions for freedom to pursue the art of entertainment!" The five-foot-tall woman marks a line in the sand, daring me to step over it.

"In my land, high-born women are considered more desirable if they possess any talent to entertain." Thanks to my intuition ability, I add with confidence, "If the duties of the family can be assumed by other siblings, I see no harm in a child exploring a dream to see if it can be realized."

"I could agree with you, if the dream suited the child, but she is a girl desiring to be a bard." The marchioness draws the attention of those around us as they pause in their discussions to listen.

"And what would be a more suitable pursuit for a woman of stature?" I add with a tight smile, "Perhaps there may be a time when I can give you a demonstration of what a woman can accomplish when one sets her mind on a higher purpose."

"If a demonstration of talent is what the gracious Archmage Reba has to give, now seems to be an opportune time." The woman thrust out her chin, figuratively slapping my cheek with a glove.

In a long blink, I take stock of my inner determination. Finding myself up to the challenge, I give a nod. "I assume you have the instrument at hand?"

Asdis of Rhymon indicates the guitar leaning against the baluster.

I look toward Szames. "Your Highness, will you continue to provide an escort?"

Moving toward the stairs, only my firm grip on Szames's arm keeps my hands from shaking. *Why am I so determined to defend the dreams of a child whose name I don't even know?* Trying not to panic, I whisper under my breath, "I need to cast a spell."

Szames nods and I chant.

"Voice ring henceforth strong and true,
Like Whitney, Julie, and Patsy too."

The short rhyme is followed by a tickling in my throat as we arrive at the foot of the staircase.

"You do not have to do this." Szames gazes into my eyes as if seeking an answer to a puzzle.

"I truly wish I didn't. If I back down now, I admit defeat. I can't do that. The future of the women in this country may depend on me setting an example, here and now. Szames, can you provide an introduction for me?" I implore before turning to retrieve the guitar from where it sits up against the baluster.

The guests watch the new instrument with unfeigned curiosity as the prince's deep voice booms out. "Nobles of Cuthburan, the gracious Archmage Reba has agreed to demonstrate the music of her world for those of you gathered here tonight." All eyes in the room turn toward me.

My knees quake. I force my back straight and stiff against the pain of the twisting cramps in my middle. Without a prelude, I begin picking out the slow, expressive, chords of a country song, one I feel this medieval culture can comprehend. I close my eyes and sing at a volume that carries my voice to the farthest corners of the hall.

> "There's a tree out in the backyard that never has been broken by the wind.
> And the reason it's still standin', it was strong enough to bend.
> For years we have stayed together as lovers and as friends.
> What we have will last forever if we're strong enough to bend."

Picking up the tempo slightly, I open my eyes.

> "When you say something you can take back,
> A big wind blows and you hear a little crack.
> When you say, 'Hey, well, I might be wrong.'
> You can sway with the wind 'til the storm is gone.

> Like the tree out in the backyard that never has been broken by the wind,
> Our love will last forever if we're strong enough to bend.
> When you start thinkin' that you know it all, a big wind blows and a branch will fall.
> When you say, 'Hey, this job takes two,'
> We can sway with the wind 'til the skies turn blue.

> Like the tree out in the backyard that never has been broken by the wind,
> Our love will last forever if we're strong enough to bend.
> Our love will last forever if we're strong enough to bend."[i]

The tune comes to a halt. I drop my shield, trying to gage the audience's response: mild approval mixed with confusion. Only the outpouring of appreciation, admiration, and awe coming from the musicians flanking me keeps me from hurling myself from the room with tears streaming down my face.

Glancing at the marchioness of Rhymon's smug face, steel slides through my veins. Searching my magically enhanced, photographic memory for a more suitable song, I lock eyes momentarily with Princess Szeanne Rose. The perfect melody springs to mind. *Time to act like the performer I am pretending to be.*

"This song is famous throughout my land. However, it will require a prologue in a kingdom so far from my home." My voice picks up volume as the room quiets. "There once was a beautiful maiden of high repute. One spring her father, the lord, brought her to an outlying property to introduce her to her betrothed. Their stay had only begun when word came of a hostile force marching on the city. The great lord immediately sent his beloved daughter home, escorted by two knights and twenty armsmen, all of whom were instructed to guard the lady at all cost." Several of the men nod, agreeing with the noble's decision.

"The lives of twenty-one brave men were the price paid, for the news of the invaders was but a ruse to draw out the real target—the lord's most cherished possession: his beloved daughter. Only one man survived, one who was not even knighted. But through cunning, bravery, and not a small amount of luck, this common soldier managed to protect the lady and evade capture. The commoner delivered her to the family's dwelling five nights later. The ordeal did not leave the young lady unscathed. She had spent five long days alone, except for the company of an uncouth, unschooled soldier." I pause. The faces of the men darken as they presume the daughter's virtue has been compromised.

"Yes, she had taken a grievous wound, one that would haunt her for the rest of her life. In the quiet hours they spent huddled together, their bodies the only warmth they dared in the cold of nights, they exchanged stories from their childhood to chase away the fears that stalked them. To the lady's astonishment, in those quiet moments, this common, uncourtly man had stolen her most precious possession: her heart. The pain of it was not as great as she expected, though, for he had replaced it with a gift equally precious: true adoration and love so pure, it pierced her soul. Duty called both. Each was obligated elsewhere. The words went unspoken until her love sat mounted, ready to depart. She looked down from the battlements. This is the song they sang as he rode away. It is meant to be performed as a duet but is often sung solo by both men and women." I begin a cappella, sounding remarkably like Whitney Houston.

> "If I should stay, I would only be in your way.
> So I go but I know I'll think of you every step of the way.
> And I will always love you. I will always love you.
> You, my darling you.

> Bittersweet memories—that is all I'm taking with me.
> So good-bye. Please don't cry. We both know I'm not what you, you need.
> And I will always love you. I will always love you."

Using the guitar I add the country rendition of chords with a slight blues twist. I pitch my voice a fraction higher for the lady.

> "I hope life treats you kind, and I hope you have all you dreamed of.
> And I wish you joy and happiness, but above all this, I wish you love.

> And I will always love you. I will always love you.
> I will always love you. I will always love you.
> I will always love you. I, I will always love you.
> Darling I love you. I will always love you."[ii]

I end the song softer than the blues singer but still drawing out the syllables, pouring emotion into every word. Refocusing on the crowd before me, I see several women wiping their eyes. The exuberant tribute I get from both sexes makes using empathy to gauge reaction superfluous.

With a bow, I prepare to take my leave. One stoic-looking gentleman shouts a request for a fighting song. Several others

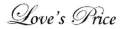

second it. I rack my brain for one that contains no references to modern weapons.

"One last song I will sing. This one is about my country's fight for its freedom." Setting down the instrument I begin.

> "Oh, say, can you see, by the dawn's early light
> What so proudly we hail'd at the twilight's last gleaming?
> Whose broad stripes and bright stars thro' the perilous fight.
> O'er the ramparts we watch'd were so gallantly streaming?"

I substitute words that will make sense to this world, noticing all of my gang has come to attention with hands over hearts.

> And the magic's red glare, the spells bursting in air
> Gave proof thro' the night that our flag was still there.
> Oh, say, does that star-spangled banner yet wave
> O'er the land of the free and the home of the brave?"[iii]

I glance toward the band of crusaders that were yanked from my world with me. A lone tear slides down Charles's face. Once again applause fills the silence. With a nod at Szames, we retreat to the area of the floor where the royalty is gathered.

Alex takes a position beside me. "Milady Reba, it seems magic is not the only field in which you excel. Your performance is undeniably something none will soon forget." He is the first to regale me with compliments. Even though I am forced to acknowledge the flattery, I feel uncomfortable doing so; without the magical boost, I wouldn't have kept the beat, much less hit a single note.

"Marchioness." Conversation halts as I address my aggressor. "Do you still see musical pursuits as undesirable?"

"Milady, you have a remarkable voice and talent. It makes one reconsider. Perhaps a skill such as you have displayed could be beneficial."

Knowing there is nothing more I can do, I nod, grateful when she makes a not-so-graceful exit. Conversation flows on. Servants come by with refreshments and hors d'oeuvres. So monumentally boring is the whole affair, I am almost pleased when Alex asks me to dance again, this time to one of the faster tunes.

When we arrive in the center of the floor, the prince gives a courtly bow, extending his hand. The mischievous twinkle in his eyes and a quirk of his perfect lips sends off alarm bells as the music begins. *I am an archmage. I will not*—I hasten to the next turn—*let this man make a fool of me.* By relaxing and relying on my intuition, I am able to follow Alex's multifarious meanderings. He dips his head as the song ends, raising his elegant eyebrow, conceding me no victory on this battlefield. *At least I've managed to hold my own.*

"Milady Reba, would you care for some fresh air?" Szames extends his arm in invitation as we approach.

"A wonderful idea. Jamison, would you care to join us?" I look for a safety net, trying to avoid any complications that may arise from a private tryst.

We pick up Merithin and Rose on the way as Szames leads us down the hall where the dining chamber is located, then out a backdoor. The lovers, Jamison and Rose, immediately break away from the group, leaving me alone with the two men.

"Szames, thank you for providing this wonderful escape. Tell me, how much longer does propriety dictate I be present?"

"You are not enjoying the celebration?" Szames inquires.

"The party is something I'm happy to have had a chance to experience in my short stay. I warned you, though, politics are not my forte." A sigh creeps into my voice. "I could dance all night back home, but I'm afraid I find all this jockeying for stature a total bore."

"Then I shall do my best to keep you out on the floor for the remainder of the evening." A smile shows he is looking forward to it.

"Reba, though you have heard it from a hundred lips today, I want to convey my appreciation for what you have accomplished. I know, probably better than anyone, how sorely we were overmatched before you and your men arrived." Merithin bows his head, showing the depth of his respect.

"I appreciate your sentiment. I'm happy to have the opportunity to help. You deserve much of the credit yourself. After all, it was you who summoned us."

"It was my first such." The sorcerer grins. "Meditation directed me to prepare the portal spell. I knew without substantial help we would be overcome by the demons. It was the oddest thing, when I first scried for you and your men. I inexplicably knew beyond the shadow of a doubt, you were the answer to our fatal dilemma."

"Tell me, Merithin: What did you see when you pulled us out of our world?" For the first time this evening, I am intrigued by the topic of conversation.

"Not much more than your auras, to tell the truth." The kindly grandfather wrinkles his brow in puzzlement. "But with that and your conversation about repelling something called 'gremlins,' it was enough. I knew I had been led to what we needed."

I chuckle. "You've just confirmed what I've suspected since our arrival. Tell me: Is contact between two worlds always so limited?"

"I, myself, have not done much research in this area." His brow furrows. "But studies show contact depends on several factors."

No longer feeling the need to mislead my new friends, I laugh. "You must have been directed by forces greater than either of us. The Crusaders of the Light are just five strangers placed on a team to win a prize. What you saw was a game, nothing more."

Their puzzlement deepens, so I elaborate. "My men and I come from a world that is based on science, not magic. We no longer fight wars with swords. Sorcery only survives in fables. The first spell I ever cast was on this world. I felt it best to keep our inexperience a secret, lest we lose credibility."

"But how can this be? All of you display skill far above what we possess." Szames asks, appearing distraught by the revelation.

Merithin is merely contemplative.

"That is why I chose not to reveal our true stature. When we were transferred to your world, we were imbued with the looks and abilities of the characters we were pretending to be." My voice turns solemn. "As unrealistic as it sounds, we were granted instant knowledge and skills." *Should I have held back this revelation?*

"I have never felt so certain of anything as I was of you. You are what I sought, else I would have done more research before I brought you here," the sorcerer repents as if guilty of murder in the first. "You have my sincere apologies for taking such action without your consent."

"We have a saying, 'No harm, no foul.' This has been an unforgettable experience. A much better vacation than my husband ever dreamed it would be when he booked the stay at the Renaissance Hotel for my birthday." Their brows crinkle in puzzlement at the strange, twenty-first-century terms. I shrug, adding, "I am just sorry I'll be leaving so soon."

"But I am afraid there has been a wound, and a grievous one at that. I should have given you a copy of the laws when you first arrived." A chill of premonition sends icy tentacles down my spine. "The Second Law of Magic states that traveling between two worlds is only possible if the sorcerer can harness the magical energy on both worlds."

"Merithin, what are you saying?" I demand. My perfect memory struggles to bring to the forefront of my mind the premonition that overwhelmed me after the battle. I thrust it ruthlessly down into the depths of my subconscious.

"Milady, I am afraid if you cannot use magic on your world, you cannot go home."

"I have to go home." I feel the world tilting beneath my feet. "I have a husband waiting for me." Shaking my head, I dismiss his proclamation. "I will not be marooned on this godforsaken planet. I will find a way around it. I have already broken one law."

"Yes, you have broken the Fourth Law by soaring aloft, but if you try to break this one, you may forfeit your life and the lives of those with you. I don't know what it is that allows you to be so successful with the spells you cast, but in this you must take heed." The words are spit from the sorcerer's mouth, the harshness at odds with his look of sympathy. With a sigh, he adds, "Let me relate a tale which I have revealed to few others.

"Once there was a master sorcerer, Meisteri, more powerful than any of the other masters. While scrying, he discovered a sorceress in another dimension. For more than a year, they communicated. Then Meisteri went to join his beloved, Meyja. They lived happily for many years and had two sons." A faraway look steals into his eyes. The wise elder draws us into his story, almost as if we are experiencing it with him.

"The paradise they found didn't last. A civil war broke out between the gifted and normals. The lovers' castle became a refuge for all those who wielded corporeal magic. A council was held. After months of research, it was decided that they had to risk transporting all the remaining gifted back to Meisteri's world, although none would be able to use their abilities. A master sorcerer in the destined land was contacted. He had used his umfang, his portal essence, on a prior venture but agreed to perform the second half of the transfer after it was begun by Meyja."

"Meisteri's children, the two boys, survived the transfer. The rest of the gifted were linked to supply the necessary energy for the portal spell. All 120 perished. The older son was rendered unconscious when the master on this world pulled the portal essence from his immature gift, trying to stabilize the deteriorating link. My brother never regained consciousness."

A renewed determination enters his voice. "I have never disclosed my origins to another. I will do all within my power to keep another from dying in that manner. That includes you, milady."

"I literally cannot go home." My heart rebels, though my mind knows the truth of the matter. "No! It can't be. . ." The chill hands of fate maintain their grip on my spine, despite my denial.

"I will send you their research if you wish," Merithin begins.

I shake my head in denial. "There must be another answer, somehow, some way."

"I fear not, child. Portal magic is like juggling; a sorcerer must be able to weave magic both on the world he comes from and the world he travels to, just as a juggler must be able to catch a ball as well as throw. If you cannot finish the weave once you have traveled, the spell will not be complete. It will unravel, leaving you and those within the spell somewhere in between."

The gray-haired sorcerer reaches out a consoling hand. "I would gladly assist you, but both the opening and the closing of the spell must be completed by someone with the essence still intact. There is no way for you to travel back to your home."

Unwanted tears gather in my eyes. I blink rapidly to contain them. "I will find another way. I have to." Unwilling to reveal the crushing pain in my heart, I turn, power-walking toward the concealing darkness of the forest.

"Let her go." Merithin lays a restraining hand on Szames as he moves to follow. "Let her grieve." Mage-sensitive hearing brings every word to my ears.

Grieve? Grieve for what? I will not give up! I am the most powerful person on this planet. I will not be marooned here without my husband! Pain stabs through my chest, making it harder and harder to breathe. I stumble over a large stick. The premonition I have been running from bounds into my distracted mind:

❦   ❦   ❦

I am sitting at a small table across from Alex. The dim interior of the massive pavilion is aglow with candlelight. Everything is slightly out of focus, fuzzy. In a flash of insight, I realize that I am intoxicated.

I miss the exchange of words. My weakened senses reel as I bound to my feet after downing the contents of the cup before me.

"Yes, I will survive, even if it is alone." The mumbled words mean little to my distorted mind. I take a step toward the door but stumble in my inebriated state. Alex's strong hands steady me. Surrounded by his arms, my tongue runs free. "And who will be there to hold me then?"

All the anger, frustration, and fear tumble out of me. "What am I going to do? I'm not who everyone thinks I am. I have no training, no upbringing for this." Tears come unbidden, streaming uncontrollably down my face. "Being an archmage is going to be so very lonely."

"Shush, it is all right." Gently Alex strokes my hair, comforting me as he would a small child. "It will all be all right."

"Yeah, here is the all-powerful savior of—hic—your kingdom, weeping like a child." Gradually I compose myself. Exhausted by the emotional outburst, I struggle to remain standing.

In a smooth motion, Alex sweeps me off my feet. Carrying me as easily as a child, his long strides bring us quickly to the bed.

~　　~　　~

I wrench my mind away from the distasteful vision. Bending down, I retrieve the offending branch that tripped me.

"I will not be taken"—I swipe at the bushes with the stick—"by that egotistical, male chauvinist, crown prince!"

Through blurry eyes I find the flattened boulder. The reminder of my failure to circumvent the First Law pushes me over the edge.

I beat the rock with the branch, punctuating each word. "No. . . it. . . can't. . . be!" The stick snaps in two. Left with nothing to take out my frustration on, I collapse into a sobbing heap. Throwing myself down on the slab, I give in to the sorrow engulfing my heart. When gritty eyes refuse to release another tear, I become aware of my surroundings. The oddness of it brings me out of the well of self-pity.

No night birds sing; no frogs or crickets chirp. The woods are eerily silent, too silent. A breeze wafts, bringing a putrid odor that hints of death.

"Magelight." The whisper brings a glowing orb floating over my right shoulder. A thought increases its illumination. I rub the exposed skin on my neck, which feels dry, as if I've been in the sun too long. I brush the feeling aside. Examining the clearing, I find the bones of a small animal—*a rabbit?*—and several pieces of skin and fur scattered under a bush.

Peripheral vision catches a dark shape, streaking out from the left. *"A demon, come now!"* I send a telepathic shriek in the general direction of the castle, hoping Jerik is still there.

I pivot, scanning the meadow. Releasing my empathy shields, I fumble through my skirts for the knife strapped to my boots. I sense malevolence seeping out from the demon before I see it.

"Laser!" The small, humanoid creature digs its claws into the ground, moving quicker than eyes can track them. The bolt of light blinks out halfway to the creature. The mage-globe winks out of existence, plunging the area into darkness.

Oh, no! I've constructed two portal spells and a shield spell on this rock in the last week. The magelight and laser fire were too much of a drain. I've created a dead zone!

With demonic magic aiding the jarovegi, it sinks into the earth before I complete the thought. In the dead zone my empathy is blank, as silent as the eerie forest. I search for the creature, sprinting for the boulder. Stumbling, I curse the skirts that wind themselves around my legs, determined to trip me. Heightened hearing endowed in my new form tracks the creature as it surfaces on the other side of the meadow. Standing in the center of the slab, I flip the dagger around in my hand to get a better grip.

Sounds of pounding footsteps reach my ears as the demon darts toward me. My dress writhes. Two-inch talons, sharp as daggers, rend the material into shreds. I grab a handful of skirts trying to get at the demon with the blade. A scream tears from my throat as claws sink into my knee. In the dead zone, where no magic will function, the defensive spell protecting me is nonexistent.

A massive hand takes hold of the demon's neck. Having appeared at my side almost as fast as the jarovegi, Szames wrenches the monster off my leg. A bellow of rage and pain echoes from him as he thrusts his knife through the creature's middle. With a sneer of disgust, Szames tosses the limp body to the ground.

"Are you injured?" he demands, fumbling through my skirts. "Are you bitten?"

"It's only a scratch. It's bleeding like mad. I'm sure it will be fine." As the words leave my mouth, I feel strength disappear like ice cream in the African sun. For the second time in twenty-four hours, I fall into the arms of a prince as consciousness is torn from my grasp.

Chapter Three

I wipe gunk out of my eyes, struggling to open them. "What happened?"

Memories of the attack come back with the precision of a perfect memory. I bolt upright. Noticing I have company, I pull the covers over my half-naked form. "Rose? What are you doing here? What time. . . ?" My sentence trails off as dizziness brings inky blotches into my vision.

"Reba." The princess hands me a cup of silver healing potion. "Drink this. It will help."

She lays her hand on my shoulder. Energy seeps into every cell of my body like ice-cold water after a long run as Rose uses her healing magic to speed the nutrients in the potion into my system. "The jarovegi, although small in size, is an awesome foe. Like the demon's bite, their claws inflict wounds that drain the aura. If Jamison had not been close, you would not have woken for days. As it is, your recovery has been swifter than either he or Merithin predicted."

"But is it soon enough?" Swinging out of bed, I reach for the clothes laid out on one of the chairs. "Is the campaign waiting?"

"Yes and no. Yes, you are awake in plenty of time; you have been out for marks, not days." Rose motions with a roll of white cloth as I pick up my pants. I sigh, letting her rebandage the knee. "And no, the campaign is not waiting on you. My brother has taken charge of your platoon until you can join him."

My shoulders sag in relief. "Thank God for small favors. At least Szames will be able to set up the shield and send out the call tonight while he waits for me."

Rose ties the ends of the bandage snugly. I wince at the stab of pain as she remarks, "Oh, you are unaware: Szames received some minor scratches from the same demon. He woke less than a mark ago."

"What? Alex leads my squadron without his brother!" I jump in to my pants, throw on my boots, and grab my robe. "Take me to your father."

Entering my foyer, I nearly stumble as I halt. Andrayia is perched on the edge of a chair. Guilt assails me. With all that has happened, I didn't even think to ask if the voluptuous warrior had made it through the battle for Castle Eldrich. *My actions placed her in the direct line of fire, yet I totally dismissed her from my thoughts. Is it because she's Alex's mistress or because I'm still unsure she is not my enemy?*

"Andrayia, why aren't you in your assigned position with the army?"

"I have been elected leader of the Royal Guard." Bounding to her feet, she bows as she continues. "As such, it is my duty to personally see to your safety."

I give a decisive dip of my chin, gesturing for her to follow us. Rose leads the way to King Arturo's apartments. At a brisk walk, we reach the door in less than ten minutes. The reception chamber is lined with bookshelves on both sides of the desk after the twin fireplaces on each wall. The room extends back to the outside wall where a set of French doors with opaque glass leads to a balcony, letting in an abundance of light.

The march to the royal suite leaves me feeling as if I have run a mile. The sunshine sends sharp pains stabbing through my skull. I squint to block out some of the light. I bow as I approach the pair engrossed in conversation. "Your Majesty, have I been informed correctly? Is Alex leading the army in my place in search of the demon's gate?"

Arturo puffs out his chest. "Our god, Andskoti, told us to proceed with all haste to find the rogue sorcerer and close the demon's gateway if we are to win this war. We felt it best if the crusade continued as planned."

I turn to the commander of the armed forces of Cuthburan. "I plan to leave at once; Alex could be in great danger."

"My thoughts exactly but I am afraid we must wait until morning." The irritation in his voice speaks volumes about his displeasure. "It is well past midday. We will never reach the camp by sunset."

"Then I will find another way, fly half the way if I must."

"What is this about Alex being in danger?" King Arturo demands.

My head pops up as I remember the presence of the sovereign. "I have given Szames the ability to see magical forces, but Prince Alexandros insisted that Szames could be his eyes for him. Neither Allinon nor Merithin are with him, if the two groups continued as planned. This means no one will be there to verify for Alex that he has properly activated the shield. Come sunset, there is no guarantee he won't have a hoard of demons at his throat while he stands unprotected without the force field for protection."

"Prince Alexandros is able to work the shield spells," Arturo declares.

"Yes, nine times out of ten he can. What if tonight is that one time he mispronounces the activation?" It takes mere seconds for the king to reach a new conclusion.

"We understand the urgency of this matter. Take extra mounts; ride them until they drop if you must." With the monarch's dismissal, Szames and I turn, striding for the door.

"Robert, have our horses readied," Szames instructs his squire.

"One for me as well," Andrayia interjects, coming up beside me.

"Andrayia, you have seen me safely delivered to the general, who will see me safely to camp. There is no reason for you to endure the grueling conditions of a crusading army."

"As I stated, milady, it is my personal duty to see to your safety. I will not shirk it."

Is it her tenacity that Alex admires? In the same camp with Alex for two weeks. . . "Robert, ready three horses. Szames, which is the fastest route north?"

The brightness of the day sends pain spiking through my skull as we exit the castle. With Szames marching silently beside me, I know he must be likewise affected. Trying to form a coherent thought through the haze of pain is impossible. It takes all my concentration to place one foot in front of the other.

"Why north?" Szames asks as we enter the shadow of the stable. "Alex is headed west."

"I noticed something strange about the forest. Call it a hunch." Seeing his brow draw down in puzzlement, I rephrase the information. "Scrying told me whatever presence holds those woods is either benign or basically good." I continue explaining as we mount. "I figure about now we can use all the help we can get. Besides, if we don't enlist some aid, we will be flying. The distance this takes us out of the way won't make a difference."

Both Szames and I need to conserve our diminishing energy for the ride, so conversation is sparse as we make the journey at a gallop. Frustrated, I yearn for a car as an hour creeps past and we crawl toward the woodland. When the trees are looming about us, I tighten the reins, bringing my mount to a halt. I ask the others to stay back as I approach the forbidden forest.

In a small clearing, ten feet from the trees, I sit cross-legged. Broadcasting mentally as well as vocally, I open my senses. "I come in peace, offering a treaty against those who threaten all sentient beings on this world. Will you speak with me?"

The forest remains silent. I feel a presence, perhaps more than one. "These demons threaten not only mankind, but all life. Have you not felt their malignancy? How long until they take one of your kind?"

"One wandered south to observe what occurred and fell victim two nights past," Alien thoughts are projected into my head.

"Would it not, then, be prudent to join forces?" I add a telepathic invitation, *"Come, if you will, and see what plan I have in my mind."* Minutes pass as I feel a feather-soft probe scanning my thoughts.

"This is the form you wish us to take?" A jet black cat, larger than a lion, almost as big as a horse, steps into the clearing. Steel rings in the silence of the meadow. I raise a hand to stay my protectors.

Muscular and lithe, statuesque, the beast is majestic. *"Tell me: What are you willing to give in return for our aid?"*

"I sense kindness and integrity within you. I will give anything within my power," I respond without hesitation. "If you can do so without harm, I invite you into my memories to perform a thorough reading of the being with which you are to make a pact."

The spirit beast raises its head, giving a very catlike twitch of its nose as its ears swivel. Gliding across the meadow, the being tries out its new form. Warm breath riffles my hair, and whiskers tickle my skin as a feline essence mingles with my own. Firm and direct, memories flash through my consciousness, lightning fast. I lose track of them before the beast withdraws.

"Rather disorganized for a being, more compassion than sense." The cat's voice takes on a note of resignation. *"Call me Jesse. I will be your partner. We will reach the encampment well before nightfall. In return I require you march east, swinging north first on your next campaign. Will you agree to clear the Ethereal Forest of demon kind?"*

"Agreed." As the word leaves my mouth, two more figures advance from the foliage. Jesse looks over his shoulder at the new arrivals. The cat lifts his head, giving a warning growl, the hair on his neck standing on end. A golden beast roars back a challenge, flexing its claws as it crouches as if to pounce.

Huffing air out of his nostrils, Jesse's gesture resembles a sigh. He turns back to address me. *"This pair wishes to lend aid to your cause. If your companions will agree to a reading as you have, these two will become their partners in this crusade against the invading demons."*

"These cats have offered themselves as mounts. They will be able to convey us to the camp by sunset." The prince immediately unsaddles his horse then comes to stand beside me. Alex's concubine hesitates as the color drains from her face. "This is the only way you will be able to accompany me. You may return to the castle with our mounts if you wish."

With a grimace of determination, Andrayia begins to unsaddle her mare. She hauls the saddle over, dropping it at my other side. "I have given my word to stand beside you. We stood against a horde of demons. Come what may, I follow where you lead."

"I am Tawny." A glow encompasses Szames as the greeting echoes through our minds.

After a few minutes, Szames mumbles, awestruck, "Tawny knows I will worry about the horses getting back. She says one of her kind will see them delivered to safety."

A silver feline, somewhat smaller than the other two but still bigger than a pony, edges toward Andrayia. *"Do not be afraid. I will not harm you."* A soft purring accompanies the silver beast's mind-speech. *"Heather, call me Heather."*

Andrayia extends a trembling hand. "You sound different. All of you talk in my head, but with different voices?"

Heather nuzzles Andrayia's fingers. A whitish glow expands from the feline, surrounding the young woman. Szames and I move to saddle our new partners. "I'm sorry but I am afraid the equipment is necessary if we are going to remain on your backs."

"You believe, after I have given my word, I would let you fall?" Jesse growls.

"No, but the saddle and the reins strapped to a halter will help the others feel safe, as if they have some control," I say telepathically.

Laughter resounds in my thoughts with a halting cat purr.

I secure the seating. Magic encompasses the equipment, transforming it into a lighter, jockeylike seat with high stirrups. We mount, Andrayia moving with stiff, jerky movements.

"Will she be all right?" I send to Jesse.

"Heather is the youngest of our kind, a mere few centuries since she became." The depth of Jesse's voice speaks of age, experience, and confidence, much different than the light, almost breezy voice the silver cat used. *"She let some of herself be glimpsed, so the reading was more of an exchange. Your companion was not harmed, but it will take her some time to assimilate the knowledge she has been granted."*

I lose the ability to form coherent thought as the ride begins. My feet are back, knees bent almost to a kneeling position. The first few steps feel normal. The feline slinks in a rocking motion similar to a galloping horse. The rolling hills spread out before us as we pick up speed. Soon all pretense of being normal animals disappears. The wind is shielded from us, but a slight breeze caresses our hair as we glide over the ground. The scenery zooms past at more than thirty miles an hour. I relax into the saddle, comfortable now that I have related our speed to automobiles.

"You adjust quickly to change," Jesse states.

"It is not an uncommon trait in my race, although some are more adaptable than others." Perceiving a tension in him concerning this topic, I let it drop, not ready to test the new bounds between my partner and me. "You have chosen a gorgeous form."

"I selected this form from your mind, with an enhanced physique, of course." The vanity coloring his statement makes me giggle.

"Panthers are my favorite cat. You've done a beautiful job. Tell me: Are you bound by the shape you've chosen? You seem to be surpassing normal standards."

"As long as we remain in these forms, we will have to live by their requirements. For the first time in centuries, I will be forced to ingest meat for nourishment." The distaste for such menial consumption is evident in the pitch of his telepathy. *"Our physical abilities will be limited somewhat."*

"I will personally see to your physical comfort. We will endeavor to make the experience as pleasant as possible." I make a mental note to continue this discussion later as smoke from the camp is already in sight.

Our partners slow to a normal speed as we approach the sentries. Szames returns their shocked salutes, crossing his right arm over his waist and touching the hilt of his sword as he bows. With more than a mark until sunset, we have arrived in plenty of time. Two large tents stand fully erect, but the majority of the camp is still in the process of setting up.

Alex has several officers gathered around him. Their light-hearted tones hint at a nonessential meeting as we lope in their direction. A weary sigh escapes as I anticipate the coming confrontation. Responding to my wishes, Jesse stops a few feet from the crown prince. Alex eyes the immense feline warily.

"Your Highness." I slide out of the saddle, grinding my teeth to hide a grimace of pain as my right leg makes contact with the ground for the first time in an hour. "Prince Alexandros, I present our new partners in the conflict against demonkind: Jesse, Tawny, and Heather."

The officers take a step back when the gigantic cats put one leg out, bowing their heads. Alex, however, holds his ground.

"These are the beings which inhabit the Ethereal Forest north of Castle Eldrich. They have agreed to assist us."

"Allies against the demons are welcome news. As our legends dictate, we have respected your domain, so shall we now respect any treaty that has been made," Alex replies diplomatically before motioning for me to join him in his tent.

"Andrayia, if you will see that the cook releases some supplies for our partners?" Alex is forced to wait while I delegate responsibilities. "Szames, will you mind seeing to Jesse for me?"

I follow Alex to his tent, pain fueling my temper to new heights with each step.

"What manner of beasts have you brought into our midst?" the prince demands as the tent flap closes behind us.

"Allies for which you should be grateful." The fire in my leg sharpens my tongue. Losing the grip on my anger, I sneer. "Allies I wouldn't have dreamed of approaching without royal permission had you not been as impetuous as a colt learning to run."

"Impetuous?" His tone implies I am treading on dangerous ground. "And just what have I done that is so foolhardy?"

"It figures!" I am as snide as Allinon at his best. "You haven't even thought through the consequences of your actions." I retreat to a center of icy calm, my voice dropping to barely a whisper. "Last I checked you weren't able to activate the shielding better than nine times out of ten. Is that still so?"

The prince stiffens, giving a curt nod. "How long do you think these men would last if tonight happened to be the one time out of ten you bungled the pronunciation?" Color drains from his face, but I don't relent. "Maybe you thought you'd activate both stones tonight, giving yourself better odds of success?" I pin him with a glare. "You are still playing the odds with the lives of every man under your command. I don't care what motivated you. I thought you had better sense." Not giving him a chance to reply or justify his actions, I turn, leaving him alone in his pavilion.

I spot Andrayia struggling with a bulging water skin and three platter-sized saucers. Her eyes are glazed, movements stiff. I take her load, urging her to seek rest. I whisper, "Schwarzenegger." The legendary strength of the former Mr. Universe, times ten, makes the added weight inconsequential, but my leg begins to throb in earnest.

I gaze ahead to where Szames strokes a purring, golden feline. His brilliant, blue eyes dart up and look toward his brother's tent. Two shadows come together, embracing passionately in a kiss. The warrior's hands clench into fists around the golden fur. His knotted hands begin to tremble as he struggles to control the searing fury burning through his being.

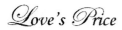

"The ride was tiring for you too?" Szames jumps a mile high at my question.

"Tiring? Not really. But an. . . interesting day. Perhaps a little overwhelming." Szames moves to finish the grooming while I divide the remaining milk into two portions.

"I appreciate you taking care of Jesse for me. For a mage who is supposed to be superpowerful, I seem to need saving quite often," I jest, trying to lighten a mood that seems tense for no reason I can fathom.

Putting my hand on his arm, I look into his eyes. "Thank you for last night." A surge of feelings blaze into being. Instantly they are carried away like a tendril of smoke in a brisk wind. *I wish I could read more than these random, stray emotions from him. The intense feelings are so brief, I don't even know what to make of them.*

Again, I hide behind humor. "I mean, there is nothing like being rescued by a handsome prince to make a girl feel special." Szames blushes from neck to ears at my off-hand remark. I begin to chuckle. The hilarity is cut off as I bend down to retrieve the plates. A bolt of pain streaks up my leg from knee to hip.

I bite my lip. The scream in my throat turns into a grunt. When Szames asks me if I am all right, unshed tears gathering in the corners of my eyes make deceiving him impossible.

"I'll be fine. I just need to sit for a while," I mutter through gritted teeth.

"Are you going to give me a straight answer, or am I going to have to carry you to your tent?" Standing with his feet planted, I have no doubt that is exactly what he plans to do.

"Okay already. It feels like someone took a hot knife to my knee." He steps toward me, and I stumble backward. "But you aren't carrying me!"

"Reba, you are in pain." Szames's brows draw downward in concern.

"And can't afford to show it, not where some of the men might see. How would it look if the all-powerful archmage, their protector, had to be carried to her tent? We can't afford to damage morale like that."

"The Flame-haired One riding her new mystical mount to inspect her quarters may raise a few eyebrows." Not waiting for my consent, Szames lifts me bodily, placing me sidesaddle on Jesse's bare back. "It will not damage morale."

"Whose partner are you anyway?" I scold as Jesse gives a purr of approval.

The short ride to my quarters is so smooth, it is like sitting on a stationary cushion. Szames lowers me to the ground then strides off at a trot toward the largest of the three tents: the infirmary. I scratch Jesse's forehead, sending a "thanks" before entering my quarters.

"Milady, shall I fetch your dinner?" asks a familiar voice as I enter the dim interior.

"Crystal!" I smile, glad to see a friendly face. "I seem to recall instructing you to stay behind."

Although she curtsies with my arrival, her tone is anything but submissive. "Your exact words were, 'You cannot ride; therefore, you cannot accompany me.' I couldn't ride at that time, but I have been taking lessons from the stable master since your arrival. I can now keep a seat on a horse."

"And I finally know the reason behind all those yawns." I sigh. "Well, you're here now. I can't say I am sorry to see you." The pain shoots up my leg as I put pressure on it, turning my walk into a pathetic limp.

"If you wouldn't mind, I could use some help out of these pants. Tupper will be here soon to take a look at this wound." I explain as she drapes my arm around her shoulders. "Removing the clothes will help speed things up."

No sooner do we have the breeches off than a scratching sounds on the outer tent flap. Crystal escorts Tupper in. To my surprise, Szames follows.

"Milady, news of your swift recuperation is sweeping the camp, but Szames, here, informs me it wasn't a full recovery." The healer unwinds the bandage around my knee and thigh. "Mauling by a jarovegi can be nasty business," Tupper remarks as he places the blood-soaked bandage off to one side. "The poison they secrete keeps the wound from closing. Even with the added gift of healing, the process is stymied. You should've stayed off it for one more day at least."

"I didn't have much choice," I grumble.

A grin spreads across my face as a red-faced Szames drips potion over the wound while trying to avoid looking at my naked legs. Tupper closes his eyes in concentration. Within seconds the pain vanishes, replaced by a prickly sensation. The gash melts then bends, closing until only faint pink lines remain.

"Now stay off this leg until tomorrow evening. The healing isn't complete. If you strain it, the cuts will break open." Taking a clean cloth from his bag, the master healer rebandages the limb.

"That excludes the short walk to the staging area to activate the shields?" *I didn't come all this way just to go back to bed.*

"It would be better if you limited your movement to the confines of this tent." Tupper doesn't give an inch. "Wasn't Prince Alexandros planning on activating the shield spell?"

"Reba, I will be there to verify the activation," Szames interjects before I have a chance to reply. "You rest. We need you completely recovered before tomorrow's battle."

"That is why you came along, isn't it?" I sulk with a halfhearted smile. "To make sure I follow the doctor's orders?"

"Someone has to make sure you take your tonic." Szames grins, turning to follow Tupper out.

Watching after me. That's Kyle's job. Using a liberal amount of self-control, I keep the tears from flowing as I recall the very real possibility that I may never see my husband again.

Having been effectively relieved of my duties, I agree to let Crystal bring me a meal. I devour the roasted meat, potatoes, and carrots, enchanted with the rustic fare as I gaze at the oiled canvas tent around me. *Rustic, yes, but not exactly cozy.*

The structure is more than a dozen yards on each side. The table in one corner has six chairs. A canopied bed that is larger than a king size and a nightstand on either side is centered on the opposite wall. The sparse furniture makes the room seem huge.

Directly across from the dining room is a curtained-off section. "Crystal, there wouldn't be. . . facilities behind that curtain," my voice raises an octave as my bladder makes its overfull condition known.

"A chamber pot and tub lie behind the curtain. She hustles before me, holding open the curtained entrance.

I shake my head at the giant spittoon stationed in the corner behind a second curtain. "You gotta be kiddin' me." With my knees pressed tightly together, I begin to chant what is quickly becoming my favorite spell.

"The day has been so long; really tired I am.
This pot won't do, even if they call it 'the can.'
Of magic you will be made and maintained. That's right.
Porcelain, but warmed, so clean, so shiny, and so white."

Deep blue energy caresses my being as it surges out of my outstretched hand, racing to encompass the tin pot. In the blink of an eye, the antiquated bathroom winks out of existence. A porcelain toilet with a heated seat awaits me. *No headache. Looks like my aura has had time to catch up.*

Crystal moves to answer a scratch at the tent flap as I use the new equipment. My nimble fingers lace up the pants. Securing the belt, I peek behind a second curtain and find a small cot. *At least I know where to find Crystal.* I hustle back into the main room to see who has come calling as the contents of the toilet are whisked off to the center of this planet.

"Jerik, I would offer you something, but I've managed to eat everything in sight." I gesture toward the table where Crystal is removing the empty plates.

"I couldn't eat a bite, even if it was covered in chocolate," his deep, gravelly voice rumbles. "We dwarves have a nose for food. I've eaten three times since we made camp."

"You probably needed every calorie after the full day on the march." I grin at the four-foot man who can be called anything but little. His wide shoulders and muscular arms would be right at home on a linebacker.

"At least no one tried to make me ride a darn horse," he grumbles. "This dwarf form is built for long treks. Even hauling my personal supplies, it felt like a leisurely stroll."

"Jerik, I've already apologized for that trip to the gate. . ." A smile creeps into my voice as I recall our first outing on this world. I clamp my lips shut, determined to keep the laughing on the inside.

The dwarf shrugs. "And more importantly, you've acknowledged what this new form is capable of. You must have a little dwarf in you to recover so quickly from a poison."

"Dwarf, eh. . . no. But I do have an enchanted bed."

He gives me a whiskery smile, nodding as if we have been friends for years. "I've adjusted to this world, but Reba, how are you doing?"

"Word gets around quick." I close my eyes, shoring up the walls against the tears building. "I haven't found a way around that portal thing yet, but you can bet your ass I'm not giving up 'til the day I have to send Allinon and Charles home."

"Weren't you trying to find a way to stay here?" Jerik's voice turns unusually soft. "How did you put it: 'This world is so vivid. It's like all my senses have come alive. Colors are brighter and odors stronger. . . When I use magic, I feel a rightness, wholeness.'"

I shake my head in denial. "That was when I thought my husband would be joining me. Trapped here without Kyle would be a nightmare."

Jerik's brows draw down in puzzlement, so I elaborate. "This world reminds me of Rome at the height of corruption; monogamy is considered folly. They don't even state fidelity in the marriage vows; it's just a union to provide heirs. How could I possibly find a lifetime companion on this planet?"

"Isn't one already picked out for you? After all, the Prophecy of the Flame—"

"Don't *even* go there!" I growl over the rest of what he was trying to say. "I will not marry that narcissistic pig they call a crown prince. With the power I wield, I'd like to see them try and force me into it!"

A rumbling echoes in the tent. It takes a few minutes to realize that Jerik is chuckling. "I always wondered what it'd be like if a woman had unlimited power. This world is in for one hell of an adjustment. Woman's liberation has begun."

"I take it you are still set on staying?" I change the subject.

"Reba, we are in the middle of a war against demons straight out of Hell that are trying to destroy mankind, and I am having the time of my life." A boyish grin makes my empathy unnecessary for gauging the truth of his words. "I just hope I get the dwarf lifespan so I can explore this world for the next couple hundred years or so."

"If only Charles and Allinon would change their minds. . ."

"Prince Charming won't. You'd think someone whose extracurricular exploits are becoming legendary would be satisfied." I chuckle at his unintended pun concerning Charles's sexual conquests. "But he isn't. Every day he slides more toward a bipolar personality."

"Then I'll find another way to be reunited with Kyle." In English I add, "I just wish I didn't have two princes to look after on this campaign."

"You didn't expect Alex to take a backseat to Szames, did you?" Jerik chuckles with a twinkle in his eye. "You being out in the countryside, parading around for two weeks with his brother could seriously compromise his position as heir."

"Well, I am married, regardless of any stupid prophecy." A yawn overcomes me, despite the early hour.

"You need rest if you're going to figure out a puzzle like that." He pats my arm. Empathy relays his brotherly concern. "I've kept you from it long enough."

I pull the stocky man to me in a rough hug. "Thanks, Jerik. Not only for the intel, but for letting me know that I'm not alone."

"Of course you're not alone. Jamison and I will always be here," he grumbles to cover his surprise as he pats my back. "Now get some rest. We'll need the most powerful mage on this planet ready for battle tomorrow." He stomps out of the tent as only a dwarf can without being offensive.

Finding I still have plenty of magical reserves, I whisper, "Superman," to activate the flight spell I installed days ago. I rise slowly toward the ceiling with a thought. My hand grazes the canvas roof as I begin an enchantment.

"Nosy people will want to see
What's taking place inside of thee.
What is spoken inside these cloth walls,
Will be heard by none, however they call."

A lazy smile spreads across my face as orgasmic energy surges from every cell in my body, cascading up my arm and through my hand. Radiant energy the color of pale sapphires gathers in a pool before shooting out in all directions to cover every inch of the tent.

After implementing a stronger personal shield, I take Jerik's advice. I crawl into bed only marks after arriving in camp. Sleep overwhelms me while I meditate on a way to rejoin my beloved.

Chapter Four

"Shall I bring you breakfast, milady?" Crystal's voice rings out seconds after I push back the velvet curtain surrounding my bed.

"Only if you will join me." I move to dress in the same clothes I wore yesterday, still relatively clean. "We are in the middle of a crusading army; I see no reason to stand on formality."

"As you wish." At a loss for words, she leaves to attend to the task. The maid takes her place across from me as if easing down on a bed of tacks.

"It looks like your trip here was a little rough." I smile sympathetically.

"The journey was most pleasurable for the first couple of marks. After that I began to realize sitting on a horse is much more work than it seems." Crystal's reply is almost as formal as a report.

I halt with the fork halfway to my open mouth. "Crystal, is something wrong? You seem different."

"Different, milady?" Her face is blank, but I perceive uneasiness below the surface.

"Yes, different. Did I do something to offend you?"

"Oh, no, never that." Crystal looks abashed as she struggles for words to voice the feelings tumbling inside her. "I guess I was trying to make the relationship more proper since it now seems you will be staying." She colors slightly. "With you, though, this is proving to be more difficult than expected."

"Well, stop, please. I don't see why things have to change. I will be the same person I have always been." I resume forking eggs into my mouth.

"That is the other thing I need to discuss with you." Crystal waits for a response, so I give a nod, inviting her to continue. "I was informed before I left that there may be occasions where I will be needed for some additional duties. . ." She implies the sexual portion of her job description.

When feelings of aversion and reluctance assert themselves, I interrupt her. "You don't have to do anything you do not want to. You are my maid now."

"Milady, I am technically your maid, but I am still a member of the castle staff. As such, I am obligated to perform whichever duties fall within the position for which I am trained." She picks at her food as she explains. "Unless I choose to leave the staff, I must do as the master steward demands."

"I see. I take it you no longer wish to perform additional duties?"

"I am unsure if it is the duties that I will mind or being treated like. . . like I have no value. I thought if I acted less familiar with you, you would treat me more like the other nobles do."

"I don't follow you." The heat of embarrassment causes sweat to break out on my palms. My eyes refuse to look anywhere but my plate. "Are you saying you don't wish to be friends?"

"It is not that I do not want to be friends." With a sigh, she pushes her plate away, her breakfast half eaten. "But if I get used to being your friend, how can I go back to being only so much furniture? I see no other choice. We must modify our relationship."

Comprehension dawns. *So she's my true friend.* A slow smile spreads across my face. "I see. Well, what if I took you on as part of my personal staff? It is not exactly a step up, but you will no longer be under Hestur's control. I won't be able to guarantee you much. Who knows where I will end up? But wherever it is, I am bound to need your services." My offer stumbles to a halt as her mouth hangs open.

"You'd do that?" she whispers. "Make me your personal servant?"

"Crystal, you have been nothing but honest and helpful. Who would make a better guide in a world I know nothing about?" Feeling her disbelief, I add, "Besides, I don't think what I am offering is so great. There is no telling where my future lies."

"Wherever it is, milady, I will be with you." The declaration brings a determined smile before she takes our plates out to be cleaned.

I'm lacing up my boots when Crystal returns with Charles in tow. "Dawg, your motor's revvin' for a woman who was unconscious twenty-four hours ago."

"Thanks." I grin. "I think."

Prince Charming ducks his head. "Uh, I meant you're looking back to your beautiful self."

Jerik was right; he is edgy. "I hear you're living up to your reputation." I switch to a topic I'm sure he'll like. "Your promiscuousness didn't cause you to lose your paladin ability to heal for no reason. Your bedroom conquests are renowned."

The black man's cheeks darken in what I assume is a blush. "I'm living lavish. I got them dreamin' of me night and day, linin' up in twos and threes just so I can tap it." Regaining his composure, he leers. "And the stamina to make them all *come* true."

My cheeks turn crimson at the sexual pun. The dark man's laughter echoes in the tent. Getting a hold of himself, he adds, "You got yourself a nice threesome in the making. I can give you some advice on how to—"

Ice fills my veins as well as my voice. "I have a husband I plan on being reunited with. I will have Kyle by my side if I have to sweat blood and piss diamonds."

"My bad. You're still dealin'," Charles mumbles. "If only we knew of someone on Earth who could do real magic."

"Tap into Earth's magic. . ." My head snaps up. "Charles, that's it! You've done it again!" Impulsively I wrap my arms around him.

"What's it? What have I done?"

"You may have given me the key to unlocking the secret of being reunited with Kyle." Standing on tiptoe, I give his cheek a peck.

"The first is free. If you want another taste of this dark suga', it's gonna cost ya." Charles gives me a come-hither look that would put Alex's best effort to shame.

I give him a playful elbow before striding to my nightstand. I retrieve the newly created communication glass. Standing before the ornate mirror, I concentrate on Cuthburan's master sorcerer.

I intone, "Merithin, Merithin, Merithin." Confident that the mirror in the Cuthburan sorcerer's possession will now shine forth with my likeness on it and that Merithin will know that I am requesting to speak with him, I set the looking glass aside.

"I'd better get suited up." Charles sketches an elegant bow, striding toward the door. *His feelings of lust have failed to dissipate after our risqué conversation. He'll be out of his clothes before he gets his armor on.*

"Schwarzenegger," the word, spoken in English, sends a warm thrill through me as magic is released with the key word for my Conan spell. Knowing I now have Herculean strength, I proceed to activate my other battle spell, "Paladin shield."

The drain on my power is minimal. After setting the major spells, only a trace amount is needed to activate it. The Sixth Law dictates a drain on the environment occurs with each enchantment: I resolve to initiate the spells at the tower next time.

I sense the mirror's activation as the hair on my neck stands on end, warning me magic is working. There is a face waiting for me on the glassy surface.

"Reba, you're looking well, considering your journey yesterday. Nemir informed me of the horses' return." Merithin's natural curiosity asserts itself. "How did you manage to fly three people all that way in your weakened state?"

I am forced to fill the Cuthburan sorcerer in on our new allies before I can get to the reason for the call. "Merithin, we have to go over the battle results in the morning. Maybe between now and then you might have time to meditate on something for me?"

"Anything, my dear." His eyebrows perk at the inquiry. "What is your need?"

"I have found a way to bring Kyle to join me! All I need is a master-level sorcerer who is willing to travel to my world and train one of my people in magic." I glow with pride.

"An inspired idea, milady, but to find a sorcerer of that caliber willing to leave a comfortable life. . . that is truly a task."

"I don't think so, Merithin. What would a sorcerer be willing to do in order to obtain unlimited knowledge of the language of magic?"

"If one could fully comprehend the language, his abilities would double. His spells would seldom, if ever, fail. Even a master who has been practicing for a hundred years would give all he has. There is no price too high, milady."

I grin from ear to ear. "That is the language of my kingdom! Whoever agrees to go, I will imbue with my knowledge of it. I've spoken nothing else since birth. Also they will spend several years being immersed in the language." A smug smile tightens my lips. "I'll need your help in selecting the candidate, though. In the wrong hands, the knowledge gained could be more destructive than the demon invasion."

"You can give your knowledge instantaneously?" Merithin stammers in disbelief. "You would do this?"

"To be reunited with my husband, yes, that and more. But I don't have much time. The sorcerer will need to join us at the castle when we return. I have agreed to use my one portal spell to send home any of my group wishing to leave at that time."

"I will have to think on this some. I should have some names for you by morning." Distracted, Merithin disconnects the transmission after a perfunctory farewell.

Buoyed by my success, I saunter out to take my first look at a military camp. I discern profound curiosity beside my doorway as I leave. Lieutenant Craig comes to attention as he recognizes my form.

"At ease." I wait for him to state his business. When he fails to do so, I demand, "You need something?" *I'm glad I took time to secure my tent. All I need is this long-haired rogue eavesdropping on me!*

"I was assigned, milady. At all times a guard is to be posted no less than twenty feet from your presence." His drawl has eased a bit, confirming it was as fake as his smile. "Shall I escort you?"

"That will not be necessary." I turn quickly, hustling on my way. I ignore the man stalking me. *The threat of turning him into a toad seems to have only slightly deterred him from his amorous pursuit. What part of "no" doesn't he understand?*

The encampment lies off the road about fifty feet, taking up several grassy knolls. Tents are evenly spaced encircling a fifteen-foot portable tower. A wooden shaft extends from the top of the tower's platform. Cradled within the wooden lattice on the end of the shaft is an emerald the size of my fist.

The gem has been endowed with enough magical power to project a force field around our position. Just as the one I erected around Castle Eldrich upon our arrival, the magical barrier will vaporize any malevolent being coming into contact with it, using the magic within the demons to recharge the force field.

I gaze about me in stunned wonder at the precise order in which the camp has been laid out. Three humongous pavilions make up the center ring: the infirmary, the royal quarters, and my tent. Dozens of smaller A-shaped tents radiate outward like spokes on a wheel. Hobbling toward one of the smaller domiciles is a familiar figure in a white robe. "Brother Nemandi," I hail the priest, looking for something to distract me from the puppy dog trailing at my heels.

"Archmage Reba." Brother Nemandi bows his head.

"I'm glad to see you made the first leg of the trip." Now that I have his attention, I find myself at a loss for what to say.

"Yes, milady." Nemandi's shy reply doesn't help.

"Well, before the battle you should see Tupper for that stiffness." He colors with embarrassment, so I hurriedly add, "I'm sure he will be able to use your help with the wounded as well."

"Thank you, milady. I will offer my services immediately." Nemandi makes a quick escape. Shaking my head at his timidity, I continue on my way.

"Your mind is eased at last," comes the familiar mind-voice.

"Yes, I no longer fear facing this alien world alone," I send back.

"Is the presence of one man so important?" There is genuine puzzlement in Jesse's thoughts. *"After all, are you not more powerful than any other human on this world?"*

"Power isn't everything. 'You can't buy love' is a popular saying in my world. Trying to find love, someone willing to commit for a lifetime, on this planet—the thought terrifies me. With the prestige I have, men would either be overly awed or seeking political gains." I shake my head in disgust. *"Not to mention the blasted prophecy."*

"You are attracted to Alexandros. Would complying with the foretelling be so terrible?" Jesse nuzzles me, pushing his head under my hand, a very catlike behavior.

"Absolutely. You've searched my memories, felt my upbringing. Can you not see how his way of life would cause me an endless amount of heartache?" I scratch the feline behind the ears.

"You humans adjust so well in truly remarkable ways. Perhaps a similar adjustment could be made here." The kindness accompanying the thought reassures me that the choice to bond with this spirit, who has assumed cat form, was the right one.

"Reba, you seem much recovered today." As if thinking of him has been a summoning, Alex appears. Always the diplomat, he bows to Jesse.

"Very much recovered." I turn to face him. "Are we ready for sunset?"

"The minor call went out last night. It pulled all the demons near our vicinity toward us. Dozens of demons perished by throwing themselves into the shield. Just as with the spell that surrounds the castle, anything intending harm to this kingdom was burned to ash as it came into contact with it. Szames stood guard to verify that the numbers were few enough that shield would not be breached. He activated the major call this morning so that all the demons within a day's travel will be brought here by sunrise. All that remains to be done is activating the moat."

"Will you be attending the transmission of tonight's progress?" I inquire.

"Of course. Knowing what Armsmaster Stezen and Merithin have faced at the other encampment will help us strategize for the next battle." Alex flashes me a brilliant smile. Glancing at the horizon, he adds, "Would you care to accompany me to the council meeting?"

I give a nod. Accepting his arm, I hold in a sigh. *Why does he have to be so darn handsome?*

We enter together. Pleased looks from the officers compound my annoyance. Thanks to the pussyfooting and political posturing of the nobles, the meeting drags on for marks even though our strategy is simple. It is the same plan we used at the Great Battle: surround the camp with the shield and stun field to protect the men. Once the demons lay unconscious, the men will dispatch them. The soldiers can dash behind the force field if any of the monsters manage to recover before they can be killed.

"Archmage Reba, you, of course, will be stationed beside me on the platform," Alex states.

"What?" My temper sparks at the thought of sitting on the sidelines. "My place is on the field."

"We have considered the matter carefully. The demons we have faced so far do not seem to travel in packs like the animals some of them resemble." The prince reveals the need for the change like a parent explaining to a spoiled child the necessity of eating vegetables. "Our task might be much easier if they did. No, our foes, though hideous in appearance, seem to be formed into units, like any army. Ap-bjans, those two headed snake monsters, usually lead several types if demons. The raloliks may look like a raptor hopping around on fuzzy haunches, but they shoot quills from those haunches that are as deadly as any archer. Throw in those blacker than night, crossbow wielding, igildru and a few ogres into the mix. . . The only effective way for a magic wielder to protect the entire circle of men is to take advantage of the added height of the tower."

"It seems my ineptitude for tactics has been uncovered at last." I surrender with glowing cheeks.

"If we failed to uncover something at which you are not exceedingly proficient soon, we would be forced to consider elevating you to sainthood." Alex earns a chuckle from the men and a grateful smile from me with his exaggeration. *At least I hope he was joking.*

The meeting is concluded with a few closing maneuvers from several of the top-ranking nobles. Prince Alex escorts me to where the men have formed up. Szames is followed by Jerik and Charles, the Royal Guard, then the rest of the nobles. The crown prince and I make a stately procession to the center of the camp. The sun paints the sky a dusky pink as Alex turns to address those gathered.

"Men, the time has come for us to draw out the enemy who has hounded us, the foe who has killed our friends and relatives, the demons who threaten our very existence." The feeling of righteousness Alex exudes as he addresses the soldiers is almost overwhelming, even shielded as I am.

"You men are the tools that will exorcise this monstrous cancer!" Alex's persuasion gift projects a sense of security. "Archmage Reba and I will watch over you from above. Wielding all the power at our disposal, we will aid you in the fight, protecting you from the worst our demonic foes may conjure." Now he radiates confidence and hope. "But it is your strength, your skill that will overcome the danger that threatens this kingdom. The time of the prophecy is now!"

"Shall we fly?" I whisper as the crowd sends up a roaring cheer.

Alex gives a brief nod. I lift us gracefully on to the platform. The men pound swords to shields in adulation at the display of power. The officers bark out commands, bringing the men back to attention. In a smart formation, they advance, taking their places around the perimeter of the camp. Szames gives Alex a salute before he and Jerik take their positions on the south side of the shield. Charles moves to the north. The women of the Guard assume a defensive stance below the tower.

"Stun field," I mutter, grasping the defense pole in my hand. A stun field extends twenty feet farther than the force field. In between the two is a safety zone, what the men call the "moat." The monsters in the moat will be dispatched as they lay unconscious from the blast from the stun shield.

A teal mist gathers around the top half of the stave, increasing in thickness as seconds pass. A fog shoots out in an arch above our heads, congealing in a thin barrier twenty feet from the force field. The gem brightens, now glowing with an aqua brilliance.

Patiently we wait for full dark to settle in. Heightened hearing brings the sounds of creaking, leather armor and the jingling of metal to my ears as the soldiers shuffle in anticipation.

Horns blare. The lampposts, set around the perimeter of the camp when the others arrived, surge to life as the men beside them intone the English word, "Illuminate." The battlefield is revealed. Hundreds of demons wait just beyond the light. With a deafening cry, they hurl themselves against the shields.

"Magefire, magefire, magefire." Holding my fingers in a triangle before me, I send streaking balls of desolation when the monsters gather in number.

"Laser," I whisper as an ogre pushes its way up from the bottom of a pile of dispatched creatures in the moat. The humanoid giant with a sloping cranium and fur-wrapped body falls at the feet of the soldier it was ambushing.

With the three alien moons high in the night sky, I soar aloft, taking advantage of a break in the assault. Mud, inky with the black blood of our attackers, squishes under my boots as I land in the moat. *If these weren't monsters, I don't think I could stomach this war.*

"A burial pyre is undeserved by thee;
However, dissolved by fire demons shall be."

The azure flames devour the beasts, while leaving human flesh unharmed. Several men buried underneath the demons are revealed like spring grass under a winter snow. The wounded are placed on stretchers by the teams of healers waiting behind the safety of the force field.

I fly swiftly back to my perch and resume my deadly chant. "Magefire, laser, magefire. . ."

An ache creeps into the back of my head as the legions of demons dwindle in number. Heaven's light brings a new day. The forces of Cuthburan stand undaunted and victorious. Having slept for more than twelve hours, the battle fails to tax my physical strength. I even have a bit of corporeal energy left. *Mages are known for their ability to do with little sleep. I wonder how long I could stay awake if necessary?*

"Your support was indispensable, milady." Alex dips his head.

"My powers did not win this battle; the bravery of the men of Cuthburan did," I mumble, thinking of the bodies lying in the moat as the magical fire turned the demons that had trapped them into ash.

Alex's lips curve in a devastating smile. My mouth twists of its own accord in a cynical grin. Even though I am unsure why we are smiling at what seems such an inappropriate moment, the exchange brings me out of the melancholy threatening to overwhelm me.

I extend my hand to the prince of the land. A word and a thought send us into the glory of the rising sun. I bring our feet to rest at the center of the encampment.

The crown prince escorts me to my tent, where Szames is waiting. Placing the mirror on the table, I intone, "Nemir, Nemir, Nemir," to summon Merithin's apprentice at Castle Eldrich.

The response is immediate. Nemir instructs as his face ripples into view. "Archmage, King Arturo is ready to speak to you,"

"Your Majesty." I bow as Arturo's face takes Nemir's place.

"Archmage." He dips his head in return. "How fares the army? Was Alexandros successful in implementing the strategies?"

"We were victorious, Your Majesty. Alex is here; would you like to speak to him?"

"Neither our son nor we can use magic," the monarch grumbles.

"As with the other objects I have created, this takes no magic to work. Activation requires only a trace of sorcery that all possess, along with the key word." I relinquish my seat to his heir.

I leave the brothers alone in my tent to brief Arturo on the battle. Jerik and Charles offer to accompany me as I meander around the camp.

"Why the frown, Hot Momma?" Charles grins. "You roasted dozens of demons tonight."

"Yes, and we still lost men to those monsters. The first thing I did when we got here was reinforce their armor with the best spell I know. I've got two shields surrounding the camp and the castle. I even made paladin stones so the men have a small force field surrounding them. Still, they are being overwhelmed by the superior strength of the demons."

Jerik harrumphs, sounding like a boulder coming to rest. "Reba, you may be the most powerful person on the planet, but you're not a god. This is war. We were called here to save this world from being enslaved by demons and turned into nothing more than cattle for their consumption. So far I think we are doing a bang-up job."

"Yeah, but—"

"No buts about it, Hot Momma. No war is fought without causalities."

I mumble acceptance of the inevitable. The dwarf gives a huge yawn for the third time. I glance at the stoic warrior. "How long has it been since you got some rest?"

"Dwarves need less sleep than mages," Jerik growls.

"Knowing you, I bet you didn't take a break from setting up camp long enough to catch some z's or snooze long enough to qualify it as a nap."

He shrugs.

"And before that there were the weapons to enchant with dwarf magic for strength and sharpness."

"I've been busy." Again a yawn overcomes him. "We're at war."

"I seem to recall that when dwarves lose sleep, they have to make up for what they have been neglecting. You'll probably sleep for at least fifteen or twenty hours. Off to bed, we will need your legs at full strength for tomorrow's journey."

The three members of the Royal Guard who accompanied me on this leg of the campaign gather around a fire, apart from the other soldiers. "They seem almost as estranged as we are from the rest of the army."

Charles's eyes follow the women as we pass. "Little Momma, with Mikaela's temper, it's no wonder," he mumbles.

"Perhaps all she needs is the right man to show her a little TLC."

His brows knit in puzzlement.

"Before we endowed her with your fighting prowess, her husband used to beat her, daily from what she said."

"Ah, Sweet Momma, it makes sense now." The dark man leers; I feel lust begin to pound in his veins. "Well, I am 'the man.' A good ride from a dark stallion should do the trick."

"Charles!" I throw a mock punch in his direction. "I said TLC, not a good thumpin'!"

"Boo, don't ya see. Here, it is practically the same thing."

I give a disgusted sigh.

Heedless of my opinion, he continues. "The right kind of lovin' is the ultimate TLC."

"Well, good luck with that."

"They don't call me Prince Charming for nothin'." He bows slightly before striding to the woman's campfire.

A twinge of pain runs through my knee as I continue alone on my walk. Knowing I, too, need to be at peak condition for a full day of riding that will begin in twenty-four short hours, I duck into the infirmary for a quick touch-up from Tupper.

"Milady Archmage Reba, how is the knee?" Tupper's brown eyes sparkle with his smile.

"Not bad. Just thought I would save you a trip to my tent." Seeing several occupied beds, I add, "If you are up to it, that is."

"Never too tired for you, milady." He ushers me behind a screened enclosure.

Deftly the healer unwinds the bandage. The wound hasn't reopened, but the skin is red and irritated. "I thought I told you to take it easy. It is a good thing you stopped by. Any more stress and the laceration would have reopened."

I sigh. "How much longer until I have full use?"

Tupper comes out of his trance, patting my leg in reassurance. "With minimal use and one more treatment, the wounds should be healed by the time we break camp."

When I hear a moan from the next room, guilt assails me for my whining tone. "How many did we lose tonight?"

"Less than five but I don't think Oheppinn is going to make it through the day." Tupper indicates the soldier on the closest bunk. "He got mauled by a jarovegi when he stepped outside the shield's protection. The wounds are grievous. The poison had seeped too far into his spirit by the time we got to him. Without family to draw on to restore the aura, the only thing we can do is ease the pain and prolong the inevitable."

We approach the cot where the boy, for the fuzzy-cheeked youth can barely be called a teen, lies motionless.

"No need to whisper. I know I'm dying," the kid's feathery voice murmurs.

Maybe he'd like a display of magic? "Is there something I can do for you?"

"I hear you sing more beautifully than a night bird?"

I lean closer as Oheppinn's voice weakens.

"If I pass into the next life, listening to such sweetness—a love song—from a beauty such as you. . ."

I touch his hand, nodding my agreement and urging him to save his strength. I ask Tupper to bring me something wooden and a strip of leather. Placing the items before me, I recall the first time I cast this enchantment for a group of kids. The fond memory brings a smile to my face, despite the dismal circumstance.

> "With words that rhyme, I am doing fine.
> Songs will improve with a guitar's chime.
> With these materials here for my use."

Energy surges from the center of my being to surround the wood and leather. The wood expands, contorting into a long-necked guitar. The leather melts and bends, wrapping around the instrument to become the case.

Taking a seat provided by the healer, I begin strumming the first few chords to "I Will Always Love You."

I open my eyes as I finish the toned-down recital. *He's so peaceful.* I extend my empathy to see if halting the music has disturbed his sleep.

A startled yelp tears from my lips as the chair scrapes noisily against the floor when I rise too quickly. *He's gone. It feels like a cold, dark hole where his body lies.* Tears stream from my eyes.

"You, a noble lady, weep for a common soldier whose name you didn't know a mark ago?" The question sounds loud in the silence of the room.

"All life is precious." I wipe my eyes, drawing closer to the man lying in the bed across the room. "Does station prohibit feeling?"

"Like your song? Just sympathy instead of love?" the brown-haired man asks.

"Exactly. Would you like to hear another tune?" I attempt to prolong my visit, unwilling to seek my bed with the feeling of death engraved in my senses.

"Probably the last time a man like me gets sung to by a woman," the soldier grouses when he notices my glance at his leg or, more pointedly, the stub where a foot used to be.

"Another love song, then." I pull up a chair, undaunted by his rough acceptance.

> "Crazy. . . I'm crazy for feelin' so lonely.
> I'm crazy. . . crazy for feelin' so blue.
> I knew you'd love me as long as you wanted,
> And then someday, you'd leave me for somebody new."[iv]

A muted round of pounding echoes into the silence as I key the last verse to the Patsy Cline classic. Wondering if I am doing more harm than good, I look to Tupper. He gestures for me to continue.

"You sing beautifully." The listless tone of the maimed man causes me to probe further with my empathy. Self-doubt, inadequacy, and shame greet me.

"I wish I could say it was a God-given talent, but unfortunately most of it is due to magical enhancements." Giving a disgusted shake, I extend my hands, palms up. "Two perfectly good hands, yet not a lick of rhythm or the time to learn what I've always loved: music. So I cheated."

Intrigued by the idea of a mage, or perhaps a lady, admitting to such a disreputable thing, he leverages himself into a sitting position. "If the results are the same, what makes using one of your talents to develop another cheating?"

"Maybe *cheating* is a harsh term. But time and effort could have produced something as good as what I used sorcery to accomplish. It seems nobler if you earn something rather than pop it"—I snap—"into being."

"And you believe performing like this to be noble?" A spark of hope enters his eyes.

"Music lifts spirits and brings joy like little else can. It may also serve as a teaching tool, expressing morals, or to invoke sympathy for a cause, not to mention leaving the ladies swooning. Yet music is something almost anyone can learn if they have the time and patience. Yes, I believe it to be a noble profession if used with the proper motivation."

"Hmm, you know, my girlfriend always did say that I have nimble fingers," the wounded man mumbles.

I chuckle at the remark. He flushes, darting a glance in my direction. "I beg your pardon, milady. I was just thinkin' out loud."

I smile. "Would you like to hear another song?" The soldier nods so I begin "Strong Enough to Bend," playing the opening chords twice. The man eyes my fingers, taking note of the positioning.

Marks later, fingers aching from the effort of the last instrumental, I look up to see the soldier lying peaceful and still. My head snaps up in alarm. I release my shield, extending my empathy.

"He's resting, as you should be," Tupper whispers.

"You said I should stay off my feet." I stretch the tense muscles in my back. "Tupper, I believe this is the longest stretch of sitting I've done since my arrival. Will you see that he gets the guitar when he wakes?"

"You wish to leave this instrument for him?" the healer asks.

"Playing it doesn't require two feet, just a small amount of talent and a greater amount of desire. And Tupper, something tells me he has more than a small amount of talent." I smile, grateful for the intuition imbued in my character in the transfer to this world.

"Call me Tupp, if you will, as my friends do." The physician gives my arm a fatherly squeeze as he ushers me toward the door.

"Good night, Tupp." As I push open the tent flap, I squint against the light. "Or should I say good day?"

Before I get within five feet of my quarters, I feel Merithin's call. It is siesta time, so not even Crystal is up and about. There is plenty of privacy as I respond to the summons. Kicking myself for forgetting about the promised meeting, I rush to the table where the mirror is standing. Taking a seat, I chant the sorcerer's name three times.

"I'm sorry about the hour; I was tied up in the infirmary," I apologize as the wizened face appears on the surface, replacing my own.

"Were you hurt in tonight's engagement? I've heard nothing of this."

"No, just receiving some additional healing for the jarovegi bite. I spent some time with the recovering men and lost track of time."

"Mmm, well, I only sent out the call less than a mark ago." The sorcerer's speech goes from a low mumble to stronger resolution as he continues. "Speaking of healing, I have a message from Jamison. He said you left before Szeanne Rose could give you the news. He apologizes for relaying it this way, but he thought you should know. I quote, 'I took the liberty of doing a full healing while I was at it. I was able to heal all past damages.' Do you understand his message?"

"A full healing?" *He healed the damage done by the endometriosis! Sure, now I can have kids, now that my husband is on another planet.* "Thank you, Merithin. Please send Jamison my appreciation. Any luck with the search for a suitable candidate?"

"I have some good news and some bad news." Merithin hesitates.

"Can I have the good news first?" *I should've known it wasn't going to be easy.* "I could use some."

"I have found a suitable individual who is willing to take on your quest." His eyes gleam as he makes his delivery.

"And the bad news?" I insist before my hopes rise too high.

"The sorcerer is demanding additional terms. He has taken a somewhat prestigious position. The candidate wishes you to take his place in the interim. He estimates it could take as long as five years of concentrated effort to find and train someone to perform the necessary incantation." Merithin's eyes probe the surface of the looking glass.

"Take his place? You can vouch for this sorcerer?"

He nods.

"Unless you can see something I'm missing, I think his counterproposal is reasonable. I see no reason why I shouldn't take him up on the offer." *Five years without Kyle. At least I will be away from the princely brothers.* "How soon can I meet him?"

"You're looking at him." The sorcerer hurls a bombshell, smashing through my defenses.

"But. . . but what about the war? I have to send the others back after the first round on the campaign. What if we haven't found Gaakobah or the portal? The rogue sorcerer who's holding open a gate to a demonic world was your apprentice. The whole reason we are crusading around the countryside is to find him and close that gate. As much as I appreciate your willingness to take on the assignment. . ." I stumble to a halt, not wanting to offend the elder.

"Reba, I understand your concerns. They are the same ones I've wrestled with since we discovered that the first apprentice I taught was coordinating the attack on our kingdom. The reality of the matter is that I only trained Gaaki for a short time, as apprenticeship goes. I have already passed on all I know about his training to you. I talked it over with Archbishop

Prestur; my not being here shouldn't affect the outcome of the battle for the gateway. King Arturo has authorized my leave with the stipulation I find a suitable replacement: he was delighted to hear I would be recommending you for the job. Besides, I would trust no other with the knowledge you offer." Merithin lays out his cards: a royal flush.

"I don't know. . . what to say." I stumble over the words, my mind reeling. "It never even occurred to me that you would be willing to go. I thought you were too dedicated to this campaign."

"It is the responsible thing to do. The wizards council absolved me of any responsibility for Gaaki's actions. It's considered unethical to pull someone through a portal without their consent; therefore, it is my responsibility to correct it." The grandfatherly smile never leaves his face. "I regret the necessity of having to hand over the responsibility for Gaaki's apprehension to you, but I see no other option."

He continues to explain. "There is a chance a return voyage won't be possible, but it is a chance I would take on most portal journeys." With an impish grin, he adds, "I have always dreamed of visiting another world but vowed never to work with portals. If not for the siege, I wouldn't have had this opportunity."

"I am sure you know what we are both getting into. I only have one hesitation: Why would a master sorcerer be willing to be confined in a castle?" I chew the inside of my cheek. "With the Sixth Law limiting the number of spells preformed in one locale, it seems less than ideal. In less than a week, I managed to create a dead zone!"

"My dear, I apologize, I should have given you the entire tome on the laws. I assumed since you placed the force field spell on the outer wall, you knew of its properties, else the spell would have failed inside an octal. Casting a spell will drain corporeal energy from the atmosphere, but marmari-sterk is known among the gifted as sorcerer's abode. Laymen prize the rock for its strength and durability, but those who weave spells know that the stone is a wellspring for corporeal energy. That is why my position is so highly prized. The tower dedicated to my use is a place of great strength."

"I see. In that case, I'm still game." I relinquish the shadows threatening to overwhelm me to the light of hope blooming in

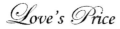

my heart. I duck my head, embarrassed to ask, "While we are on the topic, how big was it? That dead zone at Eldrich?"

"Not to fret, milady. It was merely the size of the meadow." Merithin chuckles. "I'm not sure any other sorcerer on the planet could have created one such in less than six months. In truth, the Sixth Law has been so carefully observed that this is the only dead zone I know of besides the Great Waste."

"The Great Waste?" I ask, suppressing a yawn.

"A fabled legend tells of a dead zone that occupies the northeast above the impassible great cliffs. It is said that the Great Waste inspired the creation of the Sixth Law."

Giving another yawn, I get us back on track. "Do you have a method by which you can join me in my dreams? I know how disorientating a new world can be. Even though I'll be giving you knowledge, I think it is best if we get you acquainted with my world before dumping you in the middle of it."

"A brilliant idea. Dream-coupling will make it impossible for another sorcerer to eavesdrop. If we make it a nightly practice, I will have a firm grasp of your world before I make the pilgrimage."

With the battle high, the infirmary, and now this, the emotional stress is too much. A tear traces its way down my cheek. "Thank you so very much. You don't know how much I appreciate this."

"My dear, it is my pleasure. After all you have given for my country, how could I do less?"

"And here sits your invincible archmage, unable to even stop the flow of her own tears, weeping like a helpless maiden," I mumble. *Crying is a huge weakness, often coming unbidden.*

"Tears don't make you weak. They serve to show that a heart lies beneath your strength, else the power you wield might be feared."

A smile steals across my face. "Sometimes I forget how intimidating I seem to others." Desiring time to process this new development, I try to escape while my emotions are still held somewhat in check. "I guess there is nothing else to do but bid you good night."

"We will talk again tomorrow?" he queries. "About sunset?"

Signaling my agreement, Merithin relates the dream coupling technique to me. I terminate the connection by intoning, "Mirror, mirror, mirror." Emotions whirling, I settle down for a midafternoon nap. *Like I'll be able to sleep.*

Intoning the spell Merithin gave me for the dream-coupling eases me into peaceful bliss like no drug on Earth can.

Chapter Five

Light from the restrained curtains streams into my bed. My mouth stretches wide as I push myself into an upright position. Crystal continues to tie back the remaining curtains.

"How are the muscles?" I ask her.

"Very well. The healing you performed before the battle relaxed me so much, I slept through the entire thing!" Crystal expresses herself with more candor than usual.

"I'm glad to hear it. I know you are a city girl." I smile, recalling the touch I gave to send her into a healing slumber. "I was worried about your adjustment."

"Milady, that's the nicest thing anyone has said to me in days." The maid continues about her business as I take pen and paper in hand, determined to sort my thoughts.

When my stomach emits a loud growl, Crystal excuses herself. In seconds she returns, bearing a large tray. "Lieutenant Craig sends his regards."

"Please join me. The lieutenant provided more than enough for two, even with my incessant appetite." A look of distaste passes across her face. I open my senses: *sexual tension?* "Am I inviting further advances by eating the meal he provides?"

"No, milady," Crystal mumbles, taking a seat across from me, her attitude having done a complete one-eighty in the past two minutes.

"Well then, let's take advantage of these berries he scavenged up, not to mention this butter-cheese." I fill my plate, hoping she will open up to me in her own time.

Finishing my second helping, Crystal still hasn't said more than ten words. "Is Craig as big of a pain to you as he is to me?"

"Nothing out of the ordinary. He is noble born, even if he isn't an heir." Crystal begins stacking the dishes, preparing to leave.

"Crystal, even someone who is not a mage can see you're upset." I place a restraining hand on her arm. "I will try to help if I can, but first I need to understand what's wrong."

"Why do you care so much?" The blonde's eyes fill.

"How could I not?" Bewildered by the woman's sudden show of emotion, I move to comfort her, enfolding her shuddering form in a warm embrace.

"It is this. . . it's all of this," she sputters between sobs. Maintaining a tight grip on the back of my shirt, she buries her face in my shoulder like a small child.

"Shush. . . shush now. . . everything is going to be fine," I whisper, rubbing her back until she has cried herself out.

Haltingly, she begins, "Milady, I'm sorry. Please don't think I am unappreciative of all you have done for me. It's just, I find myself suddenly so confused. When I took a position with the staff, I knew what would be expected of me. It took mere months before I became known as the best in my field. I took pride in that; I still do, in a way. But you have shown me kindness, consideration, love even." I nod my head as her blue eyes shed tears again.

"Both men and women have come and gone in my life, but no one has actually cared about my well-being since I left my parents. The more time I spend in your company, the harder it is to accept what others see when they look at me." I nod in understanding as she continues. "All they see is someone who is a pleasure master." Anger gives her words a harshness. "As if all someone has to do is offer to please me for a change or give me some pretty trinket to get me to do their bidding. What makes him think I would betray your trust? I know the meaning of you wearing that necklace Craig gave you. If I encouraged you to wear his gift, thus inviting further advances, it would be the worst kind of manipulation."

"So Craig is doing more than following me around? That's good to know. What can I do to help?" The Indianapolis 500 is slow compared to my racing thoughts. "I don't think a spell will make people see you in a way they are unaccustomed.

"Humph. . . even in my world, a woman as beautiful as you is admired for her body first and mind second. But at least there, if a woman sticks to a strong moral code, she can develop a support circle of friends and family to combat the negative attention received elsewhere. Here, though, where women are still struggling to be seen as anything other than sex objects—"

A flash of light blinds me. It takes nanoseconds before my vision becomes clear. I see my husband collapse to his knees in front of a buxom blonde. The woman's back is toward me as she rushes to his side, attempting to comfort my grieving husband. Another minor flash and Crystal is before me again. I push the vision into a corner of my mind for further examination at a later date.

To my surprise, Crystal's mood lifts of its own accord. "Thank you milady, but I don't think an enchantment is necessary. Good advice is almost as valuable as a magical spell. I will try to let those closest to me know my true self, see if that helps me deal with the Cretans as well as every noble's third son whose eye I happen to catch." More composed but still suffering, she ambles out with this morning's dishes.

A quarter-mark later, I mosey out the door to survey the camp morale and visit Jesse. Still struggling with the unwanted turn my brain has taken, I decide to visit Jesse first.

"More guilt? This time over a brief glimpse into the future?" Unable to put my feelings into a question, the cat nonetheless responds to my concerns. *"The human mind is a complex puzzle. What makes you think the cause of a premonition is something I can decipher?"*

"Can't you trace it? See if it was invoked from a hidden desire?" I ask.

"The process would be very painful and more than a little dangerous. Why do they matter so much, these 'hidden desires'? You have behaved in the most ethical and moral way, according to your beliefs. Why punish yourself for inconsequential clatter in your brain and an ability you seem to have little control over?" The irrefutable reasoning of the majestic spirit helps me push the guilt aside. Taking a wooden brush in hand, I begin the work I have come to do.

The black feline revels in the massage the brush-down gives his muscles. Telepathically, Jesse shares his pleasure with me. *It's almost like I am giving myself a massage.* The tension that has been building unwinds.

"I have never seen a beast in more ecstasy." Szames chuckles.

"Having a touch of the healing gift, not to mention telepathy, makes hitting all the right spots a walk in the park." The brush strokes remain fluid, the familiar presence disturbing neither my partner nor me.

"Ahh." Jesse's pleasure is broadcast as Szames scratches between the luminous eyes and behind the ears, redoubled pleasure cascading through him. The affection translates to me as a temple and neck rub.

"Mmm." I echo my partner's sentiments.

It's like Szames is giving me a massage! I break the telepathic link. Feeling as if I have crossed an unseen line, I end the rubdown.

Not wanting Szames to think he has offended me, I ask, "I was going to take a stroll through camp. Care to join me?"

The prince inclines his head. We meander through the tents, walking side by side in companionable silence. I open my empathy, soaking in the general state of the soldiers in the vicinity. Full darkness arrives. Torches are set out, the lampposts lit before our tightening circle brings us to the center of camp.

Men gather around the innermost campfire. Feelings of pride, contentment, and honor are prevalent as they have been throughout our promenade with only a slight fear lurking in the background. When an officer calls for Szames, I turn to take a closer look at those gathered around the glowing warmth while the two men discuss business.

"Milady, tell me: Is becoming wounded near to death the only way a soldier will get to hear that legendary voice of yours?"

I look over at the stringy, long-haired man who has plagued both Crystal and me. Several of the soldiers near him chime in, voicing their agreement, if somewhat meekly.

"Surely soldiers wouldn't be interested in the sappy love songs I know?" I direct my comment to all of the twenty or so men in Craig's vicinity.

"Ma'am, I've got a girl back home," a blond soldier states. "If I can learn a few verses that are pleasin' t'hear, the nights away would be a little less lonely." More than a few men nod in agreement.

"Well, an instrument is needed if you want the proper effect. I need a scrap of leather and a piece of wood." Men jump to provide the necessary materials. Szames concludes his discussion, coming up beside me as the items morph into a guitar and a leather case for the instrument.

"Would you care to join us?" I give a weak smile. "It seems word has gotten out of my musical abilities."

"Most assuredly." Szames places two logs next to each other, gesturing for me to precede him.

Sticking to love songs, I begin without preamble. "Strong Enough to Bend" gets a thunderous round of applause. *Looks like the common folk are more familiar with either nature or compromise, perhaps both.* I gesture to the man next to me, trying to give him the floor.

Disapproving ohs and ughs ring out along with a couple of brave shouts of, "One more," and, "Another."

Who knew warriors would like sappy songs? Oh, now this is right up their alley. "How about the love song I sang for the nobles?" Greeted by enthusiastic cheering, I recite the preamble I gave at the ball. After the second song, I turn to the blond soldier who had been bold enough to speak to the archmage. "If you know a song, perhaps I can try to put some chords to it."

By relaxing and letting the magic flow, I am able to strum the guitar methodically to the marching song the soldiers chant. When a more colorful ditty begins, I pick the instrument like a country bumpkin while my cheeks brighten at the innuendoes.

Marks later I take my leave. The joy of singing has made me as tranquil as the night surrounding us. I invite Szames into my tent, having business to discuss that requires the privacy of my warded pavilion.

"I wanted to let you in on the new developments. Merithin will be leaving with Charles and Allinon; he will go to my world to search for an apprentice."

"And if he is unable to find anyone with master-level potential?" Szames plays devil's advocate.

"He feels the danger of that is minimal."

"Is there some way for him to contact you and to inform you of the outcome of the search?"

"Hmm, let's get Merithin in on this. Having another person to brainstorm with us might not be such a bad idea." I set up the mirror and call the sorcerer's name.

"Brain. . . storm?" Szames looks baffled.

"It's an Earth idiom, a phrase that means more than just the words. In this case, brainstorm means to bring several minds into focus on one topic, tossing out any and all related ideas." A face swims into view. "Merithin, Szames has some interesting ideas about your journey."

"An inspired idea, milady." Merithin bows to Szames. "Since this will be the first time one of the members of the council will visit your world, it is entirely appropriate that a royal representative be included in our plans."

"Reba was saying that you expect the journey to take nearly five years?" Szames gets right to the point.

"Three under the best of circumstances if I have immediate access to the magic on her world. But most likely four to six years will be needed to learn to weave magic, find a master-level apprentice, and train him to harness enough magic to cast a master-level spell."

"Perhaps we could produce something like the communication mirrors to keep appraised of the progress?" Szames's question makes Merithin raise an eyebrow at the warrior.

"It seems the lessons I taught you on deductive reasoning are still being applied." The sorcerer smiles. "But unfortunately until we know just how much access I will have to corporeal magic, and many other particulars, the mirrors are not practical across such a vast distance."

"How about a simpler form of communication? Something more. . ." Unable to find a suitable word for *binary,* I add, "On or off?"

Merithin rubs his chin. "Hmm, if we linked two pairs of items with enough power to cast a light from within and enough power to maintain the link across the vastness, I believe it will work. I know an enchantment that will cause a stone to glow with a mere thought."

"If both pairs are linked, why not light one stone to signify a safe arrival?" Szames asks.

I nod. "And I will cause it to blink, acknowledging I have received your message."

"Then I will darken the stone, ending the communication," Merithin agrees. "But how to tell which stone is which?"

"If we used an emerald and ruby," I suggest. "After the original green for arrival, green could mean you've found an apprentice, and the red, it may be longer than five years."

Szames is amazingly swift in catching on to the new idea. "If you send a red for a problem, then you could send the green when you have solved the problem. This way we can estimate the time of your return." He once again plays devil's advocate. "But what if you are unable to complete the mission?"

Silence drags on as we search for a suitable answer. Sure that we will never use it, I throw out the first thing that comes to mind. "Could we use a double light?" The men look baffled, so I elaborate. "After I make the stone blink, you could cause it to become a steady light again. Two steady lights will mean that the mission is over, one way or the other. If it is the ruby, you will not return. If it is the emerald, you are on your way."

Merithin smiles, confirming the code. "I will send a solid green when I arrive and when I locate an apprentice and the blinking green to signify a solved problem. Reba, milady, I bid you good eve. Prince Szames, your aid in setting the communication code was insightful." The sorcerer bows to us, taking his leave to tend to his other duties.

Turning to Szames as the mirror dims, my brow crinkles with puzzlement. "You're much smarter than I thought you'd be."

"Thank you, I think." Szames's brow furrows but a grin shows he is not offended.

"I'm sorry. That came out horribly wrong." I chuckle at the faux pas. "I should know better than to stereotype."

"Stare. . . ee-o. . . type?"

"Presumptions about someone based on looks, position, or upbringing. In my country people are usually willing to accept you for who you are or at least give you a chance to prove yourself." Seeing the confusion leave his countenance does little to ease the shame boiling inside. I keep explaining. Holding up my hand, I motion for him to do likewise. Matching up our palms, I illustrate the difference in size. "Even on my world, your size is well above average." My fingertips just reach his top finger joint. "With your position as leader of Cuthburan's armed forces and your good looks, I guess I never figured you for a scholarly type."

"Most people make that assumption." Szames smiles. "It allows for a strategic advantage. I must say, I am not sorry you saw past the facade."

The look of sincerity in his blue eyes gives me a cozy feeling. With our hands still pressed together, a warm, tender emotion accompanies it. The silence expands between us, neither of us daring to move as we gaze into the other's eyes.

"Milady, shall I prepare a bath for you?" Crystal queries into the stillness.

I jerk my hand away. "Thank you, Crystal."

Szames sketches a quick bow, making a hasty exit. "Milady, I will take my leave."

I smirk as the tent flap closes. "The bath isn't necessary until morning, but I assume you know that."

"Yes, milady. And you truly aren't irritated at the interruption?" Crystal's head is bowed, her eyes downcast.

"For following orders? Of course not!" I chuckle in relief. "You just saved me from what might have become a very awkward situation."

Crystal still looks puzzled as she asks, "I know you cherish your vows, but it may be five years before you see your husband. Surely you don't plan on remaining celibate?"

"I do and I will." I sigh, thinking about the situation I have created. "Szames is the first male friend I've had since I got married. I guess I am going to have to put the relationship on a business-type exchange. Either that or create a spell to send me a *zap* when the inevitable physical attraction asserts itself."

"You expect the same of Kyle?" As she pursues the point, my bladder begs for attention.

"Hold that thought. I've gotta run to the chamber pot." I hasten to the corner of the tent that has a toilet. Grateful for the time to reexamine my thoughts on that topic, I relax on the porcelain surface after closing the curtain. Reaching a decision, I stand, pulling up my drawers.

"As a matter of fact, I was just thinking about Kyle. Crystal, how would you feel about taking on an away assignment?" I raise a single eyebrow, a trait inherited from my grandfather.

"You wish me to take care of your husband until he joins you." The color drains from her face as she grasps where I am heading.

"How did you know?" I'm stunned. *It didn't occur to me until this morning. It took Jesse's reassurance to pursue it.*

A flush infuses her cheeks. "You've been worrying about his being alone."

My empathy confirms what she is thinking. "I wasn't referring to any special services, although, I will compensate you greatly. I just thought, since you hold such respect for the vows we've taken, you'd be as valuable to him as you have been to me. Besides, as I was saying earlier, since my world doesn't judge as harshly as this one, you might even choose to stay." As worry reasserts itself, I forge ahead. "I trust if you decide to take me up on my offer, you'll provide me with a suitable recommendation for your replacement. It needn't even be someone who offers additional services."

"And if Merithin were unable to provide a return trip?" I perceive desire rising in her and something more, something softer. "Then what of your husband and his vows?"

I do a double-take. "You aren't worried about coming back. You want to know about Kyle's availability?" *What have I gotten myself into? I thought I was sending him a watchdog. Instead I might be sending a future bride.*

"It's just that I. . . well. . . you have talked about him so much," Crystal stammers, her entire face turning beet red. "That he might be too shy to find another partner."

Jealousy dries my mouth, turning the words bitter. "I suppose if Merithin were unable find a way to return, he would be considered a widower." I grind my teeth. *He deserves happiness if we can't be together.* "And available."

An idea sparks. I push the feelings into a dark corner of my heart, following the inspiration. "It is a long trip, and it might be one way. It's a big commitment." I hate myself for the deception I am weaving. "If you want, I can show you what he looks like, as if he is standing here beside us."

The blonde regains control of her composure. "Looks matter little to me, milady. However, knowing he isn't a mud-faced troll would ease my mind."

"What you will see is an exact image of him." Keeping Kyle's appearance implanted in my mind, I begin a rhyme.

"Kyle is not here for you to see.
A hologram will appear for thee."

The top of Crystal's head just reaches the top of the five-foot-eleven, ebony-headed engineer's shoulder. Standing a mere three inches taller than I, Kyle is not what you would call a commanding presence. But as he materializes, a peacefulness surrounds me, a comfort I have not known since my arrival. With reluctance, I finish the rhyme.

> "Love's light will surround each
> If love will dawn when they meet."

A pang of regret stabs through my heart as a soft white glow radiates from both Crystal and the holographic Kyle. My hands begin to tremble. My concentration falters, causing the likeness of my husband to disappear. *Just because they can develop feelings for each other doesn't mean that they will. And it definitely doesn't mean they'll act on those feelings,* I rationalize, holding my chin high.

Still perceiving a sense of awe from my maid, directed at the man whom she hasn't yet met, I apply reason. "He's average height for a man on my world. As I have said, only cute. There are many handsome men who will vie for your attention."

Holding in a sigh, Crystal lowers her eyes from the spot where his likeness stood. "Yes, but the compassion and sensitivity of which you spoke, I can see it in his eyes."

"Crystal, I need to know you can and will remind him of his vows if you travel to my world. I understand I ask much and will take no offense if you decline the offer." *Maybe she won't accept.*

"May I have the night to think it over?" Crystal hedges, though I sense she has made up her mind.

"I need an answer by the time we set up camp tomorrow night. If you go, I will need at least eight days to acclimate you to my world." Dismissing her to her bed, I turn to answer a scratch at the entryway.

"Milady, I saw your light and wondered if perhaps you would care for an evening snack." Craig bows with a tray in hand.

"Thank you," I reply curtly, taking the tray and letting the flap hit him in the face. Heaving a sigh at one more problem I

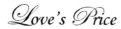

have yet to solve, I stalk over to the table to compose a few spells before I turn in for the night. Unsure whether I have accomplished something good or something that will be my undoing, I chant the revised prayer spell.

"Now I lay me down to sleep,
I pray the Lord my soul to keep.
If I am here when I awake,
Recharged power I now make.
As I slumber, peaceful and deep,
Magic into me will now seep.
Thoughts of Earth, Kyle, home too,
Fill my dreams accurate and true."

Darkness overwhelms me. I slip into unconsciousness, still struggling with the events I have put into motion.

Chapter Six

"You, your contents, everything inside,
Shrink smaller and smaller, Barbie size."

The canvas dwelling that will be my home for the next few weeks shrinks until it is the size of the Malibu Mansion. Concentrating, I continue the spell until it is half that size.

"Extremely efficient. Tell me: Could this spell work on the entire camp?" Szames's inquiry earns him a dirty look from his brother.

"I'm afraid not. The enchantment is for a single object. Even if I rewrote the spell, we would have a hundred tiny tents to pick up and pack." I stow the miniature domicile in a box created for its transportation while Alex smirks at his brother.

"Is everything tied down?" I ask Tupp, who nods. I perform a second incantation on the infirmary.

"How about if we had a wooden floor or something for the camp to sit on?" Szames, undaunted, continues with the same train of thought.

"And find a place flat enough for the entire camp every night?" Alex's innocent look doesn't fool me for a moment. I sense the sibling rivalry boiling under the surface.

Lani and I got over our competition issues years ago, mostly. They need to grow up! A flash of insight makes me add, "Wood wouldn't work, but how about canvas? It is flexible enough. If we can find a way to secure the tents to it, it just may work."

"Would a few leather stitches be enough?" I nod and Szames smiles. "I will inform my father tonight. He can have the mobile camp ready when we return. If we are forced to go on a second campaign, our supply load will be considerably lighter, not to mention reducing setup time to practically nothing."

"Reba, can you attach a permanent activation spell to the mobile camp, like the lampposts?" Alex acts as if he were backing the idea from the start.

My lips twist as I nod. "Now that I have initiated a new field of application for magic, I can see my to-do list is going to be a long one." I complete the breakdown that would have taken a dozen men almost a mark to perform.

The sun is cresting the distant hills by the time the camp is ready to move out. Hundreds of men form up, marching in eight columns. Squadrons of light infantry and officers space themselves down the line on either side. With a motion from Alex, Szames barks, "Forward march."

"Szames, you and Andrayia will scout out the area ahead," Alex orders.

"I think it will be better if I take point with Szames. My magical resources will be needed if we run into trouble."

"Your magical resources are exactly why I need you here, guarding the main force," Alex persists.

"Alex, with your leadership, I am sure the men can hold out until I arrive. Jerik can summon me if there is a problem," I insist. "It will take me less time than this discussion to come to your aid."

The nod he gives is a grudging one, but it is all the approval I need. A quick look to Szames and we are off at a lope. A cheer rises from the men as we pass. I release my magical shielding, taking in the feeling, luxuriating in the freedom of being away from Alex, where I have to keep my empathy guarded. Within a half-mark, we reach the crossroads, taking a left to scout south.

When the Cuthburan troops are a distant spot on the horizon, Jesse and Tawny slow to a walk. My breath catches in my throat. The azure sky hangs over russet knolls; the hues looking alien in a way I am unable to pinpoint. It is a picturesque vision to behold. Our secluded position gives a privacy I haven't enjoyed since my arrival. A mark passes without a word exchanged, both Szames and I reveling in the solitude and the silence.

"You seem pensive today," Szames whispers.

"I'm debating the wisdom of a recent decision." I hesitate, unsure of where I should draw the line with him. Having no other human to talk to and finding Jesse's alien contribution sincere but lacking, I decide to take Szames into my confidence yet again.

"I offered Crystal the opportunity to accompany Merithin back to my world. Since she has developed a healthy respect for the marriage vows we've taken, I thought she could provide companionship while serving to remind my husband of our covenant."

"To see another world sounds like a wonderful opportunity, but Crystal?" The incredulous tone does little to help my misgivings.

"My husband isn't the typical male. He doesn't even know how to make a move on a girl. As long as she doesn't offer him her 'special services,' he won't ask." With an explosive breath, I shake my head. "I know it sounds bizarre. I have no idea how I got myself into such a mess."

"Sometimes a sixth sense—intuition maybe—causes us to do things that, on the surface, might not seem like the wisest of decisions." Szames offers a lopsided smile, making my lips curve in return.

I recall the vision of the blonde standing beside my grieving husband. *He hit that way too close to the mark!* I shake off the minor vision. *It could be anything; he was probably upset at being separated from me for so many years.* I continue to rationalize, *Yin is getting old, perhaps he had to put down the dog he loves like a child.*

The lies do little to comfort me. "I wish I could accept that intuition was the reason behind my actions, but unfortunately I know myself too well. Guilt probably has more to do with it than anything else." I glance back at the troops who are still barely in sight.

"Self-reproach? About what could you possibly feel guilty?" The softly spoken question strikes straight to the core of the problem.

"With all my abilities, there is still a very real possibility I won't be able to reunite us. Because of my inadequacy, our marriage might fail!" Blinking to keep the tears in check, I use anger to hold them there. My voice becomes harsh. "All I know is that I can't bear the thought of him being alone should I fail."

I close my eyes, resigned, as if speaking the words out loud is a magical release. "It is out of my hands now. I made the offer; I will not take it back. It's up to Crystal whether or not she takes it."

"Not many women would think of their man's comfort while plunged into an alien world where customs are strange and the people stranger," Szames mumbles.

"I'll admit, stranger people I have not met." I chuckle at his hanging jaw. My broad smile brings one to my companion as he comprehends my dry sense of humor.

The blue skies are cheery, even in the harsh, winter landscape. I drop my temperature shield to gauge the comfort of those without magical assistance. *Can't be colder than forty-five, and it's not even noon yet. It's going to be a beautiful day, almost spring.*

"We should pick up the pace," Szames suggests. "We need to scout ahead before we return for lunch."

"How about a real stretch of the legs?" I grin in anticipation. "I'll race you to tonight's campsite."

"You are on." With the acknowledgment, our steeds are off like a shot.

"Jesse, can you get the site's location from Tawny? I'd hate to fly right past it!" A mental nod is his only response. I relax into the saddle, enjoying the wind as it ruffles my hair. The feline pair is evenly matched, running neck and neck, neither one able to gain more than a nose on the other.

"Hold on tight," the raven cat sends. With a burst of speed, Jesse leaps, surging into the lead. Seconds later he drops his hind end, making furrows in the earth as he plants his claws, pulling up tufts of dried grass.

"You were holding back, weren't you?" Tawny and Szames make a less hasty stop, circling around to us.

"Well, I didn't want to discourage the youngster." Chuckling, he adds, *"Then again, I couldn't let her win either!"*

"Wow, what a ride!" Taking the loss with extraordinary sportsmanship, Szames's grin widens. "If we had the entire infantry unit mounted on steeds such as these, this campaign would be completed in a few octals!"

"Humph! It would take a realignment of the stars for the rest of my kind to volunteer for such a thing. They believe such as this to be below their evolved status. I had similar feelings until experiencing your full personas."

"I suppose some of us humans are not so bad, once you get to know us." Szames speaks aloud to include everyone in the discussion.

"Jesse, what exactly is your species?" I rake my fingers through his fuzzy scruff, which is as soft as a rabbit's pelt but much longer.

"Once we had a corporeal form, but that was centuries before your kind came to this land. We have taken on many identities since then, exploring cultures from within their own societies." A profound sadness echoes with his next statement. *"Now most feel they have explored all there is and have done everything there is to do."*

Tawny growls at Jesse who halts his mind-speech.

"Doesn't that stagnate your culture?" I interject when he fails to resume the topic. "What does not grow, dies."

Before Jesse responds, Tawny's ears flatten from what must be a telepathic argument.

"As we have been doing for centuries now. Many of us have passed beyond. For that reason as much as any other, I agreed to accompany you. I am well respected among my kind, perhaps a few more can be persuaded to form a likewise treaty if this one proceeds as well as I feel it must."

The startled look on Szames's face transforms into a wide grin as he comprehends Jesse's suggestion. "With your permission, I will speak to my brother of this. It may take him a good while to warm up to the idea."

"Actually, I got the idea from scanning Reba's mind."

I recall the fantasy books I've read.

"A similar agreement will suffice. Since she is familiar with the topic, perhaps it will be best for her to broach the subject."

"I'm not so sure the direct approach is the best course. Alex seems to have a hard time accepting things of a magical nature. He might reject the idea without even thinking it through." I pause while the wheels turn, bringing more solidity to the plan I considered before approaching the forest for help.

"From the mischievous glint in your eyes, I take it you have got something in mind?" Waiting for me to reveal my scheme, Szames gestures for us to start back.

"I'm sure it will only take a few demonstrations of the admirable attributes of the cats, along with a couple of subtle hints, for your brother to arrive at the same conclusion you have." With a sly smile, I reach down to rub my leg. "You know, all this riding is tough on my knee, perhaps it will be best if I ride in the wagon after lunch."

Szames is quick to follow my lead. "Having Alex confirm this campsite might be wise."

"Jesse, you got another sprint in you? I think it's time we head back." Springing forward, going from a walk to a dead run, the partners keep a pace that equals a horse's gallop, practicing for the upcoming demonstration.

I snap my empathy shield in place as we arrive. Our timing is impeccable; the troops are just falling out for a quick snack. I give Jesse his head, knowing he will be able to pick out Alex's location faster than I can.

"Why do you do that?" The massive midnight feline sends a visual of me surrounded by black nothingness.

"Alex has a talent that allows him to manipulate people's emotions. I'm not sure he's even aware of the gift, but I'm enthralled beyond the ability to control myself when unshielded: My empathy makes me putty in his hands." Speaking mind to mind, it's impossible to keep the disgust out of my thoughts.

"He desires you?" Jesse questions.

"He desires all women. For him, we are something to be conquered; then he moves on." I state my assumptions as fact, having run into his kind many times before. *"I consider his actions an abominable abuse of a precious gift."*

"Have not women used the gift of looks to sway men for centuries? How does this differ?"

Exasperated at the insinuation that Alex's magic is mere flirting, I endeavor to remain calm as I grit my teeth. *"Women cannot make men act against their will and their better judgment."*

"I believe some men would disagree with that statement." His response is immediate, as if anticipating my defense.

"Fine. You want to know the difference? Just remain in contact." Capitulating under the scrutiny, I open up my empathy once more. *Sometimes even thought sharing isn't adequate to see the reality of the situation!*

"Reba, Szames, how is the road ahead?" Alex greets us, moments later.

Szames dismounts before he gives his report. "Very manageable for the wagons. It should be an easy trip to the campsite."

"To the campsite? You have not gone that far and come back?" The prince motions for us to join him where his squire has set bread, cheese, and glasses on the table.

"These partners"—Szames motions to the beings who lounge on the grass—"have many useful abilities."

I shuffle toward the table, limping on the leg that no longer has any outward trace of a wound.

"Reba, are you unwell?" Hastening to my side, Alex motions for his page to find something for me to sit on. "Your vitality makes one forget only a few short days ago you lay mortally wounded."

"I'm fine, really. Unfortunately, riding one of these special cats is much like riding a horse." I sigh, taking possession of the chair, which seems to have materialized before me. "Hard on the knees."

"My dear, you are too indispensable to wear yourself out like this. You must let another take your place." I discern Alex's sympathy. I also feel an urgent desire to yield to him. "I insist that you ride in the wagon for the rest of the afternoon."

"Well, I suppose I could contact whoever takes my place, in case of an emergency. But it is considered impolite to mind-speak someone without their invitation." Shaking my head, I shrug. "I don't know anyone well enough to ask that of them. It is a rather intimate connection." I try to dismiss the idea. "I am sure I will be fine; my knee is already feeling much better."

Szames takes a half step forward as if to approach, but his brother is closer.

The dark-headed prince squats to my level. "You have done so much for my people." Pure, sweet love, the kind I have for most of the human race, washes over me. "Let me do what I can to relieve you of this burden? I will personally take your place if you will let me."

Having backed myself into a corner, I hesitate, unsure why I have invited a greater amount of familiarity with a man I despise. In the silence, Alex brings up his hand, brushing my jaw line with a curve of his finger. "This once, let me do something for you." His seductive whisper is accompanied by an infusion of intense passion. It requires every ounce of my willpower not to fall into his arms like a rescued maiden.

Refusing to respond to his gallant gesture is impossible, so I do what would seem to be a necessity. "I must know for whom I search. May I mind-speak?"

Superfluous, except to keep him from falling off Jesse if the need becomes a reality, I hate myself for giving in to the aching, driving need to make contact with him.

Alex's back stiffens at the thought of magic, but still, he scoops up my hand, capturing it in one of his. "It will be an honor."

"It is impossible to lie to someone mind to mind, as far as I know. I only have a minor gift in this, so you must think clearly of what you wish to say." I revel in the rich flux of the thoughts of this complex, intelligent man. There are so many currents, it is like being in a warm tide pool ebbing with motion.

"Like this? Can you hear me?" Whether it is fear or his telepathic charisma, I don't have a clue, but his questions are shouted into my head.

I squint against the stab of pain in my temples. *"Loud and clear."*

"This is not so bad once you get the hang of it." Sheepishness accompanies the toned-down response; the pain he caused was transmitted with my words.

I sense desire begin to rise in Alex as our minds brush up against one another. Feeling his lust sparks my own. Reluctantly I break mental contact, knowing we are treading on dangerous ground.

I continue with out loud for the benefit of the rest of the group. "There is one more thing we will need before you assume my place. Jesse, my partner, must agree to carry you. He uses a mind-gift too. You can either speak out loud or mind to mind, as we have been doing. Shall I see if he is willing?"

"I will handle the negotiations, Archmage Reba."

My cheeks color as I recall his role in life; he is one of the top delegates of this kingdom. "Of course."

"Did you catch any of that?" I send to Jesse while the brothers are absorbed in talk of supplies and duties.

"On both sides." With a mental blush of his own, he adds, *"I never stopped to consider it might be inappropriate to listen to another creature's thoughts."*

"Since you were unaware of my species' feelings concerning mind reading, no offense taken." Pausing, I acknowledge Szames's offer to refill my cup.

Jesse takes the opportunity to send a sense of relief.

"So as long as you were listening, what did you think? Is Alex aware of his gift?" I interrogate my partner. *"Is he abusing it intentionally?"*

"You were right. It is a little different than—what do you call it? Womanly wiles? The magic he wields can deprive you of freedom of choice. But from what I gathered, he looks at his gift as if it is just that. Most of him feels it is natural charm. Because of his fear of the arcane, he refuses to see that it could be anything else."

"Well then, if I get an opportunity, perhaps I will set him straight on where his charm comes from." After my recent exposure to his gift, the thoughts are more smug than I usually allow myself to be.

"Tread carefully. With his dislike for magic, he might bear you ill will for being the bearer of bad news. He seems the type to hold a grudge for life." The concern coming through with the admonishment takes the sting out of the blow.

"I will keep that in mind." The others are beginning to assemble for the rest of our march, so I quickly add, *"Thanks for watching my back."*

"We are partners, are we not?" Although I have never seen a cat smile, there is one in Jesse's parting.

Alex ushers me to the wagon where the wounded are being transported. The crown prince lifts me up, placing me next to the driver, earning a scathing look from Andrayia.

"Until this evening, milady." Alex's bedroom voice begs for a kiss as he takes his leave. However, with my shields back up, I can, and do, restrain myself. With my hesitation, he settles for brushing my hand with his lips. To my chagrin, my body betrays me and butterflies take flight in my middle.

"Even shielded he seems pretty persuasive." The chuckle of my partner changes my sappy smile to a scowl as Alex pivots in his direction. *"With your temper, I don't know how you've remained civil for so long."*

"We still have a deal?" Andrayia's caustic remark causes me to refocus on my surroundings.

"Definitely. As a matter of fact, Jesse was just remarking what an awful couple we'd make." I expound, "If forced to be together, one of us would probably wind up dead."

"You certainly do not give that impression." Some of the bite has left her tone, but her feathers are still ruffled.

I shake my head, feeling as if I have swallowed something unpleasant. "Believe me, only the fact that he is the crown prince of the land in which I'm now forced to reside keeps me courteous."

Tupp approaches. "Reba, Alex's page said there is something wrong with your leg?" He glances from Andrayia then back to me. "I'm sorry. Am I interrupting?"

"No, I was just leaving." Alex's lover excuses herself. Having dropped my shielding once more, I sense most of her resentment has left—her resentment toward me, that is. *Alex is in for one heck of a night!*

"You must have been exceedingly rough on it. It was almost as good as new." Tupper reaches for my pant leg.

"Tupp, this isn't necessary." At his no-nonsense look, I put a hand on his arm. "I have taken care of it," I fib.

Tupp trances. Opening his eyes, his lips purse. "Right you are. And so capable that not even a trace of damage is left to be found."

Knowing I am a terrible liar, I opt for honesty. "Yes, and I will be happy to give you a full disclosure concerning this healing, perhaps over dinner tonight when we have more privacy?"

After what seems like hours under his scrutiny, the healer pats my knee. "You know, milady, I may take you up on that offer sometime. But I will have my hands full setting up tonight. I trust that you've handled it to good avail, whatever the issue."

"Whenever you have time, then. Your company is always welcome." I smile as he climbs onto the wooden bench with me.

The wagon lurches forward as the driver urges the horses farther south. Our conversation pauses, as we accustom ourselves to the jarring movement of the archaic mode of transportation lacking one major convenience: shocks.

After ten minutes of bouncing down the road it feels like my mom caught be smoking out behind the barn and took a paddle to me. *I don't have a clue how shocks work, but this shouldn't drain too much power.*

> "Up and down, up and down, painfully
> A cushioned seat under our tush, thankfully."

The driver of the cart looks about wildly as a red leather buttoned seat appears under him. Locking eyes with him, I smile. Gulping, he looks down between his legs, touching the seat with one hand. The stoic soldier give a nod of resignation, turning his attention back to the horses.

"Milady, thank you for making this instrument." The wounded man, whose name I still don't know, is seated in the wagon behind me. "How much do I owe you?"

"It is a gift, and a small one considering what your bravery has cost." I turn, anxious to see how the new healing techniques have aided his recovery.

"It's too much for you to give to someone like me." His face crimsons. *Women are subject to the rules about gift-giving too? Without a price, he thinks I am inviting a sexual relationship!*

"Perhaps it would have more meaning if I put a price on it?" Relief washes over the soldier's face.

"I don't have much in the way of savings, but with the bonus I'll be getting because of this"—he gestures to his missing foot—"I should be able to come up with a fair price."

"I was thinking along different lines." The man's eyes narrow as I pause. "Up until now you have been willing to give your life for this country. What I ask is nothing less. I will show you some additional chords to play. Master that guitar, sing for pleasure, your livelihood, and also to glorify this monarchy."

The man refuses to meet my eyes. He holds the cased device out to me. "Milady, I'm afraid the price you ask is a mite too high. I may be quick, but I'm over twenty, too old to master a new trade."

I push the guitar back toward him, forcing the lame man to look in my direction. I hold his gaze when our eyes meet. "You are speaking to the Flame-haired One. I know when something is within your power. Only your lack of dedication will prevent you from becoming the rightful owner of this instrument."

Although he pales at the reference to the Prophecy of the Flame, he doesn't take possession of the tool. Revealing the grit that enabled him to obtain a position in the Cuthburan Army, he boldly challenges, "And who will be my teacher? Who will apprentice me?"

"Was not the builder of your city, Rikard of Kempmore, apprenticed to a new craft at your age?"

He nods.

"I will send a personal recommendation to the musician of your choice stating my belief in your potential."

"If I am to master this. . . guitar." He wraps his mouth around the foreign word as he removes the stringed instrument from its case, offering it once again. "Then I humbly ask for another demonstration."

"Gladly." This time I begin by showing him the chords, how to place the hands to strum each. After giving him a chance to practice the finger positions, I launch into the same love songs I sang night before last.

Marks later, when the day is two-thirds gone, Andrayia, carried by her partner, Heather, does a snazzy pivot, bringing her to my side. "Milady, you sing beautifully." Her remark feels more like an apology than a compliment.

"It is only magical enhancements, not true talent." I shrug. "I don't know about you, but I could use some. . . ahem. . . feminine privacy."

"It was before lunch when I last managed a brief jaunt on Heather." Andrayia accepts my invitation.

"Flying will be quickest." I extend my hand. "Shall we?"

We soar westward. I spot a secluded-looking gully. Wasting no time, I select an appropriate bush to take care of the necessities demanding my attention for the past two songs.

"Son of a. . ." The yellow stream bounces off the ground splattering everything within two feet of it, including my shoes. The disgusting waste seems to defy gravity rolling straight toward my shoe instead of directly to the ground. I pick up my foot a second too late. The side of my boot is saturated. "I'm going to create my very own port-a-potty before the next leg of this campaign!"

"Is something amiss, milady?" Andrayia inquires from the other side of the shrub.

"Besides my newly decorated shoe? I swear, I have absolutely no depth perception; I thought I was standing uphill! I really hate squatting."

Andrayia's smile, along with the twinkle in her eyes, tells me she appreciates the irony of the situation. "You have my deepest sympathy, honestly. I don't think I will ever look at my shoes the same way again. It's almost as disgusting as walking around with a pair of chamber pots on your feet!"

Giggling like a couple of schoolgirls playing hooky, we walk down the dry wash.

"It feels good to get away from things for a little while," Andrayia says.

"I know what you mean. If eyes were daggers, I'd be a pincushion. I despise having my every move scrutinized." I sigh. "I hope people will get used to me, now that I'm resigned to staying."

"I doubt it. . . that they will get used to you, I mean. Alex is watched by everyone, in all he does." Andrayia sulks. "It was one of the hardest things for me to get accustomed to when we first became a couple."

"Hmm, just one of the many drawbacks of being royalty. I have no wish to become queen. I hope you realize this by now."

Andrayia stares at me as if trying to solve a mystery.

"Magic is my first love. The responsibilities of the position would interfere with my studies. Besides, I'm at a loss where political maneuverings are concerned. On my world only one out of every hundred thousand has an opportunity for the realm of politics. I never had the slightest desire to even try for it."

"And if you are forced into the position?" Andrayia queries, her voice a hoarse whisper.

A wry smile twists my lips. "That would be pretty difficult for them to do. I am not exactly helpless."

Andrayia raises her eyebrows, so I relent, answering the question. "If I was forced into it, I would make a lousy queen. I know nothing of how a kingdom in this era runs and nothing of politics on this world, not to mention that I would be consumed by hatred for a husband who is unfaithful to my bedchamber."

"Letting me push you into making that statement proves just how inept you are." A smile frames her heart-shaped face, displaying the beauty Alex fell in love with. "You know, I believe you."

An incoming thought from Jesse causes my eyes to glaze over for a moment. *"The army is in sight, but when I looked for your presence, I could not locate you."* I glance toward the west where the sun is approaching the horizon.

"That was Jesse, the army is almost at the campsite. We'd better start back." *The conversation was finally getting to where I wanted it.* I shake my head. *Will I ever find out where her hostility is coming from?*

Joining hands again, I lift us into the air. On the flight, Jesse fills me in on the details of Alex's first experience with a partner. With the telepathy I am drawn into his thoughts as if riding beside the prince the entire way.

∾   ∾   ∾

"Jesse, I am honored by your willingness to carry me to the campsite." Alex bows before the cat. His composure is serene, but underneath his heart pounds fiercely. The beast before him is as large as one of the great bears of the north. His life would have been forfeit to such a one if not for his brother's swiftness with his spear.

"It is I who am honored to be carrying a direct descendant of Sheldon the Wise." Jesse tries to ease his discomfort.

Alex's eyes widen with surprise as he throws a leg over the oval cushion strapped to the feline's middle. "You know of King Sheldon?" the prince asks, slipping his feet into the stirrups that Jesse lengthened.

"Know of him?" Jesse gives a mental harrumph. *"He was the first human I called 'friend.'"*

"Your gait is smooth." Alex dismisses the boring talk of history. "Like a galloping stallion. How much speed are you capable of?"

"How much are you comfortable with?" The cat evades a direct answer, knowing Alex's intolerance for magic.

Swallowing hard, Alex looks to his brother, who has remained respectfully silent. "Shall we see tonight's

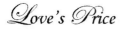

campsite?" Holding the reins stiffly, Alex addresses Reba's partner again, "Let's see your gallop."

"As you wish, Your Highness." Jesse's mind-voice becomes formal, sensing Alex's apprehension rising.

The submissive tone placates the prince. Taking a few minutes to accustom himself to the movement, Alex asks, "Can you accelerate to that of a racing horse?"

"Undoubtedly, Your Highness." Jesse complies with the request. The cat's gait smoothes out, the rocking sensation barely detectable.

"Your physical prowess is remarkable." Alex flatters his mount.

"Thank you, Your Highness." Jesse's tone remains subservient.

"Tell me, Jesse: How long can your kind keep up this pace?" Alex queries.

"For a day, at least, Prince Alexandros." Jesse can't help the confidence in the thoughts.

"Reba was right; you are a remarkable species." Instinctually Alex pats the neck of the cat. "Jesse, show me just how remarkable you are."

Knowing the arrogant royal sees him as nothing more than an intelligent animal, the cat remains silent. The growl that would accompany his thoughts would end any hope of a lifetime alliance with the kingdom of Cuthburan. He, the leader of a race far superior to these humans, will endure the insulting affection of this witless prince.

Instinctively, Alex's hands sink into the lush fur of the cat as panic threatens his self-control. The scenery speeds past at more than fifty miles an hour.

"Are you sure it is wise to reveal this much of our abilities to him?" Tawny sends to Jesse.

"A partnership cannot exist if one of the parties is looked upon as a lower life form. Continuing to let him assume we are lesser beings will do us more harm than good. Either he will deal with the fact that we are spirit beings or he will not," Jesse growls back.

Alex's hands relax as Jesse begins to slow. *"We have reached our destination, Your Highness."* The exercise gave his temper a chance to cool.

Both princes slide from their saddles. "Camp will take up these six knolls." Alex gestures before him.

"Yes, but if we moved it over there"—Szames indicates an area farther west—"we would have a higher hill on which to place the tower and a steep incline on the west."

"I agree." Alex nods. Looking back to their mounts, he asks, "These cats are not like horses, are they?"

"Not at all. They are allies, not beasts of burden."

Alex saunters back to Jesse. "Do you have a formal title by which I may call you?" the prince asks, stopping before him.

"Before Reba approached us, we were spirit beings." Jesse's pleasure at being addressed as an equal to the human race is broadcast through the link. *"Now we have become felines to aid in ridding this world of the demonic invasion. I believe SpiritCat would be an appropriate title."*

"SpiritCat Jesse it is, then." Alex smiles, not totally comfortable with these new allies but willing to explore the benefits they bring. "Shall we return to our position as scouts?"

∾   ∾   ∾

Having followed Jesse's mind-voice, my vision clears as we come within sight of the army. I set us down close to where the partners are lounging on the outskirts of the encampment. I chuckle at the soldier scurrying by after he plants a light post beside the big cats.

Alexandros is just taking his leave. He dips his head in greeting. "Reba, thank you for allowing me to assume your place. It has been a most enlightening experience."

"Thank you for allowing me to rest my knee. It feels good as new." I smile gratefully as he continues past me on the way to the center of camp. *Looks like he has a lot on his mind.*

"Prince Szames." Andrayia bows to the prince. She waits for his approval before tending to Heather's needs.

I pick up a toothy comb and begin the task of grooming my own partner. Running one hand through the velvety fur while combing with the other relaxes me almost as much as it does Jesse.

Not wanting to get any more familiar with someone I am already too close to, I send my thoughts through Jesse, with the request that he broadcast them to Szames and Tawny. *"If you don't mind, we can talk through the cats for more privacy."*

"It is probably the most secure way to discuss our progress," Szames agrees.

"Jesse filled me in on your outing. What was your take on the outcome?" I ask.

"As I said, Alex takes a while to warm up to new ideas." Szames pauses in mid stroke, thinking his reply through. *"Considering this is magical as well as new, it didn't go too badly."*

"Well, at least he didn't freak out on us."

The slang causes Szames's brows to draw down in puzzlement.

"Go ballistic?" causes even more puzzlement. Finally I add, *"Run screaming from the idea."*

A deep rumble echoes into my mind. *"Your world uses vocabulary in such an interesting fashion."*

"Is there anything else you guys need?" I ask Jesse, placing the brush in the saddlebag.

"We will hunt for our dinner tonight. Look for us as the last moon rises." Jesse sends, purring as he shakes his mane back into place.

"Milady, shall I escort you to the command center?" Szames extends his arm.

Strolling in a courtly fashion, my empathy reports the morale boost the sight has on the men. "Will you assist me in setting the tents?" I ask.

The strength and size of his hand is comforting. I lace our fingers. Guilt assails me for the intimate contact. *Holding his hand means using less energy.* The rationalization helps me focus on the task before us.

"For traveling, this size will do.
From now on, just say 'Malibu.'
When your spaciousness is to be set free,
Just say, 'home, sweet home,' and there you'll be."

I draw power in a steady stream from Prince Szames. With the closing line, the cerulean force surges from me in a tingling wave. It encompasses the three miniature dwellings, sinking into them.

"The spell has been set," I inform the waiting audience.

"So now all we have to do is think of the tents getting bigger and say 'home. . . sweet. . . home'?" Tupper pronounces the alien words I taught him on the trip here with care.

The infirmary he was looking at begins to grow as the last word leaves his mouth. The healer's jaw goes slack as he hastens back a few paces to give the growing pavilion more room.

"Looks like you've got the hang of it." Enlarging my own domicile, I take my leave, ducking into the darkened interior.

My gosh, how I need a bath. Hiding in the shadows of my mind is the fear of hearing Crystal's decision and what it could mean.

Stepping into the curtained enclosure, glaring at the wooden tub fit only for bathing animals, frustration consumes me. Crystal steps up beside me with a bucket of water as verses of a rhyme spring to life in my mind.

> "Heat and hauling is too much work for thee.
> Faucet, drain, and showerhead, now *be*."

A lazy smile graces my lips as magic caresses my being. The picture I focus on becomes reality as the enchantment takes the working details from my mind.

Humming to myself, I demonstrate how to use the new equipment. The enchanted brass knobs and the hand-held showerhead need no connecting pipe or reservoir of water. Without low-flow restrictions, the tub fills in minutes.

I climb into the warm water. Releasing the temperature spell surrounding me, I immediately regret the loss of its protective warmth. My breath comes out in white puffs, and my nose feels as if it has grown frost.

> "For a bathroom this will never do,
> So seventy degrees you will heat to."

An azure mist clouds the small, curtained enclosure. In the blink of an eye, the mist disappears.

"Ooh, it is like there's a fire in the corner. Being a maid to a sorceress is much better than I ever imagined." Crystal's casual behavior hints at her decision even though she has not voiced it yet.

"So is it a maid that you wish to stay?"

"If I were to remain a maid, I would enjoy being permanently assigned to you, milady, more than anything else I've done." Her voice drops. I strain to catch what she says next, "But here, that is all I will ever be. A chance to travel to a place where there are other possibilities. . . I will gladly take on the assignment, if you still trust me to fulfill it."

"Although what I require is contrary to your normal duties, I see no reason not to put my faith in you. I've asked much of you; you have yet to fail me." Stretching the truth a bit, I add, "I trust your abilities and your honor."

"Thank you, milady. I will do everything in my power to see your husband does not betray the vows you have taken." Crystal's back straightens as she states her mission.

"In compensation for forsaking the world you know, I will grant you the knowledge I have of my world and my identity. Those who know me will assume you are me, except Kyle and my family."

Crystal's hands freeze in the middle of washing of my hair.

"Will I become you?" She clears her throat. "I will not be me?"

"It will only be an illusion, as with the likeness of Kyle I showed you. People will see my likeness when they look at you. That way people will think you are me. The only difference will be your knowledge of my land. My world is very complex, and you will need the information to function. Also, I have had schooling: twelve years of basic school and two years of higher learning. This will give you employment opportunities, but you might need to further your education to obtain a higher position."

"How different could your world be?" The maid continues the shampoo, more comfortable with the idea now that she understands the need for it.

"That is the other thing. Between now and when we get back to the castle, I want to do something called 'joined lucid dreaming.' This way you can explore my world with me before you are forced into it."

Crystal acknowledges the wisdom of the idea, so I continue. "Also, I will give you sufficient monetary compensation so you can support yourself until you get accustomed to your new life."

"You are more than generous, milady. The knowledge alone is worth a fortune."

"I'm not so sure, having been on the receiving end of a similar situation." I wrap myself in a robe. Entering the next room, I level a gaze at her. "And payment is not up for negotiation. I know the task ahead of you, so I will decide what is enough."

"Yes, milady." Crystal takes my robe as I dress in a clean set of clothes. "I trust your judgment completely."

A mark later a scratch sounds on the outer flap. "I'll get that. If we are going to begin the lucid dreaming, you will need to get cleaned up as well."

Sheepishly she dips her head, bewildered that someone of stature would not only assume a maid's duties, but also allow a maid to use her personal accommodations.

"Milady, is there anything I can do for you this evening?" The appearance of Craig makes me grind my teeth in frustration.

Now why didn't I think of this sooner? "Lieutenant Craig, I have some important correspondence in need of a courier. I've been wracking my brain trying to come up with a person of suitable reliability as well as noble lineage for this important errand." Shaking my head, I feign dismissal of the sudden inspiration. "But I couldn't ask that of you."

"For you, milady, I would welcome any task." A wide smile encompasses most of the lieutenant's face.

"Have you heard? I am sending part of my group back home. I'm not going with them."

Craig looks shocked.

"Those accompanying them will endeavor to return in five years. However, the possibility exists they may not be able to return at all." Sighing, I continue after a brief pause. "Never mind. I shouldn't have mentioned it. I wouldn't feel right asking you to undertake a personal mission for me, no matter the compensation I offer. What would be worth leaving all that you know? You may very well wind up stranded on an alien world."

"Tell me: What manner of errand would it be?" His lust for glory has him firmly in its grasp.

"I would call it 'intelligence courier.' I have several reports to be delivered to my peers." Craig gives a satisfied nod, so I continue. "In payment I will give you knowledge about my country, an identity in my world, and one bag of gold coins. The knowledge portion will begin tonight. You will have to participate in something called lucid dreaming, a kind of introduction to my world."

"That seems just compensation." He oozes self-importance with an undercurrent that speaks of some ulterior motive. "Milady, you have found your messenger. When are we scheduled to depart?"

"Eight to ten days. I will need you to report back to my tent in a mark." I make a hasty departure, knowing where my next stop has to be.

Long strides bring me to the partners' post, where the cats are lounging. *"How was the hunt?"* I send to Jesse in greeting.

"I had forgotten how exhilarating stalking prey can be, especially when your stomach is rumbling," Jesse purrs, licking his lips. *"Tawny knows where Szames sleeps."* My partner answers my unasked question.

I roust Tawny from a light doze. The groggy cat isn't in a chatty mood. A map of the camp flashes into my mind with a single tent highlighted.

I scratch on the flap. A tousled, blond head smiles at me. "Reba, what a pleasant surprise." Szames gestures, indicating I am welcome to enter.

"Yes, well, I hope I haven't caught you at a bad time."

The smile he gives is one of pure indulgence.

"I'm afraid I have to beg an even greater imposition. I seem to have gotten myself into another situation."

"Sounds like you have had a busy evening," Szames teases. "With Alex assuming command of this contingent of the campaign, my schedule is clear. What can I do to help?"

The events of the past couple of marks gush outward almost of their own accord. I tell him everything. "So now I'm not so sure I haven't gone from the frying pan into the fire. To conserve energy, I will need the participants as close as possible. Somehow I just don't trust Craig to hold to his honor when we have to touch while horizontally reclined."

"You want me to stand guard while you conduct the dreaming." Szames nods, agreeing to the conclusion he has drawn.

"Actually, I don't think such extreme measures will be necessary. You, too, will need to rest. I was hoping you will join the group and make it a foursome?"

His jaw hits the floor.

"You did mention an interest in seeing my world."

"Yes. . . yes, that would be. . . wonderful," Szames stammers, glowing with enthusiasm. "Not an imposition at all. But who will monitor the shield?"

"I can cast spell I used to give you magical sight on any soldier. After that it will only take a trace amount of energy to activate their sight. Which of your men has the least aversion to magical workings?"

"Captain Youngmen, the soldier you healed of the jarovegi wound, has expressed interest in the arcane since he recovered," Szames replies without hesitation.

We hustle to the captain's quarters without another word.

Szames explains our need then asks, "The attacking forces should be light tonight with only the minor call activated. Will you be willing to stand guard at the tower tonight?"

"It will be an honor, sir."

Szames gives a nod, a tight smile playing about his lips as if the captain has just passed a crucial test. "You will need an aide close by. If the blue shield lightens, you must send for Archmage Reba immediately."

With darkness gathering, I hurriedly chant the sight-granted spell, tapping the soldier on the forehead as I finish the rhyme.

Moments later Szames and I rush into my tent. The other participants have already arrived. I scramble to gather my thoughts for the dream-coupling. Before we begin, I take the necessary precautions.

"Knowledge of my world you will gain.
From divulging facts, you'll refrain."

As the final words are uttered, a soft blue light surrounds my hands. I touch first Crystal, then the lieutenant, and last of all, Szames. When reaching to touch the prince's brow, I refrain from giving a push to stabilize the magical spell. An azure glow streaks from my hand. A soft blue emanates from the hands and heads of Crystal and Craig as the enchantment settles into place.

Having felt nothing of the magic that now controls him, a sarcastic smile twists Craig's lips, "And this will help me retain information better?"

"Yes." *Retain within yourself, that is.* "Are you ready to begin?"

I usher the dream circle over to the bed. "Crystal, you and Craig, having the least experience in joining with me, will take the outside positions on the bed. Szames, you will be between Craig and myself."

The lieutenant looks disgruntled. I feel courage swelling. Drawing his shoulders back he dips his head at Szames. "Your Highness, you will be accompanying us on our dream quest? Will you be traveling on this mission as well?"

"Szames will observe the culture so that if the occasion arises, he may act as diplomat to my kingdom." *An excellent reason for him to be here. Glad I thought of it.*

"Humph." The lieutenant shuffles his feet, clearly unhappy with his position on the bed.

"I can find a replacement for any of you who no longer wish to be a part of this expedition. I'll need a commitment by morning." I raise an eyebrow at the long-haired nobleman.

"I said I am your man," Craig declares, stepping back and motioning for Szames to precede him onto the huge mattress serving as my bed. I saunter around the side of the bed, crawling to the middle, lying parallel to the prince. Crystal assumes her place beside me. Taking the hands of the people next to me, I walk them through the procedure.

"Just relax; breathe deep." Recalling my last trip with Merithin, I give some final instruction. "You will feel a tickling at the base of your skull when I make the connection then a little drowsiness. Let it carry you into slumber. It will be as restful as if you are sleeping in your own bed. As you dream, you will dream of my world. We will all be together, and you will remember everything." With my empathy wide open, I perceive nervousness along with excitement and anticipation from Craig and Crystal. But to my senses, it is as if Szames isn't even in the room. I thread a narrow stream of magic through each consciousness until I feel their minds as solidly as the hands I grasp along with a void that is Szames.

"Heigh-ho, heigh-ho, it's off to sleep we go,
To see my land as we hold hands,
Heigh-ho. . . heigh-ho, heigh-ho, heigh-ho.

Heigh-ho, heigh-ho, it's off to sleep we go,
The dreams will come, and when we're done,
Learning some, rememberin' fun,
Heigh-ho. . . heigh-ho, heigh-ho, heigh-ho. . . heigh-ho."

With the last "ho," I feel my consciousness drifting. Hastily I partition off a section of my mind. I ride the sensation like bodysurfing a wave, letting it carry me into a deep slumber. The piece of my mind I pushed into the corner allows me to keep a close count of the strands of awareness wrapped up with mine. The REM stage approaches. When the dream begins, my thoughts are ensconced in visions of home.

"Crystal, Szames, Craig, welcome to Earth." Sitting up in bed, I wait for my guests to orient themselves. Merithin's form shimmers into existence. "Right on time." I nod to the elder before getting down to business.

"This is my home." The demand for explanations begins when I turn on the light using a switch on the wall. The tour of the house takes twice as long as I planned. Though the sorcerer has already explored the modern residence, the trio of off-worlders is intrigued by even the simplest of items. Someone wants to know the purpose of every device, so it takes more than an hour just to get out of the bathroom!

Though it has felt like we spent an entire day on Earth, the night is only half gone. I stretch, releasing the handclasp. I wiggle my fingers. Overpowered by a yawn, my mouth stretches wide. "That was the first step. At the next session, we will actually leave my property."

"Will we get to ride in one of those. . ." Crystal tries to remember the term.

"You will find it hard to express things from my world while you are still in this one. That's normal. Don't strain yourself. If you try too hard, you will get a fierce headache."

As an afterthought, I add, "And yes, we will take a ride next time."

The others stumble off to bed with instructions to sleep as long as possible so the knowledge can integrate into their minds. Taking my own advice, I let myself drift into a more natural state of slumber.

Chapter Seven

"Mmm, that smells good, even if it is only scrambled eggs." The enticing odor pulls me out of the comfort I have been unwilling to desert.

"I thought you would never rouse, milady." Crystal is quite chipper.

"Yes, well, I'm finding it difficult to withdraw from the luxurious familiarity in last night's journey," I mumble, wiping gunk from my eyes. "It was so nice to be home."

"I can see why. With a home like that, who needs servants? Everything is practically done for you." This time my maid takes a seat with very little prompting. "You must miss it horribly, milady."

"Miss it? I think I miss knowing what is expected of me more than anything. Then again, having a brand-new set of rules, not to mention this lifestyle, is incredibly exciting." I pause, swallowing a mouthful of sausage. "How about you? I take it your first look didn't scare you out of your decision?"

"Not in the least. I think I am going to love your world." Crystal digs into her breakfast, talking around a mouthful. "Who knows? If Merithin is able to send us back, I may choose to stay."

Much later, I drop in on Szames. "This stopping by your tent is becoming a bad habit."

"One that continues, I hope." A smile plays about the corners of his mouth but fails to take hold.

My acute hearing picks up the lieutenant assuming sentry just outside the door. "Let me do a quick warding for privacy."

"This is business, then?" My favorite prince seems positively gloomy compared to Crystal's sunshine.

Finishing the lines of the rhyme that secured my pavilion, I reply, "Kind of. There are a couple of things I needed your thoughts on: First, how do you feel about continuing with the dreaming, now that you've had a trip?" *Have I pushed the bounds of our friendship too far? If only I could get a reading.*

"It was great. I would love to see more." His tone is more bland then the eggs I had for breakfast as he gestures for me to take a seat at the small table crammed next to his bed. "And second?"

"I didn't place the retaining spell on you like I did the others. I hoped to have someone to chat with." My forehead furrows as I pause. "But perhaps that was selfish of me. You seem to have enough weighing you down."

"So are you reading me?" His back stiffens as his voice takes on a harsh tone.

"My gosh, you're as prickly as a wet tomcat!" Letting out a sigh, I relax, figuring I have finally pinpointed the cause of his distress. "I can't read you any more than any other woman could. Don't the women on this world always assume a dark mood has something to do with them?"

Szames's eyes scrunch at the corners as if trying to gauge the truth of my words.

I close my eyes, my hair bouncing as I shake my head. "I probably should have told you sooner, but I wasn't sure if I could trust you. Szames, you are the person from whom I can sense the least. Nothing really. But I am pretty good at picking up on people's moods by body language." *Not to mention my intuition.*

"I meant no offense by my reaction. I have always been a private person." Szames smiles for the first time this morning. "That and putting up with my brother trying his 'magic' on me was too much today."

"I hope you know by now that I'm not the sort to use knowledge I gain with selfish intentions. Lord knows I hate it when Alex plays with my emotions. . ." My sentence trails off as the tent flap sweeps back. *Speak of the devil!*

"Reba, it is fortunate I have caught you here." The irritable suspicion washing through Alex says he is anything but happy about it.

"We were just discussing a reconnaissance mission." Szames is unabashed by his brother's agitation. "Please, join us. My tent has been secured so we may speak freely."

"Security is exactly what I wanted to discuss with you, Reba. I am finding myself trapped in my tent." Alex takes a step in my direction, and I feel myself pulled in by the intensity of his eyes. "Can you make some sort of portable warding so I can discuss business on the move?"

Snapping my empathy shields into place, I give a nod, both in reply and to clear it. "The warding spell is a simple one, but it needs something physical to give it solidity. I should be able to center a revised spell in a stone, like the shield spell. A gem of some kind should do the trick."

Alex removes the signet ring resting on his right middle finger. "Will this work? I can think of nothing better in which to set such a ward."

"It will take some time for me to come up with a proper spell with so many variables." Examining the facetted sapphire in the center of the engraved ring, I nod. "I can have it back to you before the battle if I begin now."

"That will suffice." Alex gives a brief dip of his head. *I've been dismissed.*

I walk back to my tent at a brisk pace. Seated at the table, I place the ring before me. With my magically endowed photographic memory, the privacy spell is a cinch to recall. It isn't much help.

Going to the drawer next to my bed, I retrieve the ballpoint pen and paper I conjured up when I first arrived. A mark later I have worked out a suitable spell.

"Nosy people always want to see
What I do, wherever I may be.
'Secure' allows the wearer's words to remain,
'Open' and freedom will now be gained.

Blue light will shine when magic's working.
A red light to show trouble's lurking.
Warmth will tell me I am not safe.
Shatter when there's no saving grace."

Magic pools in my cupped palm. As the last word is uttered, the radiance sinks into the stone of Alex's ring. I sigh. *There's nothing like working with magic.*

With the pen in front of me, I begin brainstorming on a spell that will help aid us, should we actually find the gate through which the demons are accessing this world. *Andskoti said there was a demon lord trapped there. I'm not sure what that means, but better over prepared at this point.*

"Milady, are you ready for your dinner?" Crystal asks cautiously.

My brow furrows in anger. I slash out the lines I composed. *I'm sure that'll hold the monsters we've been facing, but what if the demon lord has magic?*

The dimness of the tent means it is only a couple of marks before we assemble for battle. Heaving a sigh I nod, "I suppose this will have to wait till later. Dinner would be great."

Chatting with the Crystal over dinner, I begin to realize how much I've give away for Kyle's comfort. I clear a lump from my throat as Crystal removes the dishes. Clean clothes have been laid out on my bed. I dress for battle. Strapping on the knives and donning my robe, I look for my staff. *Where did I leave it? I thought it was next to my bed.*

"I can't seem to find my staff. Do you know where it is?" I ask when Crystal returns.

"I put it under your bed for safekeeping." She retrieves the magical stave.

Shaking my head in irritation, I mutter.

> "Magical weapon belonging to me,
> I call 'staff' and in my hand you'll be!"

My palm tingles fiercely. *I won't be looking for this again.*

"Milady Archmage Reba, His Royal Highness, Prince Alexandros, desires an audience." Crystal's behavior takes on a new level of formality.

"Please show him in." *Turning him away at the door would probably be considered rude.*

"Milady Reba, I hope I am not intruding." Alex gives a slight inclination of his head. "I thought perhaps you would like an escort to the tower."

Lest I show up beside Szames? "How thoughtful. Before we head out, perhaps you should retake possession of this?" I extend the bejeweled metal band.

"It looks no different." Alex frowns, sliding the ring back on his finger. "It feels the same."

I knew Doubting Thomas would need proof the thing works. "Activating the spell will require a word *secure*. The stone will glow a soft blue when active. Nothing said within a five-foot radius will be overheard by one outside the circle of protection. If magic attempts to penetrate the projected field, the stone will turn red. Once privacy is no longer needed simply say, 'open.'"

"And if the warding should be compromised?" The prince examines the stone more closely.

"The ring will heat if something penetrates the shield. If the stone shatters, someone has broken the spell I placed on it." *It's nearly a mark before assembly.* I gesture to the table.

"A very thorough enchantment." Alex's praise is delivered without a touch of his gift.

"You are the crown prince; the security of the nation is at stake." I shrug. "Anything less would have been irresponsible."

"Reba, you have truly changed the world. Two octals ago I would not have dreamed of asking for magic to act as personal protection; now it is embedded within my signet."

My brow wrinkles with thought. "Could this be a fulfillment of the prophecy?"

"It would solve a lot of issues." Alex sighs. "But we are not that fortunate."

"Then a partial fulfillment at least," I insist, trying to keep the desperation out of my voice.

Patiently, as if lecturing a teenager, Alex crushes my hopes. "The prophecy states that magic will be brought to the crown..."

Unwilling to hear the words from his mouth, I interrupt him, "Hearken to my words: our salvation is revealed by our beloved Andskoti. In the darkest hour, when the fate of mankind is threatened by a great evil, our savior will come with hair aflame, by that you will know him." I repeat the words given by the priest who was burning alive, trying to distance myself from them. "Change will sweep the land like fire across a summer meadow. Embrace that which is brought, for it will be your only salvation. Magic will rise as the entire fabric of our kingdom is rewoven. Through the bond of marriage, magic will be brought onto the throne of Cuthburan at last. So I have been shown. So let it be known."

Alex opens his eyes, whether trying for patience or out of reverence for their sacred prediction, I cannot tell with my empathy shielded. "And your exotic appearance tells us that the time of the prophecy has begun; the changes you bring confirm it. However, the rest has yet to be completed."

I take a long drink of the water before me, giving my temper time to cool. *If he thinks I'm going to become another doe in the herd he's collecting, he had better think again!* "And this prophecy is what? Two hundred years old? It was wrong about the savior being a man. There may be other mistakes we have yet to discover."

"Yes, I had thought of that as well." Alex seems regretful. "I had the priest research the original document. It seems 'him' in the first line was originally *hana*, 'her.' When the royal copy was made and put on display, it was changed to *hann*, for the scribe assumed that the original must have been in error."

My thoughts scramble as my emotions erupt at the idea of marrying the chauvinistic womanizer. "Perhaps there are more such assumptions as in—"

Alex interrupts my rebuttal, his tone strangely remorseful. "The original was brought before the royal family. There were no other discrepancies." Seeming to rally his optimism, he continues. "But perhaps you will find a unique way of fulfillment. Your culture has sent us a remarkably resilient woman. Perhaps it will also inspire you to one more feat of wonder that will allow us to escape what it seems fate has ordained."

Suddenly I realize that Alex hasn't used his gift once tonight. I ease down my empathy shield to gauge the honesty of his words. *He's on the level!*

"Let me ease your mind, Alex," I reassure the prince. "I have already set in motion plans that will buy us time if not solve this dilemma." Quickly I fill him in on the plans to retrieve Kyle.

"Did I call you 'resilient'? It seems resourceful is more accurate." Alex smiles. Empathy shows the honesty of his words.

My cheeks brighten. The compliment makes my knees weak and my stomach tighten with expectation.

"Thank you, Alex." My lips curve as I gaze into the deep green of his eyes.

"Milady." Crystal waits until I dip my chin. "If I am to plait your hair before the battle, I must begin soon."

"Shall I wait outside to escort you to the tower, milady," Alex inquires.

"Thank you, yes." I nod.

"That was quite inventive, Crystal," I remark as soon as we are alone.

"The danger didn't seem imminent." She begins to braid my hair, fingers weaving it close to my head. "However, with the crown prince, I could think of no other way to remind you of the time."

"Although I wasn't in danger, the situation was becoming quite uncomfortable." She hands me the communication mirror. With a nod of approval, I stride from the tent, ready for battle.

Alex extends his arm as I exit my domicile. Not having to defend against his constant barrage of charming guile, I find myself relaxing in his presence. Strolling toward the tower, my heartbeat speeds up. I slide a glance at Alex. *Damn, he's good looking. I'd love to fall into his arms.* Knowing I am probably being toyed with, I shake off the feeling. With a thought, I lift us onto our perch. Refocusing on the reason I am here—men's lives are at stake—I gaze at the soldiers before me.

At this height I am able to view the full circle bristling with steel. To the south, Szames and Jerik are easy to pick out; their respective heights are noticeable even from this distance. The fact that they stand side by side makes locating the mismatched pair a breeze. Charles's shining armor is a beacon on the west side of the circle.

Night falls, smothering us in an ebony blanket of nothingness. Illumination extends less than ten feet from the moat's barrier. Grunting echoes from the gloom like a pack of wild pigs in rut.

The troops shuffle, steel hisses as weapons are unsheathed in anticipation. We await the onslaught. My patience evaporates. I add a touch more power to the attraction stone. A hoard of black shapes seethe out of the darkness, tumbling into the light of the moat.

I lose track of time as the slaughter waxes. The ground turns into an inky quagmire of demon blood. As before, the violence both sickens and stimulates; senses are heightened as battle rage infuses every fiber of my being. My normal revulsion to brutality takes a backseat to the finely honed reflexes instilled with the portal transfer.

"Szames!" Alex shouts from beside me then mumbles under his breath, "You stupid fool."

I place a restraining hand on Alex's shoulder as he steps toward the ladder. "Stay here." I hand him my staff, knowing I may need two hands to retrieve both prince and soldier. "Guard the stones."

Alex holds my magician's rod as if it is a snake that might bite him at any moment. My feet leave the platform without a backward glance. *What the hell is he doing outside the shield?* I soar toward the darkness where two shapes are being herded away from the safety of the moat. Fliers pelt the invisible shield above me, disintegrating in a fiery display.

I race across the encampment as three jarovegi pop up inside a ring of monsters surrounding Szames and a wounded soldier. The poison-clawed demons chitter among themselves, mere feet from the prince. The warrior prince's gaze is focused on the new arrivals. An ogre lashes out, crushing his sword arm. His blade clatters to the ground, his right arm hanging uselessly at his side. With gritted teeth, Szames stoops, taking his sword in his left hand.

I increase my flight speed. Seconds before I land beside him, Szames assumes a protective stance, straddling the soldier lying in a crumpled heap. A shout of inhuman gibberish comes from the monsters as my feet touch the earth beside my cherished friend. The beasts surge forward.

Taking hold of Szames, nudging the downed soldier with my toe, I shout, "Fire ring!" Blue flames roll out from my body, boiling like water from an overfull pot. Like wildfire caught in a cyclone, it expands, growing taller as it travels outward.

"Fireball." I aim a bolt straight up at the flier plunging toward us.

"Fire ring," I call again as another wave of blackness threatens to engulf us. By the time a ring of flames surrounds us for the third time, the enemy has grown leery. The demons' chattering grates on my nerves as they circle our position from a safe distance.

"Schwarzenegger," I intone, extending my hand to Szames. "Ready to leave yet?"

Despite the agonizing pain I perceive cascading from shoulder to hand, he gives a weak smile. "Thought you would never ask."

The agony is so intense that I grind my teeth as I block my empathy to keep the pain from my senses. Taking the prince's left hand, I reach down with my other. Picking up the soldier by the mail he is wearing we soar swiftly back to the safety of the shield. Seconds later we land in front of the infirmary. Now that we are safe, fury overwhelms me.

"What the hell were you doing out past the shields?" I demand as a pair of healers move the unconscious man onto a stretcher.

"What took you so long to come get me?"

"What took me so long?" I sputter. "If it wasn't for Alex trying to run after you to save your hide, I might not have known until it was too late!"

"Alex?" An involuntary shrug ends as the color drains from Szames's face.

The thought of losing one of my few friends snaps the fragile thread of control I have on my temper. "In case you haven't noticed, there is a battle going on. You are lucky your arm is the only wound you took!" Eyes narrowed in anger, I glance at his damaged limb. Blood drips steadily off his limp hand. I feel like a total jerk. "Oh my dear God, Szames. I'm so sorry." Guiding him gently by his good arm, I usher him inside the healers' tent. "Let's get that arm taken care of."

It takes both Tupp and an assistant to remove Szames's chain mail and undershirt. A jagged piece of ivory protrudes from the prince's triceps. When Tupp begins the setting process, I take it as my cue to get back to the battle. Turning to go, a hand takes hold of my arm.

"That boy is Stezen's son, Zach. He got knocked out of the moat by a demon who managed to stay hidden until he recovered from the stun effect." His eyes plead for understanding. "I could not watch him be torn apart. He is like a brother to me."

"Next time you play hero, signal Jerik to call me." With a brief smile, I add, "My aid might be a little more timely."

"I will see you in a mark," he gets out between clenched teeth.

"I don't think so. You've lost a lot of blood. You can count on staying right here." My lips are pressed so firmly together, they disappear completely, which is signal enough for Szames not to argue the point.

One step out the door, I lift myself heavenward. "I don't know which is more stubborn, your brother or a mule," I grouse to Alex, letting him know his sibling is okay. "Laser." I dispatch an ogre wreaking havoc inside the moat before Alex has a chance to reply. The prince calls out sightings while I release a continual stream of deadly azure light.

"I would say the mule has lost that stubborn contest," Alex remarks when a blond head appears over the top of the ladder.

"Tupper was running out of room. He dismissed me." Szames grimaces when he attempts a shrug.

"Dismissed you to your bed, I will wager." Alex's sarcasm echoes my thoughts.

"Who knows how many lives another pair of eyes can save? I might not be fit for battle, but I can still see." Szames glares at his brother.

Mule is the right comparison. "You take northeast. Alex northwest. I will focus on the south." The three of us scan the night sky, the moat, and the distant horizon.

The sun lightens the eastern sky as a huddled mass of demons hurl themselves into the moat. Demons half the size of a man, but twice as wide, surge forward. Their skin is inky black and the monsters wear no discernable clothing. Even with the added light of the lampposts it is difficult to make out any details of the individual monstrosities as the beast fling themselves toward us. Exhausted men jump to dispatch the fallen enemy but the numbers are too great. A pair of ogres and one of the flying insects with appendages resembling a tarantula's, push themselves up from the bottom of the pile.

I snag Szames by the shirt. "I'd rather not pull the stored power out of my magician's rod if you are up to it?"

He nods and it takes only seconds to clear the last of the enemy out of the moat.

Though the dawn is cold, I wipe sweat off my brow as rose tints the eastern sky. Looking at Szames for the first time in an hour, I'm shocked at his ashen appearance. "You look dead on your feet. Let me give you a lift back to your tent."

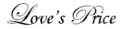

He nods nearly losing his balance. Quickly I turn to his Alex. "Would you care to join us?"

I hand my staff to Alex and, taking a brother in each hand, I ease us down to where the Royal Guard is stationed, hovering feet from them. Alex dismisses the women as we glide swiftly to the smaller tent located across from the infirmary. Szames's broad shoulders slump with fatigue as our feet touch ground.

"What you need most is rest." I switch to healer's sight, eyeing him dubiously. "Are you going to be able to get out of that mail by yourself?"

"I will be fine. . ." Szames's deep mumble trails off as he stumbles toward his doorway.

I take a step in his direction, determined to see to the needs of my friend. A hand grasps my shoulder. "Let me take care of him," comes Alex's soft whisper.

I give a grateful smile, acquiescing to his brother. "He'll probably feel better if you're the one to help him in his current state. I'll check on Zach and meet you back at my tent for the debriefing."

"Zach? Stezen's son?" Alex shakes his head, gaining immediate insight into his brother's actions as he slips Szames's good arm around his neck.

A scratch sounds on my tent wall as I finish setting up the communication mirror. Crystal hasn't yet risen, so I move quickly to answer it. "Perfect timing. I was just about to place the call."

Setting a small cask of wine on the table and placing two wooden cups next to it, Alex sighs. "I thought we both might need aid in sleeping after tonight's battle. Will. . . ?" Emotion threatens to overcome him as he begins filling the cups. The prince clears his throat. "Will Zach make a full recovery?"

"He hasn't regained consciousness, but his injuries have been stabilized. I'm told the biggest danger is the coma." I report the patient's condition before putting out the call to King Arturo. "If he hasn't woken by tomorrow night, his chances of coming out of it are not good."

"At least there is still hope," Alex mumbles as his father's face materializes on the smooth surface of the glass.

"Your Majesty, how stands the castle's forces?" I make the initial inquiry before handing over the report to Alex.

"Archmage Reba." The king is composed, but the skin around his eyes is pinched, signaling his discomfort. "Nemir inform me that the demons have failed to task the shields strength."

I only half hear the conversation between Alex and Arturo as my stomach rumbles. I examine the fare Alex brought. *If I eat some of the bread and cheese Crystal left, the alcohol shouldn't affect me too much.* Swirling the liquid, staring into the burgundy depths, I consider Mr. Suave's possible intent.

Too tired to contemplate the consequences of my actions any longer, I help myself to some food, sipping the wine. The port is much sweeter than expected, tasting light and fruity. I have finished half the loaf, several slices of cheese, and the entire glass of wine by the time Alex finishes his report.

"Would you like to try placing the call to the Armsmaster Stezan and the other contingent?" Feeling a little mellow but not yet buzzed by the alcohol, I am content to sit on the sidelines.

"What do I need to do?" Alex's smile is hesitant but even more endearing than the stunning one he usually gives. This one speaks of honesty.

After I walk him through his first calling, I help myself to another glass of the red. My thoughts roll inward, my perfect memory replaying everything I have experienced since my arrival as if set on fast forward.

"You look worse than I feel." Alex's voice brings me out of my introspection.

"Huh?"

"Tonight's battle seems to have dragged you through the coals." Alex moves to refill both our glasses.

"Hmm." Unsure of how to respond to this new caring aspect of Don Juan, I shrug, hoping he will go away before the wine gets my hormones surging.

"You know, it might help if you talk about it." When his prod fails, he adds, "I do know a little of how you must be feeling."

"Really? Mr. War-Is-Glorious can sympathize with my uncertain ability to cope with the violence in which I am forced to participate? Phft." My grumble trails off when I register the shocked look on his face. In a flash of insight, I realize the prince has probably never been criticized by anyone but his immediate family.

"I apologize. It's late. I'm tired." Running out of excuses for my blatant honesty, I rise, gesturing toward the door.

"It is. . . all right. I suppose I deserved that." Alex scrubs a hand over his face. Cautiously, I lower my empathy shield a fraction, trying to gauge his sincerity. *He's really upset.*

"Maybe but it was insensitive of me to put it so harshly. Wine has a tendency to make me even more direct than usual. Perhaps now is not the best time for us to talk." Determined not to throw him out, I retake my seat.

"Are you saying I cannot handle a little honesty?" A half-sarcastic smile twists his mouth.

"A little, probably. But the brutal dish I'm bound to serve? I'm not sure I will retain my position when all is said and done." I echo his sardonic expression.

"Then tonight I will be Alex, just Alex." With a firm nod, he dismisses my concerns. "Nothing said will have any reference to the crown."

Discerning his sincerity, I sigh. "If you're sure you are up to it."

"I deserve whatever it is you will say." Fascinated by his perfectly shaped lips, I watch as they wrinkle into a grimace. "When this began, I could not wait to prove how much of a superior strategist I am, to go down in history as the fulfiller of the prophecy. The war is not even half over, yet I regret the complete idiocy of my naïveté."

Surprisingly, instead of exulting in his humble admission, Alex's plight strikes my heart. "You didn't start this conflict. It's not your fault."

"No, I did not start this war, but I rejoiced in its coming." Tossing back the rest of his cup, he refills it, topping off mine too. "Until I saw Szames surrounded by demons, the consequences of this conflict never meant anything." His voice drops to whisper. "As much as he aggravates me, I do not know what I would do without him by my side."

"Perhaps it is easier for me. I have always known the realities of war. My world recalls them vividly." Already buzzed, I swish the liquid around, trying to slow down. "But still I was swept up in the momentum. So much to do, so much help to give. Surely I would be able to keep a chosen few safe. Tonight I came way too close to failure."

"But you were victorious, saving the day once again." Alex pauses to refill his cup yet again and my half-empty one as well. "I have the proper teaching. I read all the words. But I failed to see the severity of war, failed to respect its destructive capability. How could I have been so blind?"

With wine-dulled senses, I answer the rhetorical question, "It was your pride. And your vanity didn't help much."

"Yes. You have said what no one else will dare. In my eagerness to prove my greatness, to make sure I am remembered forever, I would have gotten us all killed without your auspicious arrival." Alex's guilt is real and beginning to overwhelm him.

"I'm impressed." I pause, shaking my head to clear it, absentmindedly taking a long drink.

"Impressed? By my stupidity?"

"By your ability to take into consideration new experiences and reevaluate a belief you've had probably since childhood." I take another sip to let him digest that. "In the history of my world, it has taken generations for a kingdom to reach the conclusion you have reached in only twelve days: There is a cost to any war. A cost most of us would rather not pay."

Alex's attention is focused on the maintenance of our drinks when he casually remarks, "You are going to make some lucky man an extraordinary wife."

"I already do," I hasten to inform him. "I will not forsake him, not while there is even a glimmer of hope."

Alex chuckles. "Reba, I am glad to see that sometimes you are just as blind as I am."

I come dangerously close to throwing the wine he has provided back into his face. The controlled rise of his brows stokes the fire. "Regardless of whether or not I am being blinded by hope, I will hold to my vows. It may be years before either view can be proven, but there's no way in hell—" Putting a stranglehold on my temper, I regain my composure. "I refuse to be goaded into giving up."

"After what has been revealed from our short acquaintanceship, I would expect no less." It is his turn to hide behind his cup. "I would be disappointed in you if you did not."

"You, disappointed in me? You, who has probably bedded half the women in your kingdom?" My hands ball into fists as I glare across the table. "You, who has pursued me relentlessly, would be disappointed in me for not remaining faithful?"

"Yes, I would. You have resisted my best effort, hurled them in my face, actually. You have held up your values like a shield, the vows you have taken like a sword."

It is my turn to hide a blush in my drink.

"I have been avoided, put off, and even run away from, but never before have I been stood up to and defeated. You have shown me a strength I did not know a woman could possess."

Alex administers the alcohol again as I mumble, "And five years is going to be a long time."

"But you have friends to support you through it: Rose, Szames, and myself." The gorgeous smile he gives reminds me of exactly how long those years are going to be.

"Szames. We almost lost him tonight, didn't we?" I deftly flow into a new subject. "There's no guarantee any of us will survive this ordeal." Depression takes over, which is better than the other effect this much wine usually has on me.

"I would say you have one."

Knowing I had better get to bed before I am unable to make it there, I cut him off, bounding to my feet after downing the last of my drink. "Yes, I will survive, even if it is alone." I take a step but lose my balance in my haste to be away from temptation. Alex catches me. Surrounded by his strong arms, my tongue runs free. "And who will be there to hold me then?"

All the anger, frustration, and fears hiding in the corners of my soul tumble out of me. "What am I going to do? I'm not who everyone thinks I am. I have no training, no upbringing for this." Tears come unbidden, uncontrollably streaming down my face. "Being an archmage is going to be so very lonely."

"Shush, it is all right. It will all be all right." Gently Alex strokes my hair, comforting me as he would a small child.

"Yeah, here is the all-powerful savior of—hic—your kingdom, weeping like a child." Gradually I regain control of my composure, but the emotional outburst has left me so weak, it takes every ounce of strength I have just to stand.

In a smooth motion, Alex sweeps me off my feet. Carrying me as easily as a child, his long strides bring us quickly to the bed.

"Being held, does that break the vows you have taken?" Tall, Dark, and Handsome's voice deepens as I shake my head. "Everyone needs a shoulder now and then, even archmages and princes."

Saabat Studio

Chapter Eight

I snuggle deeper into the chest upon which my head is resting. The warmth of another human body is infinitely comforting in the aching loneliness of my alien status. Arms squeeze in response to my cuddling. Full consciousness reasserts itself.

Eyes wide with fear, I spring up and away from the large man sprawled on my bed. The sudden motion sets my head throbbing and my stomach churning. I begin to panic. I search my photographic memory for last night's events. My recollection has several large gaps concerning parts of last night activities.

"Whoa, it is all right." Sitting up slowly, Alex attempts to soothe me as he would a spooked horse. "Easy now, nothing happened."

"Of course it didn't!" I snap. "But the last thing I remember is. . ." I blush, refusing to vocalize the sensual memory of his arms around me.

"Probably me laying you down. You had quite a bit to drink. You fell asleep as I held you. I did not have the heart to desert you."

"So nothing happened?" *I know better than to drink when I'm upset. I never drink, especially when I'm emotional. What was I thinking?*

"You believe that I am a rogue who would take advantage of an intoxicated woman?" Alex nearly shouts. We both wince at the volume.

"I'm sorry. I should be thanking you. It seems you were a perfect gentleman." I stumble to a halt, recognizing the nagging murmur in the back of my head as Merithin's call. "Oh, crap!"

Jumping out of bed, I race for the table. Pain stabs through my temples. My stomach gurgles, threatening to rid itself of last night's snack. I apply a touch of healing power to relieve the dehydrated membranes and calm my acidic belly.

"Merithin, Merithin, Merithin." Immediately the face in the mirror changes to that of the graying elder with a hawkish nose.

"Rough night?" The sorcerer smiles at my mussed hair and disheveled clothes.

"To say the least." I straighten my shirt, trying to dampen the adrenaline that has my blood racing. "I really sacked out. Have you been waiting long?"

"It's nothing urgent." Merithin eases my conscience a bit. "I heard about Zach's injury. Are you familiar with the calling technique that will bring him around?"

"Calling technique?" His words are better than a full pot of coffee. "Is there something to draw him out of his coma?"

"Yes. I assumed you knew of it. It is the same procedure used when a sorcerer overtaxes himself. It is just a matter of summoning the consciousness back into the focus of the body. If he has slipped past the point of perdition, you may need to join with someone who is familiar to him in order to pull him back." I listen intently as Merithin goes over the procedure for the cognizant call.

"I appreciate your help. Is there anything I can do for you this afternoon?"

"I will let you get to your preparations for tonight, unless you've got a useful technique for memorization," the aged sorcerer grumbles. "I'm trying to master that new miniaturization spell of yours. The wording keeps getting tangled up in my mind."

"You mean you haven't performed a memory spell?" I ask.

"The Fifth Law dictates one may only increase intelligence." Merithin's eyes twinkle in anticipation. "Something tells me your world's scientific advances have allowed you to circumvent this law as well."

"In a learning academy, I wrote a paper on memory. I have more knowledge on this topic than most of my people. Our world has discovered a direct link to. . ." My mind scrambles, looking for the appropriate Cuthburish term for *synapses*. Finding none, I continue. "How fast certain parts of the brain work and how it organizes information when we observe it."

"So if I concentrate on organizing information for faster assimilation and speeding up brain function, I will have an improved memory?" Merithin tries to get a grip on the revelation.

It takes half a mark to adequately explain the frontal lobe as well as the hippocampus with enough detail that he is assured of success. Gratefully, I disconnect from Merithin, who has given himself a photographic memory.

"I think between the two of you, you could come up with a spell for just about anything." I swivel in Alex's direction, reminded of his presence.

"Will it be lunch for two, milady?" Crystal asks from the other side of the room.

"As enjoyable as that sounds, I'm afraid I haven't got the time." My stomach rumbles at the thought of food, but with a remedy for Zach within reach, I refuse to put off the summoning.

"I, too, have an appointment for which I am late." Alex, smooth as ice, takes his leave.

"Nothing happened," I assert as soon as Crystal and I are alone in the tent.

"I know, milady. I was prepared to intervene this morning if necessary." Her reply isn't scathing with disappointment, but guilt weighs me down nonetheless. "Luckily, Alex was the gentleman he is known for being."

"I guess since my arrival I haven't stuck to the rules by which I usually conduct my life. In these unconventional circumstances, I keep telling myself they don't apply." I give a sigh of resignation. "It looks like I need to hold to those policies even tighter on this world. I have been here fourteen days, and I've already been in more trouble than I've seen in the last eight years of marriage."

"These rules, did you read about them in a book?" Crystal inquires.

"No book that I know of keeps 'em. It's a lifestyle, a moral choice of how to live." I pause long enough to run a brush over my teeth and hair. "Basically I try to avoid any situation that might put undue stress on my marriage vows."

"I see. . . so your vows have never been truly tested." She helps me get changed while I mull over her speculation.

"The vows themselves hold no power. The ability to stand by them must come from within each of us." I struggle to put what I have always taken on faith into words. "We, all of us, are only human, with human weaknesses and desires. If you are wise enough to know what your weaknesses are, then you can put restrictions on yourself so those shortcomings will not cause you to hurt the one you love."

"Perhaps if someone wrote that down in a book of instructions, more of your marriages would survive, milady." Crystal gives a smile as she ushers me out the door.

My feet carry me over to the infirmary as I review Merithin's instructions on magical calling. With a nod to Tupper, I make a beeline to the bunk where Zach lies. The young man looks peaceful, as if merely asleep. Szames is next to him, his full concentration on the young man.

"Any improvement?"

Szames's back stiffens. He refuses to look up from his bedside vigilance. "Tupp says he hasn't stirred."

Speedily I inform the prince of my morning, or afternoon, discovery. "From his symptoms it looks like I'll need your help to bring him around. If you will join with me in a cognizant call, there's a good chance we can pull him back."

This time the blond hunk turns to look at me. The hurt in his eyes stabs my heart. "Would you rather I fetch Alex for the joining?"

"Alex doesn't have your aptitude for magic." My eyebrows rise in puzzlement. "I would prefer to work with you, if you don't mind."

"I am surprised last night did not increase your ability to work with my brother," he states in a calm monotone.

"What I do with my nights is none of your business!" The unfounded accusation gets my back up. "I get the distinct feeling you were closer to Zach than Alex was. This will improve our chances of reviving him. If you insist, though, I am sure Alex will assist me."

"For Zach's sake, then." The despondency in his blue eyes reveals more emotion than my silent empathy. Szames pauses as if deciding whether or not to continue. Finally, with gritted teeth, he extends his hand.

My flesh meets his. I sense a pain, a hollow echo as if coming from a distance. Even muted, the feelings cause me to suppress a gasp. It is like a giant has sat on my chest; it is painful and hard to breathe.

"Think of the times you were together; keep those events firmly in mind." As I focus on the spell, the feelings begin to fade. "I will begin the calling."

"Zach you are needed.
Our plea must be heeded,
Your time has not yet come.
Your work is not done."

Intoning the poem three times, I put all my will behind it, picturing a bright light in a black void. After the last words are chanted, I continue my effort. Minutes pass as we carry on with the calling. The murmur of an arm moving under the blankets blasts into the silence of the medical ward like a shout of joy into a dark night.

Szames drops my hand like a hot rock as a gravelly voice whispers, "Attended by a prince and the Flame-haired One herself, I must be special."

"Not so much special as a thorn in the posterior. You have given us quite a scare." The fond smiles they exchange make me feel like an intruder. I turn to go.

"Szames, you too. Zach needs rest now that he has decided to rejoin us," Tupp orders from the foot of the bed.

"I will come by later." Szames gives Zach a nod as he rises.

Mute as strangers on the streets of New York, we walk to the door. *My privacy isn't worth his pain.* "Szames, you also spent a night in my chambers. What happened between us?"

The blond head snaps back as if I have landed a slap across his stubbly cheek. "But I am not my brother."

"Yes, and I'm not like the women you've known. You think I could betray my husband so easily?" I neglect to mention how close I came to that betrayal. "It hasn't even been two octals, and you think I am so pathetic as to be persuaded by any man, no matter how drunk he got me?"

"It seems I owe you an apology." Szames's shoulders sag with relief. "I suppose the pattern seemed so familiar. I assumed wrongly. I will not do so again."

"Just ask. I won't lie to you." I give my best scowl. "Being up on that platform with both of you tonight would have been torture if we hadn't sorted this out!"

"On the platform? We are staying another night?" The general of the forces of Cuthburan is caught off guard.

"Yes. Didn't Alex tell you?" My smile drops. "He and your father discussed that last night. The decision was made that we are to take another day to clear out this area."

"That was the one thing Alex failed to mention when we ran into each other this afternoon." His disgruntled timbre makes his feelings about being left out of the loop crystalline.

Taking a deep breath, I plunge on. "Szames, about last night. . ." With those four words, I have his complete attention. "The situation I put myself in was unacceptable."

With a steely countenance, Szames agrees.

"If I am going to make it five years without Kyle I'm going to have to change some bad habits I've formed since my arrival."

Again he nods his understanding.

"As fond as I am of our friendship, unfortunately that holds true with all men, you included."

His stoic response tells me I have made the right choice.

"I will no longer allow myself to be alone with a man in my quarters or theirs, and especially not overnight. I know it will make matters somewhat inconvenient." This time it is my eyes that refuse to meet his.

"I can see the wisdom in the restriction. I will respect it." When he places a hand on my shoulder I want nothing more than to crawl into his arms for a hug. My back stiffens and I stand tall. *I have got to keep my distance; no more familiar contact.*

"Thank you. I just hope your brother is as understanding." With a list of things I want to do before the night's reveille buzzing in my head, I quickly excuse myself.

Intent on grabbing a huge meal, I duck into the darkened confines of my tent. Even without seeing her face, I recognize the form. From the stiff set of her shoulders, I know it may be a while before I get to that breakfast.

"Milady, may I ask if the bargain we made still remains?" Alex's mistress pivots to face me, seething with animosity.

"Unless you have changed your mind."

"Are you sure? Perhaps you should examine your feelings toward Alex," the curvaceous blonde persists. "You may find they have transformed in the night."

"I am afraid I'm at a loss." *I've had it with people making assumptions and taking it out on me!* "To what, exactly, are you referring?"

"Oh, Alex wasn't glowing nearly enough for any strenuous activity to have occurred." Acrimony colors her icy tone as she voices her grievance. Golden locks, not yet tied back in a restrictive braid, tremble as Andrayia tosses her head like a proud mare. "Knowing Alex like I do, he more likely provided comfort and companionship while acting like a perfect gentleman." The distasteful words are spit from her mouth. "He will attempt to endear himself to you before he tries to beget an heir with you."

My knees collapse from under me as I melt into a seat. "Yes, that about sums it up." *I was nearly fooled by one of the oldest tricks in the book.*

"Basically the same technique he used on me." I use my empathy to reexamine Andrayia. The animosity isn't directed at me. Hiding behind it is a wellspring of hurt. "Until now it has been a great source of pride. Alex has never befriended another woman. I have remained his only source of that kind of companionship."

In one fluid motion, Andrayia takes possession of the other chair, burying her face in her arms. For the second time in a handful of days, I find myself consoling a hysterical woman. Eventually she cries herself out.

"I'm sorry," she mumbles, wiping her eyes.

I give a gentle smile, urging her to continue.

"I always knew there would be other lovers; with him, that is a given. But we had a commitment, he and I. After his relentless pursuit, I finally gave in when we developed a significant level of friendship."

Andrayia continues to explain the object of my greatest curiosity: their relationship. "I knew the marriage he promised might never come about. He knew my greatest fear: being the unwed mother to a son of an heir. He soothed that fear, telling me we had more than just a physical relationship; we had an understanding, that no matter what came, we would always have each other." Tears overcome the barricades she has erected.

"And you still do." I pat her hand. "I could never make an arrangement like that with him, no matter what friendship develops."

A light of hope enters her eyes, chasing off some of the shadows growing there. I expound. "My biggest flaw is jealousy. Any man I love enough to take as husband, to have in my bed for more than just one night." I pound the table with my fist. "Hell will freeze over before I stand by while he chases other skirts."

Her eyes widen at the emotional outburst. "It would really be upsetting to you?"

"Oh, and then some. I thought I was controlling myself quite well."

Andrayia laughs; a swift recovery is on the way.

"You know, I think my opinion on this matter should be spread around a bit. If you happened to mention you heard me say that any husband of mine will be spelled so his manhood won't function when he is in contact with any woman but me, well, that just might do the trick."

The concubine blushes a bright pink before she collapses in a fit of giggles. "Oh, if just one hint of a rumor like that reaches Alex, he will be thinking long and hard." Our laughter is unbridled at the unintended pun. "You must join me at dinner tonight with the Royal Guard. Besides the privilege of your companionship, I might need you to back up my story!"

"What time will you get together?" I ask, going over the list of things needing my attention.

"We usually meet a marks before sunset." She gets up to leave. "Can I have Heather call you when the others are ready."

"That's a great idea." I smile. "Do you guys"—I sense puzzlement at the earthly slang—"er, girls want to gather here?"

"That would be lovely." She nods as if we will be having tea, not dinner right before a battle.

"Three more for dinner?" Crystal asks, placing the eggs, sausage, and bread before me.

"Yes." I sigh, wondering how social obligations can arise in the middle of a war.

Devouring the breakfast in a rush, I squint as I dash out into the afternoon light. I skid to a halt. Jesse is right outside my door. Craig stands tense as a bowstring beside the entrance to my private quarters. Remaining at his post while the husky, pantherlike beast the size of a pony stalked my doorway must have been a test of his courage.

"Jesse, I was just coming to find you," I send to my partner.

"I felt tension building and thought I might be needed." Jesse's reassurance is tinged with irritation.

"How about a lift to your nest?" I bound gracefully onto my partner's back. *"I'm doing okay. I'm just not used to so many things piling up around me."* I shrug aside my concerns, concentrating on my partner's discomfort. *"It looks like I'm not the only one having a trying day."* Feeling the feline's powerful muscles under me is both exhilarating and calming.

"It isn't something you need to concern yourself with," the cat evades, concern for my well-being echoing through the link.

"Jesse, just having you here to share my thoughts with is comforting." The truth of the words would have made the beast misty eyed if cats could cry. *"Let me help, if only to offer the ear you always give me."*

"Your race truly is a compassionate one," Jesse muses before he growls, *"Or at least most of your race is."*

"Has one of the men done something to offend you?" I interrupt, ready for a new battle.

Jesse sends a mental shrug. *"It was not an intentional harm."*

Sensing embarrassment, I give a reassuring mental nudge as I stroke his fur.

"We have been in spirit form so long, I had forgotten how finicky the feminine species can be. With the unrestrained curiosity your race is displaying toward our new forms, the females"—I have to restrain a giggle as he gives a disgruntled purr—*"find they lack privacy with the nests we have created."*

"Oh, my," I mumble as I get the mental picture of carnal urges through our link. *"I'm so sorry. It should have occurred to me. Although you look like mere animals, you are not. Of course you require a certain amount of. . . privacy."*

Arriving at their chosen nesting place, I slide from his back. Irritation still clings to him, but it dawns on me that its source is not even human related. *Jesse is feeling like a husband nagged by two wives!*

Sensing my revelation, a very humanlike sigh escapes the cat. *"I will remedy the problem if you will authorize an addition to the camp."*

"Of course, whatever you need. . ."

Jesse interrupts my offer of help; the male has all the feminine aid he can handle. *"I will create a cats' tent, one that will allow no entrance but to Spirit Cats and their partners."*

"I will see that the restrictions on your domicile are known." I nod, realizing that I am needed as only a ruse; my partner does not want his full abilities known.

Unlike the magic I cast, the air doesn't waver as if a desert mirage were before us, condensing to a new image. My neck hairs stand on end. Before they are fully erect, they relax back into place. I blink my eyes to reassure myself of the new reality. A tent, smaller than my own, is staked out on the brown grass.

My brows draw downward as I long for the caress of the arcane forces. *"That was an easy fix. I wish casting spells was all I had to do. In this case I didn't even have to do that. All you needed was a distraction."*

"Which brings us to the true source of your tension." Jesse's head tilts inquisitively. *"It has nothing to do with menial duties."*

"In the last twenty-four hours, I have almost lost a good friend and nearly betrayed my wedding vows." I fight to keep the tears from my eyes, but my partner senses them in the link.

"The males from your homeland don't seem to worry about vows taken on another world. I seem to recall that females, of any species, add complexities to every situation." Sensing my affront to his male insensitivity, he adds, *"They seem imbued with a greater desire to explore emotional issues. Complexity is just the natural result of their beings."*

"Good save," I growl grabbing a handful of his neck ruff and shaking it briskly.

The mental chuckle we share makes the day a little brighter. Jesse's mind-voice is surprisingly somber. *"We noted Szames's injury. We have been using the midnight hours as a time to contact and update the others of our kind on the battle's progress. So entranced were we in our joined form, we noted* an injury but failed to sense the seriousness of it. We feel responsible. From this day forth, we will be true partners, in every battle as well as the war."

"Jesse, I didn't mean to imply—"

"And you didn't. Our agreement was for transportation. I sensed this hope in your thoughts when we met. We are now ready to proceed along the path you foresaw." Jesse doesn't negotiate for better terms on our agreement; he just gives the incredible gift of true friendship.

I run my hand caressingly over the tops of his ears. "You have given me much more than I had in mind, my friend, much more."

A delighted purr rumbles into the quiet. The intimate touch I have given, without his permission, has been accepted as a hug from someone who is more than just an ally.

I smile, turning to leave as I send a brief tendril to Jesse, "I will let the partners inform Szames and Andrayia of the change."

Chapter Nine

I stretch my aching fingers, looking up from the yellow pad of legal paper. The soft stroke of another mind alerts me to Jesse's intent before he sends, *"The Royal Guard inquires if this is a good time for dinner."*

"Jesse, thank you for relaying the message," I send back. *"Now would be excellent."* I switch to audible speech. "Crystal, our guests will arrive shortly." I roll my neck, trying to release the tension. *My first dinner party, and in the middle of a war campaign!*

With Crystal away tending to our supper, I answer the scratch at the tent flap. "Milady Reba, thank you for your gracious invitation. We are honored to dine with the Flame-haired One," Mikaela says, bowing.

"Please, it is just Reba. There will be no formality tonight. It is past time we women got better acquainted." Sensing shock reverberating from the pair of females accompanying Andrayia, I smile. "We are truly the same, you and I. You are normal women, fulfilling a need in this time of great trouble. I am an average woman on my world, called to Cuthburan to do what is needed to protect this wonderful kingdom." I gesture to the table and set of chairs I conjured up earlier. *Should I have called up a meal from Earth while I was at it? I hope I don't disappoint them with my lack of hospitality.*

The women take their seats, and Andrayia smiles warmly. "Reba, I never looked at it that way before. Our family and friends have been treating us. . . *different* since the Great Battle. I thought they were honoring us for our sacrifice, but now I can see they weren't. They were treating us like heroes."

"Perhaps your family did." Mikaela's voice is surprisingly timid. I nod, encouraging her to continue. "Mine thought it was time I gave up the ridiculous game I was playing at."

"I'm glad you didn't let them talk you out of joining us." I smile at the redhead. "I'm sure we'll need your sword before this campaign is through."

"I don't think Scott will try to talk me out of anything ever again," Mikaela growls.

"I only wish every woman in your situation had volunteered." I scowl. "Then this male-chauvinist world would've had a real wake-up call."

"Reba, I think I speak for all of us women when I say we appreciate everything you have done for us." Mikaela begins to open up, easing into the topic with heartfelt gratitude. "But most women our age have a couple of kids. I am sure there were many that would have loved to volunteer but were not in a position where they could."

Crystal places a steaming crock of stew and a loaf of warm bread on the table. Bowls, knives, and forks follow. I ladle stew into each bowl as Crystal slices the bread. My mouth begins to water at the heavenly aroma wafting from the thick, brown soup. "Do you think it would help if I hired servants to care for the children?"

"Oh my!" Auricle blurts, turning crimson when she realizes she has spoken out loud.

Cocking my head, I give a slight nod of encouragement.

She continues, staring at the bowl in front of her. "It's just as Andrayia said. You're from a place that is much different. No woman wouldn't never let her dears be kept by a stranger. The nobles may allow servants to raise their youngins, but we will depend on family."

A slight blush tinges Andrayia's cheeks. *She must have left Andertz with a friend at the castle.*

"Hmm, I see." I lift my spoon to give myself a few minutes to think this through. Having waited patiently for me to begin, the women dig into their bowls.

"This is wonderful," Mikaela manages around a mouthful.

"Thank you," I mumble. *I didn't even prepare the meal.* "Auricle, my world differs from yours in more ways than I can even begin to explain." Crystal humphs in agreement. I continue toward the goal. "I guess relationships are a large part of that difference. You guys. . ." The male noun gets a perplexed look from my guests. "I mean, gals, have heard about my matrimonial fidelity?"

Mikaela is intrigued by the topic. "Andrayia said you intend on being with only the man you marry."

"And you don't?" *Does the social rank play a part in the promiscuity of this society.*

Mikaela glares across the table. "Why do you think men keep us home, busy with as many kids as possible? If they can't afford a charm, they could wind up raising another man's son. Both men and women make this pledge where you come from?"

I pause in my attempt to scoop a carrot into the fork. "On my world most people take a vow to remain faithful to the person they marry. It is mandatory in my religion for both the husband and wife to abstain from love's day with anyone but one another. Are heirs the only thing stated at your marriage?"

I sense pain welling up inside the redheaded warrior before she smashes it down. "In all the joining I've heard of. Wasn't a day that went by that Scott didn't remind me what a favor he was doing by keeping me since I haven't carried a baby to term in the five years since we joined. He should have sent me home in shame."

"Mikaela, science in my homeland has proven that women lose babies they are carrying due to beatings like what you endured." I yearn to reach out to her but know better than to invade the personal space of an abused woman.

"You're saying it was Scott's fault?" Mikaela whispers, hope chasing away the dark clouds. "All those times?"

Intuition urges me to continue. "If it will make you feel better, I can cast a simple spell to verify my assumption."

Crystal begins clearing away the dishes as the stoic warrior nods. Tears gather in her eyes as I close mine. I take a moment to find the right phrase. "If you are able to carry a child to term as well as any woman, you will glow," I state before I begin to chant.

"If an OB would say you're fine,
With a light, you will now shine."

The minor healing ability imbued in my form is augmented as the magic intertwines into it. The euphoric energy blazes to life around the abused woman. Auricle jumps away from her comrade, falling from her chair.

Mikaela stares at her radiant hands, murmuring, "It wasn't my fault."

Auricle climbs gracefully back into her chair. The plain, mousy woman whispers to the leader of the guards, "Andrayia, I am sorry we didn't believe you. I do now."

I raise an eyebrow inquisitively. Realizing she was noticed, if not heard, Auricle's face turns a blotchy red in embarrassment. Gulping as if facing a horde of demons, she mumbles, "Reba, you use magic—a lot. You'd use it on a husband, wouldn't you?"

My lips twist sardonically. "In my world, if your husband lays with another woman, you can leave the marriage and take half of what he has, along with the children he has fathered. If I was tricked into marrying someone who promised faithfulness and I could not leave the marriage, I wouldn't hesitate to put a hex on him so he couldn't rise in the presence of another woman. After all, he promised faithfulness. I have the power to make sure I will get it."

Mikaela snorts. "You're too nice. I would want a spell to give him man cramps if his spear got close to another target."

Andrayia pales. "Reba, you can't add that to the curse on Alex; he'd be the first king in the history of Cuthburan to die of man cramps!"

The room erupts in laughter. Crystal moves to answer a scratch at the door. "Milady, Prince Alexandros has arrived to escort you to the tower."

The color drains from the warriors' faces. I reach for my robe. "Don't worry. He wasn't able to hear. Magic, remember? Will you ladies join me again tomorrow for dinner?"

The group nods enthusiastically.

Heather slides up beside Andrayia as she leads the women from my tent. The Royal Guard marches behind as Alex escorts me to the tower. Szames waits for us at the top. Heather joins Tawny where she sits below. Though the cats look calm, their ears swivel and eyes scan the area for signs of danger.

This night's battle is much smoother than last night's. We lose no more men to the demons besieging us. Whether it is because we have already cleared out the majority of the enemy or because we have three spotters for laser fire is anyone's guess. Taking a prince's hand in each of mine, I fly us to my pavilion.

"Merithin, Merithin, Merithin." I make the call, activating the communication mirror.

The princes wait patiently. Szames is slumped at the table, while Alex paces. Casting a worried glance at the hulking blond, I place my staff in the corner. The large pavilion seems crowded with the presence of both brothers. When the call fails to be answered in a candle mark, I look to make a hasty exit.

"I will make the rounds of the camp—" A face ripples into view in the reflective surface, cutting off my retreat.

"Alex, Szames." Stezen's arm is in a sling. His lack of formality sends a bolt of tension through both princes. "Archmage Reba, I would like you in on this strategy session as well."

I don't need intuition to tell me something is amiss. As if an ogre has just entered the room, my senses go on high alert.

Alex closes in on the mirror. "Stezen, what happened at your camp tonight?"

Stezen steps back to give us a view of Merithin and Jamison in the background. Allinon's absence sends prickles of fear down my spine. Dread turns my bowels to liquid.

The master sorcerer steps forward. "Prince Alexandros, I shall do better than tell you. To get the full scope of the issues at hand, I have prepared a spell that will allow you to view tonight's battle."

Recalling his fascination with TV, I nod in understanding. Merithin's hand extends toward the glass.

"From the minds of the men who have survived,
Reconstruct the battle as if on television."

The release of arcane forces causes the hair on the back of my neck to stand on end. The master sorcerer seamlessly incorporates his recent exposure to my homeland into the new spell. As before, though Merithin didn't rhyme, the spell performs flawlessly.

Upon the mirrored surface, the room fades from view. Few stars can be seen through the lamppost blazing to life around the perimeter of the other camp. The moons are cresting the western hills. The communication mirror has been transformed into a movie screen. With the hundreds of points of view, it is a production Spielberg would be proud of.

~   ~   ~

Atop the tower the shield stones send brilliant energy to surround the encampment. Several dozen demons lay sprawled across the moat. Only half a dozen monsters penetrate the stun shield at a time. Stezen barks out a command. Horns blare. Half the men retreat to take their rest.

The scene fades. Two moons are high in the night sky. A fresh company of soldiers takes the field. As the tired men march to the campfires in the center of camp, the tower begins to shake as if an earthquake tipped the Richter scale to 8.5.

A pair of cavernous holes opens beneath two of the legs of the structure. The tower lurches to one side. Allinon swings over the edge, leaping lithely from one support to the next until he is safe on the ground below. The earth opens beneath the elf's feet and Allinon springs back a couple dozen feet to safety.

Merithin shouts, "Hawk's wing!" and glides to safety as Stezen is thrown over the edge. The warrior seizes the upper support pole in one powerful hand. The tower continues to convulse, jostling the massive man like a rag doll. With a thunderous crack, the tower collapses, pinning the leader underneath.

The shield stone lays on the ground, its magical barrier affecting nothing but a few feet around it. Demons no longer fall stunned into the light of the lampposts. Monsters charge the startled men. The beasts are three times as strong and five times as fast as their human prey. Along the perimeter of the encampment, dozens of men are torn to shreds.

A singsong voice fills the air. Allinon's arms begin to lengthen; the skin is tinged with green as fingers penetrate the betraying earth. The ground stills. Almond-shaped eyes light with victory as the roots of the vines find the burier demons, crushing them in the earth they call home.

The elf's song strengthens once more. The ground beneath the tower begins to writhe. Verdant vines lift the battered structure until it stands upright; the foliage holds the rickety tower sturdy.

A fireball races toward the ogres charging the structure. The elf looks wild eyed about himself. A couple dozen demons tear through the camp, leaving corpses in their wake. A fire ring collapses back upon Merithin and Stezen. The sorcerer slumps against his staff, gasping for breath.

A voice slides into the night as the druid bends to retrieve a handful of wood from the scattered wreckage where the tower had fallen. Allinon throws the debris as if it were a javelin. Wind rustles the leaves of the vines as splinters grow to the size of spears, whizzing past. The projectiles bury deep into the demons converging on the tower.

Elfin reflexes propel Allinon into the fray. The wiry warrior leaps from one monster to the next. The slender blade of his sword leaves death in his wake. Battle fury clears from the ice blue eyes when no more enemies are found.

Jamison lays his bloodied sword on the ground, hurrying to a motionless human form. The master healer triages the living, ignoring the dead.

Allinon's nasal voice rings out in perfect English, "Chad, call 911. You can't handle this alone. We need the National Guard, the army, Marines. . . Someone!"

The words shouted in his native tongue cause Jamison to glance up from his patient. Shaking his head, he ignores the elf, pouring energy into the man beneath his hand.

Using his magician's rod like a cane, Merithin stumbles up to Allinon. The last of the cerulean energy seeps from his staff, surrounding the elf's platinum locks. The tall man shakes his head as if trying to get his bearings. "Merithin, are you OK?"

The elder wavers on his feet but nods. "I'm fine. Just give me a moment to. . ." Merithin crumples. The elf catches the sorcerer before the elder hits the ground.

The smooth surface of the communication mirror wavers. The command pavilion is once again in view. Stezen clears his throat, breaking the deafening silence. "We lost four hundred men tonight. But Merithin and Jamison inform me that is not the worst of the news." The graying leader looks to his arcane adviser.

"Allinon has portal dementia. It is a rare condition, more of a rumor really. According to the legends, some who travel between worlds fail to make the journey completely. I always assumed this meant they were not physically whole." Merithin gestures to Jamison. "As soon as Jamison got the critical patients stabilized, he sent Allinon into a healing slumber."

The healer steps forward. "It began soon after our arrival. He would call me Chad. I thought it was a just a slip of the tongue. But each day it has gotten worse. Sometimes he refers to Stezen as Bob. From the way he kisses up to him, that must be his boss back home. Yesterday I couldn't get him to answer to Allinon, only George."

I remove the hand covering my mouth. "And I thought he was just being insolent when he used my Earth name. His condition seems to have progressed rapidly, though."

Jamison nods. "I've noticed that Allinon's memory slips tend to occur more often under stress. Perhaps, like a heart condition, portal dementia is inflamed by circumstance."

I grind my teeth. "We are in the middle of a war and one of our strongest defenders must avoid stress? You've got to be kidding me! Merithin, you cast a spell to snap him out of it. If you join with Jamison, can you heal him of this dementia?"

"I could if I knew what was wrong. But even a deep scan reveals he is *physically* healthy."

Merithin places a consoling hand on the shoulder of the exasperated healer. "Up until now portal dementia was a little-known tale. I thought it was a story started by our forefathers to frighten children and deter portal magic. But Allinon's symptoms fit the legend."

"Well, you helped him. Surely you know something!" I calm the panic threatening my composure. "What spell did you cast?"

"I cast the only spell I could think of that strengthens the mind: increase intelligence," Merithin responds with the patient demeanor of a grandfather. "I have never encountered someone of his race. Apparently he is very intelligent, for it took far more energy it should have."

I scrub a hand across my face, thoughts scrambling for an answer. Szames touches my arm. I feel compassion that forces me to gaze up into his eyes. Exhaustion pinches the corners of his face. The sympathy shining through makes me ache with longing for the strong arms of a man. When Szames turns toward the mirror, all traces of emotion are stolen from my grasp.

"What does 'increase intelligence' do?" he asks.

"It strengthens the normal pathways used in speech, vision, and memory," Merithin replies.

Szames's lips press together in concentration. "It seems that memory is the vital portion of that spell, perhaps if we concentrated on strengthening his memory only?"

Merithin nods. "Concentrating on that portion, I may have enough energy to stabilize him until we can return to Castle Eldrich."

I push the shadows of despair out of my mind. "Jamison, perhaps this is similar to one of those problems where you need to be using a certain portion of the brain while a CAT scan is being preformed?"

"Reba, you may have something. As soon as I have the three score men out of danger, I will try a functional diagnostic. Which reminds me: if we are done discussing Allinon, I need to get back to the infirmary." Jamison waits for the briefest of nods before dashing off.

"Jamison saved my life when the kingdom was grieving for my death." Alex doesn't take my hand, but the comfort his aura exudes is more intimate than a bear hug, naked. "He will find a way."

Wrenching my eyes from his, I snap my empathy shield into place. I still feel the caress of his aura, but the sexual undercurrent is muted.

Alex steps forward, anxious to take command. "We must find a way to ensure the safety of the tower. Was this an ambush, or have jarovegi found a way around the shield?"

Both Merithin and I shake our heads, but the master sorcerer leaves me to defend my creation. "The demons had to have been in place as the army made camp. Even if the burrowers made it through the moat, one touch with their claws and the monsters would have been vaporized."

Alex nods his agreement. "Then it was a trap laid out by the demons. They have been noting our progress. The underground fiends were waiting where they assumed you would make camp. If they are coordinating their efforts, then only our delay at this site saved us from the same fate." Alex pales at the thought of facing the waves of darkness that have battered our shields each day.

Szames breaks the uneasy silence. "Reba, your communication mirrors have saved hundreds today. Is there an enchantment that will detect the beasts as they lay under the earth?"

Merithin and I lock eyes. He jerks his chin with a tilt of his head, giving me the floor. I close my eyes, searching for the answer. I smile, though I feel like slapping my forehead. *Duh, it's so obvious!* "I can modify the shield stones, directing the force field to travel down the pole 'til it hits the ground. Then it can grow like a bubble, clearing out any demons it comes into contact with. Merithin, can you make the modifications on your stones?"

"Yes. The idea is one I can easily employ." Merithin sighs. "But I don't have the energy required for the spell. It will take me one day to recover my strength and two more to store the necessary energy."

"Is there enough magic in the area to sustain the shield for that long?" I ask.

"I will monitor the situation, if it becomes necessary, I will move the camp out of the immediate area."

I nod toward Merithin. "Have Jamison give Allinon the diagnosis when he wakes. If he doesn't believe you, show him last night's battle like you did us. There may be some Elven magic that can aid his condition."

Alex steps up beside me. The heat of his body seeps into my flesh. Memories of last night's embrace fly through my mind, causing me to blush. With a dismissive nod, Alex closes the strategy session. "I will relay the news to Castle Eldrich. You have enough to attend to."

I step toward the mirror. "Arturo, Arturo, Arturo." I open the connection for Alex.

The king's visage shimmers immediately into view.

I move aside, as far from Alex as I can get and still be in the picture. A hint of a smile plays about the crown prince's lips as he addresses King Arturo. "With your permission, Father, I believe privacy is best for what I must disclose to you tonight."

Arturo raises his eyebrows but nods his agreement. I bow to the king, taking my leave. Szames and I step outside.

"Milady, would you like to accompany me on my rounds before you retire?" Szames extends his good arm.

His touch is cold and his eyes are sallow with dark circles underneath. His pallid face and slumped shoulders testify to his condition. "I will make the rounds. You are going nowhere but to bed."

Szames protests, "Reba, I will be fine. The men need to be reassured—"

"And they will be," I cut him off, steering us toward his tent. "I am the Flame-haired One, am I not?" We stop before his pavilion, but he still refuses to go in. "Look, Szames, your advice tonight was priceless, as it has always been. We need you better, sooner rather than later." His jaw is stubbornly set, so I pull out all the stops. "And I need you at full strength or at least coherent tonight." His weary mind still isn't grasping the situation. I add, "The lucid dreaming. . . remember? Who's going to intimidate Craig into behaving if you aren't there?"

"Ah, yes, the dreaming. For you, I will rest." The fatigue makes him much more open than he has been in the past. He brushes a loose strand of hair from my face. "Prophesied you may be, but you are a woman. Have Charles or Jerik accompany for propriety's sake."

Before Szames turns to go, Alex hails us. Szames snorts. "Of course, Alex will escort you. The men will love seeing the two of you together." Stumbling to the entryway, I can just make out his mumbled whisper, "And I must get used to it. You are his prophesied bride, after all."

If you weren't hurt, I'd slap you silly for saying that.

I plaster a smile on my face as Alex bows in greeting. "Milady, I thank you for the use of your mirror." Empathy tells me he would sooner sleep with a snake in his tent as a magical device like that.

"Thank you for its speedy return. I am anxious to hear more about Allinon's condition from the other camp."

With the deftness of his political upbringing, he gracefully changes the subject. "Will you accompany me in a promenade through the camp?"

I did promise Szames I would reassure the men marching with us. I place my hand on Alex's arm, giving a slight affirmative nod. "How did your father take the news?" *At least I can get some intel out of this.*

"As I expected. Magic and sickness mentioned in conjunction was enough to make him lose his composure." He shrugs off the encounter. "At least there were no witnesses to his breakdown. By the time we return, he should have time to adjust to the new circumstances."

"Please let me know if there is anything I can do to help." I shrug "Right now I feel like my best position is staying out of his way."

"Reba, your patience is a boon I did not expect." Alex smiles. Untouched by his aura, I feel a natural urge to snuggle closer to the man. "He knows this is the time of the prophecy. Given time, he will adjust."

"You seem to be adjusting well." I smile back.

"I had the good fortune to find a skilled teacher in the arcane." The gracious dip of his head causes my cheeks to brighten.

What am I doing? I can't be egging him on. He already expects me to marry him. "Yes, well, we must learn to work together if I am going to find a way to 'bring magic to the throne.' Perhaps your son's healing skill will be the fulfillment of that line of the prophecy." I attempt to steer the conversation back to business.

Alex refuses to concede me victory on that point. "I am sure there are many possible ways for the prophecy to be brought about."

We round a corner. The infirmary stands a short distance off. "Thank you for providing an escort. I should see if Tupper needs a hand with any of the wounded." I dip my head, hoping to make a hasty retreat.

"I shall leave you to your duties." Alex raises my hand to his mouth in a swift motion. His lips bring a warmth that races up my arm, causing my heart to pound and my loins to ache. "I look forward to a time when duties do not steal you from me so swiftly."

Indecision renders me speechless. I'm torn between wanting to slap the snot out of him for taking such liberties and wanting to fall into his arms. *He isn't even using his aura persuasion, and I have the hots for him!* I apply logic to the situation. *He's a flirt who knows I'm married. Alex is just testing the boundaries I've laid down.* The thought does little to absolve my guilt; desire for someone who is not my husband rarely plagues me. I turn on my heel, purposefully walking at a steady pace into the sanctuary of the medical pavilion.

"Milady Archmage Reba." Tupper bows. "What a pleasant surprise."

I give a nod of acknowledgment. "I thought I'd drop by to see if there were any AV cases you needed assistance with."

"The woodsmen Allinon has instructed in the druid ways have successfully exorcized the aura virus we've encountered." Tupper gives a wide yawn. "Pardon me, milady."

More contagious than the flu, my mouth gapes in return. "I think it's time we all got some rest."

Though my tent is not far, three times more I am involuntarily overcome by a jaw-cracking yawn. I shuck my boots on the way to the bed, slipping off my pants before I slide in between the sheets.

I begin to whisper my prayer spell when the hair rises on the back of my neck. *Magic?* I bolt straight up in bed, whispering, "Sight."

Scanning the room, my eyes narrow as they slide across the mirror Alex left on the table. *Who's summoning me at this ungodly hour?*

I stumble to the table, mumbling, "Light," to activate the lantern on the nightstand. On the glassy surface waits the beautiful face of Princess Szeanne Rose. Another yawn cracks my jaw. *I did enchant her mirror. Why isn't it Jamison she's calling.* "Rose, Rose, Rose," I mutter, rubbing my eyes that have gone back to being only half open.

Immediately the glassy surface shimmers, and the petite, blonde princess wavers into view. "Reba." She takes in my disheveled state in a quick glance. "I hope I have not disturbed your rest."

"I haven't actually gotten to the resting part yet," I grumble. "I suppose you've heard about the other camp?"

"If I had thought it through, I would have waited until this evening to contact you," Rose apologizes. "Jamison didn't call for me this morning. When I heard that the shields at one of the camps had been breached, I didn't know where else to turn to get more accurate information."

"It's just like this chauvinistic world to leave women in the dark." Swiveling the mirror, I collapse into one of the chairs. "Jamison is fine but I can't say the same for Allinon."

Relief washes across her tightly pinched face. Proving once again she is a true friend, Rose adds, "Reba, I am so sorry to be a burden at this difficult time. Has Allinon been wounded?"

"Rose, you could never be a burden. It's good to hear from you. Allinon wasn't injured in the fight." As quickly as possible, I brief Rose on the elf's deteriorating condition before adding, "For the first time since I got here, I am truly afraid we may not all make it home."

"I, too, am suddenly aware of the precarious position those I love are placed in." A cynical smile twists her lips. "How is it that it took so long for two intelligent women to reach a logical conclusion?"

A dejected sigh slips past my tired lips as she hits the nail on the head. "I think knowing the realities of war and seeing someone you care deeply about placed in mortal jeopardy are two very different things."

"Alex lay mortally wounded when you arrived to pull him back from the edge of the abyss." Rose closes her eyes briefly as if fighting off a vision of her new lover facing the same circumstance. "And I am just now haunted by fear?"

Guilt spikes into my soul. *It's the friendship with him I'm worried about losing; that's all.* I push all thoughts of the towheaded prince from my mind. "Yes, I showed up and saved the day. But in the last octal, we have nearly lost an entire encampment and even your brother, who was within my range of influence." I stumble to a halt, hating the moisture gathering in my eyes. I clear my throat. "Reality is a monster we now face."

"Ah, you may have it there. It seemed, with your arrival, all would be fine." Rose's cheeks imitate her name.

I shrug. "Yes, apparently we have discovered that even my powers have their limits."

"Reba, I didn't mean to—"

"You didn't. I came to the same conclusion not too long ago." I give a tired smile of reassurance before changing the subject. "Merithin and I have come up with a solution I am sure will facilitate their safe return. I will contact you personally if they hit a snag. If my face appears in your mirror, then worry."

Rose gives a timid smile. "In this time of crisis, with all you have to do, you seek to take on my concerns." She dips her head, acknowledging the gift. "It seems like ages ago you boldly put forth your hand in friendship. I know now I was blessed with a fortune beyond measuring that day."

"Rest assured, we both gained equally that fateful afternoon." Another yawn pries my jaws apart.

"I have kept you from your bed long enough, my friend." She bows formally.

"Call me whenever you want an update," I invite before mumbling, "Mirror, mirror, mirror."

Reciting my prayer spell takes more effort than I want to expend, but I know I need to be fully charged in the morning. I barely manage to control the surge of energy I push from my being, sliding into sleep moments after.

Chapter Ten

"Milady," Crystal whispers, "you asked to be notified when it was midday."

"Thank you, Crystal," I mumble. I curl into a ball around the feather pillow, burrowing myself under the covers. *I've been going at this sixteen hours a day for almost two weeks! Surely I'm entitled to a few more hours of rest,* I rationalize. Sleep begins to cloud my thoughts.

Scenes from this morning's debriefing play across my consciousness. I throw back the covers. *That wasn't a movie I was watching. It was real men—and real death.* I scrub my face. *Man, what I wouldn't give for a cup of coffee.*

With the few hours of rest, my aura is halfway charged. My lips curve with anticipation. I begin to chant.

"With little sleep, I'm moving slow.
I need a jump start with a cup of joe."

Energy ripples up and down my body, sending electrifying pleasure along every nerve. On my nightstand, the caramel macchiato sends steaming tendrils of flavor into the dim canvas tent. Sliding back into the same pants I wore the day before— *It's not like they're dirty; I didn't even get to engage the enemy*—I take the ceramic mug my father bought me at last year's Renaissance faire in both hands.

"Ahh." *I should have thought of this sooner.*

Seated at the table with pen and paper in hand, I begin scribbling lines of rhyme. *There has to be a way to provide more protection for the soldiers.* I tap the pen on my mouth. An hour later, I scribble two last bits of prose, my lips curving. *With this spell, every blow against them will increase the strength of the soldiers' armor.* White blinds my vision as I am drawn into a premonition.

The night shines nearly as brightly as noon to my magesight. The spell I cast grows stronger with each blow the enemy delivers. Each soldier glows like a million-watt bulb. Demon bodies litter the moat. More monsters surge into the fray. Like an EMP bomb hitting New York, the lights are snuffed out.

It takes only milliseconds for my night vision to kick in. The enemy tears through the soldiers' armor like a butcher carving a goose. Light blinds my eyes once more.

I wipe the tears away. *It'll create a dead zone. We will lose the war, not to mention our lives, if I implement this spell. Maybe the guys were right. No war can be fought without loss of life.*

"Milady, would you like to break your fast?" Crystal gestures to the tray she holds. Meat, bread, and apples await.

As she sets the table, I sense her curiosity. "This is a type of coffee," I explain.

Crystal nods. "Made by the machine you showed us in your kitchen."

Purposefully I push the thought of death aside. I gesture for Crystal to join me. Grinning, I begin serving myself. "Yes and no. You can make coffee at home, but this is a special coffee drink you buy at a place called a coffeehouse. This is my favorite coffee drink. Would you like to try some?"

"Milady, you'd allow me to share a specialty from your homeland?" Crystal is dumbfounded.

"Food and drink are two things that are always better when shared." I reach my hand out for her stein.

Crystal downs the contents before handing it over to me.

Holding the pair of vessels over the ground, I pour some of my macchiato into her mug.

Crystal takes a hesitant sip. "Mmm, it is sweet and slightly bitter. A very unusual combination, milady."

"Thanks. I'm glad you like it. Speaking of enjoying a meal, the women seemed to really enjoy our dinner. Am I being served something different than the rest of the camp?"

"Not different. . . just enhanced." Crystal shrugs, taking another sip of coffee.

Whispering, "Sight," I reexamine her aura—not a trace of blue or green. The maid's aura is dominated by shades of gray I have come to associate with those void of magic.

Concentrating on the subject matter causes the world to go white in a flash of brilliance.

The camp cook is filling the crock the buxom blonde holds with stew. Crystal sets the pot on a large stone next to the glowing coals. Taking two small pouches from her cloak, she adds a pinch of salt from one and a palm full of spices from the other. The maid stirs the stew then replaces the lid. The world flashes white as my maid waits for the stew to return to a boil.

I shake my head to clear the vision from the forefront of my mind. "Crystal, I apologize for the oversight. The food here has been wonderful. I assumed it was the cooks' doing. It never occurred to me that you had a hand in these scrumptious dishes."

Crystal blushes prettily. "Thank you, milady. I will pass on your compliments to my mother. Before I left home, she taught me all I know."

I chuckle, recalling the stories of her home life. "I can see why she is known throughout the quadrant for her fine meals."

I lift my nearly empty mug, shaking my head in regret. *I will have an entire night to recover before I'll be needed for battle.*

> "Alas, to the bottom I have now come.
> Fill up to the rim each time I am done."

I picture in my mind the coffee refilling again and again. In a blink, the perfect caramel macchiato, complete with steamed foam and melted caramel drizzled on top, sits before me. A heavenly smile graces my lips. *It is a good life, here in Cuthburan.*

"Would you care for some more?" I ask Crystal.

"Thank you, milady." Crystal's eager reply gives me another moment of brilliance.

I fill her mug again then, retrieving the pen and pad of paper from my nightstand, I ask, "Do you think the Guard would like to sample a meal conjured up from another world?"

"Milady, it would undoubtedly be the highlight of this entire campaign." Crystal's reply is enthusiastic, but I feel a hesitation.

"But. . . ?" I prompt.

"Auricle's reaction to your minor spell on Mikaela. . ." The blonde shrugs. "I'm not sure she would be comfortable eating food she saw magicked up."

"Thank you for your helpful insight. I will prepare the meal before they arrive." I sort my to-do list in my head. "Can you find me a couple large stones? I will need them, along with the dishes you have brought, a full mark before dinner."

Crystal bobs her head, accepting my orders. The maid begins opening the canvas window. A breeze teases the yellow pad. *I have several hours before sunset, the typical time for dinner when we aren't going out to battle.* I close my eyes. Picturing the needed result, I begin to meditate on the lines I'll need to complete the shield modifications.

I've just finished the last line when my neck hairs prickle. Maneuvering the mirror into the metal stand, I intone, "Merithin, Merithin, Merithin."

"Good day, milady." The aged sorcerer bows. "I thought perhaps we could try this brainstorm technique for the shield modifications."

I give a shake of my head. "I appreciate the offer, but I've just completed the lines of poetry. Would you like to go over the enchantment?" Merithin gives his immediate assent, so I ask, "Are you in an ensorcelled room that will prevent eavesdropping?" Receiving a questioning gaze, I reveal my security spell.

"Until this attack, it would have been unfathomable to use magic in warfare. It seems I have overlooked a crucial application."

My brows knit with thought. "I have no preconceived notions concerning magic. Perhaps that is what the prophecy meant by 'Magic will rise as the entire fabric of our kingdom is rewoven.'"

"Perhaps." Merithin hesitates to disagree. The familiar prickling of intuition creeping down my spine doesn't appear, signifying that I'm not prophesying, so I am making only a normal human guess.

"Perhaps not. Time will tell." As the words leave my mouth, a shiver races down my backbone. *Sure, more time, probably three to five years with my luck.* "Let me give you the security spell first." I jot down the enchantment then hold the paper in front of the mirror.

Now that Merithin has a photographic memory, it is just a matter of explaining the terminology to him. Most of the words are simple English; the sorcerer is quick to grasp the definitions, but detailing the thought behind the words takes more time than I expect.

I try once more. "When you speak, your voice travels through the air, much like a sorcerer projecting his mind into places he cannot physically travel, right?"

Merithin nods.

"The force field keeps out things intent on causing physical harm. This spell will keep all consciousness out of the confines of my tent. At the same time, it traps all voices within."

"Outstanding!" the wizened wizard crows. "Such a unique perspective with such mundane words. I can't wait to explore your world."

"It will definitely broaden your scope of possibilities." I glance out the window, trying to gauge time by the shadows. "Shall we proceed? Do you wish to secure your room?"

"Milady, I am afraid that will have to wait 'til morning. I have not yet recovered enough strength to be sure of my success with such a powerful enchantment."

I blush. *The spell was easy for me. I keep forgetting just what a tremendous gift I have been given.* "Are there any soldiers in your camp with energy in their aura?" I ask.

Merithin recoils as if I had struck his cheek. It takes only a moment for him to regain his composure. "I realize you meant no offense, milady, but I will not allow one not called to magic to participate in *my* endeavor."

"I don't understand. You have seen me use Szames and Lieutenant Craig. . ."

Merithin shakes his head, causing me to stumble in midsentence.

The sorcerer begins a lecture, explaining his position. "You are from another world. You cannot be expected to adhere to our customs—"

"And neither can you!" My voice is hard as I remind him of exactly who he is speaking to. "I am the Flame-haired One. 'Change will sweep the land,' remember? Or does that prophecy exclude you?"

Merithin clears his throat. "Time is crucial. Perhaps I can take a look at the men."

"Good." Knowing that teaching an old dog new tricks can be painful, I explain, "If we are going to win this war, we don't have the luxury of staying within our comfort zone." When his brows draw down in puzzlement, I rephrase. "We must broaden our prospects to things with which we are not comfortable. We must push the limits of what we consider proper and even socially acceptable."

Merithin nods in agreement. "Somewhere inside, I knew this was a necessary step. I even have two soldiers in mind, but to include the unwary—the magically blind—in my work. . ." He lets out a heavy sigh. "I only fear that once the world witnesses our power, it may begin the cycle that brought about my family's doom."

Ah, now we get down to it. "Thank you for pointing that out, Merithin. The less seen, the less to be feared. Once this war is through, I will have to put some serious thought into the best course of action where magic is concerned."

Merithin wipes his cheek with the back of his hand. "That is a comfort, milady. I pray that Andskoti will grant you divine guidance."

Unsure how to respond to the pagan blessing, I merely nod. "I will leave you to your preparations."

"I should be ready to discuss the shield modifications a mark before sunrise tomorrow." Merithin terminates the connection by whispering, "Mirror, mirror, mirror."

I'm tucking a stray hair behind my ear as a scratch sounds beside the entrance. Crystal hustles to answer it. "Prince Szames," she intones, holding the flap for my royal guest to enter.

"Milady Reba, I thought perhaps you might use my assistance in the shield modifications?" He bows, more formal than I have seen him in quite a while.

"You seem much better." I gesture for him to lead the way. "How's your shoulder?"

"Nearly good as new." Szames extends the wounded appendage as if offering proof, and I place my hand on his arm. He continues as we begin to stroll toward the tower. "Tupper has released me for scouting as well as the battle tomorrow night."

"It seems a little rest—" I clamp my lips shut as the words *that I had to make you get* fly through my mind. "Has done you a lot of good."

Szames smiles as if hearing the unuttered words. "Yes, thanks to your insistence." The hunky prince halts in front of the tower, turning to face me. "I feel I owe you an apology. Rose tells me that I am the worst patient. I fear I have not behaved as—"

I cut him off. "You were there to make sure I was following the doctor's—" I rephrase when his brow crinkles in puzzlement. "I mean, the healer's orders, I was merely returning the favor." Gazing into his gorgeous, blue eyes filled with compassion, I'm unable to look away. Blood pounds through my veins.

"After you, milady." Szames tears his eyes from mine, gesturing to the ladder.

"Shall we fly?" I ask, extending my hand.

His massive fingers gingerly touch mine. I move to thread them. The strength of his hand, the warmth of his flesh, causes a blush to infuse my cheeks. Guilt hammers me. *You're only flying so you have an excuse to hold his hand.*

I shove the thought from my mind, focusing on the needed result. I whisper, "Superman."

I lift us past the platform, continuing until we reach the shining globe entwined at the end of the hundred-foot post. *More magically efficient to touch the object.* I attempt to justify the action before addressing my helper. "Shall we begin?"

Szames nods.

Pulling capacious amounts of energy from him, using my force only to guide his flow, I begin the mantra.

> "Like New Year's Eve when midnight arrives,
> Protection descends before our eyes.
> Making contact with the ground, the bubble will grow,
> Destroying demons above and below.

Ecstasy surges through my tired body. I clench Szames's hand as I fight to control the forces I have unleashed. Perspiration glistens on every curve of my form as the enchantment settles into place.

Silently we glide downward. *I suppose I can see why Merithin doesn't want to share such an intimate contact with another.* "Sight," I whisper in curiosity. Szames's aura is depleted of half its energy.

"Thank you, Szames." I manage to speak as our feet make contact with the ground. "I don't know what I'd do without your help."

"I am glad I can be of service, milady." His stiff reply makes me wonder if I have overstepped that line again.

I plunge ahead. "Will you be available for our dreaming session tonight?"

"I look forward to seeing more of your wondrous world," he reassures me. *Is that fear in his eyes? Blast the stupid empathy! It wreaks havoc with Alex and is blinded to Szames. What good is it?*

"I've got a ton of stuff to get to." I back away from the puzzle I don't have the time or patience to decipher. "I'll see you tonight." Turning, I speed-walk to my tent, not even caring if he understood my twentieth-century jargon.

Closing the tent flap, I let out a sigh of relief. Crystal bustles about, lighting candles and lanterns. Three large stones await me on the table. Recalling the poem I composed before Merithin's call and the energy it took to place the enchantment on my mug, I retrieve my staff.

Standing before the table, I begin.

> "For holding food, you won't do.
> A stoneware crock now shape to.
> Inside this bowl, time is suspended.
> Nutrition preserved and never ended.
>
> The food will not cool, spoil, or rot.
> Refill when we see the bottom of the pot.
> The contents of this cauldron can be changed.
> Double tap upon the bottom to rearrange.

Though the enchantment rhymes as badly as some folk songs, cerulean forces surge into action. Energy races from my staff, surrounding the largest of the rocks. I repeat the spell for the second rock and the bowl Crystal has been using. I wipe sweat off my brow. The power in my magician's rod is down by a third as I use the second spell for the last rock. *We aren't battling until tomorrow night. I should be able to recharge my staff and be at full power by the next battle.*

Seeing I have completed the task, Crystal reaches for the midsized bowl. "Milady, what beautiful serving pieces." The green earthenware set comprises three bowls and one platter. Each dish has a matching covering.

"The items are enchanted to refill as they are emptied." I explain unseen properties. "To change the contents, merely turn the item upside down and tap twice on the bottom then put your new contents into the pot or platter. They are designed to stack securely, one on top of another."

Crystal is wide eyed, more impressed than I have ever seen. "Milady, we must be careful with these. If word gets out, they will be the target of every thief in Cuthburan."

I shake my head in denial. "But, Crystal, they're only enchanted dishes. I just wanted to be sure I had your special touch on the next leg of the campaign."

My maid turns the stone pot over in her hands. "With these you could open an inn and make a fortune with very little work."

I slap my head with my palm. "Or an army! This will solve our food crisis. I will enchant the cook's cauldron."

Crystal nods her head. "You'd best enchant his lips while you're at it. Half the men would starve before eating something magic has tainted."

Her words speed me into motion; the Guard will be here soon. I lay the dishes out before me, licking my lips in anticipation. In measured time, I begin to chant.

"My mother dear, how I have missed you.
Your love, your advice, and your cooking too.
Gumbo, pepper steak, and pineapple upside-down cake will
have to do.

The air around the dishes wavers then coalesces into the requested items with rice filling the fourth pot. Though it wasn't mentioned in the rhyme, the last bowl is filled with a diverse salad sprinkled with balsamic vinaigrette.

A scratch sounds at the tent flap as Crystal retrieves the individual dishes from the packing trunks. The blonde ushers in the trio of women as I gesture toward the table. "Ladies, I present to you my mother's specialties."

The delight I sense from the women confirms that I have made the right choice. Explaining the principles of Cajun dishes—that more rice will make it less spicy—I demonstrate, serving myself first. Using the bowl Crystal provided for the gumbo to create soup with a little rice. I make a bed of the starch on my plate and place the tenderloin with peppers and onions on top. I use the tongs to fill the rest of my plate with the salad.

Andrayia and Mikaela take my advice, spooning just enough soup into their bowls to moisten the rice. To my surprise, Auricle serves herself exactly as I have. The warrior gives me a shy smile. "My mother is from the west. I have missed her spicy fare on this campaign."

"I would love to try your homeland's specialties." I manage around a mouthful. *Will it be Mexican or Middle Eastern or some other flavor?*

"My family would be honored to prepare a meal for the—" Auricle blushes as she corrects herself. "For you, milady."

I smile encouragingly. *Maybe she'll let me conjure it up from her memories.* I shove the thought aside, refusing to voice it. Conversation ceases as we sate our appetites.

Mikaela murmurs, "Mmm. The heat is subtle, and it grows with each bite." The redhead reaches for her glass once again.

"A bite of cake will help negate the heat." I nod toward the dessert platter. The oohs and ahs make empathy unnecessary for judging the success of the meal.

"Reba, your world has such interesting flavors." Andrayia's diplomacy is exquisite as she makes an early exit. "Thank you for the opportunity to broaden our palates."

Sensing mounting sexual anticipation, I know where her mind is and where she is heading next. "Thank you for the pleasure of your company."

The other women rise with Andrayia, echoing her sentiments and her feelings. *With no skirmishing, I guess everyone is looking to expend some energy. At least Charles and Alex should be in a better mood in the morning.*

I shrug off the jealousy threatening to dig in roots. *Kyle will be here soon.* Crystal bustles about. First the stackable dishes are stored, then she hustles out to clean the dirty ones. I shake my head in wonderment at my fortune: both a confidante and a helper have graced my life. Struggling with thoughts of her impending departure, I remove the communication mirror from the drawer and intone, "Jamison, Jamison, Jamison."

The healer's form appears on the glassy surface. Shocked by the suddenness of the reply, I ask, "I take it I caught you at a good time?"

"I was just readying the mirror when your call came in." Jamison's tired grin makes me ache in sympathy for my comrade.

"How'd Allinon take the news?"

"Better than I expected. He'd been losing chunks of time for a few days now so he was open to our explanation." The healer's eyes close briefly as if gathering his thoughts. "We lost another soldier this afternoon. When Allinon started shouting for an ambulance, I scanned his cerebral cortex. It was the craziest thing I ever saw. Patterns were stable but only on a portion of the brain. Then when he snapped back to this reality, the entire spectrum lit up. It was as if part of the normal pathways didn't exist during the reality break."

I rack my brain, trying to think of a spell to aid Allinon in overcoming the portal dementia. Heaving a sigh, I ask, "I'm not sure I have a firm enough grasp on the medical aspect to come up with an enchantment. Did Merithin's memory spell help?"

Jamison snorts. "That's where Allinon's patience evaporated. He stormed out of the infirmary refusing to—How did he put it?—let an ignorant Neanderthal tinker with his brain."

"Yeah, sounds like the right guy. I hope the elf's magic is able to aid him in securing the entirety of his mental capacity since he's being so pigheaded."

Jamison's lips twist as he shakes his head. "The arrogant SOB." Seeing me wince at his harsh tone, he dips his head. "Excuse my French, but that stubborn jackass wouldn't even let me put him into a healing slumber. He swiped that enchanted dagger you gave me, insisting that focusing on a powerful magical artifact can keep him stable."

The tent flap opens. I look up from the mirror. "Milady Reba, Prince Szames and Lieutenant Craig," Crystal announces, waiting for my acknowledgment before letting in the men.

I give a brief nod then turn back to the mirror. "The dreaming group is here. Keep me posted on his progress. If his condition doesn't stabilize, I'll take a day and fly over there if I have to."

"No problemo. With the camp being rebuilt, he's bunking in the infirmary. I should know before we move out if his technique is working. Sweet dreams. . ." With a dip of his head, he says, "Mirror, Mirror, Mirror," severing the connection.

Yawning, I gesture toward the bed. "Glad you guys are here. If you're ready?"

Stifling a yawn of his own, Szames nods, stumbling on his way to the massive bed that dwarfs a California king. Crystal follows me to the mattress and the guys get comfortable beside me.

We join hands and I intone the lucid dreaming spell. Drifting into slumber banishes my lethargy. We materialize in the garage. "This is a horseless carriage. We call them cars." The men circle the SUV, looking over this new type of vehicle. The last time we were in the garage, my husband's pickup was the only mode of transportation. "I won't go into any detail about the different types of vehicles or even too much about how they work. Before your journey to my land, I will give you the necessary knowledge you need to operate them. For now I just want you to get used to how it feels."

Merithin's form wavers into being in a corner where I pictured him being. The sorcerer's mind must have just reached the REM stage necessary to complete his portion of the enchantment. "Milady, I do hope you haven't been waiting long."

"We arrived minutes ago. We were just preparing to take a ride in the car." As the elder goes to inspect the vehicle capable of towing a four-horse trailer fully loaded, I climb behind the wheel. The group from Cuthburan takes to modern-day travel much faster than I anticipate. We have time to explore a grocery store and gas station before the end of the tour.

Seconds after the tent flap closed behind the men, I shuck my pants. My shirt will be my nightgown once again. I snuggle down in between the sheets. My mouth stretches wide, disrupting the flow of the words for my nightly prayer spell. Frustrated, I forgo the ritual, slipping silently into slumbering bliss.

Chapter Eleven

Taking a long pull from my coffee mug, I push back the tent flap. The crisp air is fresh with morning dew. A timid smile dawns as I gaze into the brightening eastern sky, listening to the sounds of the camp being broken down around me. Jerik saunters up beside me, wiping crumbs from his beard.

"Thought you'd sleep the morning away," he grumbles.

"The sun hasn't even crested yet," I grouse, recalling the lit candles I had to dress by. A smile peeks out beneath his whiskers. My lips twist sardonically. "Dwarven humor is almost as dry as the English."

Crystal hustles out of my campaign quarters, carrying a wooden box. I turn back to my comrade as she boldly says, "Malibu," to shrink the tent.

The grin disappears faster than dew in the desert as I recall my duties. "Can you get Charles? There's been a development at the other camp."

Jerik bobs his head. "Shall we meet you at the tower?"

"Let's meet at the partners' tent; there will be more privacy there."

Jerik stomps off as only a dwarf can. I turn back to Crystal. She has positioned the miniature domicile in its container. I give her a grateful smile. "How did you like the ride last night?"

"It was most enjoyable, once I became accustomed to the speed." Her eyebrows rise with concentration. "The way you must hold the. . . wheel," she pronounces carefully, "and the movement of the big wagon as it turns sharply, it reminds me of the drills stable master Mik put me through. Handling a robust horse isn't much different."

I chuckle. "Crystal, I don't think you are going to have any adjustment issues. I will see you at the new campsite."

I march toward the cats' quarters, hoping Jerik has managed to corral Charles from whatever bed he has wandered into. The pair of Americans appears at my shoulder as if conjured by my thoughts. I whisper, "Secure," watching as the diamond in my ring begins to shine with a blue radiance.

"You gonna give us the 411 on the situation at the other camp?" Charles's broad smile and the feelings he emits hint of his morning recreation.

"I take it word has gotten out, despite our efforts at secrecy? How are the men taking the breach in our defenses?"

"Morale is good," Jerik rumbles. "Many of the men saw you and Szames flying over the camp to update the shield."

"From what I hear, most feel lucky to be on campaign with the Flame-haired One, like they've hedged their bets for survival." Charles gives me a sexy leer. "So, Hot Momma, why call this secret powwow?"

"There's an issue with Allinon. He has what Merithin is calling portal dementia." My heart aches for the comrade who may not make the trip home as I detail his disability, finishing with the elf's tantrum.

Charles sighs. "Man, I know the guy's a major jerk, but to wind up a total nut-job. . . Wouldn't wish that on my worst enemy."

"I'm stumped," I admit with a shrug. "I'm open to ideas for a spell."

"A sorcerer asking for help concocting an enchantment?" Jerik's eyebrows climb to his hairline. "You really are a newbie at all this stuff."

I stare at my toes, blinking to keep the moisture in check. "Maybe if I wasn't, I'd be able to find a way to help Allinon not to mention fortify this camp better. All I do is try and adjust our defenses to the new form of attack."

"Don't go there, Sweet Momma." Charles slips an arm around my shoulders. "These aren't men we are facing. This army was so outgunned when we arrived, holding our own is a major improvement. Don't you realize? You've so many lives by crossing boundaries that you didn't even know were there. I mean, you've done some really cool stuff." He wiggles his fingers at me.

"And asking for our help is a good example of what you do best." Jerik tucks his thumbs into his belt. "Not only stepping outside the box, but disregarding it all together."

"Thanks, guys." I turn to give the ebony knight's neck a squeeze and nod to Jerik. "I don't know what I'd do without you two."

"Probably do just fine," Jerik grumbles before adding, "The only thing I can think of that might help is a stasis spell. Maybe if his bed was turned into a type of cryogenic tank. Then when he's not needed, his condition wouldn't worsen."

"That just might work." My lips twitch, wanting to smile yet not quite able to get there. "If he'll let Merithin cast the spell."

The cats saunter out of their tent, cutting the conversation short. "I'll suggest it tonight when I talk to Merithin," I add, making a beeline to my partner.

Standing beside Jesse, I whisper, "Open," to remove the privacy shield. Looking up from my ring, I smile. The tent has shrunk, and beside it sits a wooden box, waiting for me. The magic the cat used was masked by my spell.

Andrayia rounds a corner from the infirmary as the tent begins to shrink. The warrior bobs her head. "Milady, I will take care of our partners' quarters. Alex and Szames await you at the southern edge of camp."

I throw the saddle over Jesse and slide the halter over his head. Rubbing the cat's neck, I ask, "Ready, partner?" I chuckle at the unintended cowboy slang.

"Looking forward to stretching my legs a little," Jesse sends back.

Side by side, we stride to the center of camp. Szames, Alex, and a band of nobles wait for us at the tower. "Humph, looks like an ambush," I mutter, sensing tension emanating from the crowd surrounding the pair of princes.

"Milady Archmage Reba," Alex addresses me formally as we halt before him. "SpiritCat Jesse, good morn to you."

I dip my head in salutation. "And to you, Your Highness."

"I see your quarters are secure," he continues with the platitudes. "Shall we proceed with the tower?"

Why does he insist in making a public show of my working of a spell I designed to make my workload easier! There must be more behind it. I wish he'd just get to the point already. I turn on my toes, grinding my teeth in frustration. Jesse's rumbling purr echoes beside me. The cat is unable to conceal his amusement. "Malibu," I snarl.

Alex's page, William, scurries up with a box. He secures our defenses within. A deep breath helps me regain control of my temper.

I swivel around with a smile plastered on my face. Ignoring Alex, I turn to his brother, "Prince Szames, are you ready?"

"Milady Archmage Reba." Annoyance colors Alex's words as he endeavors to get my attention. "It has been decided that a new procedure will be needed."

I cock my head, inviting Alex to continue.

"I assume you have a way of detecting any hidden enemy?"

I nod, still refusing to speak, wanting to be on my way as soon as possible.

"Then if you and Prince Szames will circle the camp to clear the immediate area of any hidden enemy, the general can fill you in on the other changes." Alex turns to the nobles, making it clear that he is the one who is ending the conversation.

I roll my eyes at his back. Mounting Jesse, I turn to Szames. "Shall we?"

"Surely." He smiles encouragingly.

The cats lope to the edge of camp then begin a spiral pattern leading outward.

I turn to Szames. "So the nobles found out about the breach?"

"Your powers of deductive reasoning continue to amaze me." Szames shakes his head. "They were fine with the campaign as long as we had the assurance of the shield. With the possibility of an ambush vividly pointed out to them, Alex has had to use every ounce of his persuasion to keep most of them from bolting. Only his insistence that the Flame-haired One can detect the enemy kept them from running back to the protection of Castle Eldrich."

"I see," I mumble, sending a tendril of thought to Jesse. *My empathy will only sense things relatively close. If I have to maintain a spell the entire day, it will seriously compromise my power level. How far do your feline senses range?"*

"In this enhanced form, I should be able to detect their foulness within a league of my position."

Tawny's ears flatten as her superior details his abilities.

"Szames, the enemy cannot hide within a league of our scouting position."

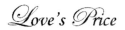

Tawny's ears return to normal as she realizes I will keep the cats' abilities a secret.

"Will that do?"

He bobs his head. "Perfect. We will ignore their paranoid request to cut today's journey down to half. There will be no need to weave our march through the hills."

Completing the circuit of the camp's location, we ride to the head of the column of men, where Alex waits with three of his officers. Szames briefs his superior while I wait in silence. The grateful smile Alex gives me causes my cheeks to brighten with embarrassment. *I should cut him some slack. After all, he's carrying the weight of the kingdom on his shoulders.*

Scouting in companionable silence is a soothing balm to my frazzled temper, but I reluctantly breach it. "Szames, is having the nobles on this campaign necessary? I've always felt that too much politics only complicates a military situation. One of the few engagements my country lost was because they let policy dictate their military's decisions."

"I must say that I agree with your opinion, but in Cuthburan we have always held with the tradition that all officers need to come from a noble birth."

"And the men need their leaders." I sigh.

"Yes. So it seems we are stuck with politics for the time being. However, your suggestion of knighting a warrior for actions in this war may just be the wedge I need to change some of our more inconvenient military traditions."

I gaze about us at the undulating hills and the road weaving its way through them. *Besides the slow progress, traveling seems almost too easy.* "Will the terrain become more difficult for the army as this crusade progresses?"

"To ferret out the gate's hiding place, our route must remain in a somewhat circular direction. It will take months of travel at the army's pace before we are no longer in the tightly settled lands surrounding Castle Eldrich."

And of course the settled lands have plenty of roads which make the going easy. Every novice would know that!

Not wanting to reveal just how inept I am concerning politics, strategies, and campaigning in general, I clamp my lips shut on my other questions, determined to talk to Charles later. The sun is caressing the horizon as Alex's page places the tower in the middle of the southern junction of the main road.

The now-familiar noise of the camp being erected echoes around us. I reach for the buckle on Jesse's saddle, unsure why the silence between Szames and me suddenly seems strained.

"Will you be able to join us for the dreaming tonight?" I ask.

The smile he gives is sincere but not beaming. "I wouldn't miss it. Midnight bells again?"

"Sounds good." My lips curve. *Probably just stress; we are in the middle of a war, after all.*

Because of the long march, the shield stones are activated, but the call to bring the demons to us from the surrounding countryside is not. Szames, fully recovered, returns to the front line for the first half of the night. Without the attractant, the enemy is scattered and few. It is quickly decided that the company's magical resources are not needed. The appointed officers will man the tower and summon me if laser fire becomes necessary.

Crystal insists on drawing the bath, though with the magical equivalent of a modern bathroom I could have seen to it myself. "I never thought preparing for bed could feel like a luxury," I mumble as Crystal massages shampoo into my hair.

Her strong fingers rub my scalp as she whispers, "There were many ballads sung in my parents' inn about the harshness of an army on campaign, but this is the first Cuthburan has seen of it in many generations."

"Cuthburan has been fortunate to have peace for so long. Has the country flourished in the last few decades?"

"Trade has been good. The healers established their school. Many new uses for ironwood have come to be. Yes, I suppose my world has seen many improvements since I was born."

I rise from the bath, gesturing to the tub. "You may want to take a soak before morning. I can see to my needs while you do."

"Yes, milady," shock colors her whispered answer.

Less than a mark later, my flaming locks are still wet as I greet our dreaming partners. Craig's eyes rove over the comfortable clothes I'm wearing as if picturing me without them. The long-haired man's passion spikes to a new high. *I'd lay odds that he's stiff as a board.* I shoot a grateful grin at Szames. *Thank you, God, for my princely protector.*

The morning dawns bright and sunny. Ansil, the soldier who lost his foot, returns to the safety of the castle along with the rest of the wounded. I am certain he won't let go of his new guitar the entire way. Reinforcements arrive before sunset. The hundred or so fresh men are a welcome boost to the soldiers' morale.

I touch the shield stone's pole, activating the demon-calling spell. Andrayia joins us on the platform. Heather paces below with the other Royal Guards. The night's battle, while still heavy, leaves me with enough storable energy to get my staff humming with power.

The days blur together, forming a monotonous string of battles and scouting. The only break in the routine is the nightly sessions of lucid dreaming. The trips to my home make the loneliness bearable. We continue the campaign, turning toward the northeast.

The new restrictions I place on my behavior are a constant reminder of my position. Even though the Royal Guard and I share evening meals, none truly understand who I am. My strange views keep us from becoming true friends.

The soft glow of the diamond in my wedding band proves we can talk freely as Szames, and I scout together. "This road is great. We should make good time today."

"EastRoad is the main thoroughfare to Brightport, though it looks like a four-wheel driving trail compared to the roads on your world."

"Without cars, you really don't need pavement."

"We should pick up the pace and take a look at today's campsite." Szames doesn't seem interested in exploring the new English word.

My foreignness is pushing even him away. Maybe I shouldn't have included him in the dream sessions?

At each encampment, Szames and I take another journey to my world. Each day we seem to talk less and less. It seems a lifetime has passed by the time the army reaches EastRoad. I feel more alone than ever before.

The moons rise behind a curtain of clouds. Again it is decided that my talents aren't needed. Instead of heading for my quarters, I meander through the camp.

"Hot Momma, you runnin' about unescorted?" Charles's midnight face blends into the darkness, but his teeth flash brilliantly in the quiet night.

I grin at the ebony paladin. "Szames is holding the eastern edge of camp, dispatching the occasional demon that finally makes it into the calling area. Jerik is with him." Recalling the last time I let Alex into my quarters, I growl, "And hell will be snowed-in before I ask Alex to accompany me."

Charles, ever the Prince Charming, holds out an elegant arm. "Looks like I showed up in time to rescue a fair maiden after all."

"Charles, I can walk myself. No one would dare accost the Flame-haired One. Heck, they'll hardly make eye contact."

Placing a hand over mine, Charles shrugs. "But a woman alone in a company of soldiers wouldn't be proper."

Heaving a sigh, I open my empathy, trying to gauge my comrade's true intentions. *Surely Mr. Hound Dog can't be worried about propriety.* Unease bordering on nervousness and worry with a subtle undercurrent of arousal come through. *Well, he's definitely a man.*

"You doing OK?" I give the dark man a nudge. "Allinon's meditation has stabilized him. He'll be back at the castle with us tomorrow. He is going to make it."

"Sweet Momma, you're apt at usin' that empathy, aren't ya?" Prince Charming isn't fooled by my ploy. "And you care enough to try." Silence expands as he switches to English. "The elf's dementia got me thinkin'. Things have been wild since we got here, and I'm not talkin' 'bout the demons." He slides me a glance out of the corner of his eyes.

I begin to steer us toward the partners' quarters, where we will have some privacy. "We've been here a little less than three weeks and your exploits are becoming legendary." I chuckle. "Wasn't Rose conned into relaying messages via Jamison for those who are clamoring for attention before our departure?"

In the deep shadow of the large pavilion, I turn to face the paladin. Gazing up into the darkness of his face, his smile lights up the night. A flash of white sparks blinds me momentarily as intuition is turned into a foretelling.

The bright sun shining behind the hulking form hides the identity of the figure. Light glints off the metal of a blade. I hear grunts behind me. I'm in the carriage house, out by the barn. Charles's hips thrust and the woman under him pants his name.

"How could you betray me like this?" I swivel back to the doorway, sensing murderous intent. I hold my breath, eyes squinting as I try to discern the identity of the intruder.

Incredible softness envelopes my lips. The world before me shimmers. I grasp at the shredding threads, trying to hold on to the vision. Silky wetness teases my mouth. The realization of what is occurring tears the premonition from my grasp as I am snapped back to reality.

Brilliance eclipsing my sight brings pain stabbing through my skull. Vertigo turns my limbs to jelly. Hips swivel into mine, and a surprisingly large bulge grinds into my pelvis as strong arms surround me, crushing me into chain mail. A tongue snakes in between my lips.

Using all my strength, I push against the massive wall of the chest crushing me, pulling my head sharply back. Freed from the iron grasp, I wipe the foreign spit from my mouth.

"Charles!" Sensing confusion surrounded by currents of passion so strong that it sets my own hormones surging, I strangle the urge to slap the man.

"Sexy Momma?" he mumbles.

I place a hand on my throbbing head. "You oversexed idiot! Someone's going to try and kill you."

"What?" I feel the lust begin to ebb. Tortured embarrassment rises in a sharp peak. "You weren't. . . ?"

"No, I wasn't swooning under your magnificence." I snarl. Pain stabs into my brain as I try to recall the details of the premonition. "A vision showed you banging some girl and an angry man with a knife." A touch of healing magic helps settle my aura.

"Little Momma, my bad. I thought with your jawin' 'bout legends."

"Charles, you gotta get a grip." True regret and humiliation war with the need for sex still throbbing inside him. "You were in the carriage house. . . I think."

"That's what I was trying to tell you, Sweet Momma." Charles still isn't listening. "I'm afraid I'll be permanently screwed up by the time we get back."

"Charles, what is going on with you!"

Unabashed, he points at the bulge his clothes are unable to hide. "It's this. Look at it." Regardless of the rose tinting my cheeks, I am unable to keep eyes from the sight of the massive shlong threatening to escape the breaches.

"Man, it's like I'm back in high school, not only three times as big, but ten times as intense. Not only babes, but battle makes me horny as a rose bush is thorny. Not getting any for more than twelve hours just makes me need—I mean really *need* two or three just to be able to get him back into my pants."

Unable to hold it in any longer, laughter erupts. "I'm sorry." The giggles break free again. "But you did base your character on scenes from a romance novel."

"Yeah, but will it go away once I get back?"

I glance at his still-bulging member. "Either that or you've got a great career as a porn star." I relent as I feel terror creep into his consciousness. "Look, you are just experiencing your character to the fullest. . ." A giggle escapes me as my eyes dart to the third arm that shows no sign of tiring. "Extent. When the spell takes you home, you will be reconfigured. Everything. . ." Another giggle sneaks out as my eyes seem to have a will of their own. "And I do mean everything, will be just like it was before we left."

"You don't need to scry or something?"

Sensing desperation I heave a sigh. "I can trust you not to—"

"Sweet Jesus, woman! Just cast the spell so I can go get me some good lovin'," Charles insists.

Feeling his lust spike at the thought of another female, I don't quite trust him enough to close my eyes. *Is it possible that it's even bigger?* I shake my head, forcing my eyes to look into his and away from the mound that's nearly as big as my forearm. *Hung like a horse could actually be accurate.*

"Give me a minute." A deep breath focuses my brain.

"Going home you will soon do.
What shape will you transform to?"

Dizziness makes me swoon. I grind my teeth, seizing the needed results in a stranglehold. A holographic form shimmers into life next to us. Allen's scarecrow body and balding head are a welcome sight.

"Never thought I'd be so glad to be me." Charles heaves a sigh as the image fades. The paladin leans forward to thank me with a bear hug.

I spring backward. "You can thank me later." My lips curve as I chortle. "Time to get him reined in."

Charming ducks his head but still manages a leer. "I'll get right on it."

My laughter crows into the night as Charles adjusts himself in mid step. My eyes pop open in disbelief as he eases between the tent flaps of Andrayia's quarters. *I guess the relationship really isn't exclusive.*

Knowing sleep will help more than anything else, I stumble toward my quarters. Grateful that we have completed the lucid dreaming early, slumber overwhelms me before I can even begin my prayer spell.

∾   ∾   ∾

With the castle in sight a mark after setting out, Szames and I aren't scouting. We maintain a forward position with Alex and the rest of the officers. I search for Charles as the company falls out for a midday meal.

Glancing westward, I see a black stallion cresting a hill just past the last of the soldiers. Two figures are mounted upon the massive horse—a dark, towering form and another that is almost child sized in comparison. Cursing under my breath, I whisper, "Superman."

A glowing buttock shines in the noon sun as the pair trots over the knoll. I turn back to the main body, unwilling to interrupt their afternoon delight. *Couldn't even wait until you were off the horse!*

"I hope he remembers to be careful." I shrug off the prickling of fate twisting in my gut. *He's a paladin and better armored than any other man. Surely he can handle an angry boyfriend.*

The prophecy crusade remains unfinished as we cross into the city well before sunset. Alex, Szames, and I lead the troops through streets crowded with throngs cheering of townsmen. The cats hold their heads high in true parade style.

"If any of the peasants are taken aback by the Flame-haired One riding a giant cat, they are too excited to show it," Jesse sends to me.

"After seeing demons, a furry feline doesn't seem threatening, no matter the size." I smile, not exactly feeling as if I've returned home but at least feeling I've come back to safety.

I give a nod to Crystal as she hastens down a side street to her parents' inn. She will visit with them briefly before coming back to the castle to prepare for tomorrow's departure.

A sigh escapes me as we pass through the massive gates and enter the castle grounds. Grooms rush toward us then skid to a halt as they get a good look at our mounts. A wry smile tweaks my jaw. My fingers, used to the task, mechanically unclasp the buckle. Sliding the halter over the ebony ears, I take the saddle in hand.

"Have Mik find a place for these in the carriage house," I say, handing the completely unnecessary equipment to the groom. Icy tendrils creep down my back with the final words. *Is it just me, or has Charles been avoiding me since last night?*

I search the milling crowd for my comrade. Jerik takes possession of Alex's mount. I catch Charles's eye before he heads to the barn with the dwarf. I mouth, *Be careful.*

The dark man gives a wink and thumbs-up of reassurance. Still, my stomach is tied in knots as I turn toward the fanned steps of the castle. I take my spot behind the cats, waiting patiently for Alex and Szames to lead the way.

"My sons, news of your continued victory has spread hope throughout the city." Arturo greets his sons formally.

"Father, we return not only victorious, but fortified with new allies against the evil of demonkind." As rehearsed, the princes step apart, arms gesturing toward the massive cats standing directly before me. Alex's voice rings out clear and strong, "King Arturo of Cuthburan, I present to you SpiritCat Jesse, SpiritCat Tawny, and SpiritCat Heather."

The felines extend their front legs and dip their heads, bowing in the presence of the sovereign. Sensing the shock of the gathering nobles, I snap my shields up. I ignore the politics around me. Unable to let go of the unease curdling in my middle, I send my mind outward, looking for Jerik.

The dwarf is in the forge. Before he lights a fire, I send a tendril of thought, *"Jerik, I've got a bad feeling. Play guard for Charming outside the carriage house, will ya?"*

"Sure, no problem," he agrees, sensing the worry I feel.

"In gratitude for the honor our new allies do Cuthburan by gracing us with their alliance, we will travel east, clearing the Ethereal Forest as we continue the crusade." I refocus on my surroundings, grateful that I've missed the rundown of our campaign. Agitated that I'm forced to endure the ceremony instead of heading off possible danger to one of my crew, I force my feet to stay still.

King Arturo smiles to show his favor as he turns to me. "Archmage Reba, do the SpiritCats have any special requirement?"

"Our allies prefer privacy. The stand of untamed woods on the northeastern side of the castle will provide most of what they need." Having prearranged the accommodations, the request is more for spreading the word to the populous than anything else. The untamed park has been set aside since the castle's inception. The area is complete with a natural spring leading to a glistening pool. "If a young steer will be let loose tomorrow in the forest, they will require nothing else."

"It shall be done as the archmage requests," Arturo announces. The king lets the silence expand as he eyes each of the noble born. "Change has come. . ."

I tune out the rest of the monologue, uninterested in more propaganda that will only serve to push me closer to a union with Alex. Jesse sits, intently observing the monarch. *I wonder how deep the cats are able to read into a person without their knowing it?* Dismissing the annoying topic, I concentrate on creating the spells I will need tomorrow instead of the foreordained marriage I seem to be hurtling toward.

"Reba, get Jamison to the carriage house." Jerik's panic-filled thought slices into my consciousness.

I whisper, "Superman." My toes leave the earth as I broadcast to Szames, Jesse, and Tawny, *"Find Jamison. Bring him to the carriage house now!"*

I ignore the uproar spreading outward from my position like a boulder tossed into a placid pool. Dread sucks the moisture from my mouth as I concentrate on flying as swiftly as possible. It takes milliseconds for my eyes to adjust to the dim interior of the enclosed structure.

Déjà vu sends icy strands up my spine as I peer around the dusty garage that houses the royal carriages. I join Jerik and Allinon, who are huddled over a listless Charles. An inky pool is spreading outward from where the paladin lies. A weeping woman huddles inside a carriage.

"I can't stop the blood," Allinon mumbles. "I don't have the ingredients."

I close my eyes, reaching for the healing power within. In a full healing trance, I see the half dozen knife wounds that pierced straight through the mail on his back. I let the energy flow from me. The magic surrounds Charles's torso, seeping into his skin.

"Ugh." I gasp for breath. I have only managed to lessen the flow of blood. "That's all I got. Charles. . . Charles. . . stay with us." Tears fill my eyes. "Jamison is. . . here." I amend as Jesse leaps through the doorway, the healer on his back.

Without a word, Jamison vaults off the cat. Emerald energy envelopes the wounded man before the healer's feet hit the ground.

Charles's face twists in pain as he begins to convulse. He coughs, spewing blood from his mouth. Between choking gurgles, he mutters, "Take. . . care. . . of. . . Sam."

Charcoal eyes stare at nothing as the warrior's features go slack. "No! Charles!" Blinded with tears, I put my palms on his torso. Rhythmically I begin pumping the immobile chest.

"Reba." Jamison places a hand on my shoulder. "There's not enough blood left to—"

I shrug off the comfort. "I'll cast a transfusion spell."

A strong pair of arms wrap around my upper body. "It's too late. He's gone."

Fury sweeps all emotion from me. My hands ball into fists. "Who. . . ?" I shake my head, ordering my thoughts. "Jerik, you were standing guard. Who did this?" I demand acidly.

The dwarf releases me from his iron grip. "I don't know. Ask Allinon." The dwarf jerks his chin toward the elf. "He went in after the first woman left."

The elf's chin drops to his chest. He refuses to meet my eyes. My blood runs cold. "No. . ." I mumble, "It couldn't be."

The vision flashes back into my mind. The dark figure is tall and lanky. . .

"I. . . I don't remember anything." Allinon clasps his shaking hands together, hands covered in blood.

I spring to my feet. I begin chanting as power surges from me.

> "Each mind will give what it knows.
> A hologram will reveal the show."

Cerulean energy bursts from me, surrounding not only the elf, but the cringing woman in the vehicle as well. A sob catches in my throat as a radiant image of Charles bends over the seat of the carriage.

Nearly undetectable over the moans of the woman, I catch the whispered words, "Vicki, how could you? And you. . . you betray me like this after all we've been through?"

The murderer remains hidden. No one has a clear view of the owner of the whispered voice. The holographic warrior straightens, as if trying to brush off an annoyance. "Man," he pants, his silky voice guttural in his passion, "give me. . . a minute."

"Allen, you bastard! I trusted you, fought beside you!" The words are spit out as Charles spins, but his legs give out under him. The paladin falls into a twisted heap. A scream fills the air as Allinon's image shimmers into being. The elf stands over the paladin, knife dripping crimson blood. I release the strands of power.

"No." Allinon shakes his head in denial, but his pallid face betrays him. *He knows.* "I was coming here for some privacy, t-to meditate."

"You had the knife." I close my lids. "*My* knife. The one enchanted for sharpness, penetration. . . and against pain." *Nothing else would have gotten through his paladin shield, much less his mail. Charles didn't even feel the stabs.*

The elf's eyes dart to the blade lying on the ground beside the carriage door. "Oh my God. What have I done?"

Tears streaming in agony, Allinon springs lithely onto the balls of his feet. "Charles. . . My God. What have I done?" Swifter than a flash flood in a desert canyon, the killer sprints out of the room, sweeping up the enchanted knife in one swift motion.

"Jesse!" I scream for my partner, sprinting after Allinon, knowing I have no chance of keeping up with the fleet-footed elf.

I swing up onto Jesse's back as he lopes up beside me. *"We have to catch him."*

I hunker down into the soft fur as the cat glides across the ground. Silent as a soft breeze, we slide into the woods behind Castle Eldrich. Moonlight glints off metal as the clearing appears before us. In the middle of the melted slab of rock, Allinon perches on his knees with the blade resting against the carotid artery in his neck.

"Allinon, it wasn't your fault," I whisper, sliding off Jesse's back, hastily wiping moisture from my face.

"It was someone else who took the life of my best friend?" The elf's hand hesitates for a moment. "Someone disguised as me? Tell me who it was, and I'll take his life instead of mine."

"Without that knife, Cha—" I choke on the name. "He wouldn't have been scratched."

The knife begins to tremble. Allinon turns his eyes toward me for the first time. I wince at the pain I am unable to share in this dead zone. "He died by my hand. Justice must be served. A life for a life."

"Then take responsibility for your actions; don't run from them." The elf's jaw jerks as if I landed a slap on his cheek. "Devote your life to his family, the son he won't be able to provide for. Be there for Sam."

Like a puppet without strings, Allinon collapses into a heap, sobs wracking his slender form. I reach for the knife, and drop the gore-covered weapon on the grass. Tentatively I place my hand on his back, rubbing in small circles. When the elf regains some of his composure, I pat his hand. "The biggest challenge will be in having very few people you can talk to about this. I suggest trying to reveal what has happened to your wife, after you prove you are different by being the same great guy you have grown into on this crazy journey."

Wiping his nose on his sleeve in what I am sure is anything but an elfish manner, he croaks, "She'd have me locked up within a week."

"I'll send an enchanted note so she can see the others for who they are." I shake my head. "No, better yet, I will give them each a key phrase so they can reveal the truth to whomever they choose. When you are ready, they will come."

"You'd do that?" He grimaces. "You think they'd do that. . . for me?"

"Of course they will." *I hope they will.* "It wasn't your fault. Back home you'd be off on a temporary insanity plea; you really were out of your mind."

"Will you call Jamison to spell me to sleep until we are ready to leave?" he asks as we rise. "I've had my fill of this world."

"He'll meet us at your chambers." I pick up the knife and wrap it in a spare bit of cloth. I send Jesse for Jamison. "Let's take the direct route." I extend my hand toward Allinon and glance heavenward.

Without a word, he extends his hand. Our flesh meets and I perceive the crushing weight of his guilt. "Superman," I whisper, trying to keep my tears in check.

We soar silently upward, circling around the castle to the balcony of my chambers. I clear my throat as our feet make contact with the stone. "I will prepare the body to look like a mugging. A miniaturization spell with stasis will make transportation easier. I charge you with finding a suitable location where he can be discovered."

A muffled sob escapes the slender man.

I place a hand on his arm. "You need to be strong; the son he leaves behind will be in need of guidance. Perhaps you can pass on some of what Char—" Again I am unable to get the name out. "Some of what he taught us all."

Wiping a tear from his cheek, Allinon turns to face me before we enter the hall. "You know, I thought you were dead wrong for leader. After all, it takes more than just power to be a real leader of men. But I was wrong."

Hot moisture seeps from eyes as I squeeze them tightly shut. "No, you were right the first time. I lost one of my men. I should have never demanded the leadership role."

Allinon's hand holds the door firmly shut as he stares into nothingness. "Do you know why I was in the disenchanted meadow? I wasn't tired. I could have easily scaled the wall and been halfway to the northern woods, where I could have held even you off indefinitely. No, I chose the dead zone, figuring that without your magic, you'd be powerless to stop me."

Hollow eyes turn to stare me down. "Sorcery aside, today you proved you deserve to be our leader, and no leader, no matter how great, can save everyone, not in the real world."

In a fluid motion, Allinon glides through the door, leaving me struggling to catch up to his long strides. I leave him with Jamison, hastening on my way. My mind struggles to make sense of all that has happened as I wander the twisting halls of the castle. Arriving at the sparring room where I enlisted Andrayia aid, I lean my face against the wall.

God! Why have you forsaken me! My mind cries out. *You have given me so much here, so much power. But, God, where is your wisdom, your guidance? Where are you!* I wipe the tears from face, feeling more alone than alone than I have since my arrival.

Chapter Twelve

"Milady." The pair of pages bows in unison.

"William, Keth. Is my correspondence in order?"

"Yes, milady. Laid out on the dining table in order of importance, as you requested," the young page reports with a stiff salute.

"Keth, any problems with the chronicling?" *He looks like he has shot up a few inches in the last couple weeks.*

"No, milady. The process continues even now." Keth mimics William to a tee.

"Keth, if you are up to a little more magical adventuring, I could use your assistance." I weave a spell to form replies to the letters received in my absence. To save strength for the upcoming portal spell, I draw nearly all the required energy from the young man I have decided to offer an apprenticeship to.

"Milady, a bath has been prepared," Crystal notifies me as I enter my bedroom for the first time in seventeen days.

"That is thoughtful of you. Thanks." Even though I prefer morning baths, she knows I like a long soak to get off the road grime.

"I wanted to give you one last formal service before my duties with you are concluded." For a brief moment, the shy smile she gives me makes me homophobic. The first time she helped me bathe, she propositioned me.

I dismiss my fears as unfounded. In all my time with her, since that first bath when I stated my heterosexual preferences, she has not implied even a hint of sexual interest. "I am honored by your graciousness."

Disrobing in the dimly lit bath chamber, I peer at my maid, noting her red rimmed eyes. *Word spreads fast.* "I take it you've heard about. . ." I shore up the floodgates threatening to burst.

"Yes, milady," she whispers, concentrating on the task of filling up the porcelain pitchers.

"Allinon. . ." I clear the lump in my throat, trying to come at it from a more logical angle. "Arturo has agreed that, since those who are involved are under my authority, I will decide the corrective actions." *I'm glad cats can outrun elves, or we might not have gotten to him in time.* "It was Allinon's illness that caused the attack. According to the laws of my land, a person is locked up until they can be cured of the mental malady if such a thing happens. Jamison has placed Allinon into a sleep from which he cannot wake until it is time for him to travel home. The elf will be under guard until the departure."

Fear spikes within the diminutive woman. "He will be traveling with us?"

"Once Allinon returns home, he'll be fine." I step into the water, releasing my temperature shield. "Jerik will guard him 'til he leaves. Once he gets home, his mind will be restored along with his appearance."

"Is he much different on your world, milady?"

"As different as my world is from yours," I mumble, beginning to relax. "Allinon will need your help to convince his wife of his miraculous journey. My comrade will need someone to help him adjust once he returns to his old life." Sensing her reluctance, I add, "I was responsible for the men here, and I would consider it a personal favor if you help him readjust in my stead."

Feeling her pain, a dull echo of my own, I snap my shields into place before the dam I've erected is breached. *She was closer to Charles than I thought.* A bemused huff escapes me. *She no doubt got a taste of that dark chocolate.* I shove the thought from my head, wiping an escaping tear.

"For you, milady, I traveled through a countryside filled with demons. This sounds no worse."

I chuckle at her relaxed acceptance, leaning back against the tub. Crystal begins kneading my shoulders. The painful knots begin to ease. "I am going to miss you." I sigh, unexpected moisture gathering in my eyes at the thought of losing another ally.

"I will miss you as well." Emotion causes her to choke out the words. "I have tried to gain a little distance in these last few days to make the parting easier. Nevertheless, you have become one of my true friends."

Minutes pass while we both shore up the floodgates. "The feeling is mutual," is all I can manage to get out around the lump in my throat. We complete the nightly ritual without uttering another word; kind gestures speaking louder than any lines of poetry can of our mutual adoration.

Crawling into the downy softness, I begin to chant. The words catch in my throat. Unable to keep sobs at bay long enough to complete the enchantment, I give in to the sorrow I've denied for hours.

෪ ෪ ෪

Nose clogged from my hysterical fit, I wake in a puddle of drool. Eyes gritty, I reach for the water on the stand beside me. My hand knocks over the renaissance mug. Steaming liquid sloshes over the rim and onto the table.

"Son of a—!" *Damn enchanted mug. . .* I snap my temperature shields into place, sending a tendril of healing power to the scalded flesh.

"Milady?" Crystal's worried voice precedes her into the room. "Is something amiss?"

"I need a towel, a rag or something," I mutter, wiping gunk from my eyes.

"Phedra, fetch the cloth from under the counter," Crystal calls over her shoulder. My helper takes the mug from me, drying it on her pristine uniform. "We will need to get you ready if you are going to make all the appointments you have set for the day."

I turn myself over to Crystal's tender administrations. *What made me think sending her away was a good idea?* The normally scrumptious meal tastes like someone has used my plate for an ashtray. I force down some eggs, knowing the protein will do me the most good.

My hair has been reset in the enchanted combs by the time Szames is ushered into my reception chamber. "Reba, are you sure you want to do this?" Worry colors his deep tone. "Merithin can—"

"Merithin doesn't have the necessary energy for half of what needs to be done. I'll be fine." I stride toward the door.

Szames hustles to grab the handle before me. Ignoring his offered arm, I stalk from the room. Boots pound the wooden floor as he rushes up beside me.

I say, "If I've interrupted any homecoming plans, I can find a replacement." *Discussing what happened is the last thing I need today.*

"I am happy I may be of assistance," Szames whispers. "If you need me, all you have to do is ask."

I grunt my acknowledgment, ignoring the sentiment. Recalling the needed spells, I hammer steely determination into place. *I will concentrate on the tasks at hand and deal with my feelings later.*

I squint as the doors swing open on a cloudless morning. *The skies should be hailing great golf balls of ice in remorse for the knight. At the very least it should be raining.* Words of rhyme begin to form, but I shove them aside, knowing I don't have the power to waste.

Sunlight glinting off the sparkling water of the fountain causes my eyes to narrow again. Not caring what the consequences may be, I begin to chant. Shades settle into place on the bridge of my nose. *I should still have enough power; it didn't even dent my energy.*

The darkened glasses give me a sense of privacy, as if hiding my eyes will hide my pain. Turning the corner to the practice fields, we stagger to a halt. Five sections of canvas have more than a hundred tents stitched to them with leather thongs.

Without a word, I march to the first section. Reluctantly I hold out my hand to Szames. The duplication enchantment comes out in clipped, short words. It takes a couple of marks just to finish the soldiers' quarters and the containers to carry them.

"Reba, you will need food if you are going to be able to complete the list of enchantments on the agenda for this day."

Entering the mess hall, the aroma of the common fare causes my stomach to grumble.

I nod my agreement, grateful for the moment of solitude as Szames dashes off to retrieve our lunch. My mouth begins to water as he places the food before me. I shovel and swallow as quickly as I can without choking.

Enchanting the cook and the helpers along with the barrels of prepared food occupies the majority of the afternoon. Two of the mess hall workers pass out from fear of the arcane. *All things considered, not too bad.* The sun is setting as my princely escort and I arrive back at my quarters.

"Milady Reba, Jamison and Jerik." Crystal ushers them into the room then scuttles back out as a knock sounds at the outer door. I ignore their somber countenances, tending to the business at hand.

"This is it. After tonight there is no going back." I test their convictions. "You will be stuck on this world with me."

"For me there was no going back the first time I picked up a hammer," Jerik's deep voice grates.

"The first time I touched someone with the gift, I knew. This is where I belong," Jamison's firm voice echoes my thought about the arcane.

Crystal reappears with Merithin and Craig in tow.

"Then let's get this over with. Craig, please stand facing Jerik," I whisper, my voice growing hoarse with overuse. "Craig, I will grant you not only Jerik's identity, but also the ability to reveal your true self to those you trust most. I would use this ability sparingly. The key word will be implanted in your memory with the completion of the spell."

Jerik gives a nod, agreeing with the necessity of the trigger.

"Take a deep breath and relax. Open yourself as if you are aiding me in magic or lucid dreaming. Jerik, think of home. Fill your mind with memories of Earth."

Taking hold of Szames's hand, I begin.

"Traveling home you will never go,
But your appearance will still show.
Along with memories, DNA, and such,
Fingerprints, schooling are needed much."

With magic glowing around our two hands, I tap Jerik's forehead.

"Darren is who people will know.
Friends, family will believe it so

Unless 'ijostrae upp' ends the show.
You have a place in my land,
His knowledge in your hands."

I end the spell, tapping Craig's forehead. The lieutenant is enveloped in a bright azure glow. As the radiance disappears, he sways like a sapling in a brisk spring breeze.

"Jerik, will you help him to his bed? He'll recover by morning." The dwarf hefts the soldier onto his shoulder, carrying his replacement from the room.

Jamison's hand grazes my shoulder. My throat feels a soothing balm as I move on to Merithin. I begin with a variation of the language spell I used to grant my group the ability to speak Cuthburish.

"The knowledge of my land that I have gained
Shall be passed along to you, unrestrained.
Formidable you are destined to be
As I pass to you what's inside of me."

The magic from our hands envelops Merithin's head like a cloud of smoke. Used to meditation and scrying, the sorcerer is only dazed by the knowledge transfer. When the fog clears from his eyes, I speak in English, "Do you understand what I am saying?"

"Perfectly. Those horseless carriages, you call them automobiles as well as cars." A smile spreads across his wizened face.

"Yes. Now I have another favor to ask."

Crystal appears at my side with two glowing gelcaps.

"These should protect you from contracting any disease, among other things. They haven't been tested yet, so I don't know how effective they will be, but they aren't harmful."

"I appreciate your thoughtfulness." Merithin takes both pills from the tray. As I give a nod, he quickly swallows them in one gulp.

A teal light appears in the area of his chest. As seconds pass, the energy intensifies to encompass his entire being. Within moments, the brilliant radiance is almost painful to look at. Finally, minutes later, the glow subsides.

Crystal covers her mouth, smothering a surprised exclamation. Jamison grins from ear to ear. A tight smile is all that manages to get past my grief. Without saying a word, I take Merithin by the hand, leading him over to the vanity on the other side of the bed.

The sorcerer stares at his reflection then glances back at me then back to his reflection again. "Holy Andskoti!" Eventually, his eyes travel down to his hands. He flexes them, turning them over. "Woman, what have you done? You've broken the Third Law of Magic!"

Standing next to me, staring into the mirror, is a brown-haired, slender, young man. Only an inch or so shorter than I, the hawkish beak he sports and the blue eyes are the same, but now we look roughly the same age. I gaze into the magician's emotion-filled eyes. The twinkling azure orbs have a depth to them that mine are lacking.

Perceiving his praise and delight and taking no offense at his rough-sounding response, I explain. "If you search your new memories, you will find that aging is caused by cell degradation. Losses of certain vitamins, minerals, and changes in hormones are what cause the aging process. I merely used magic to keep the body at its peak efficiency."

Merithin's eyes glaze over as he searches the information still integrating into his memory. "Yes, that's how you did it. I am unsure if five years on your world will be enough. There is so much to learn!"

With the added knowledge still processing, transferring Jamison's identity to the sorcerer turns out to be more than even his disciplined mind can grasp. Szames and Jamison catch him as he begins to crumple. After the prince assists the healer in positioning Merithin over his shoulder, Jamison stumbles out the door.

"Are you ready?" I turn to Crystal.

"Yes," the flaxen-haired woman's reply is stout, although her hands visibly tremble.

"This spell will bind us closer than any family. With this link, we should be able to accomplish a type of lucid dreaming despite the distance." Still sensing unease, I add, "It won't hurt, but I must warn you, some of the memories will not be pleasant. I would spare you if I could, but to take some of the memories, you must take them all."

Crystal gives me a tight nod.

"In my place you must go,
Traveling far, but few will know.
Your person and DNA and your prints,
My form they will perfectly represent.

Kyle, my family, are the only ones
Who will now perceive what we have done.
Until 'ijostrae upp' from your trust is won.

My memories I give unto you,
The good, the bad, and the ugly too.

Linked we will be. In our dreams we shall meet.
Our lives revealed when into slumber we sink."

When she collapses, Szames drops my hand to catch her. The handsome prince delivers the slumbering maiden to her bed. In deafening silence we walk back out through my bedroom, entering the reception chamber.

He reaches out, taking a hold of my arm. "Reba, are we still friends?"

"I don't know. Are we?" *He's been drawing away from me for over a week. I don't need his pity now.*

Szames's eyes widen fractionally. "Have I done something to offend you?"

I grind my teeth as I struggle with a swirling pool of emotions. Reason finally wins the war with grief. I stare at the ground, stating my assumptions as fact. "It's not your fault. I overstepped the bounds of our relationship by taking you on the dream-coupling. If not for. . . for. . ." I can't bring myself to say the words. "You probably wouldn't be here. Being friends with an off-worlder is just asking too much."

"Reba, please believe me, nothing could be farther from the truth." The prince evades the issue. "You have allowed me to fulfill a dream I had given up on years ago."

"Szames, my empathy may be blank when it comes to you, but I am still a woman." I bring my eyes up but focus on the fireplace. "Every trip to my homeland took you farther from me. We haven't really talked in an octal."

The silence expands between us. I shuffle toward the door, blinking to hold back the flood. "Forget I brought it up." I shrug, gesturing toward the door. "I appreciate your concern."

"You are right." The suddenness of his confession causes me to turn and look. "The trips to your homeworld have affected me. . . and the way I view us. The more I saw of your home, the more I realized we were destined to part."

"I will tell you the same thing I told your brother when he tried that destiny crap. Destiny is the king's trickster. I take responsibility for my actions. So should you."

"Fine. You want me to own my actions? Answer one question: How can you be friends with someone who must seem a barbarian compared to the sophistication of your society?" He gestures around him. "Our glorious kingdom is smaller than most of your cities."

It takes me a few minutes to form a reply. I choose my words carefully. "Advanced we might be, but some believe our society is a little too advanced." I struggle to put what I have always felt into a logical concept. "I told you I was playing a game, even showed you the hotel. Well, the reason that place came into being is that some people believe a utopian society could exist if magic were available. There is a drive inside us, an irrepressible desire to accomplish something. What's more, the slower pace of this time, the innocence of it, appeals to us. We wish to live in a time where courage, strength, and the force of a person's will are still respected, a place where those things are enough to allow someone to succeed."

"I wish we had talked long ago." He shrugs with a self-deprecating grimace.

"Me too."

We both sigh. Suddenly his close proximity; the clean, masculine smell; and that goofy grin make me realize how long it has been since I have been held by a man. . . when I am sober, that is.

"I should've guessed my homeworld would be a little intimidating." I stand, moving toward the door.

"Reba, I can imagine how hard—"

Not wanting to hear the words, I interrupt. "You will be the first shoulder I reach for. Right now I just need a good night's rest."

"Of course." Suddenly more awkward than a teenager on his first date, Szames excuses himself as William and Keth enter with the requested supplies. "Until tomorrow."

With more assistance from Keth, I finish the preparation for tomorrow's ceremony. The midnight bells are ringing by the time I find my bed. Exhausted beyond anything I have yet endured, I lay staring at the ceiling, willing myself to sleep.

Slumber is as elusive as fog on a hot, summer morning. When the morning bells toll, my gritty eyes feel as if I haven't closed them for more than an hour. I roll off the mattress, sore enough to have battled demons the whole night through. *My personal demons.*

"Milady, I'd like to present Constance." The ivory-complexioned, ebony-haired, middle-aged woman next to Crystal curtsies.

"Nice to meet you, Constance." I nod, still trying to slough off the sleep clouding my thoughts.

"Her mother was first maid to King Arturo's first wife. With your approval, she will assume my duties. I advise you to place your trust in her as you would me."

"And Phedra?" I inquire about the orphan who shares Crystal's quarters at my request. "Will Constance act as a guide for the young girl in your absence?"

The maids exchange glances. When Constance gives a brief nod, Crystal relates, "Constance is the illegitimate daughter of Arturo. Despite that, her mother and Arturo's first wife became close friends. I will let her reveal the details, but suffice it to say because of her situation, Constance never had a desire to produce children of her own. She and Phedra have formed a relationship in our absence."

Looking closely, I can see a resemblance to Alex in the long-lashed, blue eyes and perfect, full lips. My new maid stands a few inches taller than most women I have met on this alien world. And while the years have added roundness to her buxom figure, beauty still shines through.

As the two of them begin to undress and redress me, the haze of sleepiness begins to lift. "Constance, any aversion to magic?"

"No, milady."

"As I tell all my personal staff, I have one rule. Coming from a different culture, I insist that if you have any questions about my behavior or anything you may find around my chambers, simply ask." Stifling another yawn, I add, "At the appropriate time, of course."

"Yes, milady."

Crystal and I hasten for Merithin's tower, her things piled into the bag strapped to her back. Constance is now in charge of my personal quarters. "Are you sure about her? She seems somewhat reclusive."

"Milady, Constance has just been introduced to a legend our kingdom has been awaiting for generations. She will need time to come to know you as I do." Crystal's reminder of my identity on this world deepens the gloom creeping from the shadows of my mind.

"How are you holding up?" I focus on her problems, pushing mine into a corner as we continue our leisurely stroll.

"More nervous than I was for my first roll in the hay." This time I catch the tenseness in her voice.

"Just remember one thing: you must act according to how you wish to be treated. If you wish to find a man, like the one I have, then you should portray yourself as someone with moral fiber, accepting nothing less than to be treated with respect."

The deeply perplexed adventurer gazes at me. I fall back on my blunt nature. "If you act like a slut, sleeping around with every man who gives you a line, pretty soon people will treat you with the same lack of respect that they do here."

"That is a truth I wish someone had related to me at a much earlier age." She sighs.

"The manuscript I gave you shows every moment of my time here. Make sure Kyle reads it as soon as possible." A bright flash blinds my vision. When the spots clear from my eyes, I see Crystal seated at a computer, head bent in concentration.

A light flashes again, and I turn to face the blonde at my side. "It's not a bad read. After he's done, you might seek publication; try your hand at writing a sequel or two. When things settle down, I will contact you through the lucid dreaming and clue you in to how I manage to fulfill the prophecy."

Stopping at the door to Merithin's tower, Crystal turns to face me. "Reba, I want you to know how much I appreciate all you have done for me."

I fight back tears, realizing that she has addressed me not as a superior, but as a friend. "It's been my pleasure. Everyone deserves a second chance."

"But you have given me so much more. You have even given me a piece of yourself along with priceless knowledge." Crystal's thoughts rove through the newly imprinted memories. "I know how hard this world is for you, how hard I was for you. Your memories showed me how difficult your childhood was, what part pornog. . ." the retention spell I placed on her causes her to struggle with the earthly term.

"The graphic sexual pictures," I supply.

"Yes, how that contributed to a childhood that was worse than most."

"I know of many that were worse." I shrug, trying to move away from the sensitive topic.

"But then to have love's first day taken from you by a boyfriend who tortured you with the same. . ."

I reach out to the blonde, who is on the edge of tears. "Search farther into my memories. My husband and I sought counseling for our differences. Christine helped us work through our communication problems as well as my past issues. I came to realize that pornography was Kyle's issue, not mine. I wasn't any less of a woman because he desired something else. There were chemical reactions in my husband's body produced by the excessive stimulation of those pictures. It created an addiction—a draw to the pornography—that, like any other addiction, is hard to resist." As if saying the words were a magical balm, the pain that usually stabs through my heart isn't quite as sharp. "Crystal, with your kind and well-put viewpoint, you helped finish the job. I think I finally understand Kyle's perspective."

At a loss for words, we embrace like beloved sisters before an unwanted departure. I lead the way down the long, spiral staircase, the same one I raced up less than four weeks ago. Everyone but Szames has already arrived, including Jerik and Jamison. Allinon shoots the healer a relieved glance as we appear.

"I didn't expect to see you guys this morning." I give Jerik a grateful smile.

"We came as a team." Jerik's brow furrows as he struggles for the right words. "It wouldn't feel right not being here for the dissolution."

When the door opens again, our eyes shoot up with expectation. A gasp arises from the others as they recognize the figure accompanying the prince.

"Archmage Reba," Arturo says, "Druid Allinon, we could not let you leave without showing our appreciation for all you have done."

Allinon bows to the king, who continues, "You were brought here without regard for your free will, and yet you have stood beside—nay, led this kingdom to victory in battle after battle. Your aid has been invaluable."

The elf lowers his eyes in acceptance of the praise.

With a gesture, a pair of young boys in page uniforms step forward. "A price cannot be put on the injuries you have taken, the victories you have won. However, to let you leave without attempting to show our gratitude is something we cannot allow."

A twisted smile cracks Allinon's perpetual grimace. Arturo bestows the reward we discussed with the traditional words of parting. "Safe journey and long life."

With a dip of his head, the elf graciously accepts the two small satchels. As Arturo takes his leave, I approach the elf.

"Allinon, we've come a long way together. Tell me: Do you truly trust me now?"

The druid gives a hesitant nod.

"Then in the spirit of trust, I ask you to hand your reward over to me."

The druid elf bobs his head as if deciding something in his heart once and for all. "I trust you with my life, Reba. What's a little gold?"

"Thank you." Turning away from him, I take twelve empty leather bags out of the inner pockets in my robe. I place them in two lines.

The first of the appropriated satchels contains gold coins, fifteen of them. Taking out ten, I place one in each of ten empty satchels. The second pouch contains emeralds of varying sizes. Choosing two that are as big as my thumb, I place them in the pair of remaining sacks. With Craig's assistance, I multiply the contents of all the bags simultaneously.

Removing the borrowed items from the bulging sacks, I replace them in their respective satchels. I hand a bag of gold to Merithin then move down the line.

"Crystal, one bag of coins is for you. The other two along with the emeralds are for Kyle. He will need the resources to help with the mission." The color drains from her face. Knowing it stems from overwhelming appreciation, I smile encouragingly. The blonde places the new items in her pack with my personal memoirs detailing my visit and the other things I have given her for my family.

"Craig, please give one bag of gold to each member of my family along with the correspondence. The fourth bag is payment for your services." After he dips his chin, I give a last-minute piece of advice. "Jerik, or more accurately Darren, has a wife who he is on bad terms with. If you research your new memories, you will see that when a couple terminates a relationship, the wife gets at least half of what the man has. You didn't take the vow, although you will be held to it because of your identity. If I were you, I would keep all the assets you are bringing with you hidden until a divorce can be secured. You need to keep your true identity a secret as well or they will lock you in a jail for the insane." This information he digests remarkably well, considering that yesterday he didn't know what a divorce was.

"Married?" his eyes glaze for a second. "She is a beautiful woman. Why the divorce?"

I raise an eyebrow at Jerik. "I got tired of being run over. She is a real spitfire, that one." The dwarf sums up their two-year marriage as only a man can.

I step toward the slender elf. "Allinon, you've learned to give your trust. You are now worthy to receive it." I hand over the last three bags of coins and the original bag of gems as the druid ducks his head sheepishly. "Merithin has. . ." A lump catches in my throat. I continue, avoiding the name. "The body is in the shrunken tent. Just use the activation word 'CSI' when you have located the right environment. Everything will be taken care of. It will be as if he were mugged." A tear seeps from red-rimmed eyes. I hasten to finish the instructions before

I lose control of my emotions. "Two of those bags are for his son. I trust you to find a way to make sure he is taken care of."

I keep the remaining bag of jewels for myself. The stones will be a primary component in the upcoming enchantment. Placing the emeralds in an octagonal pattern, I instruct the others to remain inside the circle. It takes milliseconds to recall the words of rhyme while focusing on the needed result. With Szames to one side and Nemir on the other, I begin the portal spell.

> "To travel across dimensional space
> A doorway is needed to leave this place.
> Everyone and what they bring,
> Standing inside this emerald ring,
> Across dimensions they'll now go
> Exactly as they now show."

Beams of sapphire light encompassing my tingling hands race across the room to the stones on the floor. Laser light spreads quickly from one gem to another. Instantly all eight emeralds shine with a teal light. An aqua force blazes out from the precious stones, engulfing the four travelers. My fingers then my arms turn numb as I funnel more energy into the gems.

Light intensifies, becoming more substantial than pure illumination. Gradually, the human forms of my friends fade, becoming shrouded in a watery turquoise mist.

> "Hale, hearty, and self-aware,
> Ready now, fully prepared.
> Safe and secure, delivered by me,
> On my homeworld they will now be.
> Wherever my husband, Kyle abounds,
> These four will now be found."

The mystical force I have summoned takes on a life of its own. Energy is pulled from me like water from a broken dam. With gritted teeth, I concentrate, determined to control and balance the energy streaming from Szames, Nemir, and myself. The aqua light begins to look more teal as the level of power intensifies. In a burst, the radiance is completely blue.

The process doesn't slow. As the unleashed force intensifies, color ceases to have meaning. Instinctively I squeeze my eyes shut against a blinding flash of white. A stab of pain slices into my skull, neutralized seconds later by the rejuvenation spell. Gradually spots clear from my vision as I become accustomed to the darkness of the room. My hands begin to tremble when sight confirms what intuition is telling me: All eight stones are gone, along with the four people who stood inside the ring.

"Awesome! Reba, that was incredible!" Jamison's enthusiasm for once isn't catching. "You did it. You really did it! You sent them home."

"Yes, I did. I felt our home; it was all around me." *As if Kyle stood beside me.* "Our fate is sealed." I mumble, turning to leave.

"We made our choice." Jerik's rumble sounds thunderous in the quiet room.

"Yes, you did. But I didn't," I whisper before taking the stairs two at a time, practically running from the room.

"Reba." My steps hesitate when I recognize the deep voice belonging to Szames, but I can't bring myself to turn to look.

"The transfer was successful?" His long strides bring him quickly to my side.

"Yes." The reply is terse, harder than I intend.

Swiftly he steps around me so we are face-to-face. "Would you like to go somewhere so we can talk?"

A sarcastic remark springs to my lips, but the caring etched into every line in his face forces the harsh words back down my throat. "First Charles. . . now this. . . I just need some time to deal with it."

"You do not have to do it alone. Find someone—anyone— to talk to." Szames gives a soft smile before turning to go.

The door of Merithin's tower opens again, but this time I stalk off at a brisk walk, determined not to be stopped. I make it safely to my chambers before the walls holding back the emotions crumble into a heaping pile of rubble.

Chapter Thirteen

Throwing myself onto the bed, my hand grasps a pillow, bringing it into my arms. I bury my face in its softness, unable to stop the wracking sobs. My body trembles as pent-up emotion pours from my haggard soul. Eventually there are no more tears. Hiccups set in as I seal the floodgates.

A gentle hand on my shoulder causes me to look up. "You really are no more than a woman," Constance mumbles. "How did Crystal put it? 'Underneath it all, she is only a woman alone in a strange world, trying to do the best she can.'"

She strokes my flaming hair the way a mother would comfort a small child. "My dear, sometimes the load is lighter when you share a burden."

Hearing the same advice twice proves to be too much. The tears flow, hotter this time. "Yes, Constance, and better you than someone with whom I might get into trouble." *Even though I ache to be held in those strong arms.*

"Milady, please, call me Connie. I will keep your secrets. The world need not know you, too, are human."

Under her gentle urging, all the doubts and fears plaguing me tumble out, laid bare for both of us to examine. My maid shakes her head in dismay. "Unfortunately I cannot advise you in matters of the heart. I learned at an early age that the price of love is far more than I am willing to give. But I will tell you what I know." The older woman's eyes glaze over as if looking into the distant past, reexamining it. "Life usually works itself out, given time and much patience. You might not be able to see the reasons for the course you set, but your path will reveal itself in due time."

The chambermaid's words invoke a chill of foreboding. My intuition might be declaring this to be a foretelling. Ice creeps down my spine. I attempt to shake the shiver off. "Will you share with me the lesson of love's price?" When Connie's eyes narrow ever so slightly, I add hastily, "That is not an order, only a request from one woman to another."

Closing her eyes, Connie says in a mere whisper, "They were so much in love. It encompassed everything, eclipsing everyone around them. That is what haunts my dreams at night."

Gratefully I lose myself in the woman's story.

∾   ∾   ∾

He strokes his daughter's ebony hair, holding her as she trembles against him. "Everything will be fine; I promise."

"But Momma was crying," the five-year-old insists.

"Was she now? Well, moms are only little girls who have grown a bit. Sometimes they need to cry too." Constance's father breaks off the attempt to explain something that he himself does not fully comprehend. "It will be all right; I promise."

Knowing Poppa never breaks his promises, the child is comforted. But Art's worries are far from eased. His marriage to Princess Amanda will take place tomorrow; he feels as if his life is utterly out of his control.

Constance's mother, Camden, knows that he has done everything he could, short of abdicating, to prevent the arrangement. She also knows that, even if duty forces him to marry, his heart will always remain hers. What more can he do?

Less than an octal later, the problem works itself out.

"Milady." Arturo's mistress bows respectfully, fear and hatred warring within her.

"I can see why he favors you." Princess Amanda's offhand remark lacks passion or a hint of pain. "You are pretty enough."

Fear for her life leaps into top priority. This woman can take it or, even worse, the life of her daughter. Still Camden says nothing, refusing to give up her love.

"And strong willed as well." With her lips pursed thoughtfully, Amanda circles her prey like a shark testing the waters.

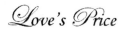

To Camden's surprise, the princess sighs. She wipes a tear from her eye. "I will not come between such love. I was forced to give up my own to come here. Compelling Arturo to do the same will only drive a wedge between us that can never be removed. Become my first maid, and I give you my word I will not bed him except to fulfill my wedding vows."

And so it began, the threesome that would become the scandal of Eldrich. Eventually both Camden and Arturo grew to love Amanda, and she, in turn, loved them. A few years later, when the princess died giving birth to Arturo's first son, both weep openly. Then cruel fate deals the lovers another blow.

"I married once for duty. I have secured an heir. Should I not be allowed to marry this time for love?" With his father's unbending gaze, Art knows he is losing the war of wills. He plays the only card he has left. "Father, I will not take her as wife no matter what the treaty. You now have a grandson who can replace me. I will abdicate!"

The king is unimpressed by his son's tirade. "Abdicate, will you? And where will you live? What trade will you ply?"

Arturo turns and stalks from the room.

The monarch's brow wrinkles. How can this stubborn child of a man continually fail to see reason? A treaty with the north is a necessity. The only way to secure it is with a marriage. The death of Princess Amanda is tragic but fortuitous nonetheless.

A plan begins to unfold in the mind of the king. "And I will have no more scandals."

A few days later, with tears streaming from her eyes, Camden pleads for Arturo's understanding. "Can you not see? It is the best for both of us. You have your duty to uphold. Now I will have the security I need as well."

"Being my love is not security enough?" Art's acid tone scars her heart as surely as if he wielded a whip, but she stands her ground. "Being a nobleman's wife in some tiny border providence means more to you than my love? Go, then, but do not expect me to favor your whelp. You have obviously deceived me into believing she is my daughter."

"But, Art, she is yours; you know that. And I cannot take her with me." Camden beseeches him but Arturo's heart is stone within his breast.

"Without you to prove the extent of your love, I will recognize her as no kin of mine." The prince's glare is knife edged. "How can I trust a woman who leaves for mere stature? How could I have loved such a woman?"

Camden brings a hand to her face as if she has been slapped. Hurling herself from the room, hysterical sobs unchecked, the beautiful, dark-haired woman flees to the privacy of the servants' quarters.

∽   ∽   ∽

"Oh, Connie, how awful to witness such a thing at the age of eight." *Her childhood is even more tragic than mine.*

"At least I knew why he was so suddenly 'not my father.' It was not until years later, after King Andertz passed, that I learned the full truth of the matter." Hastily she smothers the anguish clouding her eyes. "My mother had written me a letter, leaving it with the master steward to be given to me once Arturo assumed the throne. King Andertz arranged the marriage; that much was true. Arturo never learned the reason for my mother's decision. She agreed to the proposition because King Andertz offered the one thing she could not refuse: the life of her only child. The monarch made it clear that if Arturo found out about the arrangement, both of our lives would be forfeit." A tired sigh escapes the older woman. "I was kept here to guarantee my mother's continued cooperation. Had I known sooner, my life might have taken a different course." Connie smiles again, although it is not as bright as before. "If I had been patient and took more of it in stride, life might have been much improved. You see, the answer to my grief eventually presented itself."

"It makes so much sense. I know you must be right. But some things are easier said than done." I give a weak smile in return, still mulling over the story. In the end the obvious solution to my biggest headache makes its way to the forefront of my thoughts.

"Connie, do you still have that letter?" I ask as the maid turns to go.

"Yes. You have some use for it?"

A grimace tweaks my lips. "I know a couple whose future happiness may depend on it." Connie seems leery, so I continue. "I give you my word. You won't be harmed in any way. Wait a minute. I have a better idea. Crystal was going to become the coordinator of my personal staff; the job is yours if you want it."

"Milady?" Connie's voice sounds like a strangled cat.

"I know we have just met, but this just feels right." *How do you explain that you gave yourself high intuition points so sometimes you just* know?

"I am honored by your consideration." The new chief of staff blushes prettily. "What are your terms?"

"I'm unsure of the typical duties, so I leave their definition to you. But there are two things I would like you to assume responsibility for: all incoming correspondence, sorting between 'yes,' 'no,' and 'maybe.'"

Connie is taken back slightly by the first request but nods her agreement.

"And training a successor, preferably Phedra if she's willing, able, and qualified. I will also expect you to recruit any necessary subordinates. In return I offer room and board, twelve coppers a season, and one day in every eight in which your time is your own to do as you wish." *Translating a day off into Cuthburan is not easy!* "Does this sound adequate?"

"More than adequate, milady. You have retained your head of staff." At a brisk walk, Connie retrieves the requested letter, sealing the deal.

It takes less than a mark for my page to return with a response to the quickly penned correspondence. "Milady, His Majesty, King Arturo has replied," William informs me.

Scanning the contents, I find Arturo has no openings until midevening bells. Again, the monarch requests I meet him in the gardens. After straightening my face and hair, I dive into the work awaiting me. Unwilling to relinquish my solitude, I attend to the rest of the necessary enchantments myself, moving from one duty to the next. Having finally run out of tasks, I dismiss both pages at evening bells, wandering out to the gardens early.

Roving around the barren bushes and skeletal trees does little to relieve my heavy heart. Losing myself in the twining paths, absorbed in memories, I nearly miss the hushed voices around the next bend. Turning to leave, my feet come to an abrupt halt.

"Andrayia, my love, you know I love you more than anything, but this is the time of the prophecy." The smooth persistence of Prince Alexandros hisses into the night. "How was I to know what destiny had in store for me when I made you that promise? This is 'the time of change.'"

"That is your only defense? Is that what you want me to tell your son? 'It wasn't a true promise because it is the time of the prophecy'?" Her reply is not bitter as much as it is heartbroken.

"No, my love. I promise you there will be no reason to tell him anything. I swear to you. No matter what, I will always have room in my heart for both of you." Hurrying in the opposite direction, I brush a tear from my cheek. Perceiving the heartfelt pledge from my supposed husband-to-be makes the future bleaker than a starless night.

Rounding a hedge at the end of the path, I hastily compose my haggard emotions. Arturo is waiting, alone as requested. I open my empathy wide, scanning for eavesdroppers. Finding none, I finish my approach.

"Milady, if we continue meeting for midnight trysts, there will be rumors." The mischievous glint in the king's eye is reminiscent of his eldest son, making it even harder for me to hold the tears in check.

In no mood for small talk, I set the tone by addressing him formally. "Your Majesty, rumors will abound, no matter our actions. I, for one, have heard many interesting rumors as of late."

"Oh, is it one such rumor which prompts this urgent meeting?" Arturo's curiosity piques.

"If it were only a rumor, I would have dismissed it." I refuse to disclose my findings just yet. "However, I have been presented with proof of its validity."

"And this concerns the royal family?" The king grows impatient.

"It concerns the past as well as the future of the royal line." With a tilt of my head, I change the subject. "Back home, studies have been conducted on countless families. It has been proven that boys who see their fathers beat their own mothers, who are perhaps even beaten themselves, will be more likely to one day beat their wives and children."

"One would think a child would learn from seeing a parent's mistakes firsthand." Arturo moves gracefully to the new topic. "Instead, more often than not, the son takes up a father's annoying and sometimes harmful behavior. We have witnessed it many times in the nobility. Tell us: What bad habits are we handing down to our son?"

In lieu of an explanation, I hand over Connie's letter. The monarch turns over the aged missive. Bitter love spikes in his soul as he recognizes the seal. His hands begin to tremble.

"Where did you get this?" Anger colors his voice, although it is pain lurking in the corner of his heart.

"Your answer lies within the letter." I stand my ground.

"This is a dangerous game you play, mage," the monarch growls, tilting the letter, trying to find enough light to read the ancient missive before him.

"Magelight." The whispered word goes unnoticed. Spellbound by the words of love, Arturo fails to react to the magic aiding him.

"I am sure my father had good reason to employ the tactics he did." Clearing the lump in his throat, Arturo continues. "As I recall, at the time I was behaving more like a spoiled child than an heir with duties to attend."

His gruff attitude cannot fool my empathy. The hurt writhing inside him is painfully clear. "And was the treaty you gained worth the cost?"

"It was my duty—"

I cut the ruler off. "Not only to you, but to Connie and Camden as well?"

"Royalty does have its price along with its privileges." Arturo gives a bow, whispering as he turns to go, "Thank you, Reba. I am in your debt."

"It is Alex and Andrayia to whom you are accountable, not me." I take a step back when the king pivots, anger kindling in his eyes.

"That," the monarch says tightly, "milady, is a topic we will not discuss."

"As you wish, Your Majesty." I bow with formality to show that I do indeed know my place.

Crawling into bed after meeting with Arturo does little good. I lie there, having said my nightly prayer spell, in utter loneliness that is amplified by the oversized mattress. A flood of emotions saturates my pillow, wearing me out for the second time. Still, the peacefulness of oblivion eludes me.

Having slept less than three hours, I am groggy when Connie wakes me for the first day of the last campaign. Our crusade of warriors will not return to Eldrich until we have located the rogue sorcerer and destroyed the demon gate.

Chapter Fourteen

"Rebecca!" Kyle charges over the hill where lightning flashed in the clear fall day. "Rebecca!" For some inexplicable reason, he knows his wife is just over the hill.

"George and Chad, right? Where's Rebecca?" The ebony-headed engineer cranes his neck, but the only other person in the vicinity is a busty blonde in one of those long Renaissance dresses.

Crystal clenches her hands around the letter and the book she dug out of her pack as soon as she heard Kyle's call. Her grip on the leather-bound manuscript is the only thing keeping the trembling from showing. "Rebecca sent this for you."

"What do you mean 'sent'?" Kyle demands, voice calm and collected. "Where is she?"

The fear in his eyes stabs through her heart. Crystal juggles the book from arm to arm as she searches for the sealed letter inside. "Please, just read the letter."

The maid's quiet request touches something within the expectant husband. Putting the leather-bound book on the ground, Kyle rips the thick paper in his haste to open the note.

> *Kyle,*
>
> *This is going to sound really strange, so please, please read this entire letter before you tear it up.*
>
> *I'm betting you saw the bright light in the foyer right before we disappeared. That was the work of Merithin, a mage from another dimension. I've sent him back with the blonde who gave you this letter. Everyone will recognize this sorcerer as Chad except for you while you hold this letter.*

The complete idiocy of the last sentence causes Kyle to look up at Chad, who gazes expectantly toward him. The air around the lanky beach bum shimmers, revealing a brown-haired man he doesn't recognize. Kyle drops the parchment.

"What the. . . ?" As the enchanted paper leaves his fingers, the air flickers again. Chad reappears.

Kyle retrieves the letter. The paper shakes so badly, he can barely read the words.

> *Darren isn't who he seems to be either; he is a soldier carrying messages for my family.*

Of their own accord, Kyle's eyes dart from the letter. This time the engineer retains his grip on the message when the gangly architect turns into the athletic, long-haired rogue. His hands steady as he continues reading his wife's message.

> *Crystal is the blonde. Everyone will think she is me. I'm counting on you to help these strangers get adjusted to this world. They come from something right out of King Arthur's court.*
>
> *What has happened, why they are here, that is a long story. An entire account will be given to you with this letter. Please read it ASAP.*
>
> *I want you to know no matter what happens—what decisions you make—I will always love you.*
>
> *I miss you terribly,*
> *Rebecca*

Folding the letter, Kyle slides it carefully into the book. "You can't be serious. You expect me to believe people will think you're my wife? You look nothing like her."

"Kyle! There you are." The winded manager trots up to him. "See? I told you we would find her." The suited man tucks his thumb into the belt loop hiding beneath the bulging middle. He points to Crystal with the other hand. "Just like I said: they wandered off to some obscure part of the property."

Crystal arches her eyebrows at Kyle. "You were saying?"

∽   ∽   ∽

"Connie, I leave you in charge of my quarters here at the castle. If you need to contact me, all you have to do is think of me while saying my name three times while gazing into the mirror in the bathroom. Leave Phedra there to monitor the mirror after you call. I will appear on the surface as soon as I get a free moment."

"Yes, milady," she replies sullenly.

"Connie, the Royal Guard has agreed to act as my personal servants." I attempt to reassure her. "With the five of them on rotating shifts, you needn't worry about any damage to my reputation."

Her royal lineage shows in the straightness of her back and the stiff set of her shoulders. "Milady, my place is at your side."

"As chief of staff, your place is taking care of my residence," I retort. *The last thing I need is someone else's life in my hands.*

Connie dips her chin, accepting the instructions at my insistence. "Yes, milady."

I manage a tight smile in return. I turn to go. "Staff." My palm is open as I call the rod to me. My empathy tells me it is a mild surprise that causes the sudden intake of breath behind me. Throwing open the doors to the balcony, I whisper, "Superman."

My feet leave the stone of Eldrich, and for a brief moment my heart soars with the freedom of flight. I land before the carriage house. A stake feels like it is being pounded in between my ribs making my breath come in short gasps. I squint, determined, there will be no more tears. I yank the saddle and halter from its stand and stalk from the building. No longer in the mood for soaring through the heavens, I tramp toward the untamed woods.

Respectful of their sanctuary, I halt before the forest that has been untouched since the castle's inception. I look over my shoulder. There are acres of open space between the woods and the castle. *Would be a great place for the women's quarters.* A flash tinges my vision. A sprawling complex materializes in the open space. I blink as another flash pierces my sight.

I turn at the sound of padded steps. *"Your hearing is almost as good as a cat's."*

"It was interwoven into this new form." I shrug. "We need to get moving if we want to be on time."

"I apologize for my tardiness." Jesse's voice is anything but apologetic. *"I didn't sense you coming, shielded as you are."*

Stroking the soft ruff, I ease the saddle onto his back. *"This isn't a pain I'm willing to share. Give me a little time."* The tendril of thought carries with it a shadow of the ache in my soul.

The feline's ears flatten at the rebuff, but a rumble seems to convey acceptance. I swing my leg over his back. My hands gather the reins, but the slack in them gives Jesse complete control.

The cat's rolling gait comes to a halt before the towering gates of the castle. I nod my readiness to Alex, grateful that the distance between our positions makes talking impractical. The populous cheers. My flaming tresses splay wildly behind me, declaring the Flame-haired One's departure.

We reach Cuthburan Road early on the second day. I evoke the call and retire to my tent. We only stay one night after encountering only a handful of the enemy.

Morning trumpets blare, announcing the breaking of camp. I ease out from the warm comfort of the down-filled coverlet. The paladin spell keeps me from feeling the cold, but I shiver at the lack of warmth in my unwanted predicament: a foreigner in this alien world and so very alone.

The tent bustles with activity with the Royal Guard sharing the confines of my modified tent. The enchantment to add rooms on to the structure makes my quarters unmistakable. Surprisingly the sororitylike arrangement provides little companionship. It only serves to highlight the differences between my culture and this one.

The breakdown of the encampment takes minutes instead of hours. By the time I am dressed and striding out of my temporary residence, the other canvas dwellings are packed and secured in wooden boxes. The dawn is hidden within the overcast sky. It begins to drizzle as I mount Jesse. We turn north, marching toward the Ethereal Forest.

The continual downpour turns crystalline. Luckily, the paladin stones have the added benefit of keeping the men just warm enough to avoid frostbite. Although uncomfortable, at least none will be lost to gangrene or exposure.

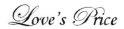

"The troops should reach the tree line by late afternoon," Szames informs me as we lope down the road. "The meadow before it will be an adequate area for the night."

"Humph." Depression allows me no other response.

With an understanding nod, Szames remains a silent sentry beside me throughout the day.

I shake the water off my robe as I hang it on the bedpost. Mikaela rushes to answer the scratch at the tent flap. *I wish Connie could see how seriously they are taking their duties.* "Milady Reba, Jerik to see you."

I nod, holding in a sigh. "Still glad to be grounded?" I ask, grimacing at the muck he's tracking into my chambers.

"A little mud never hurt anyone," he rumbles. "That bath you magicked into my tent gets me and my clothes clean each night."

Sensing his gratitude, I shrug and slide onto a cushioned chair. Switching to our native tongue for added security, I ask, "How's morale?"

Standing with fists on hips, he growls, "Outside this tent it's great."

My eyes narrow in warning. "You, of all people, should understand. It was my proposal, not to mention your backing of it, that took a father from his son."

"You warned Charles about the carriage house. It was his cocksure attitude—and his roaming cock—that got him killed."

"He told you about the premonition?"

Jerik's harrumph sounds like a boulder coming to rest. "He was bragging about planting one on the 'Fiery Momma' to some of the men. When I called him on it, he swore he was drawn to you by the pheromones in the vision. Said if it was that strong in a vision, he wasn't missing out. He figured wearing his mail would keep him safe."

I squeeze my eyes shut. A lone tear escapes. "And it would have been enough for anything but one of *my* enchanted weapons."

A massive hand clasps my shoulder. "Even though you were elected leader, each person is responsible for their own actions. He was warned. Charles gambled his life for a piece of—well, he gambled and lost. Quit beating yourself up already."

Twin paths trace their way down my face as I meet the compassion-filled eyes hidden beneath the bushy brows. "I will try."

Grabbing me in a grizzly hug, the dwarf tries to squeeze the sorrow from me.

I scrub a palm over my face as he relents. "Join us for dinner before we head out to the tower?"

"You have hit my Achilles heel; I can't seem to turn down an offer of good food." Tucking a thumb into his belt, he adds, "Need me to fetch it from the cook?"

Hustling over to the chest, I begin removing the ensorcelled crockery Crystal had so carefully packed. "Just give me a hand getting these to the table."

Taking possession of the largest bowl, Jerik gives an elongated sniff. A smile creases his bearded face. "Unless I miss my guess, you've magicked-up some gumbo in your witch's cauldron."

"And I trust you to keep that fact to yourself."

A rumble begins low in his middle. "I could be bribed to silence, say with some magicked-up pizza."

Half a grin peaks through the gloom. "Blackmail? I didn't know dwarves could forge in different colors."

The pun earns a belly laugh from the short man.

"I think I could manage another dish. Bring me a rock the next time we're alone."

While Jerik and I set the table, Mikaela fetches the rest of the Guard. We eat in silence, shoveling in food as fast as we can.

"Shall I escort you to the tower, milady?" Jerik asks with a bow.

I shake my head. "Please, not from you too." I begin packing up the dishes so the warriors won't. "Help me clear these, O gallant warrior. Then we'll charge out into the night to battle the demonic horde and save mankind." The rumbling laughter of the dwarf almost causes me to smile.

The courtly pose Jerik takes as he deposits me at the tower causes my lips to quiver, but still, my heavy heart drags down all traces of merriment. Once again the demons are few and far between. I begin to ache for magic's tender caress and pick off every beast I have a clear shot at. Still, the night ends too quickly.

Lying down on the oversized mattress does little good. Closing my eyes, even less. With gritty eyes, I stumble out into the afternoon light.

The stoutest of soldiers glances over his shoulder, expecting a boogeyman, as the Cuthburan Army crosses into the forbidden woods. Every shadow holds a monster from a childhood nightmare; every creaking branch is a fabled beast springing to attack. The dimly lit forest has the opposite effect on me. The Ethereal Forest soothes my ragged emotions, as if I can hide from my pain within the shadowed interior.

"Traveling through the trees and brush will take longer than the hills," Szames remarks as the cats pick their way through the growth.

"I could create a path. . ."

"That would not please those who call this forest home." Jesse vetoes the suggestion.

"A temporary path that disappears after the last soldier is out of its sight," I amend. "Jesse, if you can lead us to a suitable campsite, we won't make any unnecessary blemishes in your forest.

"That would be acceptable." Jesse purrs his agreement.

I extend my hand to Szames. "If you don't mind?"

"It would be my pleasure." He smiles.

> "Wherever we tread brush, will no longer be
> Until the last man is out of sight of thee."

A peaceful smile thins my lips as power caresses every fiber of my being. Our energies meld and trail behind us. The undergrowth melts into the ground. To magesight, there is a blue tint to the earth.

"I had almost forgotten what pleasure magic brings." Szames sighs.

"The campaign has been surprisingly easy so far." I glance at the big man. Despair springs like a dark panther from the corners of my mind. *You couldn't save Charles. He might not make it either.* Goose bumps cause me to shiver. Knowing the truth of the thought, I jerk my head around, looking straight ahead. I press my eyes tightly shut, using healing power to evaporate the moisture from my eyes.

"I expect that will change once we swing south." I barely register Szames's reply.

I merely nod, not trusting my vocal cords. I wrap silence around me like a cloak.

Szames respects the space I need. He gives a dip of his chin as we part.

Glancing around at the massive giants stretching toward the light above and the triangular tents speckled in between them, a sense of foreboding seeps into my bones. *How many of these men will make it back to Eldrich? I'm the most powerful person on the planet, yet I can't think of a single spell that will guarantee their safety.*

Turning my back on the beauty of the woods that look as if they were pulled out of a fairy tale, I march into my quarters. Huddled inside my tent while the camp is being erected around me, I wait patiently for the dark and a chance to use my magic once more.

A score of demons sprinkle our defenses in the inky darkness that is possible only in the deep woods. A yawn pries my jaws apart. I shake my head to rouse myself. *I wish I had something to shoot at.*

As if an evil genie sits on my shoulder, balls of fire erupt from the northern perimeter. Dozens of soldiers fly outward. Several smash into trees, never to rise again.

"Laser, laser. Alex, see the others?"

"The creatures are black as night. I don't know how you spotted those two."

Three more explosions light up the darkness. "Laser, laser."

"There!" Alex points to where he saw the shadow in the light from the bombs.

"Laser!" I growl, taking out the last of the igildru. The humanoid monsters use their long tails like spider monkeys, wrapping their whiplike appendages around tree limbs. *They must have woken up inside the moat in the safety of the upper branches.*

A couple handfuls of demons wander into the battle before daybreak but none of consequence. I take my leave, flying straight to my tent. A scratch sounds on the entryway before I can douse the lights and escape into the oblivion of sleep.

Auricle, having served as tower guard on the first shift of the night, hurries to answer it. "Jerik to see—" A yawn interrupts the announcement. "To see you, milady."

Must be the stone. "I will see him. Please feel free to retire. I won't be needing anything else tonight."

"Yes, milady," she mumbles, holding the flap for the guest.

Jerik tromps into the room. A rock twice the size of a football is tucked under his arm. "Found this on the trail. Will it do?"

"You carried this how far?"

"Used it as a stool at lunch," he shrugs.

Man, dwarves are stronger than I thought. I gesture to the table, figuring if I don't speak, maybe he'll leave sooner. Repeating the stasis container enchantment, the stone transforms into a twenty-four-inch platter complete with a lid. My energy is down to a third as I search for words that will complete my promise.

"Flat and round, fresh and hot from the oven,
Pepperoni, Supreme, and Meat Lovers sliced into a dozen."

A blue haze settles over the stoneware. Jerik licks his lips in anticipation as the aroma from the massive pizza fills the tent.

"Would you care for a piece?" he asks.

I place the lid over the platter. "I never liked pizza much." I hand him his dinner. "The pizza will reform when you clear the plate. Just don't turn it over and tap on the bottom. That is the key to changing the contents."

"Reba, your secret is safe with me." Jerik licks his lips as he strides toward the doorway.

"Lights," I mutter, extinguishing all the illumination simultaneously. Able to see in muted shades of gray, I pull the drawer of the nightstand open. I cradle one gem in each hand. *In a way I'm glad you won't come until after the war.* I snuffle into the dark. *But, my gosh, how I need you with me tonight.*

Thankful the light engagements have kept the entire company safe for yet another day in these strangely silent woods, I shuck my clothes into a heap beside my bed before sliding into the nightgown. I crawl onto the pillowed surface.

A tickling at the base of my skull nags me. I toss the covers up over my shoulders and turn over. Curling into a ball around my pillow, the tension of the day begins to ease. *Why am I not asleep? I've barely dozed for nights now.* I brush the hair at the nape of my neck. Still, the prickling won't go away.

The mirror! I leap from my bed. Taking the enchanted looking glass to the table, I peer into it. *Rose?* I call the name of my friend three times. I run a hand through my hair, trying to put some order to the unruly curls.

"Reba, you are looking, well, all things considered," the slight hesitation tells me her words are kind.

"As are you, my friend."

"I will be setting out for Mother's chambers to join her and some of the ladies so we may break our fast soon." Her eyes narrow as if she is trying to use healer's sight through the communication mirror. "I know you must be ready to retire for the day, as strange as it seems, with my day beginning. I will endeavor to be direct. I apologize if I overstep."

Her unusual boldness piques my curiosity. I try to give a grin of reassurance but realize it probably looks more like a grimace. "Rose, you worry way too much. I'm pretty hard to offend."

"I know the events of the last octal have been difficult. With all the turmoil, we didn't get a chance to visit when you were here. I merely wanted to see if perhaps you felt the need to share your feelings with another. Grief shared is an easier burden to bear."

"This is getting rather tiresome."

Her head pops back as if I landed a slap on her cheek.

I heave a sigh. "Rose, I appreciate your candor and your concern, but I am not yet ready to share what has been the most difficult issue of my life so far." Her eyes are still a little pinched around the corners. I take a deep breath and add, "You are my most cherished friend on this world. I will put a call through to you as soon as I think I can deal with saying his name."

"Even the Flame-haired One shouldn't have to carry her burdens alone. I will be awaiting your call. For now I will let you get to your rest."

"Thank you. It is good to know I have you to turn to when the time comes."

Replacing the mirror in the side drawer, I take the jewels in hand again. I crawl back into bed. Oblivion is elusive. I am denied relief of the burdensomeness of consciousness as a dark, handsome face appears each time I close my eyes. Rolling the emerald and ruby in my palms, tears of loneliness trace their way down my ivory cheeks. *If only. . . if only. . . Kyle I really need your shoulder!*

Waiting is not my strong suit. Gratefully sleep wraps its arms around me. The world disappears.

Yawning, I search the covers for the enchanted jewels. I stow the gems in the drawer, stumbling across the room into the curtained enclosure. A steaming bath greets me. Relaxing in the tub, the fog of exhaustion recedes. Determined to show the strength of a woman, I straighten my spine and go in search of Jesse.

Prince Alexandros strides toward me as I make a beeline toward the partners' tent. "Good morning." He beams a gorgeous smile at me.

I grunt and give a nod of my head. Oblivious to my mood, Alex syncs up with my steps. "Tawny helped us detail our position. We made good time yesterday." My forehead furrows at his continued exuberance. "It should only take us three more days to clear the Ethereal Forest."

"Then let's get this show on the road." I grump, ignoring the prince's puzzlement. I send a tendril to call Jesse.

"Who nettled your fur?" He pokes his head through the flaps.

"Sorry. I get kind of bitchy when I don't get good sleep."

Jesse plops down beside the entrance, tail flicking in annoyance. *"It's not me to whom you should be apologizing."*

"Fine!" I grind my teeth. "Alex, sorry if I'm a little crabby. I haven't been sleeping much."

"Quite understandable, under the circumstances," he replies, looking as if he wants to wrap his arms around me. "I will see you at midday break." Alex bows in parting.

Not if I see you first.

Szames eyes Alex as he passes him on his way toward us. Refusing to respond to the questioning rise of his eyebrows, I turn and swing my leg over the cat's back. Szames hustles to saddle his mount.

In silence we ride to the northwestern edge of camp. A strong hand grasps my own. I clear a lump in my throat then begin to chant. I stumble over the words of the yellow brick road spell. I begin a second time. Blue radiance pools around us. I give a mental nudge to urge Jesse forward.

Respectful of my need for silence or fearing my sharp tongue, we return to the crusaders at midday with the calm unbroken. "I'll let you report to your brother. I've gotta catch a few z's." I yawn, batting sleepy eyes.

Szames nods, leaving me to find a comfortable tree to lean on. Hunkering down against the base of a giant spruce tree, I wiggle around, trying to get comfortable. Whiskers tickle my neck as Jesse's head nuzzles my chest.

The midnight beast slinks to the ground, easing his head in my lap. I stroke the silky fur. A rumpling purr echoes in the crisp, noon air.

My eyes pop open as a touch gently shakes my shoulder. *I don't even remember going to sleep.* I try to shake the cobwebs from my brain as I accept Szames's hand to assist me in rising. I run a furry tongue over my teeth.

Szames hands me a wineskin. "I'm not sure who was louder, you or Jesse."

"I don't snore," I insist, taking a long pull of the not-so-fresh water in the fur-covered bag. "Unless I'm completely exhausted." I wipe at the water dripping off my chin with the back of my sleeve.

"Reba, how are you sleeping?" Szames asks as we mount and set out.

"Mages don't need much. When I'm tired enough, I'll sleep." I sigh but it turns into another yawn.

Szames nods, handing a cloth-wrapped bundle to me. "I thought you might be hungry."

My stomach emits a long growl as the aromas of cheese, bread, and a leg of fowl reach my nose. "Thanks," I manage before tearing into the food.

Brushing crumbs from my clothes, I hand the cloth back to Szames. I rub my gritty eyes. *Jesse doesn't need me. I can close my eyes for a few minutes.* My eyes spring open as I begin to slide to one side.

I give a quick shake of my head. A yawn overpowers me. I stare at one tree then the next as we make steady progress toward tonight's campsite. *Wasn't it nicotine that speeds up your system?* It seems to take forever as I begin combing through my memories. *Hell, I know coffee will give me a jolt. I'll just go with that.*

My eyes narrow with the effort as I concentrate on my healing ability. Picturing myself chugging an iced mocha latte, I release the somatic energy inside. *Better.* Taking the reins in hand, I begin twisting a pattern.

I am forced to give myself two more jolts of caffeine before we reach camp. "Szames, will you take care of Jesse for me?" I ask the prince as I slide off the cat. I force my feet still, determined not to dance in place like a potty-training two-year-old.

"Of course." He nods.

I shout a quick thanks over my shoulder while sprinting for my quarters. Trembling fingers fumble at the belt holding my pants while my eyes adjust to the dark interior. I make it onto the seat as pee bursts forth like water from a punctured garden hose.

My shaking fingers fumble with the belt again. *My staff is fully charged. I'll just zap the belt closed. Let's see, close. . . buckle. . .* My fried brain scrambles but fails to find anything that sticks. I wander to the nightstand. Still trying to puzzle out the lines of rhyme, I yank the drawer open.

The drawer flies out of its brackets, spilling the contents across the rug. After several tries, I finally manage to shove the drawer back in. Staring at the items scattered on the floor, frustration consumes me. I slam the jewels down on the top of the stand and grab the lidded cup from where it rolled onto the floor. *I just need some more joe.* Pressing the button on top to release the opening, I clamp both hands around the cup and gulp half the macchiato down.

"Jamison to see you, milady," Mikaela announces.

"Let him in." *Now what!*

"Reba, I wanted to stop by to see how you're doing." Jamison eyes the coffee mug as well as my unbuckled belt.

"I'm fine." I shrug. "Just a little tired." I take another swig. "Nothing a little caffeine can't overcome."

"Mind if I take a peek with sight?"

I shrug again.

The healer's eyes narrow. "Reba, how many of those have you had?"

"This is my first." When his stare turns mocking, I amend, "I just used my somatic energy to simulate caffeine intake on the way here."

"I see and just how many times did you give yourself a little rise to overcome the tide of exhaustion?"

I look away, uncomfortable with the healer's mothering glare. "A few."

"More than two!" the healer explodes. "Reba, do you have any idea what you've done?"

"I just needed something to help me stay awake." My eyes plead for understanding.

"Just like every rock star back home." Jamison sighs.

"Huh?" I'm dumbfounded by the sudden change of topic.

"Caffeine is a stimulant, a lesser form of speed. An overdose can do serious damage to your mental state. Have you had problems concentrating?"

I nod.

"How much sleep have you gotten lately?"

"Look, I'm a mage. I don't need much."

"How much?"

"I don't know. A few hours here and there. Without a clock, who can tell?" I discard the cup and stride for the door. "My body will sort itself out tonight. I'm bound to get a good sleep as soon as the coffee wears off."

Jamison grabs my arm, swiveling me toward the bed. "Are you going to let me put you in a healing trance, or do I need to fetch a prince?"

"It's not that bad. . ."

"And neither are the numbers attacking us." Jamison gently pushes me toward the pillowed plateau. "You will be more use to us if you can think straight."

I push myself up a little. "But I won't be able to wake if they—"

"I will leave word with the Guard. They will send for me if you're needed." The hair on the back of my neck prickles seconds before I slide into dreamless slumber.

∿   ∿   ∿

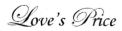

"Reba, I'm sorry to wake you." It seems minutes since the healer put me down. "We could use some laser fire."

Adrenaline surges into my bloodstream. I launch myself out of the bed, rubbing gunk from my eyes. "I'm good," I mumble, trying to throw off the haze of sleep. "Let's kick some evil ass."

Feeling better than I have in days, I whisper the name of the Man of Steel. Hovering in midair, I send fireballs streaking toward the clumps of demons grouped on the western border of camp.

"There." Alex points as my feet touch the tower's surface.

"Laser-bolt." Instead of a thin blast of laser fire, the new spell releases a mammoth beam that takes off one of the heads of the ap-bjan awake in the moat. "Laser-bolt," takes care of the other. The slithering, serpentine body writhes as the two-handed ax and the hammer fall from the creature's trio of humanoid arms.

"Archmage, your arrival is most timely." Alex dips his head. "Ogre." His greeting is interrupted.

"Laser." The smaller bolt of concentrated light takes out the Neanderthal demon. "Fireball," takes out a cluster of demonic kangaroolike creatures with a raptors beak the natives named raloliks. Their fuzzy hindquarters cease peppering the shield with the darts disguised as fur. "Feels good to—laser—to get some exercise." I lace my fingers together, giving them a good flex.

"Milady, are you suggesting battle to be—to the right—entertaining?" Alex mocks.

"Laser, laser, laser." The jarovegi that popped up inside the moat crumple into dark heaps. I wipe sweat from my brow. "Not at all. Destroying evil may just be what I need to vent—fireball—excess emotion."

Alex chuckles, pointing out a group behind me gathering for a rush at the shield. "Prophesied you may be, but you, Reba, are all woman."

I grunt, acknowledging his praise, though the feminist in me wants to send a tiny spark his way. *Not enough to hurt him. . .* I push the idea aside, concentrating on taking out my frustration on the enemy.

"West and two northwest." Andrayia points out two demons rising in the moat.

"Three west and southwest." Alex says.

I swivel about. *Those crafty buggers!* I begin drawing energy from my stave.

"Lightning." Wind whips my hair about with the new keyword. Radiance streams from my fingertips. Thunder fills the air as white light zigzags across the sky. Nine demons fall, paralyzed; three more are fried to a crisp. I swivel about. The remaining demons flee into the coming dawn.

"Shall we?" I extend my hands to Andrayia and Alex. With the Superman spell still active, the energy cost of flying us down from the platform is minimal.

A tired cheer arises from the men stumbling off the battlefield. After marching most of the day then being called into the fray, most are dead on their feet. Andrayia slides Alex a come-hither look before dipping her head to take her leave.

Setting up the mirror for Alex, I collapse into one of the chairs. The adrenaline ebbs from my system, leaving my brain in a soupy fog. Rucela, one of the Royal Guard, answers a scratch at the door I didn't even hear. I swallow in order to keep from drooling as the fragrance of fresh bread surrounds me.

Szames places a slice from the loaf and the cheese before me. The wine washes the first few bites down. *Man, am I tired.* The general of the armed forces of Cuthburan joins the royal discussion. I concentrate on the rest of the bounty before me.

"Reba, thank you for the use of your quarters." Alex bows and I struggle to my feet. "We will, of course, be staying another day. I will leave you to your rest." Szames, likewise, takes his leave.

I stumble to the bed. I stare at the leather holding my feet captive. *So many buttons. I could sleep with them on. . .*

"Let me help you with those." I look up in surprise at Jamison's offer. *When did. . . how did. . . ? Oh, who cares?*

The healer makes short work of the straps and buttons, deftly removing the boots. He swings my feet onto the bed. "Even though you will probably sleep without it, I am going to put you into a healing slumber. This way you won't wake until your body is fully restored."

Unable to reply, I try to nod. The sandman steals even that from me.

Chapter Fifteen

I roll over, realizing I am awake. My enhanced memory brings Jamison's words back to me. I stretch the tense muscles in my back. Rubbing my face, I totter toward the bathroom.

"Hmm." I sink lower in the warm water. Though I miss Crystal, this morning's privacy eases some of the tension that has been building. Reluctantly I rinse the cream from my hair. After wrapping my tresses in a towel, I slide on the fleece robe I conjured up for this leg of the campaign.

I step from the curtained enclosure ready to face the world for the first time in more than a week. Glancing to the right, a light catches my eye. One of the communication gems is lit. *Merithin sent a message!* I rush to the nightstand. *Are they coming sooner than planned? Lord knows that this message is quicker than we expected.*

Rounding the corner, I stagger to a stop, gulping air. My knees weaken, bringing me up short. The ruby, not the emerald, glows. *A problem? What kind of problems could they be having? They just got there.*

In a brilliant flash of white, I see Kyle's anguished face and Crystal's rush to comfort him. Denying the vision, I shove the picture ruthlessly aside, forcing the room to come into focus before me. Black spots replace the white ones as I fight not to swoon.

The tent flap opens and Mikaela enters. Grabbing both stones, I hold them out to her. "How long has this stone glowed? Has the green one been lit?"

"I checked last night before I turned in and again this morning before I left. Nothing glowed, milady." Taking in the sopping hair, the guard adds, "We all know the importance of the stones. We would have notified you if we'd seen something, milady."

"Thank you, Mikaela. Of course you would have." Setting the stones back on the nightstand, I reapply the towel to my hair then don my clothes.

I bring the gems to the table and take several deep breaths, willing myself to relax. Closing my eyes, I focus on the ruby lying in the palm of my hand while I picture a blinking light. A push sends energy to do my bidding. Now the gem is pulsing like a living heartbeat. *Merithin will know I have received his message.*

I cradle the gemstone, praying Merithin will send an all clear by terminating the light radiating from the ruby then setting the emerald aglow. Time ceases to have meaning as minutes slide by.

~   ~   ~

"Crystal, Merithin's not in his room. Do you know where he is?" Kyle finds now that he knows Merithin isn't really Chad. He can remember that fact even if he still sees Chad.

"He was going to the east side of the hotel to get some solitude for his experiments." Anxious to find out how the ebony-headed engineer is dealing with his wife's predicament, Reba's first maid follows Kyle as he searches for the sorcerer.

"Any luck?" Kyle fully accepts that magic exists. What else could explain the memoirs only his wife could have written?

"This is going to be much easier than I anticipated." Merithin grins as he turns to the red-eyed husband. "It seems my native tongue is the key to invoking magical energy."

"Great, how soon can we leave?" Kyle returns Merithin's smile. "We've been apart a few days, but it seems like forever."

"What did you say?" The color drains from Merithin's face.

"That I miss my wife?"

"No, the other thing!" the sorcerer demands. "How long was Reba gone before we appeared?"

"Rebecca and the others disappeared in the morning two days ago. You appeared on the evening of the second day, so. . . that is two and a half days. Is something wrong?" Kyle asks anxiously.

"I can't believe the possibility didn't occur to me sooner!" Merithin slaps a palm to his forehead.

Kyle plants himself in the path of the pacing sorcerer. "What possibility?"

"Kyle, I'm sorry." The strangely wise eyes are suddenly poignant, capturing him completely. "There won't be a reunion for you and your wife. You might as well consider her as passed away."

"Wait a minute. You just said you could use the magic here." Kyle brushes off the sorcerer's consoling hand. For the first time in years, his voice rises to a shout. "Why? Why can't you take me to her?"

"I couldn't get an accurate vision of the Crusaders. I thought it was due to some difference in the corporeal energies, but they are exactly the same, only the language of command is reversed." The sorcerer gives a dejected sigh. "I never considered that time could flow differently on the dimensional planes, that time could flow so slowly here."

"Yeah, I figured that when I saw the size of that book. Rebecca's longwinded but even she's not that bad." Applying the logic he is so comfortable with, Kyle continues. "You said that it will be easier, right? How long will it take to train someone?"

"Once I find them? Three to five years depending on their aptitude for languages." Hating what he must say next, Merithin finishes the explanation. "Reba was in our world for twenty days. This means that for every day that passes here, more than eight days will pass where Reba resides." Kyle pales as the sorcerer's voice drops to a whisper. "How long do you expect her to wait? Ten years? It will be almost thirty, even under opportune circumstances. Will you know the person she has become when she is sixty and you are half that age?"

"No!" The scream echoes into the crisp air. "Rebecca! It can't be. . ." The marriage that began almost a decade ago is cut off by strangled sobs. Kyle buries his head in his hands, weeping for the first time he can remember.

Crystal drops to the ground beside him. Gradually he allows her to hold him, the soft woman scent providing what little comfort he can accept.

Merithin focuses on the gem he holds. He lights the ruby. The response from the matching gem seems instantaneous; his ruby now pulses in time to Reba's. The archmage has received his report. He prepares his mind to send the reply.

~   ~   ~

I clasp my hand tighter around the emerald. My fingers begin to ach. I stare at the unlit stone until dry eyes force me to blink. *Send the all clear. Glow, damn it!*

When light shines from the crimson gem, the air explodes from my lungs. The green rock falls from limp fingers. A quarter of a mark later, when the light fails to blink to indicate that it is merely a very serious problem, not the end my grand plan to be reunited with my husband, my hands begin to shake. *A steady red light twice in a row means only one thing: the mission is over. No return possible.*

"No. . ." I mutter under my breath. "No! This can't be happening."

"Milady?" Mikaela questions from across the room.

Moisture gathers in my eyes. I try to squeeze the life out of the red jewel. Hurling myself from the room, I give a mental cry, *"Jesse!"*

The black feline perceives my distress. Tufts of grass fly as the cat's massive claws tear up chunks of earth as he races to my tent. Bursting from the doorway, I leap up on his bare back. Flaming tresses streaming behind me, I flee the encampment, unwilling to let anyone bear witness to the tears I am unable to control.

Jesse weaves through the trees at a breakneck pace. A death grip on the cat's fur keeps me in place. The foliage thins. The cat picks up speed, racing toward a cliff wall in the distance. Gradually Jesse slows and stops at a gulch that runs down into a shallow canyon before a rock face. Swinging a leg over, I slide from the cat. Eyes overflowing, I stumble blindly down the steep ridge in the direction of the river below, wanting nothing more than to be alone with my grief.

Heart aching, I collapse at the bank of the river. I draw my knees up to my chest. Burying my head in my arms, I rock until my backside is numb and my legs tingle with sleep. Slowly I extend my limbs. Limp hands fall down into my lap.

Looking at the lit jewel, anger replaces pain. *He must have chosen to stay!* "How could you? Kyle, how could you desert me like this?" Rising in a rush, I fling the offensive messenger with all my might.

Without the Conan spell, it doesn't go far. Bouncing off the gulch wall, the gem rolls downward, coming to rest about twenty feet from the stream. It sits there, staring accusingly, a judging red eye.

I'm sorry. Kyle, I've failed you. Extending a trembling hand, a shout tears from my lips, "Laser!" The ruby explodes into a million shards. Seeing the stone pulverized, knowing without a doubt any hope of a reunion is forever gone, anger crumbles, leaving only a hollow emptiness within my breast.

"Reba, I apologize for intruding, but less than a mark remains until sunset." The sound of Szames's approach was covered by the angry blast.

A rough jerk of my hands brushes the moisture from my face. I turn to him. "I will be returning shortly. Thank you." Glancing around, for the first time I see the dark shadows covering the gully. "How did you find me?"

"Tawny found Jesse. I hoped you would be close at hand." Szames struggles to find words of condolence, finally adding, "Mikaela told me of the stones."

"Yes, well, if I heeded what everyone else seemed to know, instead of being so determined to make fate what I wished it to be, perhaps three other innocents wouldn't be stranded on my world as I am on this one." Fury rises again. *I've got a battle to fight, a war to win.* I charge toward the warrior, intent on putting grief behind me.

"They knew the risks. They volunteered for the assignments, did they not?" The gentleness and caring of the big man's tone brings back the emotion I am endeavoring to dismiss. "And was not Crystal sent partly for this contingency?"

"Yes, she was sent for Kyle, and for that I am truly thankful." Twin streams carve new paths down reddened cheeks. Self-pity reasserts itself. Bitterness colors my voice, which is already hoarse from crying. "But who will be here for me? I have seen to everyone's needs: Kyle's, Crystal's, an entire kingdom's. . . but what about mine?"

Szames puts a broad hand on my bicep.

I shrug of the offending grip. "I'm stuck here alone on this damn world where men are encouraged to follow every urge that enters their pants!" Balling up my hands into fists, I strike out. A solid blow lands on rock-hard pecs covered by even harder chain mail.

"The Flame-haired One!" I strike him again and again with every statement. "The prophecy's fulfillment!" Gently he takes hold of both of my arms. "Who will ever be able to see past that! Who has the courage to stand up to the damn prophecy incarnate!"

Having run its course, the anger flees. Tenderly Szames pulls me toward him. He strokes the curls of my hair as I sob into his chest.

"And here I am. . . the great archmage. . . your foretold defender. . . acting like an undisciplined child. . ." As minutes pass, I regain control, but the breath still comes with wracking hiccups. "I bet this gives you great faith in my abilities, right?"

"A wise woman once said to me, I'd be more worried if you didn't." Easing me back, Szames brushes the tears from my face. "What would be more fearful than the greatest sorcerer this world has ever seen lacking emotion, human feelings?"

The compassion in the big man's eyes fills a little of the gaping void that has ripped my heart in two. I ease forward, closing the distance between us. I use his shoulder for a pillow. In the comfort of his embrace, I am able to face the truth. "I suppose a part of me has known this would be the outcome since I first arrived. Kyle would have been a fish out of water here on this world, as I was on mine. I just refused to see it."

Exhausted from the outpouring of emotion, I heave a tired sigh. "Thank you. Szames, you are a true friend."

Still wrapped in the embrace of his arms, our eyes meet. Time stands still. Heartbeats echo into the coming night with neither of us daring to move, afraid of what might happen if we do.

"The sun is nearly past the horizon. . ." Jesse's voice enters with reluctance. We step apart, both looking anywhere but at each other.

"We should get back. Dark is almost upon us." Szames leads the way up the brushy crevasse.

Dusk gives way to darkness. Full dark arrives before the lights of camp are in sight. Our mounts' speed increases. I sense our pursuers. Their malevolence is gaining ground. Jesse and Tawny strain their powers, trying for additional acceleration while weaving in between the massive trunks that are soaring skyward. Gripping the ebony fur in one fist, I look over my shoulder, extending the other hand. "Laser, laser."

"Hold on," Jesse warns.

I break off the attack, grasping his fur in both fists.

Bunching up their muscles, the felines soar over a ravine, landing solidly on the other side. *That was a small canyon, not a crevasse! "Great short cut you found. What next? A raging river?"*

"You doubt our ability to cope with whatever may come?" Jesse's sarcasm isn't offensive; I sense no condemnation in the thoughts.

"Doubt you? Never!" A tiny grin forms on lips that, a mark ago, I believed would never smile again.

Once more, I turn to pick off the pursuers unfortunate enough to be faster than the main pack. "Laser, laser, laser." *They are gaining. I can't use a fireball with only one hand!*

The blue dome of the force field looms, shining like a beacon in the night. "Laser, laser, laser." The first bolt takes down a demon less than twenty feet from my hand.

I glance ahead. Safety is still a quarter mile away. "Laser, laser, laser. . ." Firing continuously, I am able to take out the leaders, keeping the pack at bay for a few more minutes.

A cheer arises from hundreds of throats as we cross the moat. Soldiers swarm the demon bodies falling limply to the ground seconds after we clear the shield. Giving a final thank-you to Szames and Jesse, I fly to the tower.

"So kind of you to grace us with your presence." Alex sneers.

The princely attitude and the fact that I no longer have a husband sparks my temper. "I was unavoidably detained."

"See it does not happen again." Demonstrating his authority, Alex dismisses me.

Enraged, I am alert and energized through the first half of the night. My eyes are blurry with fatigue as the sun peaks over the horizon.

I ease in between the flaps of the infirmary. Shaking his head, Jamison takes me by the hand, escorting me to my tent. The attacking force was half what the army faced last night, so the casualties are few. The healer hands me over to Mikaela, who is preparing a bath. The guard even helps me undress, making sure I get settled in the tub.

"No one should have to sleep in battle grime, milady, least of all you," is her simple explanation.

Eyes wet, I fight to contain a new flood. *In this alien place, there are people who care, even if they can't comprehend what I'm going through.*

The water is warm, and because of the spelled tub, it remains that way. Reclining into the curved surface, I doze. By the time I climb out, my hands and feet look as if I have lived a full century, but I feel much better.

Wrapped in my bathrobe, I stop at the table long enough to grab a slice of bread and cheese before a scratch sounds at the door. Everyone else sought their beds long ago, so I move to answer it, shoving the last bite into my mouth.

"Milady, I beg your pardon for the late hour, but I saw your light." Alex hesitates as he takes in the robe and wet hair. "I see you are retiring for the night." He glances at the sky. "Or morning. I will only take a moment of your time."

Puzzled at his uncertain manner, I decide to hear him out, though I would rather be in bed. "I wanted to give my condolences. Word has reached me that you have received some bad news."

I'm sure it has. "News of my personal life seems to travel rather swiftly. Your sentiments are noted," I reply dismissively.

Alex reaches out a hand as if to take hold of me. I back up a step, not wanting his touch.

Uncertain, he lets his hand drop to his side. "I also wanted to apologize for my earlier behavior." He searches for the right phrase. "You have always been most conscientious about your responsibilities. It was uncalled for, and. . ."

"Presumptuous, pompous, and rude," I supply for him. The hurt I sense is too much. "I'm sorry. That was uncalled for. When I am this tired, my mouth has a tendency to run away with me. You were just doing what I am sure you saw as your duty."

"Duty partly. Uncalled for, perhaps, but unfortunately your other observations are also accurate. I could not sleep knowing I contributed to making what I am sure was a horrendous day even worse. Thank you for letting me try to make amends."

The prince bows his head as if accepting full blame for the earlier events. "I seem to spend more time apologizing to you than anything else."

"And a fine job you do at that." I give him a sardonic smile. "Alex, you have proven time and again the one quality you have in abundance is a compassionate heart—a good quality in the future king."

"And your heart is there for everyone to see." The prince takes a half step forward so I must look up to meet his eyes. "Time only reveals additional things I respect and admire in you, milady." Although his tone is sultry, it is naturally so.

"Thank you, Alex." Blushing, I back up, giving a small bow. "On that note, I think I will get to bed while I am ahead."

"Good night, milady." A wistful smile plays about his lips as the tent flap closes.

Exhausted beyond measure, I topple onto the feathered mattress. Oblivion is a welcome retreat after the tornado my emotions have blown through my life today. Wakefulness comes too swiftly. I grit my teeth, determined not to let my newfound courage dissolve into another crying fit.

Shoulders squared, back stiff, ready to face the day, I push back the tent flap. My feet lurch to a halt. The color drains from my face. The canvas drops closed behind me. My head droops as if too heavy for my neck to support.

"Milady, we thought a ceremony was in order." Andrayia's soothing tone registers in the haze of pain. The buxom blonde, once a bitter enemy and now a beloved friend, closes the wooden box where rests the unlit emerald.

Slowly my shoulders draw back. Clenching my jaw, I raise my head. Tears glisten in the dappled light of the forest. No longer afraid that some might see the emotion as a sign of weakness, I force my right leg to move. Then I push my left forward. I trail behind my friends in a stately procession past the soldiers, standing at attention, outlining a path through the trees.

I lose myself in the grief I pushed aside since the day Merithin told me I couldn't go home. A pit appears before me as if the gaping hole in my heart has leaped out before my raised foot. Puzzlement crinkles my brow. The opening is approximately two feet in diameter and a foot deep. Alex takes me gently by the arm, guiding me to stand between him and his brother.

"I, Alexander, Crown Prince of Cuthburan, declare this ceremony a duly ordained and attended rite."

Brother Nemandi, gowned in white, steps forward directly across the opening of the funeral plot. "May Andskoti guide, bless, and show his favor. . ."

"Unto us," rings out from the meadow where all have gathered.

"May Kyle, husband to Archmage Reba, find pleasure, peace, and prosperity. . ." the priest continues.

"Where his path takes him." Again the assembled finish the litany.

"We bequeath this token of his being into an earthen home," Nemandi intones as Andrayia closes the wooden box, gently laying it in the prepared plot. I grit my teeth to hold back a sob as Nemandi continues. "May his god watch over his soul as he lies far from us. May his. . ." The rest of what is said is lost forever in the void that consumes my heart. I grieve, not only for the loss of my husband, but for Charles as well as for every fallen soldier who has sacrificed his life in this foretold campaign.

Alex, Szames, my Earthly companions, and finally the Royal Guard give their formal acknowledgment of my grievous state. I am now not only the Archmage Reba, the Flame-haired One, but I am also the widow. Brother Nemandi gives a closing, and I am allowed to mount Jesse. Having risen early to break camp and prepare the funeral, the party moves out, aiming to reach the edge of the forest before sunset.

"You have known you would never behold Kyle again for some time, have you not?" The tenderness of Jesse's thought almost causes my eyes to flood again.

"Your point?" I jab the question at his mind.

"Knowing did not lessen your pain." The cat replies, ignoring the hurt I inflicted.

The feline's anxious desire to aid me breaks my resolve. Hot moisture seeps from eyes squeezed tightly shut. *"I have lost the man I have shared my life with, the man I have loved for so many years. . ."* Unable to continue, I bury my face in the scruff of his neck, trusting his power to keep me seated, though not caring if I fall.

I sob like a child who has broken something precious, something that cannot be replaced. The gentle rocking motion of Jesse's steps brings the relief his words could not as his magic ties me to him. Sleep enfolds me.

ᕰ   ᕰ   ᕰ

The swaying ceases. My eyes pop open. Grit causes me to scrunch them shut despite the approaching figure. I crack my eyes enough to make out Tupper's form.

"This I know how to help," he mumbles as he places a cup in my hand. "Drink."

His hand grazes my shoulder. Coolness floods into me as the water sooths my parched throat. The sandpits in my eye sockets drown in a blessed ocean of wetness. I glance upward but the overcast sky is no help. "How long have I been out?" I ask without meeting his eyes.

"It is a little more than a mark until sunset." The wise elder backs quietly away, knowing I need the precious minutes before dark to compose my still raw emotions.

I glance sleepily around me. *The camp must've been set up around me as I slept. Some hero I am.* Szames hastens to my side as I make my way to the shield stone's tower. "Reba, if you need—" His words halt as he sees my jaw muscles clench.

"I'm fine." Guilt at the growing intimacy between us, no matter how I tried to stymie its progress, stabs into my disheveled emotions. I draw the pain deep inside, unwilling to accept comfort from such a dangerous direction.

Grief transforms into anger as demons charge the shields encircling the camp. I pace the few steps I am allowed on top of the tower like a caged beast. The second half of the Cuthburan army assumes the field. Finally, a chance to blast something! "Laser, laser, laser. . ." I pick off the trio of ogres before they are within fifty yards of the shining barrier. Swiveling, scanning the horizon, I search for a new target.

ᕰ   ᕰ   ᕰ

Days slide past, sorrow haunting my bed so doggedly that sleep is a mere memory. Rage keeps me going when my eyes cloud with exhaustion.

"Laser," I mumble as a beast charges into the lamplight.

Szames's blond head pops up over the top of the platform. I lean on the rail, scanning the darkness for a new target outside the lamp's light.

Failing to sight an enemy, Alex turns to me. "Reba, you need to call it an early night. You could use some rest."

With magical energy still pulsing in my veins, irritation causes the power around my hands to be visible to normal human sight. "And just what is that supposed to mean?"

"Look." An exasperated sigh escapes the princely composure as he glances at my hands. "With the men splitting the night, we both have only slept three out of five nights. I need you at peak performance when—not *if*—we are hit with an organized attack."

It takes a conscious thought to smother the seething anger, which caused the warning enchantment to trigger. "You think I can't handle a few nights without sleep?"

"I concur with Alex," Szames interrupts. "Reba, on the battlefield, prince and general have the majority. Your abilities rely on rest. We cannot afford to be caught lacking."

And to think I was glad when Alex asked him to take second watch at the tower! It was nothing but an ambush. Light flashes into being around my hands once more. I grind my teeth to keep from uttering the word that will reduce something—anything—to a pile of ash. With a jerk of my chin, I acknowledge defeat. Not trusting my control of the mystical forces, I take the ladder two rungs at a time, stalking into my tent the second my feet hit ground.

Alone in the pavilion, I stare at my glowing hands. *Stop it!* The hands continue to be limned in flaming light. *I should have never invoked that stupid enchantment.*

> "A woman I am, and my emotions may reign free,
> No longer will I hint when fury overwhelms me."

The luminance bleeds from my fingers. Anger seeps from my soul. Knowing that lack of sleep causes me to become bitchy at best does not relieve the guilt I feel for the loss of my temper. *I'm the mage. How can they kick me off the battlefield?*

Men! I flounce down on a chair, too pissed to sleep. *I wonder how Rose is faring with her men?* With a shrug, I jump up for the communication mirror. Quickly I chant her name three times. *We may not have a computer or even electricity, but, hey, being a mage helps.*

I set the mirror on the table then go to the trunk to retrieve the dish of lasagna I conjured up a few days ago. I am only halfway to being full when the hair on the back of my neck rises. The blonde in the mirror isn't as well kempt as a fairy-tale princess; the robe she wears is suspiciously like my bathrobe.

"Rose, I hope I didn't catch you at a bad time."

"Not at all. Actually it is pretty good timing. I was just rising early to prepare to break my fast with Mother and some others from court."

With my confidante before me, I'm suddenly unsure why I put through the call. I turn the mirror to the empty side of the table and take a seat. "How are things there? Are the nobles handling the war reports well?"

"Too well, it seems. That is the reason for this morning's gathering. Mother and I let the ladies of the court know that even though the number of demons is low in the north, one is still enough to kill hundreds. A few well-described demons should help give them the courage to sway their husbands from a foolish move."

"Would you like a firsthand account?"

"Gladly. I have the details given to my father, but a firsthand account from a female perspective would be wonderful."

"The northwestern area seems dominated by ogres, raloliks and jarovegi led by ap-bjan. Ogres aren't too scary; they just look like giant men. The jarovegi, well, you saw the one that attacked me. But the raloliks and the ap-bjan, now those are the stuff of nightmares. The raloliks appear harmless from a distance, and that is when they are the most deadly. Their haunches look furry, but they are really coated with quills as long as a man's forearm. They shoot these small arrows with amazing accuracy. We lost one soldier who was shot through the eye. The poison on the tip of these quills isn't swift acting, which has saved many lives. But without a healer, a small scratch will turn gangrenous and the flesh will rot. If one is wounded by a ralolik, it is suggested the limb be amputated before the infection can spread if no healer is available."

Rose visibly pales as she gulps.

A smile twists my lips. "That leaves the ap-bjan. Imagine a snake that is half as tall as a human when it is coiled. Small, you might think, easy to kill. If that were all there was to the creature, I'd agree, but the snake is just the beginning. A torso rises from the snake, twice the size of most men. . . well, that's appropriate because the creature has two heads and a trio of arms."

"And you fight these beasts? These are what you killed outside the castle your first week here?"

I shake my head. "I didn't fare too well my first time out against these monsters. Allinon actually did most of the damage." The name brings thoughts of home. Tears spring suddenly to my eyes. "My God, I didn't think I'd miss them so much. The elf was such a pain."

"So it was not the nature of his race that made his behaviors so. . ."

"High minded, haughty, and pessimistic?" My bark of laughter echoes from the mirror. "No, he was like that before the transfer to this world turned him into a seven-foot elf. The only one that got a personality tweaking was. . . Charles." The name catches in my throat, but I manage to get it out. A tear slides from one eye. "He was a clown." When her brow furrows in puzzlement, I amend, "Jester. But the transfer gave him a silver tongue and a little thing called charisma."

"Reba, are you telling me that your group changed when they traveled here?"

"You mean you didn't know?" *Merithin wouldn't talk about magic to a nongifted, but Szames is a better friend than I thought. I thought surely he'd tell his family.* "Rose, I find I do need someone to talk to, someone with no preconceived notions about. . . anything. But I do not wish to impose upon our friendship. Will having too much knowledge that must be kept unknown to the outside world make things difficult with your position within your family?"

"Reba, it is not an imposition, but an honor." She glances over her shoulder. "Please allow me a moment to secure the room."

If only I'd magicked up a transporter device. Umfang *is needed to transfer things between dimensions, but I'll wager it's not need for local travel. I've got to start a journal of things I want to explore with magic.*

Rose reappears. "My dear friend, I can now reassure you that nothing said between us will be repeated." She gives a tiny shake of her head. "I wish you had appeared years ago. I have often longed for a sister to share my most intimate thoughts with."

"And I suddenly find myself without hope of ever seeing my sister again." Tears come once more, a flood this time. "Merithin was going to bring her out, her husband too. If I know them, and I do, they wouldn't miss a trip to a magical world."

"But you are an archmage. Your magic could not bring her here?"

"That's just it! That is why I can't let go. That is why it is my fault that Charles is dead." Wracking sobs cause me to hide my face in my hands. Eventually I regain a measure of control. "The guys don't get it. They don't see. . ."

Rose's composure is completely gone. She is baffled beyond her ability to hide it.

I take a deep breath, determined to explain it all, every detail of my guilt. "We were just ordinary people. Magic, swordplay, none of that exists on my world. I was a wife and a scribe." I use the term for lack of a better word. "The others were just as ordinary. No one on my world has the ability to use magic, and no one fights with swords. But when Merithin brought us here, we got all the abilities we were pretending to have. And we just knew things, like how to use weapons and tactics and how to heal."

"You mean Jamison wasn't a healer?" she interrupts.

"He was learning to be a physician. My world is more advanced than this one, so some of the stuff he could do would almost seem like magic, but no, he didn't actually wield somatic energy until we were brought here." I hesitate a moment. Her face registers understanding but nothing more. *In for a penny. . .*

"Rose, no one besides my crew knows, but I was given another gift. In the game we played, I had given myself the maximum amount of intuition. Now I get glimpses of the future. It's like a waking dream, a vision that only I can see."

Her eyes widen. "You are a prophet?"

"I don't think so. I usually only see things that I can affect or change. Kind of like a warning system telling me when I'm going the wrong way." I wet my lips. "I had one of these visions about Charles the day before he. . . he. . . the day before. I tried to warn him, but somehow it just made him more determined to see the vision through." The tears begin again. "I think it may have been a self-fulfilling prophecy. By telling him about the vision, I caused the vision to become a reality."

"Oh, my sweet dear. Oh, no. You are not to blame."

"But he told Jerik that because he was there when I got it, he had to go and see for himself." I leave out the vulgar details. "If I'd just told him to stay away. . ." *But I did,* my perfect memory shouts. "If I made up some errand to send him on."

"Reba, I've studied philosophy. Everything about prophecy states that each individual has freedom of choice. That is why much of prophecy is so vague. It must be to allow for the 'personal will' factor. Did you give him a warning? Tell him to avoid the carriage house?"

I nod. The tears begin to lessen.

"It sounds to me like your gift gave a warning. You passed on what you knew to Charles, and he made his choice."

"But he was so young. . . so sweet."

As my sobs ease, Rose shakes her head. "Oh, Reba, then to have such news from home."

I nod. "I knew how it would all come out, but I didn't want to face it. I pushed every vision I had down into a deep hole. I figured I'd have years to deal with it, not weeks." In between sobs, I whine, "Sorry, octals."

My crying jag finally comes to a stumbling halt. "You were right. I did need to share this burden. Thank you so much, Rose."

"Szames has always been there for me, but I have longed for another woman to share my burdens with. I am happy I could be here for you."

"And I will always be here for you." A ghost of a smile twitters across my lips. "With these mirrors, that is one promise

I know I can keep. I should let you get ready for your morning engagement, though."

"Put a call in if you would like a friendly ear again." Her smile reminds me of both her brothers.

"Until then. . . Mirror, mirror, mirror."

Hauling in as much air as my lungs can take, I realize that I meant every word. Though the future seems slightly daunting, I no longer feel the need to run from it.

Stripping to my skivvies, I climb onto the bed. *Since I'm a permanent resident, I might as well be comfortable. I'm sure seeing me mostly naked will be the last concern if I'm pulled out of bed for an attack.* Knowing I'll be awake for hours, I force my lids to close. The internal turmoil and stress I have shouldered for weeks dissolves, just like my marriage. Strength ebbs from my muscles. In moments I slumber, my soul more at peace than it has been for days.

Chapter Sixteen

"You asked to see me?" I duck into Alex's tent, still pissy about being outvoted on the tower the night before.

"Yes. It has been decided that we will activate only the shield stone tonight." Looking up from a pile of correspondence, Alex adds, "Light guard will be posted, but we will hold here until tomorrow night."

Irritated that I was not part of a major decision, my tone turns caustic. "And what about the gate? We were told to hasten our efforts."

"We have tripled our pace. We have stopped for only one day at each rendezvous location where the men sleep only half a night." Alex's tone turns hard as I roll my eyes. "I will not lose good men because of lack of rest."

Head jerking back as if I've been slapped, I refuse to give in. "No, but you chance losing the war."

"That will be all." Alex raises his voice. "You are dismissed."

Storming from the room, I charge to my pavilion before my temper causes me to do something foolish. Seeing a chestnut head pacing the confines of the tent does little to ease the fury writhing inside. "You need something?" My request is more a statement than a question.

"You look like you have been rolled by a big one," Jamison offers.

"I'm fed up, Jay; I have had it with all this political crap!" Before I can stop it, the whole story flies out. *Rose said it was better to share.*

"Well, Reba, you did say tactics weren't your thing. Perhaps it is better if you let them deal with strategy stuff."

I huff across the room and swing back the other way again. "I can't believe it! You, of all people, are taking his side. You think I'm supposed to just shut up and cast laser beams, is that it?"

"I didn't say that." Jamison backs up a few feet, his hands thrust defensively before himself. "All I said is try and consider your true field of expertise. How much do you really know about a campaigning army?"

I shut my eyes, shaking my head in defeat. "God! I hate it when you're right. I knew I was in the wrong when I was fighting with Alex. It's just. . . I don't know."

Jamison puts his arm around my slender shoulders. "You have chosen to champion this kingdom. With home no longer an option, it's hard not to become overly concerned about the path of the war."

"Jay, that is the nicest way I ever heard anyone say 'stop being such a controlling hard case.'" I chuckle. "But you're right. Up 'til now I have had a say in most everything. Now that I am here permanently, I have to learn when to let go, take a step back."

"And when to take a step forward." He grins. "Speaking of which, can I borrow the comm mirror? I've been asked to inform Arturo of the delay."

"You knew about the change in plans before me?"

Hearing the bristling tone, Jamison cuts me off. "I suggested it. The wounded I saw last night were on the verge of exhaustion."

"Apparently pride is something else I need to work on," I grumble, opening the drawer and removing the mirror. "Not every good idea needs to be mine."

"It's not easy being a superstar," Jamison jibes.

"Why don't you see about finding a place for this in the infirmary." I hand over the enchanted looking glass. "I have little need for it without Merithin to consult." *Surely I won't need to cry on Rose's shoulder again anytime soon.*

"No problemo." The healer hustles out the door.

The day passes in a haze. Keeping busy by meditating on new defensive spells and one for the demon lord being held captive at the gate, I am able to integrate into my new circumstance without any more weeping fits. Unfortunately when I crawl into bed without exhaustion to aid me, I can no longer avoid thinking about the current situation.

Tears roll silently down the sides of my face as I confront my new reality. By the time I fall asleep, I have come to terms with my new marital status. I am ready to deal with whatever life throws at me next.

I cast an arm over to the other side of the bed. Finding it empty, I open my eyes. *I'm single now. A widow. Better get used to it. I've had enough tears to last me a lifetime.* As camp breaks and the wagons are being loaded, life takes its first shot.

"Milady, with all the battles. . . I'm sorry. I forgot to give this to you." Mikaela hands me a sealed letter.

"Where did you get this?" I ask, not recognizing the imprinted seal.

"Crystal gave it to me before she left. She asked that I give it to you in the event she was unable to return." The redhead shrugs.

Desiring privacy, I take the letter with me to saddle Jesse. Breaking the wax with a thumbnail, I lay out the letter against the cat's broad back.

> *Reba, my dearest friend,*
> *If you're reading these words, our mission has failed and you are now a single woman.*

A sardonic chuckle escapes me. *It seems my personal life concerns truly everyone!*

> *I'm writing in hopes of repaying some of what you have given me. In our short time together, you have come to mean so very much to me. If your situation changed, I wanted you to be aware of my observations.*
> *I have listened closely to the stories of your life and seen much of what happens at the castle. I never believed in the teaching of the old, thinking them sentimental and misguided, but now I question my skepticism.*
> *It is said that for each of us there is someone who is our completion, the half we don't even know we are missing until we join with the wrong person. When we join with someone who isn't our "true mate," we discover they cannot meet with our expectations of what "love" means because*

*love means something different to each soul,
except for our other halves.*

*I believe you have found your match if you
will only bring yourself to see it. On your
world you loved someone without thought.
Drawn to him, beyond reason. When you
discovered his soul wasn't a match, you
dismissed him from your life.*

*The rumors at the castle are that Szames
has been searching for something too.
Everyone thinks him daft for it. He searches
for a true mate.*

*I only offer you what I have seen in hopes
you will consider it further. You have done so
much for me, showed me so much truth. I
couldn't do less for you.*

With sincere gratitude,
Crystal

A small guffaw escapes my pressed lips. *Yeah, me and
Szames?* I shake my head with disbelief. *Like he would ever
make it past the three-year mark!* I nearly jump out of my skin
when the deep voice sounds right beside me.

"Must be a pretty good read." Szames smiles.

"Just a final parting from Crystal." I shove the missive into
the pocket of my robe and begin saddling Jesse. *Wait a minute.
This is perfect!*

"You know, it is kind of personal. But you are one of my
best friends. I really don't mind sharing." I gaze across Jesse's
back to the warrior. "My only misgiving is that it concerns a
topic which might be a little awkward."

"You really know how to pique a man's interest." Szames
grins, showing he is game.

"I never thought of Crystal as naïve but can you believe she
thinks that we"—I motion from him then back—"should be a
couple?"

Szames freezes for a split second then continues saddling
Tawny. "And this is what strikes you as funny?"

"I'm sorry. That came out all wrong." Assuming I have hurt
his male ego, I explain. "I am not saying 'we' would be so
horrible together. Most likely we would be very good together.

I was actually planning on broaching the subject with you, just not so soon after my situation changed."

"The subject of us?" Having quickly finished with Tawny, Szames gives me his undivided attention.

"Yes. I like us just the way we are. I am not willing to jeopardize the friendship I have come to value so highly for something that will undoubtedly end in complete ruin." Easing into the saddle, I stare at my statuesque friend, sealing away all the emotion our close association has developed. "I have said what's weighing on my mind. What do you think?"

Szames's face turns stony, his voice taking on an acrid note. "I suppose Alex is worth the chance since your friendship with him is not so developed?" The warrior turns to mount Tawny.

"What is it with the two of you?" Still emotionally hot, my anger is lightning fast. "It's like I am a prize you got to win! Well, I am tired of it. This nonsense stops now." I grasp my temper in both hands, struggling to bring it under control. "As for your question, I am not eliminating you as an option because I desire your brother. Alex is not a choice either." Sighing, I gesture for him to lead.

"When I get involved, if I get involved, and the guy is unfaithful—and I don't see how he could be otherwise considering this world's moral philosophy—I will go ballistic, crazy. With the power I wield, being that upset at this kingdom's monarch wouldn't be wise. Besides, could you imagine how upset Alex would be if I put some dreadful curse on him." Snickering, I add, "And I don't mean foul language. If he ever did me the way he is doing Andrayia, I'd put a spell on him so that his manhood wouldn't work within ten feet of another woman."

"You. . . you could do that?" Szames sputters.

"Oh, yeah, in a heartbeat." I smirk. "Maybe someone should mention that to him; then he might not be so eager to pursue me."

"My brother is not easy to discourage. He is stubborn enough to outlaw magic or something equally stupid." Our joined laughter shears off the tension of the argument.

We ride on in companionable silence. My lips turn upward as the paper in my pocket crinkles. *I knew he'd need Crystal.* A nagging begins in the corner of my heart. I recall the premonition I had forestalled and refused to embrace. *Well, there is no time like the present to explore the depth of my gift of precognition.*

I concentrate on the premonition, remembering the smallest details in perfect precision. White blinds my unfocused eyes. A black-haired groom waits at the end of the aisle while a blonde steps in sync with the music, making her way slowly to him. I concentrate and the vision focuses on the blissful pair.

A less powerful light tinges my vision. Now Kyle stands beside Crystal's bed, wiping sweat from her brow, whispering words of encouragement. My former maid's face turns red from the strain of exertion. A startled cry fills the air.

"It's a boy," the masked doctor says.

Brilliance blinds me for a third time. Jesse's rhythmic steps tell me where I am before I open my eyes. I smile at the day in front of me. *They seemed happy and so much in love.* I struggle to hold a self-pitying tear in check. Lifting my chin, I take a deep breath.

He has a new life ahead of him, and so do I. Feeling like I have been granted a clean slate, at least in the realm of my love life, I smile at the blond hunk riding beside me. *At least I've made some friends in this crazy world.*

Our army makes its way southwest, dusty and dirty by the time we make camp. In the normal pattern my life has assumed since landing on this world, an opportunity to have a heart-to-heart with the other prince promptly presents itself. Against my better judgment, I join Alex for dinner in his tent.

"Milady," Alex addresses me respectfully. "I am delighted you could join me. I only wish I had a better fare to offer."

I gingerly take a place at the table, a duplicate of the one in my tent. "Fresh onions, meat, and wine—under the circumstances, a virtual feast."

"Only a remarkable woman could find genuine praise for such as this." The prince gestures to the meal before them.

"Women with whom you associate must be incredibly self-absorbed. Only a fool is unable to appreciate quality above what others are forced to endure." I begin to serve myself. "If you have better than those around you, it only takes common sense to be grateful for it."

"If half the nobles had what you call 'common' sense, their demands would be reduced by half." Alex follows my lead, serving himself, beginning to eat only after I have taken a bite.

The dinner drags on. The gentle patter of rain along with Alex's droning about his skills and accomplishments causes me to long for the oblivion of sleep. Just when I believe my fears may have been misplaced, the conversation takes an unexpected turn.

"I realize it is rather soon after your misfortune to broach such a topic, but I thought it prudent to discover your feelings on a matter before I begin maneuvering the council to approve my proposal."

"I take it this plan involves my marital state?" I swallow the bait he is dangling.

"That it does. We both know my father and the council expect us to marry." Alex swirls the contents of his cup. "I believe I have found a way around the issue."

When he fails to continue, I arch an eyebrow at him. "You have my attention."

"I propose a contractual agreement, a treaty of sorts. In the time of the prophecy, this agreement might have appeared to be a marriagelike joining. If we both sign a written agreement stating I will provide the only suitable heir to the throne through you, I believe the council may accept the arrangement, in lieu of a marriage."

I sit motionless, afraid if I twitch so much as a finger, I will betray the explosive emotions raging inside. "Instead of giving you a few choice words about propositioning me like a common whore. . ." I pause to regain the composure slipping from my grasp with every word. "I will refrain from taking insult. I realize I now reside in this world; I am no longer just a visitor. Give me time to work through what I consider the gravest of insults. I will consider the matter."

"I assure you I meant no offense. I merely wanted you to understand. I have no desire for an unwilling wife. My only intention is to prevent you from being forced into a marriage you obviously do not want."

"I thank you for your consideration, but these nobles of yours are in for a fight that will make this war seem like child's play if they try anything of the sort." Standing, I give a tight nod. "I thank you for this enlightening meal."

"Reba, I am truly sorry for the situation in which you are placed. I only seek a practical solution." Alex steps toward me, his eyes darkening with sorrow.

He's sincere. Fury seeps from me. "I'm not the only one in an awkward situation. Perhaps working together we may yet reach a suitable resolution." My mouth curves in a crooked smile of reassurance.

Brushing back a lock escaping the tight braid I have begun wearing, Tall, Dark, and Handsome whispers, "Would it be so terrible, forgetting who you are while I hold you in my arms for a night? You have my solemn word. I will make the experience most enjoyable."

I fight the desire to lose myself in the deep, emerald pools I gaze into. "Of that I have no doubt." Longing rages, threatening to sweep me away. The weeks without companionship add fuel to the flames. "But could I keep myself from falling in love?"

"Would that be so bad?" Alex closes the gap between us, narrowing it to mere inches. "Love's day blooming between us would eclipse the sun."

"I am sure it would. It would probably be most heavenly." Gently I shake my head, taking a step back. "But what about the next day, or the next year, when love's sunset comes. Surely you have heard the saying: 'Hell hath no fury like a woman scorned?'" He looks confused, so I continue. "No? Well, soon after our coupling, your society would. With the power I wield, I can't say for sure what I would do when your attentions were redirected to your next conquest."

"Is that a threat?" Alex bristles.

"Did you intentionally insult me?" Ignoring his injured pride, I pursue reason. "Like you, I only offer my observations, intent on averting possible disaster."

"It seems we both have much to consider." His smile is no longer quite so inviting. This time it is he who gestures toward the door, keeping the distance I have placed between us.

I hasten to my tent, where Andrayia is waiting, wearing out the rug with her pacing. "I take it the dinner didn't go well." The blonde assumes a seat across from where I'm fuming. "You didn't send for me, so it could not have been a complete disaster."

In short, concise statements, I relay to my ally what has transpired. "And I have a sinking feeling he hasn't completely given up. What do I have to do to convince him to quit this game of cat and mouse he's playing?"

"If I could tell you that, I wouldn't be here now." Andrayia sounds as dejected as I feel. "You have just thrown down your glove in challenge. He will go easy for a while until he has found a weakness. Then when you least expect it, he will strike again. The next time he will go for your heart."

"Maybe magic will work. I need to talk to Nemir, see if he has any ideas. If nothing else, I can make a charm that will cause me to dislike men altogether." I slam a fist down on the table. "I would rather be celibate than be his pawn."

"You could do that?" Andrayia's eyes pop up. "How long would you stay that way?"

"As long as he keeps pursuing me." Shrugging, I dismiss the topic. "I was willing to do without companionship while I waited for Kyle. I will do whatever it takes to evade the traps he sets."

"Have you considered his proposal?" Amazingly enough, the idea doesn't seem to upset Alex's mistress.

I take a few minutes to think it through, now that I'm a little calmer. "Does this scheme of his have merit, or is it just another ploy to get me into his bed?"

"It could go either way. After all, he used the opposite logic to get me to give in after he spent two years convincing me of his love. A child was supposed to make his father allow our marriage." Pain and longing washes through Andrayia as her mind turns to Andertz. "As long as the council makes a ruling before any offspring is produced, I don't see how they could deny a contractual agreement."

"And you would be all right with becoming queen and having someone else provide the heir?" I concentrate on empathy so I can catch Andrayia's true feelings.

"I don't see why not," she muses. "I am sure any agreement will include provisions for Andertz along with stipulations that I be magically blocked from producing any competition for the throne."

I'm flabbergasted. *How can she sit and discuss her man sleeping with another woman?* "I will have to think on it. Eventually it might come down to that, but I'm not giving in at the first sign of trouble."

A bugle sounding in the distance ends the discussion. We stride out to engage the demons once more.

Chapter Seventeen

Trumpets blare. The raucous noise of breaking camp heralds the new day that might have arrived unnoticed but for the watchman. Thick clouds block the dawn light so effectively that I would've guessed it was midnight. The depression shadowing me since the loss of my husband blossoms under the cover of the overcast skies.

On the second stopover heading southwest, the cloud cover lifts. The sunny sky irritates me as I mount Jesse. *"Fantastic. I have a pair of sunglasses in the drawer of my nightstand. I wonder how Cuthburan society would be affected by them?"*

"Most would just see them as a magical device." The SpiritCat answers the rhetorical question.

"Yeah, then I have to explain to everyone and his brother about the mundane principals of tinted glass," I grouse.

"Why do humans evade the real issue with inconsequential whining?" Jesse asks without a trace of humor.

"Fine, if that's the way you feel about it, silence it is." Still heart sore, I retreat behind a wall of quiet.

As each day passes, I slide deeper and deeper into a state of despondent melancholy. Alex, ever the diplomat, quickly learns to gauge my disposition by the set of my shoulders. My temperament is so foul, even Jamison avoids me, which is all the better as far as I'm concerned.

"Archmage Reba, do you have a moment?" Nemandi's chipper demeanor is not a welcoming beacon in the dark night surrounding me. "Perhaps we could talk in my tent for a little privacy?"

"Lead the way, Brother." The young priest fails to rouse my curiosity, but manners force me to acquiesce to his request.

"As the only member of the fellowship assigned to this crusade, I feel it is my duty to address whatever it is that troubles you." At my look of disbelief, Nemandi hastily adds,

"I assure you whatever is said will remain strictly confidential."

"And what makes you think there is something bothering me?" I demand.

"You must be kidding." His unpriestly speech puts me instantly on the defensive. "The entire camp walks on eggshells around you."

"So I should confide in you, someone of no training, someone who I have talked to once—and briefly at that." The maliciousness of the tone causes the young man to wince. "I should just reveal my most intimate thoughts? You aren't even a real priest!"

"O-of course. . ." The color drains from his face. Fear and disgrace tie his tongue in knots. "I have no right."

Unable to live with causing an innocent man grief, I mutter, "I apologize. I was out of line."

"No, you are completely right. I'm not a priest. I don't even know what I'm doing here." Nemandi's devotion is shaken to the core. "I am nothing but a common thief who donned a white robe for reasons I can't explain."

"It sounds like a genuine calling to me."

"Yes, but a calling for what purpose?" The young man sighs, burying his face in his hands. "I have done nothing but tag along. My only duties are intoning funeral prayers and listening to the confessions of those about to pass on. I thought perhaps you might finally need something from me."

"I'm afraid the help I need lies beyond your god's ability to produce." *And mine seems unavailable on this retched world.* Trying to ease his plight, I let out a fraction of my troubles. "The God of Abraham, Isaac, and Jacob seems to have deserted me. I feel trapped beyond God's reach in this foreign world. I've got this tremendous power, but I struggle to direct my own course. Hope is fleeing my heart, my soul. Without the shining light of hope, I fear soon I will have nothing left to fight with." I clamp my lips shut, unwilling to say any more.

A white light surrounds Brother Nemandi's head. "Patience, young one. Your destiny will show itself before spring truly arrives."

Knowing the message is more than mere words uttered by an unordained priest, that the war must be nearing a close, my spirits lift. *Perhaps I will be free to leave when this is all over.*

I could explore this world on my own terms. I give a tentative smile at Nemandi as I turn to go.

~   ~   ~

However, an octal later, when the birds begin chirping and the grass takes on a verdant hue, signs of budding love only serve to highlight my plight: a council of pious, old men are trying to force me into a marriage that will be misery beyond agony.

Scouting becomes my only relief, and a cherished one. Astride Jesse, the limbo engulfing me is left leagues behind as the wind caresses my face, teasing strands of hair free of the tight braid. The sensation of powerful muscles beneath me as we glide through the hills is a sweet tonic to my flagging spirit. Szames travels at my side. Tiring of one-word answers, he ceases to engage me in conversation.

"Is it common for humans to wallow in remorse?" Jesse's mind-voice contains not a hint of humor or sarcasm.

"Oh, please. Not you too?" The day started out sunny, but once again clouds have cloaked the sky in murky obscurity. With my robe back at camp, my ninja outfit clings to me. The shower does little to improve my temperament.

"I understood where the feelings were coming from a few octals ago, but eventually you must allow yourself to be happy again." Sheepishly he adds, *"Won't you?"*

"Happy about what? This godforsaken rain?"

In response to my sarcasm, the ride suddenly becomes exceedingly rough. In less than a mark, my bottom is feeling the reprimand. Gritting my teeth, I refuse to apologize.

> "To tame this overbearing steed,
> A pair of spurs is what I need."

Without looking down, I know the requested items have materialized on my heels. I jab the new equipment into Jesse's side.

The shocking sensation of physical pain causes the cat to screech and twist wildly. Having hunkered down in the seat, I easily retain my position.

"About time someone knocked you off your high horse!" A chuckle escapes me.

"My pain is funny, is it?" The growl of anger in Jesse's thoughts is more from being the butt of a joke than physical discomfort.

My partner bunches up his muscles, but instead of the rodeo bronco busting I'm prepared for, he takes off at top speed. At first I struggle to maintain a seat, but once I get comfortable, the ride is quite exhilarating. *"How kind of you to provide me with a look at Cuthburan's scenery."*

No sooner does the thought leave my mind, than Jesse puts on the brakes. First he drops his hindquarters and sends mud flying. Sliding to a near standstill, the cat brings his backside up in a quick fling.

"Ahh!" I fly from the saddle, flipping through the air like a pancake, landing solidly on my buttocks. Thanks to the paladin spell, I manage not to break anything.

Awareness returns. I realize what has caused the unexpected softness. Jesse's aim was right on the money. I am smack-dab in the middle of a mud hole where water has been collecting for some time.

"Just thought you might like to get an up-close look of the land you have sworn to protect," he remarks with a very catlike cleaning of his paws.

The tension keeping me wound in knots for the past several octals shatters like an icicle slipping from its perch. I twitter, giggle, then begin laughing hysterically at Jesse's joke. When Szames finally arrives on Tawny, I am wiping tears from my eyes. Streaking across my delicate, ivory face is the earth I now defend.

In between snickers, Szames says, "Now if that. . . is not just desserts. . . I don't know what is."

"Just desserts, huh?" I break with formality, beseeching his mount uninvited. *"Men really don't understand what having our hormonal drive is like."*

Picking up on more than the spoken words, Tawny gives no warning. A sudden lunge and twist sends her rider soaring into the mud pit.

"Poking fun at a woman's predicament while in the control of another female isn't the wisest of moves." I give Szames an affectionate pat on his cheek, depositing quite a bit of mud. "O, all-knowing prince of the land."

"A lesson in mud-slinging, is it?" Szames brings up a handful of slime, crowning me with a token of his affection. "Being raised at court, it is a lesson learned early in life."

With the opening shots fired, the battle begins. I make it my personal goal to see that Szames doesn't leave the bog with one inch of clean skin. We wrestle and roll in the mire as gleefully as piglets put at play.

"All right, all right, you win!" I holler as Szames threatens to dunk my nose in the murky depths.

"Say 'uncle,'" Szames holds my face less than an inch from the puddle.

"Uncle. . . uncle already!" As the words of surrender are spoken, the towering soldier releases his hold, falling back on his filth-coated bottom.

Szames chuckles. "I am glad to see your humor restored, else it would have been a long campaign."

"I was that bad?" I whisper.

"Humph, almost unbearable." He smiles, easing the blow. "But understandably so."

"Then it seems I owe you." Szames is immobilized as I gaze seductively into his eyes, slinking toward the warrior in a sexy crawl. "A rather long-overdue apology."

Sitting on my knees, I lean into him, eyes closed. As Szames's eyes ease shut, I bring up muck-filled hands above his head while planting a sisterly peck on his forehead.

"Finally!" I giggle with childish glee. "I got those golden locks!"

Determined to get revenge, Szames lunges for my lanky form. Limbs tangle and our bodies rub. We begin to pant from more than just the physical exertion. Before Szames gets a firm hold of my slippery body, a disgusted purr issues from our mounts.

"Did we partner with humans or swine!" Jesse broadcasts.

"And I bet they expect us to let them on our backs," Tawny chimes in.

We bog-dwellers exchange meaningful glances. Needing no other communication, we lunge at our partners, giving each a warm, wet, slimy hug. The cats are silent as we mount for the return journey. When the monsoon rain begins its daily torrential downpour, I turn to Szames and smile.

A mark later, Szames gives his report when we reunite with the main body for lunch. "We have yet to find a suitable location for tonight's encampment."

Alex eyes our disheveled appearances. Even though we washed in the rain as best we could, our mud bath is still quite evident.

After a quick bite, we set out again, this time looking for a campsite in earnest. *"I think I have found something that might interest you."* Jesse sends a mental picture of what he sensed a half mile east.

"Ah, Jesse, that couldn't be more perfect." I motion for Szames to follow, loping off at a gallop.

Nestled in a gorge, a winding river is shaded by overhanging trees. The shade isn't what makes Jesse's discovery such a find. Several natural hot springs feed the river.

"If you will unsaddle us, there are some shallows where we can bathe," Tawny broadcasts along with the exact location of the bounty.

"Don't cats hate water?" I ask aloud to include Szames. When Jesse sends a picture of spewing up mud-caked hairballs layered in feelings of disgust, I laugh so hard, I can hardly stand.

Szames dismounts beside me. "I will take care of Jesse if you want to go first."

"I would like to soak for a while. There is more than one tub. If you can retain your gentlemanly manners, the company will be welcome." I can see Szames's blush through the grime on his face but he assents.

While our partners wander their own way, we race to the rocky pools heated by underground thermal activity. True to our agreement, Szames looks away as I slip out of my filthy clothes and into the water.

Turning my head when it is his turn to strip, I submerge then begin the chore of washing dried mud out of suede. Unable to get the embedded slime out of my garments, I call up soap and a washboard as well as shampoo, a washcloth, and some towels.

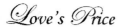

"Scouting with a mage has definite advantages," my fair-haired companion remarks as I pass him the supplies.

I lean back against the rim of the pool, easing down my temperature shield. "Between the two of us, we have it made: a member of royalty and privilege and a witch."

"Pretty much." Szames's boyish smile causes me to grin in return. After he finishes scrubbing his clothes, he begins soaping himself up. The sight of his sculptured biceps flexing as he reaches for his back brings color to my cheeks. I jerk my head away. Suddenly the water doesn't seem so warm.

Closing my eyes, I try to get the picture of his naked, half-submerged body out of my mind. "Mmm, now this is what I call a little R and R," I mumble, trying to distract myself.

"R and R?" A deep sigh escapes the prince as he relaxes into the warm water.

"Military jargon for rest and recuperation." I sink down until the liquid is just above my chin.

"The entire company could use some about now," Szames replies drowsily.

"For that, I feel partly responsible. My behavior hasn't helped morale." Gliding across the pool to the wall between his and mine, I put my head on the top of my laced fingers so I can gaze across the way at the best friend I've found on this world or any other. "Sincerely, I'm sorry for the way I've been. I know I have been a real bear."

Looking up, Szames approaches the edge of his hot tub so his face is only a couple of feet from mine. "Perhaps, but friends can be at times. You are, after all, only human."

"A true friend you are indeed." I return his ready smile.

"You ask a lot of a friend." Surprised at Szames's reprimand, my head pops up out of my hands. "Behaving as a gentleman with a sexy woman, naked and wet. . ." He gives a leer that would give Charles's best effort a run for its money.

"Is that so?" I give it back to him. "Do I sense a challenge?" I give him my best come-hither look. Leaning forward, folded arms are the only thing covering my bare breasts.

"And you think it would be me who breaks first?" With a twinkle in his eye, Szames's arms bulge as he lifts his torso out the water, lowering himself onto the grass between the pools. Our faces are inches apart.

Driven by a competitive urge and an urge of a different nature, I wiggle forward until less than an inch separates us. "Of course. You're a man, aren't you?"

The silence between us deepens, but the space remains small. It will take only the slightest forward movement for our lips to touch. The desire to run my hands across his muscled body builds as seconds pass. I gaze into the depths of his sapphire eyes, feeling myself falling, my head tilting.

In one swift movement, Szames pushes himself back into his pool. "I knew you would give first." His glib remark is husky, betraying his own struggle.

Sliding back into the pool, I slap the water, sending a spray his way. "Unfair! I have just been through a turbulent emotional crisis, two even!" I pout. "I have a severe handicap!"

Szames's only reply is a gloating smile. We recline, enjoying the soothing warmth of the bath. I ponder my sudden weakness. Chalking it up to weeks of emotional upheaval, I dismiss the entire incident. *Now I know why I have those rules.*

Deciding the plateau will be the perfect campsite, we mount the cats, prepared to inform Alex of what we have named Hidden Springs Bluff. Jesse halts in midstride, his ears perking.

"Reba, attack at the supply wagon!" Jerik's thought echoes into my mind as the ground rumbles underneath us.

"I'm on my way," I send to the dwarf as Jesse leaps into a run. "The main body is under attack!" I shout to Szames while Tawny hustles to keep up with her superior.

The army is within sight as an explosion rocks the ground underneath us. The cats surge forward.

I extend my hand. "Laser, laser, laser." The three jarovegi wreaking havoc fall. I whisper, "Superman."

I glide upward to get a better view of the ambush. Jamison and a pair of the Royal Guard square off with an igildru. A discarded crossbow is before the creature that has donned peasant garb. A blade in each hand and a tail that acts like a whip keep the trio embroiled in the battle.

"Laser," I whisper, searching for another target.

A second igildru crouched behind a bush takes aim as Jerik flings his battle ax. The weapon spins through the air. The creature, so intent on its target, never sees the blade that cleaves its skull in two. A thick bolt with a heavy tip streaks from the crossbow seconds before blood splatters on the weapon.

I hover, knowing I am helpless to intervene: the bolt flies swifter than a spoken word, and even Superman can't beat the missile to the target that close. Time stands still. Heather bunches up her haunches. The cat springs into the air. The feline lands less than a foot from the crown prince, the bolt clenched between massive fangs. The royal pales as his eyes widen. A dip of his chin acknowledges the partner's service.

I scan the chaos before me for more demons while soaring toward the cluster of nobles. Dark smoke billows from two of the three wagons. Jamison and Tupper hustle toward the downed soldier as I land before Alex. "Your arrival is as timely as you promised, Milady Archmage."

I dip my head, acknowledging his praise before asking, "How did these monsters manage to get so close? Your peripheral scouts should have spotted them long before they were close enough to fire a single shot."

"The scouts were stationed three hills out. When the soldiers fell out for a break, a pair of the scouts came trotting toward camp. Heather informed us that a demonic force was approaching." Alex gives the cat a grateful glance. "We sounded the alarm, and the demonic assassins disguised as scouts raced back. The jarovegi broke the surface about that time. We didn't realize they were the distraction until the igildru"—he gestures at the humanoids lying dead on the ground—"fired on the wagon."

Spotting his brother at the wagons' ruins, Alex gestures for me to ride with him. "If we can stabilize the wounded, we should push on to the bluff we've located."

Szames grimaces as he rubs his chin. "A well-coordinated ambush. If they had set the last wagon on fire, they would have crippled us."

"Which one did they miss?" I ask. *I'm not sure if I'd rather lose the supplies or the quarters.*

"The basic supplies were stationed in the rear of the train in the healers' cart." Szames jerks his chin northward. "The infirmary, half of the grunts' quarters, and the barrel of beans with basic cooking utensils are all that remain."

"Reba, how much can you restore with your magic?" Alex's need causes him to disregard his displeasure for the arcane.

"With Szames's help, I think I can get most of us someplace dry to sleep." I shrug. "Beyond that, I can't make any promises."

The commander turns to his brother. "Reba informs me that there is a bluff not far from our location?"

Jamison approaches as Szames nods to his superior. "At this point," Szames says, "we need the game we can find near the water. It will be days before supply wagons will be able to make the rendezvous at WestRoad."

Jamison bows his head, waiting for royal approval before entering the conversation. "The demons managed to kill fourteen, including the wagon drivers and the missing scouts. We have eight that were poisoned by the jarovegi. Without one more wagon, at the very least, we have too many disabled to make even a short journey."

"I'll get you that wagon." I turn to Alex. "With your permission, Szames and I will take the soldiers' accommodations and work on setting camp?"

I wait for only the briefest of nods before riding to the rear of the company. The duplication spell for the mundane wagon hardly registers on my energy supply. Horns blare, announcing our departure as Jesse glides across the hills toward the front of the line of soldiers.

In the time it takes to return to the bluff, I have formed a good plan of action. Doubling the size of the current tents is more magically economical. The soldiers find themselves with new bunkmates when they arrive. Darkness falls. The men settle in for a night of rest. I relinquish my tent to Prince Alexandros for a formal briefing to the king.

For the first time on this leg of the campaign, I stroll to the center bonfire. *The men need to see fearless courage, not a worried Flame-haired One.* I push the agonizing thoughts of battle from my mind. I recall, instead, the antics in the mud bog. A gentle smile graces my countenance. Hoots and hollers and a round of applause break out as Ansil appears by my side with his new instrument.

"About time we got an upgrade from Sil's caterwauling." Stezen's gentle ribbing is a welcome invitation.

I smile at Ansil. "What brings you back?"

"You were right. I showed that letter and just like that"— Ansil snaps his figures—"I was accepted into the musicians' guild. Only one stipulation: I've gotta travel with the army. They expect a full report of any songs by 'the Phoenix.'"

"Phoenix? Is that what they call me? Suitable, all things considered." My interest is piqued. "Tell me: What is the legend concerning the bird on this planet?"

"Ma'am, it ain't no legend. There's a group of phoenixes living on the northeastern ridge." The musician looks over his shoulder in the indicated direction. "The females have feathers that glow so bright, they light up the night sky. They're ten times a falcon's size and twice as smart. I hear tell ranchers keep archers with the sheep. The birds of the fire plumage are canny enough to snatch their prey in the night. Double watch is posted in the summer after mating season. The beauty of their songs are said to bring a tear to a grown man's eye."

"It is a privilege to share the name of such majestic animals." When the lame man returns my grin, I forge ahead. "We'd better get started if you're going to earn your keep." With a glance around the circle, I include the men gathered around the fire's warmth. "I thought I would try something new. For this one you are going to have to use your imagination a little. My dad used to sing a few songs as he played a guitar. Try to imagine a deep-voiced man is singing."

"My daddy left home when I was three,
He didn't leave much to ma and me
Just this old guitar and an empty bottle of booze.
Now I don't blame him 'cause he run and hid,
But the meanest thing he ever did
Was before he left, he went and named me Sue.

Well, he must o' thought that it was quite a joke,
And it got a lot of laughs from a lots of folk.
It seems I had to fight my whole life through.

Some gal would giggle, and I'd turn red,
And some guy'd laugh, and I'd bust his head.
I tell ya, life ain't easy for a boy named Sue.

Well, I grew up quick and I grew up mean.
My fists got hard and my wits got keen.
I roamed from town to town to hide my shame."[v]

The ditty is an instant hit, especially the part about "kickin'" and a-gougin' in the mud, the blood, and the beer." Marks later I retire from the rowdy sing-along, feeling much better about the state of morale, despite the ambush just marks earlier.

Outside the firelight, a figure detaches from the shadows of a tent. "I am pleased to see you are feeling better."

"I had an interesting day. Sometimes that is all you need to break you out of the rut you're in." I meander toward my quarters as Alex tags along. *I've had enough of wallowing in the gloominess of a self-pitying depression. This is my world now, my new life.*

"Would you care for a bite before you retire for the evening?" Amazingly Alex fails to use any persuasion with his offer.

"I'm afraid I'll have to pass." *I won't fall for another wine-laden ambush.* "I was just heading over to give Jesse a brush. Care to join me?"

"It would be an honor." Another shock: Alex's feelings actually match his words.

"Two princes in one day? Are you out to set a record?" Jesse snickers as we approach his chosen nesting place beside his tent.

I smother an escaping chortle. *"We are just friends, and you know it."* As my partner gives a mental chuckle, I add, *"Besides, I figured if I was close to you, I could leave my empathy shield down for once. You feel up to running interference?"*

"Having a discussion inside your mind must be convenient at times." Alex's smile takes my breath away.

"Jesse is just sending a welcome. And rather impolitely so, excluding you in his private broadcast." Sensing Alex's discomfort, I hastily add, "If you are all right with that."

"I am still working on being comfortable with a voice other than my own inside my head, but I am willing to try." Alex's grin turns lopsided, reminding me of his brother.

"I wonder. How far does that go? Your willingness, that is?" I give his curiosity a few minutes to take hold before proceeding. "Jesse was telling me that others of his kind watched as we passed through the Ethereal Forest. They continue to watch now. Close to a hundred are considering offering service such as his."

"One hundred riders with mounts who have the abilities Jesse has displayed?" A rumbling growl escapes Jesse at Alex's comparing him to a mere horse.

"None would have my exact abilities. Age compounds our aptitudes. I am an elder of my race." We both chuckle at the pride coloring his voice.

"The only thing I see blocking our path is the bonding process. To take a partner, the elected individual will need to open themselves to the spirit being, allowing a full scan of their life, beliefs, and moral fiber."

Alex's stance goes from relaxed to defensive. I pause in mid stroke as terror rises inside the prince.

"These beings are our superiors in many ways, yet they mold themselves in a physical form that will be dependent on us. You can't expect them to do that without knowing exactly who they are tying themselves to in such an intimate relationship." I wait for logic to conquer the apprehension in the prince. Idly I pick up the brush. Long strokes bring a vibrating purr from Jesse.

"And this bonding gives them no power over us?" Alex edges closer to the gigantic cat.

"None." Resuming the massaging strokes, I give the diplomat more logic to contemplate. "As arcane counselor, I fully recommend the bonding. It is a precaution that is good for us as well. Could you imagine a band of rogue outlaws on mounts like these. . . or members of a rebellion?"

With a decisive dip of his chin, Alex directs an inquiry to Jesse, "How long until we know if we have a new set of allies?"

"There are several of my kind willing to allow a bonding for further study. They have selected the members of the Royal Guard as a partner choice. Is the kingdom of Cuthburan ready to proceed toward a true partnership between our races?" Having only intended to scope out his feelings, Jesse's offer takes me by surprise.

"You never asked," the SpiritCat sends a private tendril to me.

"If I did not know better, I would think I have been ambushed for the second time today." Alex graces me and

Jesse with another devastating smile. "Have I, master of politics, been outmaneuvered by someone who claims to have no talent for it?"

I chuckle. "I take it you will allow partners for the Royal Guard?"

"Yes. I have discussed such a treaty with King Arturo. We proceed with the blessings of his majesty, the king," the crown prince replies formally.

"Are you sure I'm not the one who has been duped?" I stand with hands on hips. "I've played right into your hands."

Alex's quick stride closes the space between us. "If manipulating you were that easy. . ." He halts in midsentence. The urge to melt into his arms begins to ebb. By the time he resumes, I am free of his influence. "I am glad we have this time, Reba. There is something else I have wanted to discuss with you."

Feigning nonchalance, I resume the grooming. "This sounds important."

"It is important to me." With a heartfelt sigh, Alex saunters around Jesse until he is looking at me across the cat's back. "I have done you a grievous wrong. I realize in order to earn your trust, I must fully own up to my mistakes."

My acute hearing picks up someone approaching who hesitates just outside the range of sight. I note the presence as Alex continues.

"When we were faced by a seemingly unconquerable enemy, speculation began about the time of the prophecy. I quickly came to terms with the direction my future might take."

Alex makes his revelation, staring at his hands. Even though I cannot see the truth in his eyes, I can discern it within him. "I have been groomed from birth to be king, but now another would take my place. I could deal with that. The stranger would surely need my guidance, my help. I would ride beside him as he led our forces to victory. Perhaps most importantly, I would now be allowed to marry as I chose."

Alex raises his eyes, willing me to meet his gaze. The depth of feeling swirling in the emerald pools holds me captive. "Then you came. My plans crumbled. Yes, I will still be king, but no more than a puppet. The title will mean little if I sit next to a woman who saves my kingdom." The prince lays his heart open for me to see.

"I reacted badly, I admit. I sought to conquer you, to prove not only to myself but my country that I was still in control." Alex captures my hand, the forgotten brush tumbling to the ground. "For this I have apologized, but now I find myself needing your understanding as well."

"Tonight, Alex, you have earned it." Alex's honesty excites me more than magic ever could. Without any coercion other than the mesmerizing quality of his gaze, I find myself leaning into Jesse. Alex leans toward me. Our heads tilt.

Heather, lounging a few feet away, greets her partner with a purr. The sound brings reality crashing down. I take a step, bending to retrieve the brush.

"Oh, Your Highness, Archmage, I hope I'm not interrupting?" *Andrayia lies better than I could, as upset as she is.*

"Not at all. I was just leaving." I give Alex a brief nod. "Thank you for your company."

Chapter Eighteen

I storm into my tent. With a disgruntled growl, I begin pacing in frustration. *I've nearly fallen into the arms of not one, but two princes today!* "Somehow I think the depression was better!"

"You are being facetious, right?" Jesse interrupts my fuming. *"My companions are ready for the bonding."*

"I will get the women. Let Andrayia inform Alex via Heather." I hustle to the openings leading to the guards' private quarters.

"Royal Guard." The women come to smart attention as I address them officially. "You five women have showed that we, of the female persuasion, have strength beyond what the world knows."

The guards smile cautiously.

"Your courage will be talked about for generations. Now I must ask that you take that courage and follow me once more."

Mikaela steps forward, keeping her eyes straight ahead. "Archmage Reba, we will go wherever you lead."

I look down the line as each woman nods. "You have seen Andrayia's partner?"

All the women nod. Auricle pales.

"Five more SpiritCats wish to join our crusade—nay, our kingdom. These are not mere beasts, but intelligent beings such as you and I. Our new allies have chosen to partner with the Royal Guard. Will you accept?"

Mikaela nods her assent. Rucela, Villiblom, and Hrinia step forward to join Mikaela.

Auricle's voice wavers as she asks, "Will they be using magic on us?"

"Remember when I gave you the fighting abilities?" I wait for her nod. "It will be something like that." I sense the level of fear drop to something that can be reasoned with. "I will be right here, making sure everything is done right. When you have bonded with a cat, you will have a partner like Andrayia and Heather, Tawny and Szames, and Jesse and I."

Still fighting the fear, Auricle steps forward.

"Follow me." I get them going before Auricle can change her mind.

I bow formally when I approach Alex, the guards behind me following suit. "Your Highness, we are ready to proceed with the partner pairing."

"Let those gathered bear witness. Cuthburan enters into a new treaty with our allies in the demon war. SpiritCats will become partners with the Royal Guard."

The nobles flanking the prince look nervously among themselves. The tent flaps to the partners' quarters billow as if a cyclone fills the tent. The officers take a step back when a red, tiger-striped cat steps out, followed by four more cats of various shades of brown.

The pony-sized version of an orange tabby approaches Mikaela. A soft glow moves from the cat to the woman. A smile slides across Mikaela's face. "Her name is Miyana." Eyes a little glassy, she chuckles. "It means *rebellion* in an ancient language."

"Now that looks like a cat of the prophecy," I send to Jesse.

"But in your childhood, you longed for a mount the color of the deepest night." My partner's puzzlement hides hurt behind it.

"You are a picture of beauty I didn't even imagine could exist." I send love through the link. *"I definitely don't need anything that flashy to draw even more attention to me."*

A brown cat with a slight auburn sheen slides up in front of Auricle. The woman's eyes widen. She looks ready to bolt as the energy encompasses her. A nervous smile tweaks her cheek. "Vorkunn, what a sweet name," she mumbles.

I search my memories of Cuthburish. Vorkunn means something like pity, compassion, and sympathy all rolled together.

A nut brown feline, with white on the tips of her ears and nose, steps forward. Villiblom giggles as her eyes regain focus. "Frost. . . how perfect. My parents told me my name means *flowering forest* in the Forgotten Tongue."

A lithe, lanky cat the color of wet earth approaches Hrinia. "This is Scatiar."

"Scatiar means something like 'good scout' in the Forgotten Tongue." Jesse supplies the answer to my curiosity.

"Do all Cuthburish names have a meaning?" I ask.

"Don't all your names?"

I give a slight nod. *"I guess they do if you go back far enough."*

"Your Highness, Archmage Reba." Rucela draws me back to the proceedings. "I would like to present my partner, Euon."

I smile at the smallest of the cats and his new partner. "I thank each of you. . . each partner pair brave enough to join us in the war against demonkind." I dismiss the new recruits, knowing they need time to integrate into a true partnership.

I nod to Alex and Szames, hastening toward the safety of my quarters. I glance about for Andrayia. *"Jesse, do you mind relaying a message to Andrayia again?"*

"We are partners, are we not?" Jesse's voice rejoices with victory for his kind. There is a pause; then he continues. *"I have let her know you are looking for her."*

A few minutes later, Andrayia approaches. "Heather said you wished to see me, Archmage." Although her etiquette is exemplary, her eyes are red rimmed. Manners ingrained into her since childhood are the only thing keeping tears in check.

"I think it's time you called me Reba, and it is also time we were totally honest with one another." I motion to a chair across from me. Andrayia takes her seat, eyes never straying from me. "First I must have your word that what we say tonight stays between the two of us."

"As long as it does not endanger the ruling monarchy, I so swear." Having given her word, Andrayia waits to see what will come.

"It is necessary for you to have additional information about abilities I possess. One of my talents as a mage is to know when someone is telling the truth." Even oath bound, I am cautious about how much I disclose about myself. "Some people have a natural ability to block this. Alex can interfere with it at times, but tonight was not one of them."

"You expect me to believe that you know when someone is lying?" Andrayia leans back, instantly defensive.

"Test me." *Regaining her trust is going to be harder than I thought.*

"Alex was the first man I slept with." Her eyes narrow.

"False." I reply without hesitation.

Andrayia's eyes widen with surprise. "Alex was the first man I loved."

"True."

"I love Alex more than I have ever loved anyone."

"False, you love someone else even more. I don't even need magic for that one."

That breaks her. Tears flow as Andrayia whispers, "My son."

"Yes. So believe me when I say that what you overheard Alex telling me was the complete truth." Pouring myself a glass of wine, I hand one to Andrayia.

"It seems he is attracted to strong women." The buxom blonde sips the alcohol. "You already know that, though, so what do you need me for?"

"I was in the royal gardens the night before we left. I heard what Alex told you. Truer words have never been spoken." I down the entire cup, needing the confidence to continue. "I need an ally in a war I am losing." The shock the royal mistress displays is genuine and I forge ahead. "To prevent the tragedy of Camden and Connie from repeating itself in you and Andertz, I need your help."

"What do you want me to do?" With a solution within reach, Andrayia's tears evaporate.

"Alone, the odds are stacked against us. But we are not alone. We have our partners." I feel Jesse's mind brush mine in reassurance. "Jesse knows how miserable I will be if I succumb to Alex's charms."

Andrayia's eyes glaze over momentarily. "Heather says she'll help too."

"The way I see it, Alex can only get at me when you aren't around."

Andrayia nods.

"Well then, when you aren't with Alex, you need to be with me."

"We can use the cats to relay position, just like tonight." The guard catches on fast. "But, Reba, why are you going through all this trouble?"

Feelings of suspicion rise. I drop my forehead onto the table before me. It takes a concerted effort to pound it on the wood a few times. "Why? All this time together and you don't know why?" Fear is added to suspicion. "God, woman, because he loves you!"

"Yes, and love is dawning for the two of you. Our sunset approaches!" Andrayia is as shocked as I am by the volume of the protest. "I apologize, milady."

"Reba. . . Tonight, I am just Reba. No archmage and no titles." I wait until some of the fear ebbs. "Maybe you're right. But if love is dawning, it isn't love as I know it. It isn't love that I can accept."

"That—What did you call it?—That man-og-no-me thing?" Suspicion disappears, replaced by hope.

"And then there is Andertz." I slap the table. "I won't see a child used as a pawn. Not with the power I wield."

"But if Arturo chooses—"

"No matter what the king does, what he says to you, you and Andertz come and see me." I growl, "I will put a protection spell on you that is so strong, a building could fall on you and you'd survive."

Andrayia bats her eyes in astonishment. "You would defy the king? For us?"

"Andrayia, I will stand up to injustice, no matter where it comes from." Still sensing disbelief, I add, "Why else was I endowed with such power?"

"Your world must be an interesting place to breed such as you." Andrayia smiles.

The mention of Earth brings pain that has dulled to discomfort. I push it into a corner. A smile that doesn't quite reach my eyes cracks the hardness of my countenance. "I'm just glad that I have found an ally to help ease the transition."

It takes half the night to hammer together cohesive contingencies for the plan. By the time we crawl into bed, we have a few surprises in store for Alex. Feeling more secure about keeping my morals intact, I snuggle into the covers. Thoughts of home and my lost love creep into my mind. I whisper my prayer spell with dry eyes and a heart that isn't quite as lonely. Dismissing the thoughts, I concentrate on the new cats and try to imagine what a hundred of these majestic friends will mean to my kingdom.

∾　　　∾　　　∾

It is nearly midday by the time I wake. Warm achiness echoes from every muscle. *Maybe I should give up drinking altogether.* A sharp pain stabs into my lower abdomen. Seconds later, when I feel moisture between my thighs, I know the symptoms aren't due to alcohol.

Cursing, I crawl out of bed, striding to the bathroom. Seated on the toilet, a red stain confirms my fear.

"Aw, man!" *No wonder my hormones are running away with me: I always get really horny right before I'm due. That explains the depression too. PMS! I don't have time to deal with this now. I don't even know what they use in this world, probably torn-up rags for absorbent padding.*

Inspired by that thought, I begin a rhyme.

> "In this world being on the rag
> Is a pain in the rear, a real drag.
> For women to be equal, a solution is needed.
> When blood flows, it'll disappear, unimpeded."

Tingling centers above my pubic bone. Another wipe and the toilet paper now comes away clean.

Too bad I can't zap away PMS as easily; I have no idea what causes it, other than some kind of hormonal shifts. Without a more comprehensive idea of what I want to do, the spell could leave me worse off than I am now. I suppose that's just nature's way of keeping us humble. Cinching up my drawers, I saunter into the next room.

"Andrayia, I'm glad you're awake. I need some information about a feminine matter." Taking a seat across from her, I pour myself a cup of strong morning tea, knowing caffeine will just make the cramps worse. "How often do women get their bleeding? How long does it last?"

"The curse comes upon us once every seven octals. For most women it lasts only two to three days. Is it that season?" The blonde continues with her breakfast.

"Let's just say I had a rude awakening this afternoon." I grimace at the thought of eating leftover beans. *If the fight is short tonight, I'll have enough power to reproduce that stoneware.* I shovel a spoonful of legumes into my mouth.

"Do you need supplies?" Andrayia grimaces in sympathy.

"Actually that part is taken care of—nothing a little magic can't handle." Two of the guards were already PMSing. *They need the spell I just created. It is such a minor spell, the energy loss won't even matter.* "You know, I could use the same spell on the Royal Guard."

"Will it interfere with conceiving offspring?" Mikaela asks as she takes a seat with us.

"It will only take away fluids leaving that area of your body," I reassure her.

By the time I have performed six duplications of the enchantment, my abdomen begins to cramp with gas pains. Putting cold beans in an empty stomach probably wasn't the wisest thing I have ever done. Rather than bother the infirmary when they are trying to set up for the battle ahead, I crawl back to bed to sleep off some of the symptoms before the coming night.

"Laser, laser, laser." Before the shots hit their targets, I swivel to aim at another demon Alex spots.

"My God, how long until dawn?" I wipe sweat from my brow when the battle shows its first lull.

Alex glances at the largest moon's position. "The night is only half gone."

"Then I'm going to need your brother's help. Anyone see him?" I scan the area where I last saw the towheaded warrior.

"There." Andrayia points farther south.

Following her lead, I locate him by his aura more than anything else. Lifting off, I fly swifter than ever before. In a few seconds, I land soundlessly beside the man in question.

"Szames, my energy is two-thirds gone."

The warrior's sword comes up as he pivots his attack stance; the dispatched demon crumples to the ground behind him. As the battle rage clears from his eyes, he gives a short nod.

Szames points at the sky as we lift off. "Beware!"

I link by elbow through Szames's. I make a triangle with my fingers, intoning, "Fireball." When the flames roll off the approaching flock of demons, I whisper, "Laser!" Shielding deflects the bolt, so I try the new enchantment I prepared. "Dispel magic."

The air surrounding the fliers recoils as blue lightning zaps it. "Laser, laser, laser, laser, laser." With a deftness belying my inexperience, I take out the demons. The boulders they were transporting fall harmlessly downward, still yards from the platform.

When the huge rocks make contact with the shield, the outer layer disintegrates, revealing black, oily sacks. The lumpy bags pass through the moat, drifting harmlessly to the ground as they are shredded by demon claws. Each of the five pouches holds two monsters. The demons rise, unscathed, inside the primary defenses.

"Jerik, Jamison, attack at the tower!" I send out the mental alert. Even though it may cost the life of a wounded man, Jamison's sword skills are needed more than his healing.

The entire military force is engaged in battle on our second night on this bluff. All six of the Royal Guard are on shift. Only the half dozen women sworn to protect me stand between the invaders and the shield stones. The partner pairs spring into action, each rushing a chosen foe.

"Laser, laser. . . I can't get the others. Too much in the way!" I spit in frustration swooping toward the ground.

"That leaves six to handle the old-fashioned way." The menace in Szames's deep rumble sends a cold shiver up my spine.

Side by side our feet pound into the earth as we charge toward the tower. *"To your right!"* A cougarlike scream comes on the heels of the thought as Jesse's claws slash out. His dagger-sharp nails nearly decapitate the beast waiting in ambush around the next corner.

"Laser." I nail the other monster.

The remaining demons have given up trying to tear the tower down. Instead they scale the poles, nimble as monkeys. Alex and Andrayia are managing to keep the monsters from gaining the platform, but they are losing ground.

"Laser, laser." Two more beasts fall.

Taking Szames's hand once again, I lift us onto the scaffold. With the threesome spotting for me, the rest of the intruders are quickly vaporized.

"Jesse, you saved us. Thank you."

"That is what partners do, do they not?" The emotion coloring the reply makes me feel not quite so alone.

The battle drags on into the night. Szames stays by my side, supplying a wellspring of power, but still, before the skirmish ends, I am forced to use some of the power stored in my staff. Longing for bed, I stagger toward the infirmary. Fatigue winds its destructive force around my legs. I stumble as I push back the tent flap.

Jamison appears instantly at my side.

"How many wounded?" I ask.

"Too many. Almost twenty have been healed enough to be sent back to their tents, including one of the Guard. Six are still critical, and twelve will never fully recover." When I glare at him expectantly, he adds, "Seven dead and four unaccounted for."

Air hisses between my clenched teeth. Sympathy for the mothers and wives of the lost men force me to blink back tears. "The critical ones, anything I can do to help?"

"You're beat. . ."

"What is it?" The words are harsher than intended. Gritting my teeth, I struggle to stay on my feet. "I don't have the energy to conduct a battle of wits. You need something. What is it?"

"There are six who are stabilized, but we can't seem to get rid of the aura virus. You want to have a look?"

I grunt, rousting enough energy to cast a glare in his direction.

Jamison shrugs. "OK, it was a stupid question."

He ushers me to the back of the tent. The healer removes the bandage wound around the soldier's thigh. "Kent, Allinon's disciple, couldn't seem to get a grip on it. We've knitted the bone, stopped the bleeding, and halted the infection, but that's as much as we can do. We can't close the wound."

The gash looks more like a clean cut made by a weapon rather than jagged flesh torn by claws. One single laceration spans the width of the entire leg, revealing an alabaster thighbone. "Sight." Covering the entire area is a black, writhing mass.

"Of magic you have been made, and magic I wield.
Power surround this wound. Against me you have no shield."

The greasy glob undulates faster. The summoned force engulfs the blob. Try as it might, the AV finds no escape from my magic; in a bubbling gush it evaporates.

A flash bulb goes off as a premonition overwhelms my senses. Before me stands a demon holding a sword. Dipping it into a bucket, it mumbles a spell. Now the blade has a red-tinged glow. In another flash the world reappears.

My hand digs into the bedpost as I wait for the black spots to recede from my vision. I suck in huge amounts of air. When I catch my breath, I mumble, "These wounds were caused by a poison-coated weapon or a magical poison, not a natural venom secreted by a demon. That's why druid magic can't touch them."

"I'll let Kent know." The tension in Jamison eases now that a cure has been found for the last of the wounded. "He has been beating himself up about this for most of the night. He's pouring through the books you and Allinon whipped up on druid theory."

Too tired to delay any longer, I thrust my chin at the men on my left. "These are the other five?"

I move on down the line with Jamison removing the bandages to verify that infection has been neutralized. A mark later I mop my forehead. Through pale lips, I mumble, "If you get any more of these, call me."

"Reba, you gonna make it home? You're swaying on your feet." Though I nod, Jamison takes me by the arm, escorting me to my bed. I allow the physician to help me out of my boots and my pants before collapsing on the feather mattress. Through the haze of exhaustion, I mumble my nightly prayer spell.

Chapter Nineteen

I snap awake, noting the dimness of the tent. *It's already sunset?* I swing out of bed, searching the ground for the discarded clothes. Finding the floor bare of the outfit Jamison helped me shed, I hustle to the chest I was forced to re-create after the attack.

I run a hand across my fuzzy braid. *I really need to wash or at least brush and re-plait this.* One long growl echoes from my midriff. *Food first. I need to be ready for battle.* The flap swings back. Auricle, followed by Mikaela and Rucela, hustles to the table with two steaming plates.

A fine mist covers the women's royal blue cloaks. *Oh, I forgot about the doggone monsoons.* Auricle manages a dip of her head as she sets a plate at the head of the table. "We hoped you would be up in time to enjoy the bounty Vorkunn helped us find."

The aroma wafting from the table makes my mouth water. "It smells wonderful," I mumble, rubbing my eyes sleepily. Hunkering down, I give a grateful smile to the women. "I'd say you guys demonstrated your worth last night." I slide a spoonful of the stew through my jaws.

"About time we got to see some action," Mikaela grunts.

The delicate flavors of onion and carrot tantalize my palate. "You want to be on the front line?" I manage around a mouthful.

"Keep those bastards from jawing 'bout us," Rucela mutters. "If they see we can take any of them in a fight."

Embarrassment tinges my cheeks. *They're having problems?* "I'll see that you're assigned a rotating position. Three of you will fight, and the other two will guard the tower. The cats can signal when it is time to change the guard or if another problem arises like tonight."

The tight smiles and grunts of approval confirm I have made the right decision. Sharing the tent with the Guard, I know returning to bed will send the wrong message. Instead, I run a steaming bath and doze in the tub.

The steady drizzle eases by the time night sets in. My boot squishes inches into the mud a foot past my doorway. Grimacing, I whisper the name of the Man of Steel and fly to the tower, though my aura still isn't fully charged. Before sunrise, I regret the indulgence.

The moons rise, none of their light penetrating the dense cloud cover. From the tower I release a hailstorm of magic, yet still the enemy continues to charge our shields. I am forced not only to retrieve Szames once again, but to drain even more power from my staff: The stave's power is reduced by half. I slip into bed, knowing the few hours of sleep I get won't fully recharge my aura. Just one night, that's all I need: six to eight hours and I'd be back at full power.

"Milady, lunch is on the table." Mikeala gently shakes my arm.

I open gritty eyes, my stomach rumbling as the smell of food reaches my nose. Grunting a thanks to the guard, I lever myself out of bed, stumbling toward the table. *I've got to talk to Szames before the meeting today.* I shake my head trying to get my thought moving.

The afternoon passes in a sleepy haze. The night brings no relief to my overtaxed resources. The sun rises and I pass out, exhausted beyond my endurance.

Alex slogs up beside me as we watch the soldiers breaking down their tents. "Reba, are you sure it is necessary to push on for half a day's march?" Although I privately convinced Szames to back me, outvoting Alex on the matter, the crown prince still hasn't given up.

My mouth gapes wide. I struggle to slough off the tendrils of sleep clouding my brain. "Staying a third day did not see the dramatic lessening of invaders as in times past." I evade giving a direct answer, knowing magic is a touchy subject.

Without his subordinates present, Alex asks questions more freely. "Perhaps. . . but game is plentiful as are the winter vegetables growing by the springs."

Fine. You want to know. . . "Supplies are the least of our concerns. I cannot risk draining the area completely of magic.

If a dead zone is created, our shields would drop, and we would be easily overwhelmed. Our food shortage can be solved once the numbers throwing themselves at our shields are low enough for me to recharge my staff."

Alex's back stiffens and he visibly pales.

I sigh. "Well, I'd better take point with Szames."

"Archmage Reba." The formal address Alex uses puts me on immediate alert. "It has been decided that the Royal Guard will take point until we clear this buildup of demons."

"But—"

His head held high, the prince overrides any objection I could raise. "With the SpiritCats' ability to communicate over long distances, your abilities are needed to guard the main force and what is left of our supply train."

"Of course." I bow out gracefully. "I appreciate your taking time to explain the strategy behind the change."

Alex smiles at the compliment as a group of officers approaches. I dip my head in parting, withdrawing before the political posturing can begin. I stride toward the partners' tent. Jesse slinks between the flaps, already saddled.

"I'm not that late, am I?"

A purr of amusement rumbles from the black cat. *"Villiblom saw to my readiness."*

Frost, Villi's partner, follows Jesse from the tent. The rest of the Guard and their partners amble out behind Villi. The serene contentment I sense from the women causes my lips to twist sardonically. *"A few days ago, they were almost as isolated as I was. Jesse, cat's wisdom is proving to be a thing of compassion."*

"Compassion revived, thanks to you." He sends back warm fuzziness.

I clear the sudden lump in my throat. A dozen pairs of eyes turn in my direction. I plunge ahead. "It has been decided that the Royal Guard will take point until we can clear this hot spot." Though a minor wave of confusion ripples through the women as they elbow their neighbors, I know the meaning is still clear. A menacing growl tinges my voice. "Not only are we in greater danger as we march through an unsecured area, but the scouts will be in even greater danger. For this reason, three of you will take point. Your cats will aid you in gauging the distance the army can march in the remaining light. It is your job to find a suitable campsite and report back via your partners."

All six women straighten and salute. The anticipation emanating from them sends adrenaline surging through my veins. "Andrayia, you will remain to act as my guard. The other two guards will pace to each side of the column, scanning for demons."

"Yes, sir." I feel her regret tinged with pride at being chosen to guard the Flame-haired One.

The Guard forms up behind me. Heads turn as the cats march toward the command center. I take a position beside Alex, motioning for the others to proceed to their positions.

Szames assumes field command, delivering Alex's orders to the subordinates. Tawny lopes effortlessly beside the quagmire of mud that used to be a road. Bunching up her hind legs, the giant feline leaps the muddy bog. I glare at the mud that splatters from her paws onto my pants.

The general brings Tawny to a halt beside Alex's mount. "The men of the 18th are exhausted from slogging through the churned mud. By the time they travel the road, the mire is nearly four inches deep. Captain Youngmen suggested a rotation to bring the rear guard to the front."

"Make it so." Alex nods to Szames, gesturing me closer. "Reba, you cast a spell to make a path through the forest. Can you do something similar here?"

"Not without compromising the available power."

The prince's brows shoot up in puzzlement.

I expound. "Until we know the number of demons attacking are lessoning, I intend to conserve every scrap of energy."

"It seems the power of the Flame-haired One is not as limitless as we have assumed."

I snap my empathy shield shut when I sense smugness with the thought. Though he hasn't tried to persuade me in a while, I choose to err on the side of caution when dealing with him. "Can Jesse relay word to the scouts that the progress will be slowed?"

"I will see to it." I edge Jesse away from Alex's mount. Andrayia continues to shadow me.

The demonic forces surging into the shields fail to diminish with distance from Hot Springs Bluff. After another pair of exhausting nights, we push onward. Half a dozen stops sees a gradual lessening in the numbers arrayed against us but not enough that I am able to recharge my staff.

The leader of the crusade heaves a sigh. "The men need to regain their strength before nightfall. With tonight's calling area overlapping last night's by more than half, we should be able to use a swing shift. Even though we will make half the distance, we can be ready to march in the morning. This may let us make up distance, regardless of the traveling conditions."

The demons, however, do not cooperate with Alex's brilliant plan.

"Fireball, fireball." I swivel as Andrayia points to another group gathering on the south side. "Fireball."

"Reba, northeast." Alex spots a band of ogres gathering before turning to shout down the ladder, "Sound the call for reinforcements!"

The hailstorm of demons persists for another octal as Mother Nature continues to lament, drenching the land about us. The early monsoons have brought a nasty storm. The pace of our advancement slows to a crawl. Even though the distance we covered is shortened, the number of enemies we face fails to lesson to an amount manageable by half our soldiers.

Breaking at midday, Alex's normally pristine appearance is as haggard as I feel. "At this speed we will be lucky to make it to SouthRoad by the time the supplies run out."

"I can provide food, if necessary, but I still need to keep works of magic to a minimum." Thanks to Szames's contribution, I finally have managed to charge my staff until it hums, but I have also had to constantly rely on his help during battles, no matter how I try to conserve power.

"We need a respite from the constant battling." Szames's pessimism echoes my feelings. "We have been fighting without a break for octals. Nearly every man has taken a wound at some point. Morale is flagging, dangerously."

"Your Highnesses, Archmage, please forgive my intrusion." Ansil, hobbles forward on his crutch. The commoner waits for Prince Alexandros to dip his chin before continuing. "I couldn't help overhearing your conversation. I think I may have a solution."

Alex gives a brief gesture, and the man continues. "My family lives close to Skoguri. They sought refuge at Eldridge some time ago. They say Skoguri has been deserted since word of the demons reached them. The town isn't too far from here, less than a days' march west. It is right near the forest. Skoguri may offer some protection from the worst of the weather if nothing else."

"Hmm. It may very well be the place we need to shelter us while we wait out this storm." Alex rubs a stubbly chin, thinking out loud. "We were going to swing farther east to skirt those woods. It is worth the delay. How accurately can you point it out on a map?"

"That might not be necessary," I say. "Alex, Jesse informs me that a SpiritCat has been watching our camp. With your permission, he is willing to take Ansil as a partner. They can scout that area for us." The jaws of both men hit the ground.

Ansil recovers before Alex does. "But I can't ride."

"I don't believe a partner would offer unless he has a way around that," I reassure the lame musician.

"Your Highness, if I can still be of use in this war, I'm willing."

"You have been of great assistance. Your contribution to morale has not been overlooked." Alex closes his eyes briefly as if trying to sort something out. "Ansil, I will accept your pledge as royal musician, with leave to travel as necessary. You will not only scout ahead of us today, but will be continually vigilant while visiting every court in the kingdom."

Ansil drops to his knee, the stub sticking out behind him in an awful parody of a knighting ceremony. "I so pledge, Your Highness."

The royal musician struggles to rise while a soft purr echoes from behind. A sapphire mist condenses, a small piece breaking off to surround Ansil's calf. With a bright, lightning flash, a mount appears along with a perfectly proportioned prosthesis on the end of Ansil's leg.

Alex takes a step back from his appointee as Ansil gingerly tests the artificial appendage. Gingerly stepping toward his new partner, Ansil smiles. "It cradles my limb as tenderly as a newborn's momma."

Coming face-to-face with the new cat, Ansil's eyes glaze over. Three parallel scars from neck to chest stand out brightly against the dark gray fur of the SpiritCat. One ear is cropped short. The marred veterans stare eye to eye as minutes pass. Finally Ansil glances our way.

"This is Penumbro." The smile conquering the musician's face is priceless. "He says he will aid me in riding until I become adjusted to the new limp he has made me."

"Penumbro, if you will report your findings via Jesse, we will follow your path." Alex has become quite adept at taking full advantage of the partners.

The new partner pair lopes ahead as Szames calls for the assemblage of the troops. I keep my head tucked as far as possible inside my hood as the wind seems determined to provide a thorough rinsing of my face. Slogging through the mire of a roadway, the Cuthburan army arrives at the township a mark before sunset. Using the spare shield stones, I secure the village as well as the camp, the township being large enough to house only the officers and a couple dozen of their men.

The main body of the army collapses into their tents intent on getting some rest before night sets in. Alex and the officers in his favor take possession of the largest building in town. The small stable next to it, as much as the painted board with a bed on it, marks it as an inn. Shrugging off the lethargy nagging my limbs, I amble toward our vacation spot anxious to get my first look at a medieval village. *Surely this isn't big enough to be a town?*

"Milady Archmage Reba." Ansil bows, waiting for acknowledgment. "I thought you and the Guard might like the accommodations the town's mill might provide."

I tilt my head questioningly, gesturing for him to lead the way. *I suppose it may be nice to have some real walls around me.*

"Skoguri is known throughout the kingdom for the fine craftsmanship of ironwood." The musician ambles beside me gingerly on his new wooden leg. "The mill was built generations ago. It is rumored Heggur's ancestors were the first to discover the secret of working with the wood."

Oh, a wood mill, not a grain mill. The buildings we are approaching stand perfectly straight, though not laid out in the gridlike precision of Eldrich. *If I didn't know better, I'd swear that each structure had manufactured siding.* "This is the same wood that the barracks and most of the town are constructed with?"

"Yes, milady." Awareness of my lack of knowledge dawns on my escort. "Ironwood used to be considered unworkable. Once the wood dries, it becomes as hard as perinthess; a cutter can dull his blade beyond repair if a log is gone dry. But if kept moist, the wood can be sliced thin, dried straight, and used to build most anything. Any thicker than my little finger, and a nail will bend rather than pierce. Thanks to ironwood, Skoguri has prospered."

I halt under the eaves of the inn to give the musician a break. Though the prosthetic leg makes walking without a crutch possible, there is still some adjustment for his muscles. "I take it that river"—I gesture to the tributary behind the tavern that is threatening to run over the banks—"is the same one that winds south of Eldrich."

"Yes, Ma'am." Ansil bobs his head. "The East River, where the recruits got the sand, meets up with the Skoguri Run. The two then flow into Brightport."

Smiling, Ansil gestures for me to continue on our way as he narrates. "The only man more prosperous than Heggur in Skoguri is Djuprista. Prista the Ferryman they call him, though he hasn't manned a craft in years. Prista designed the barges to haul the raw wood to Eldrich. But ol' Heggur wouldn't be outdone. He began to draw craftsmen to Skoguri. Painted or stained wood holds the color as well as the day you put a hand to it. Those good with a brush seek apprenticeship here."

The mystery of the pristine buildings is explained at last! The wood doesn't rot or corrupt. "So this inn. . ." I gesture to the building we just left. "How old is this structure?"

"The Red Bed is one of the town's oldest buildings." Ansil shrugs. "Gisti is the sixth in his family chosen to assume the duties of innkeeper."

The steady sprinkle eases into a fine mist. I can't help but to smile now that my curiosity has been satisfied. "What a wonderful resource to have. Tell me: Are the forests around Skoguri thinning to the point of depletion of this ironwood?"

"Oh no, milady." Ansil's prosthesis echoes as we cross the bridge. The arched path doesn't even creak as we cross. "We passed through many of the lumber farms on the way here, though you probably couldn't see them through the downpour. Ironwood grows quickly; in three years the trees are still supple and plenty large enough to harvest."

The musician gestures toward the two-story structure with a water wheel to one side. "Heggur's Mill," he proclaims. The wheel is still; a vertical shaft securing it in place. "I thought the partners may like to be close by, perhaps in the mill itself, while you and the Guard assume possession of the house."

The mill itself is more of a square. The main house is sits to the side and slightly in front of the massive mill. "What a wonderful idea. I will inform the Guard of our new accommodations. Thank you, Ansil. I'm sure the women will love a change."

I glance around the surprisingly open area. Ruts have been worn in a steady path from the mill leading out to the smaller houses on this side of the river. I point to a structure nestled back into the trees. "Is that a barn?"

"You've good eyes, milady, to see so far in this dim light." He grins. "Most lumber farms grow crops between rows of the wood. Keeps the fragile ironwood saplings from succumbing to the monsoons. The common fare is good barter 'tween fellings." We begin the walk back to the main camp as Ansil elaborates. "Gisti's pa built the barn for his patrons that had a couple shilling for a night in comfort but wouldn't pay the copper for his stables for their mounts: many would turn them the horses out into the paddock. Last summer I was here, good ol' Gisti would stable your horses and wagon back there for a peck of vegetables or a string of grouse caught on the road in. Leave it to Gisti to take that piece of land nestled in the trees on the edge of town and expand his hospitality to new heights."

"Gisti sounds like a crafty guy." I chuckle. "Keeps himself in fresh vegetables and meat while making his customers feel pampered."

I give Ansil a grateful nod as he ambles off in the direction of the center of camp. The main room echoes with a quiet I haven't enjoyed since leaving Cuthburan. I take a seat in a sturdy looking chair. I eyes begin to droop. *I've got a few minutes to catch some z's before letting the Guard know of our temporary luxury.*

Spirits lifted with expectation, I wake to thunder and raging wind. With the increased area, every man takes the field, despite the weather. Sporadic attacks of small groups roam the perimeter, but few charge the encampment.

"There are a couple dozen demons out there," I report as the rain eases to a steady downpour. "Do you want me to activate the call?"

"The men need a rest, but we can't have a buildup of the enemy either," Alex explains before asking, "Can you modify it so the affected area is no more than half a league?"

A yawn overcomes me before I can reply. "Not a problem." I whisper a few lines then activate the spell by saying, "Minor call."

Demons surge into the force field. A battle cry rings into the night from the throats of hundreds of soldiers. With the enemy spread out along the expanded perimeter, the soldiers are able to dispatch the beasts before any can recover from the stun shield.

"Stezen, dismiss a third," Alex bellows at the soldier below. Subordinates are set running to the selected officers in the field.

The clang of armor being removed is drowned out by another thunderclap as Alex turns to me. "Reba, get some rest. Tawny will send Jesse for you if we need some of your la-ser"—the twist of his lips with the unfamiliar word causes me to smile—"for any large assaults."

"Yes, sir." I chuckle when I feel the surprise hidden behind the royal facade.

Hrinia and Scatiar follow me as I wander through the village. I keep to the edge of the streets, where the mud is only an inch or so deep. "Your talents would be better served at the tower." *Like I need a bodyguard!*

"Perhaps, Milady Reba, but while the enemy is engaged, at least one guard will be by your side." Her attitude is formal, but after sharing quarters for the past few months, she no longer fears me.

"Would our bargain not be fulfilled better by securing the force field that protects me? By guarding the towers?"

"Milady, we have sworn to stand by your side throughout the demon wars," Hrinia explains. "Only the direct command from Prince Alexandros has enabled us to broaden our protection this far. Not even the king could cause us to abandon it altogether."

I glance at the torrent of water rushing under the bridge as we cross. *Much more rain and I'll have to figure out how to keep the town from floating away.* I chant a few lines that will send me a warning if flooding is imminent.

The superstitious fear continuing to rise in the woman convinces me to reconsider. "And the Guard's part in the bargain must be fulfilled in order for the agreement to have worth." I smile. "I am proud to be served by such a group of honorable women."

"Mage-globe," I pronounce as Hrinia stumbles over a rut in the road. A glowing sphere materializes over my right shoulder.

She smiles sheepishly. "I think, milady, there are much worse things than being assigned to a sorcerer."

The covered porch on the south side of the house provides an excellent place to discard our muddied boots. Unlacing the soiled footwear, I glance to my partner. Jesse and Scatiar head to opposite sides of the porch. The felines turn in tight circles before lounging on their sides.

Moving toward the door, I send the light floating before us. In our stocking feet, we enter the most prosperous home in the town. The floors are wood but swept and well kept. A brick fireplace, nearly the size of the one in my castle suite dominates the wall to the right. A large kettle hangs from a hook over a metal bar, suspended over the ashes. The bricks from the hearth extend a good distance beside it. A metal door marks the oven. A table occupies the back half of the room with several stools sprinkled around it. The only other pieces of furniture are a massive chair and a padded loveseat.

The sturdy furniture is beautifully finished, though not as ornately carved as Prince Alexandros's. A stairway on the back wall leads to the bedrooms upstairs. Hrinia gestures to the door beneath the stairs. "This is the largest of the rooms, milady. We will rotate which of us sleeps in the main room. I will take this shift."

I nod. She moves to stack wood in the four-foot cavern that serves to heat the residence. When Hrinia reaches for the tinder, I say, "Lights." The stacked wood and the candle on the table sprout a flame at my command.

The guard gives me a smile over her shoulder then begins to unroll the small mattress in the corner. I duck under the low entry into the bedroom. A small chest is situated at the foot of the bed, and an armoire stands against the wall. A clean set of clothes have been neatly stacked on the end of the bed. The mattress is smaller than the full-sized one in my guest room back home. The bed appears just long enough so my feet won't hang over the end.

I left the luxury of my ensorcelled tent for this? A hummed song reaches my mage-sensitive ears. I sigh. *Because these are acceptable—no, luxurious—accommodations in this world. And I will not behave like a spoiled princess.*

Light catches a spiderweb in a corner. I shiver. *This place has probably been deserted for months. If I'm gonna stay, I have to do some pest control.*

"I have become part of this world
and am destined to stay.
All creepy-crawlies will vacate.
Go somewhere else to play."

I smile contentedly as power caresses me with its release. By the light of the globe, I see trails of tiny insects stream from my mattress. *I'm glad I intended to encompass the entire structure, I'd hate for them to scurry into my guard's bed.*

I keep my shirt on in case I'm called to duty and slide between rough sheets. I dismiss the glowing sphere with a thought before whispering my nightly prayer spell.

Chapter Twenty

Wiggling beneath the blankets, I stretch. My toes poke out the end of the covers. I kick and squirm, finally curling into a ball around my pillow. *Still, having a secluded room is worth a little inconvenience.* A rumbling echoes from my midriff. *Time I got to laze a bit; eating can wait.*

The sound of reveille penetrates the light doze. My head springs off my pillow. I throw on the clean clothes and grab my robe as I dash through the door. Someone has cleaned my boots and left them by the fire. I hop on one leg then the other, stuffing my feet into the shoes. "Any idea why the trumpets are going off?"

Footsteps pound the stairs as Rucela shrugs. "No, milady, but it is the general call to assembly."

"Staff," I call, reaching for the door with the other hand. Jesse, still as a statue, waits for me on the porch.

"Would've been nice to have some advance warning," I grouch. *"I am the arcane counselor, after all."*

"Perhaps if you were out of bed before midday." Sensing no rebuke with the remark, I let the slight slide. *"Or perhaps this doesn't concern matters pertaining to magic."*

"Whatever." I shut the uncomfortable topic down as we traipse out into the muck. The Guard and their partners march in parade style behind me as I cross the bridge. I halt beside the overpass. The trumpeter is stationed on the other side of the bridge. Soldiers, formed up in companies with the officers before them, line up in practiced rows.

Alexandros, resplendent with his cloak fluttering behind him, strides past me to the arch of the bridge flanked by Szames and Stezen. A "hup" from the officers is followed by the jingling of armor as the soldiers perform the saluting bow.

"At ease." Alex's voice carries to the farthest corner of the market square. When the jostling quiets, he continues. "The campaign has been long, but we will continue until we find the source of the invasion. We will secure this great kingdom from the evil seeping into our midst." I snap my shields closed against the waves of confidence and triumph battering my emotions as a throaty cheer rises from the troops.

Alex motions for quiet. "Fresh supplies are waiting at SouthRoad Crossing. Will every skilled horseman step forward?" A grateful cry erupts from the crowd as the men realize the supplies will include not only new living quarters but fresh vegetables as well.

Officers bark out names, and more than fifty soldiers assemble before the bridge.

"I need eight volunteers who will take Skoguri Road and rendezvous with the supply wagons."

Every man takes a step forward.

The prince grins at the display of loyalty. "Stezen, choose the new members of Cuthburan's cavalry."

Men slide out of the ranks as the arms master calls their names. "Youngmen, you will lead the cavalry to retrieve the supplies. Choose your mounts and depart immediately." Light footed, as if they haven't walked miles in the past months, the youths scamper toward the picket line on the far side of camp.

"Dismissed!" Szames bellows.

Catching Alex's eye as he makes his way back to the inn, a motion of my head gestures him over. "Good day, milady. You look well rested."

Taking in his clean-shaven jaw and coiffed hair, I nod. "As do you. Seems our detour has paid off. Any other developments I should be aware of?"

"Secure," Alex pronounces the English word flawlessly. "The enemy was sporadic until midnight then ceased altogether. We will divide the troops into two shifts, as before. You have been assigned the first watch. If the numbers of demons are as last night, then all should be fully rested by morning. Will one more day suffice for the reestablishment of the supply spells?"

They've already made the decision. He's just patronizing me. "It will do. We can all use one more day of rest." I give a curt nod and stalk off in the opposite direction.

"Jesse, can you tell if it is the fact that I am a woman or just the typical behavior to exclude the arcane counselor from strategy sessions?"

"Do you wish me to begin eavesdropping on his thought processes?" Jesse asks.

I sigh. *"That wouldn't exactly be ethical. I suppose I'll have to puzzle it out myself."*

The sun peeks out behind the thin cloud cover. A grin sneaks past the scowl twisting my lips. *"Perhaps it is for the best. Not being trapped in those boring meetings will leave me plenty of time to take care of the supplies."*

Sauntering to the mobile camp, I ignore the Royal Guard shadowing me. *It's not like she's with me because she wants to be. It's her job.* I push the depressing thought aside. With focused determination, I begin to enjoy the semisolitude. My thoughts turn inward. *God has deserted me, but Andskoti said my path will be revealed in the spring. Everything is in bloom, but where is my answer?*

The aroma of meat roasting over a fire pit guides me to the center of camp. "Smells wonderful." I greet the rotund man tending the fire.

"Thank you, Milady Archmage." Fear wraps around Kokkur as he bows low.

"Someone was lucky enough to get a deer on the way here?"

"No, milady." He glances nervously at Jesse, who is sniffing a pile of leftover bones. "Half the hunters sent out at daybreak have returned with game."

I turn to the roughhewn table piled high with meat and vegetables. A ten-gallon cauldron on the ground next to the prep area waits to be filled. "I will be enchanting this pot, just as I did the last one." Fumbling with his hands, he stumbles back a step, perilously close to the fire. "What are you preparing for dinner tonight?" I attempt to distract him.

"A mulligan stew, milady." Kokkur hustles to the table, gesturing to the sack beside it. "The winter onions and some roots have been scavenged."

Smiling in reassurance, I begin to chant. The unending crock spell makes a notable dent in my power supply, but my staff is still thrumming with power. "Just as with the last one, all you need to do is tap the bottom twice to begin anew."

Resignation settles on the man like a cloak. He bobs his head as I take my leave.

Auricle steps up in my place. I can't help but envy the warm greeting Kokkur gives her. Without a backward glance, I saunter toward my campaign quarters. Jesse drags his prize inside with me. He circles a dry corner, finally settling in to gnaw his pilfered prize as I sink into a chair. Auricle shuffles in with a pair of heaping plates as I begin to mumble the Starbucks spell.

I sense surprise laced with alarm as the renaissance cup materializes on the table. "Would you care to try a cup of my favorite drink?" I ask, my lips twisting in mischief.

The guard sighs. "I have magic in my head. Magic helps with my season time. I suppose it won't hurt my stomach none."

I chortle as the woman hustles to the chest holding the dining equipment. After the long week of little more than beans, the heavenly aroma makes my mouth water. Knowing the waiting will make the tasting sweeter, I take a seat at the table.

Carefully I pour my guard a cupful. "Mmm, this is delicious," Auricle mumbles, sipping the steaming macchiato.

I take another cautious sip. "For me it is the flavor of home that I enjoy more than anything." The guard nods in understanding, giving me a burst of inspiration. "You know, it would take very little power to exchange these beans for something your mom might cook. . ."

"You could. . ." She wiggles her fingers. "And bring my mom's food here?"

"Oh, no, nothing that extravagant." *Teleportation again. . . I've got to remember to study how magic might be able to do that.* "You will just need to concentrate on your favorite dish. Then, like when you talk to Vorkunn, magic will turn the beans to whatever food you are thinking of."

"So I just think of saag and kalajosh?"

I nod, reasonably sure the foreign words are her mother's specialty. Words of rhyme spring to mind and I begin to chant.

"Mothers dear, we have missed you,
But here your cooking will have to do.
Take from her memories her comfort food."

I sigh in contented bliss as azure energy moves from my hands to Auricle's head then to the heaping plates. In a flash, beans have been replaced by cubed meat, breaded and sautéed with a yogurt-looking gravy and chopped green leafy vegetables in a creamy sauce. A pile of pitalike bread lies between the two plates.

The diminutive woman's extraordinary beak twitches. "It is saag and kalajosh with the tandoor bread my mom made last solstice!" She pounces on a seat, tearing off a piece of the tandoor and using it to shovel food into her mouth.

Glancing at my untouched plate, she swallows hard. "Forgive me my manners, milady."

"I'm glad your exuberance has saved me from partaking of this bounty in the wrong way." I smile, picking up a piece of bread and tearing it as she has done. I gesture for her to continue.

The lamb is sweet instead of hot, the spices blend with the strong flavor of the mutton, making it surprisingly palatable. The saag is spicy as well as creamy, reminding me of the palak paneer I used to order at Cuisine of India.

"Your mom is a good cook," I mumble around a mouthful.

Auricle blushes at the compliment. "Had I known I would be eating kalajosh, I would have accepted the larger plate Kokkur offered."

"If this lull of activity lasts, we'll have to do this again." Pushing my empty plate away, I summon the pen and paper.

The stillness of the large pavilion affords me the perfect opportunity to work out the kinks in the spell I'm composing for the demon lord.

The sun is behind the tree line, but it is still a couple of marks before setting as we start toward town. I pick up a couple of large stones on the way, acquiescing to Auricle's desire to carry them for me. Welcoming smoke billows from the chimney. A wonderful aroma emanates from the brightly lit main room. My stomach begins to rumble as I scrape the mud from my boots.

"We cats will hunt. Two will remain to guard the partners," Jesse sends before leading seven of his brethren into the forest.

"May you find plentiful game," I reply, reaching for the door.

"Milady." Ansil bows as I enter. "You have impeccable timing." I nod. Cuthburan's newest musician returns to his basting of the birds roasting on the spit.

My brows draw down in puzzlement. With the added musician, the room is quite full. Only Andrayia is missing from the guards. Mikaela hustles up beside me. "Milady, Ansil snared some grouse this morning. I invited him to prepare his bounty for the guards."

Ansil's fine-tuned ears miss not a word of what is said. "It is an honor to prepare my family's specialty for the Flame-Haired One and her guards."

I smile at his very political correction. "I hope you will be joining us?"

"These are large-boned birds, slimmed from winter." Ansil shrugs. "I wouldn't want to impose."

"It just so happens that I have a solution to that problem." Taking one of the stones from beside the door, I motion for Mikaela to follow with the other. I use the stoneware spell to transform the rocks into a deep platter and lid I am sure will hold not only the birds, but the roasting potatoes and carrots as well.

I turn to face those gathered. "As partner pairs, those of you gathered here will be privileged to know many things that will be kept from the rest of the world." I gesture toward the table. "This is the first of many secrets you will be required to keep."

In short, concise terms, I explain the properties of the enchanted dishware. Ansil proves his quick wit. "Milady, with one of these in every hamlet, none would fear famine ever again."

"Perhaps, but farmers make a living off growing crops. Too many of these about, and farmers would be destitute." I chew my lip, considering the idea further. "But I won't see innocents suffer either. I will think on this some more."

Wrinkling his nose, Ansil hustles to the hearth. "I believe the glaze has set. Rucela, if you will hold the platter?"

Villiblom reaches for the plates on the shelf. Mikaela retrieves a wooden box containing a set of three-pronged forks and knives. I move out of the way. Noticing the basin with fresh water, I go to wash my hands.

My stomach begins to rumble in earnest as the platter is placed on the table. Ansil does the honors, carving the birds with strong, sure strokes. My taste buds explode with joy at the tangy-sweet glaze on the fowl. "This is wonderful! Ansil, you are a man of many talents. Where did you find berries this time of year?"

The musician's cheeks brighten at the compliment. "These are winter's-harvest berries. They only sweeten with months of cold. Gisti has cultivated several bushes along the river."

When the last bird is sliced, I take the platter in two hands. I scrape the juice from the fowl and the bone scraps into the fireplace. Blue mist coalesces on the big plate. Before I can pivot back to the table, three new hens and all the trimmings are nestled on the platter.

"Which of you is brave enough to try magic-upped food?" I ask my dinner guests.

Auricle is the first to reach for the seconds. Five pairs of eyes are glued to her as she bites into the leg.

She grins at me. "Every bit as tasty as the last one."

"If Auricle will eat magic food. . ." Mikaela stabs a carrot with her fork. "It must be good." Four others join her.

"So how is Gisti disposed toward magic?" I ask Ansil as he cuts a hen in half.

"Can't really say, milady." He shrugs. "Like most in the village, he's never seen a sorcerer, much less anything magical."

I grunt. "Well, he's creative. Filling the need of the farmers speaks well of him. Is he an honest man? A fair man?" I push my plate from me. "A trustworthy man?"

"Of all the men in Skoguri, Gisti is the one I'd say you have most aptly described."

Refreshed by the evening meal, I call for my paper and pen. "I assume he can read?"

"Yes, milady."

Though the letters are slimmer with the modern tools, my Cuthburan words are clear and precise, thanks to the penmanship spell. It takes mere minutes to finish the missive, which I hand to Ansil. "Auricle can escort you to my quarters, where she will affix my seal. I trust the two of you to see that these instructions, along with the platter, are delivered to the inn once the Red Bed is vacated."

"Yes, milady," they reply in unison, echoing a feeling of pride at being chosen for such a mission.

"Ansil, per the instructions in the letter, I trust that you will see to the retrieval of the platter next summer." The musician nods. "I hope he will follow the directions to use the ensorcelled dish to supply those in and around Skoguri with necessary provisions to prevent famine."

"With the seal of the Flame-haired One?" Ansil smiles. "You can trust that he will."

"Hmm." I follow my train of thought to the end of the line. "Are Alex or Szames preparing compensation for the supplies used in the village?"

"Not that I have found, milady."

Horns blare into the night, summoning me to the first watch of the tower. Hastily I draw a handful of coins from the pocket in my robe. The money clinks into a pile on the table. "Make sure these are delivered to each household along with a note with my seal thanking the occupants for the use of their property."

"Yes, milady," they reply.

"Milady," Ansil says as I call for my staff, "there will be a gathering in the barn tonight. We would be honored by your presence."

Sensing no guile, I nod. "If my schedule allows," I reply, striding to the door.

The dry day has allowed the mud to stiffen. I don't squelch quite as much as I plod my way to the center of town. I spot Szames on the other tower. *Alex and Andrayia must be enjoying their freedom before their shift.*

The demons are few and far between. The moons are high in the sky as the trumpets blare into the night, announcing the changing of the shift. Soldiers move to replace their comrades, some of whom haven't even darkened their blades with demon blood.

A head pops over the edge of the tower. "Good eve, milady." Alex's smile takes my breath away. "The general informs me that it has been quieter than expected."

"So far, yes." I return his smile.

"If things change, Andrayia will send for you via Jesse." He dismisses me with a nod.

I march toward the mill, wincing at the thought of the cramped room. I turn to the guard shadowing me. "Make yourself comfortable. I will see to my mount."

"Did you feast well today?" I send as I stroke the soft fur.

"It is good to hunt with so many. We brought down three elk."

A purr rumbles from the cat as I continue to stroke with the brush. Jesse begins to doze as I caress him into sleep. With quiet steps, I ease into the night. Light emanating from an enormous building on the outskirts of the village catches my eye. That and the large silhouette of a statuesque form that could only be one of the princes piques my curiosity. Recalling Ansil's invite, I saunter in that direction.

"Pleasant night for a stroll," Szames greets, recognizing me even without my silver robe.

"Yes, quite. Any idea what's up in the barn?" I motion for him to continue in that direction.

"Only a hint from Ansil. He said I should pay the loft a visit." He extends an arm, offering a formal escort. "Care to join me?"

Faint music sprinkles the night as we draw close. Raucous laughter explodes from within. Szames reaches for the door. A hush falls over the men. Standing just inside the doorway is the newly christened bard. Into the surprised stillness, his voice sounds loud and sure.

"Come in and join us, if you'll be so bold, but a warning to you must first be told." He strums a chord in between each pair of lines. "All who enter leave rank at the door, all stand equal on this dirt floor. The price for entrance is the same to all: entertainment, as if at a royal ball."

"Hmm, entertainment is the price you ask?" Szames rubs his chin, pondering the demand as a crowd of eyes ogles us.

"I am open to requests." I look to the audience. Shouts greet the offer now that the men know we are game.

Ansil hands over his instrument as one request is shouted continually. *Of all things, a love song?* With spring budding all around, the perfect tune comes to mind.

"Some say love, it is a river
That drowns the tender reed.
Some say love, it is a razor
That leaves your soul to bleed.
Some say love, it is a hunger,
An endless aching need.
I say love, it is a flower,
And you its only seed."

I find a balance somewhere between Bette Midler and Conway Twitty, easing into my selection.

"It's the heart, afraid of breaking
That never learns to dance.
It's the dream, afraid of waking,
That never takes a chance.
It's the one who won't be taken
Who cannot seem to give.
And the soul, afraid of dying,
That never learns to live."

I use the country chords. The stringed instrument sends a haunting melody echoing into the night.

"When the night has been too lonely
And the road has been too long
And you think that love is only
For the lucky and the strong,
Just remember in the winter,
Far beneath the bitter snow,
Lies the seed that with the sun's love,
In the spring becomes the rose."[vi]

After a thunderous round of applause, I move to relinquish the guitar to Ansil, but again the crowd demands another love song.

"The populous has spoken." Seeing my blank expression, he whispers, "I believe you call it 'I Will Always Love You'?"

My lips twist wryly. "Well, this will need a little preparation." Nimble fingers unbraid my hair, shaking out the wavy locks. "Now I look a little more princesslike."

A hush falls over the men gathered as I set up the song with the standard introduction for those who haven't heard it before. As Ansil plays the guitar, my voice slips softly into the night.

> "You, my darling you.
> Bittersweet memories—that is all I'm taking with me.
> So good-bye. Please don't cry. We both know I'm not what you, you need.
> And I will always love you. I will always love you."

Into the silence of the first dramatic pause, a deep, surprisingly soft, operatic baritone voice rings out.

> "If I should stay, I would only be in your way.
> So I go but I know I'll think of you every step of the way.
> And I will always love you. I will always love you.
> You, my darling you."

Szames joins me, making this performance a duet. We gaze into each other's eyes, putting on a spectacular performance. In slow, measured steps, we approach the center of the room while Ansil plays a short interlude before my next verse.

> "I hope life treats you kind, and I hope you have all you dreamed of."

Standing only inches away, Szames takes the next line.

> "And I wish you joy and happiness, but above all this, I wish you love."

The intense gaze of his sapphire eyes holds me captive.

> "And I will always love you."

Unbidden emotion swirls within me. The words of reply come without thought.

> "I will always love you."

The room disappears. No one exists except the two of us as we continue exchanging phrases throughout the next stanza.

"And I will always love you. I will always love you.
And I will always love you. I will always love you.
And I will always love you. I will always love you."

The last line comes from Szames in a husky whisper.

"My darling, I will always love you."

Breathless, I am locked in place, held by the emotion revealed in his eyes. Seconds pass. A sound comes from the crowd, as if every man in the room remembers to breathe in the same instant. The crowd ruptures with acclamation, applauding wildly.

The raucous noise breaks the spell. Blushing, Szames looks away. I ignore the undercurrent of the duet, unwilling to face what it might mean.

"You've been holding back on me." My attempt to lighten the mood only increases the redness of his face. Hastily I add, "I never knew you could sing. That was awesome."

Szames finally manages a shrug. "I have not used my voice for anything but barking orders for so long, I was afraid I forgot how."

Ansil interjects, "Don't think for a minute that you're off the hook." The smile he gives turns the harsh-sounding demand into a ribbing joke. "You will need to perform solo if you plan on staying."

"If you can pluck that instrument as well as hold it, I think I can manage. What was it called? 'A Boy Named Sue'?" The voice that had been so warm and compassionate a minute ago turns rough and gravely.

One of the men gestures to a rain barrel and a pile of cups. I sip the tepid water. *I know what this party is missing.* The reason I suddenly feel the need for a drink never rises to the forefront of my mind.

I mumble under my breath, "Jesus did it at a party one night. Water to wine as I follow His light." I feel somewhat blasphemous as I pour the cup of water back into the barrel, watching the red liquid change the rest of the barrel to wine. I hold up a wooden cup, shouting wildly when Szames gets to the part "A-kickin' and a-gougin' in the mud, the blood, and the beer!"

More latecomers arrive, Jerik gives a great juggling performance with a pair of axes and another demonstrates what can only be called interesting acrobatics. The guitar is passed my way again. Putting down my second glass of wine, I decide to try a risqué song.

I pitch my worn-out voice as low as I can, strolling around the room. At the second chorus of another one of Cash's famous songs, Ansil joins me as the men hoot and holler.

"Lay ya down and softly whisper
pretty love words in your ear.
Lay ya down and tell ya all the things
a woman loves to hear.
I'll let you know how much it means
just having you around.
Oh, darlin', how I'd love to lay ya down."[vii]

The marks slip by, my voice growing hoarse from both cheering and singing. I merely sip the wine so I won't get too out of hand. *Man, I wish my exalted position didn't demand so much decorum.* Relaxing for the first time in weeks, the long days I've been pulling catch up with me. I make a polite exit, smothering a yawn. Slowly I work my way to the door.

Stepping into the crisp, night air, I take a deep breath, clearing the musty scent of sweating men from my nostrils. In the close confines of the barn, the human stench finally overpowered the dusty hay aroma.

A smile plays about the corner of my mouth when I hear Szames's voice at my shoulder. "The clouds have come to cloak us in gloom once more. I will escort you to your quarters, if I do not get us lost between here and there." *What kind of gentleman would he be if he let a woman walk at night unescorted?*

"Not a problem. I can see even in pitch black. Just follow my lead." With a hand on his arm, I guide our mist-shrouded walk.

"I know sorcerers have exceptional sight, but you can see that well?" Having imbibed more than a little himself, Szames tests me. "Tell me: What is that clump of shadows over there?"

Thunder rumbles overhead as I answer. "A bush, and next to it, a boulder."

Midway across the clearing, the sky looses its gathered treasure. Hail the size of marbles rains down. I take hold of Szames's hand, leading us in a mad dash for the nearest eaves. We struggle to remain upright as laughter overcomes us when our backs hit the wall.

"It looks like the weather is making up for the beautiful afternoon we had," I say, but with the hail beating on the wooden roof, Szames is unable to hear. I snag the shirt that, for once, is lacking a chain mail cover. I gesture for him to bend closer.

The hulking soldier turns as I stand on tiptoe to shout in his ear. Whatever I was going to say dies in my throat. Szames's eyes have the same intense gaze he wore during the duet.

The heat of his body beneath his shirt sets my palm on fire, absorbing my attention. Immobilized, I gaze into his eyes as the blond head ever so slowly leans forward. I close my eyes, lips tingling with anticipation. Flesh meets flesh.

Our lips brush in a feather-light caress. The contact makes me swoon. Passion surges through me. Leaning into each other's arms, our trembling mouths press together. Achingly slow, my lips part, inviting him inside. Through closed eyes, stars burst in dazzling colors, dancing before me. I swoon into his arms.

Tongues begin an intricate dance, along a roof, entwining together. Desire builds. Our bodies mold to one another. The hail ends, unnoted. Echoing in the silence, the sound of the barn door slamming open as another reveler retires for the night is loud enough to penetrate my consciousness.

It only takes the slightest pressure of my hand on his chest to break the steel embrace that captured me so tenderly. Gazing into those emotion-filled eyes reminds me of the letter I read weeks earlier.

Shaking my head in denial of what will be an impossible future, I take a step back. Unable to find the words to express the sensations tumbling inside, I turn, sprinting to my house.

The dwelling is blessedly quiet. Going to my room, I shed clothes along the way, intent on losing myself in the oblivion of sleep. I grab the silver robe to chuck it off the bed. A crinkling draws my focus away from those azure eyes and the ruffled mop of straw-colored hair filling my mind's eye. My hand steals inside the satiny pocket.

"Light." A flame appears, lighting the wick next to the bed. I reread Crystal's final message once again.

"It can't be." My teeth grind in frustration. "He won't. . ." Silent tears trace paths down my cheeks. "We can't!"

Angrily I wipe the offending moisture away. "He will never be faithful. How could he be?"

My hand streaks toward the light source. The parchment catches easily, the flames consuming the entire document in seconds. The words disappear. Only ash remains. But my perfect memory replays the lines over and over as I toss and turn throughout the stormy night.

Chapter Twenty-one

Rubbing gunk from my eyes, I wake to the homey sound of a noisy kitchen. My perfect memory brings to mind last night's events. The situation with Szames takes on nightmarish proportions. Putting on fresh clothes, I run a quick pick through my hair. My hand snakes out to grab my robe before I rush into the next room.

"Milady, thought a real breakfast might be nice for a change. Found some eggs out in the chicken coop." I wince in the light of Mikaela's cheerfulness.

Reluctantly I sit at the table. The food has no taste as I shovel it in as quickly as I can swallow it.

"You got in pretty late last night for someone who was on the first platoon." Mikaela gives a wink across the table.

"Ansil threw quite a party in the barn last night." *Did she see the love song?*

The guard shrugs. "It was a real foot stomper, from what I hear. Prince Alexandros called us to the tower. He had half the Guard patrolling the perimeter and the other half guarding the towers on the shifts you were absent." The redhead pauses to glower at the air between us. "I don't know how he managed to convince us that we would be protecting you better by protecting the camp. I apologize for the lapse, milady."

"You women swore to stand beside me in this war. If I'm not in a battle, I can take care of myself."

"I will discuss that with the other guards." Mikaela nods but reserves her judgment.

I think I liked it better when they feared me. At least then they did what I told them to! Finishing breakfast in record time, I hurry out under the guise of grooming Jesse before Mikaela can probe any deeper about last night's late entrance.

"Your mind scrambles like a month-old kitten chasing a moth," Jesse sends as I stroke his glossy coat.

I glance at the shadows in the mill where the other partners lounge. "Feel up to a little scouting this morning?"

A rumbling purr proclaims his agreement. Silence echoes while I saddle the cat. Concentrating on the task at hand relieves the stress of the situation for the moment. Throwing a leg over my mount, I heave a sigh as Jesse's long strides carry us beyond the camp boundaries.

I give the cat his head, dropping the reins while I try to organize the thoughts rumbling around inside my skull. Looking up, I notice a meadow where the long grasses will provide a comfortable napping place for my mount. Having nowhere else to turn, I broach the worrisome topic with my ebony companion.

"Jesse, what am I going to do? I've made a huge mess of things."

"Why not just tell him of your suspicions?" My partner gives a detached reply.

Frustrated with his arrogant mindset, I lapse into audible speech. "You don't know men at all. The quickest way to scare one off or destroy a friendship is to go too fast, be too open. I've made that mistake more than once."

"Perhaps this situation is different from the others," Jesse sends as I slide off his back.

My voice increases in volume as I proclaim out loud what I have feared for weeks. "I'm just supposed to go up to a prince in the land, that I am now a permanent resident in, and say, 'I think that we're true mates. You know, life-bonded, meant to be together for the rest of our lives, incomplete without each other'?" With a despondent head shake, I mutter, "What could he possibly say?"

"Why not try me and find out?" An all-too-familiar baritone echoes into the still meadow.

"Szames?" I squeak. I jab a thought at my partner, *Traitor! I trusted you. You didn't even warn me he was here?"* If I could scream mentally, Jesse's eardrums would be ringing.

Clearing my throat, I smother the dread tying my stomach in knots. "How. . . ?" I am forced to evacuate the frog from my throat again. "How long have you been here?"

"Long enough." Sliding off of Tawny, Szames gives a strange half smile. "I don't know what part Jesse played, but I was lost in contemplation until I heard your voice ring out."

I turn from him, knowing my cheeks must be bright red. "I should've never taught them that silent approach." I joke to cover nervousness.

My amber eyes lock on the ground, seeing nothing. Stoically, I keep the trembling out of my voice as I try to evade the coming confrontation. "Look, Szames, just forget whatever you heard. That was a private conversation between partners."

Dry, winter grass crunches underfoot as Szames steps closer. "And what if I can't do that?" he queries softly.

I still refuse to look anywhere but at the ground. Muscles become taut as guitar strings as my hands clench into fists. I glare defiantly at the cat lounging mere yards from me, delicately licking his paw. "There is no other choice. We have to put what happened last night—and today—out of our thoughts."

Forcing myself to relax, my eyes search the forest beyond the meadow as I patiently explain the facts of love to the naive prince. "I know you are attracted to me, and now you also know I'm attracted to you. But it changes nothing. I won't destroy our friendship for sexual gratification. You don't really know me. I've only been here, what, a few months? And what's more, you have no idea what it takes to hold to a lifelong commitment. I do. It takes a heck of a lot of work."

A note of despair creeps into my voice. "Believe me, your world is not set up for that kind of thing. For the sake of our friendship, I beg you, ignore everything you've heard."

With unusual stubbornness, Szames persists. "Only if you tell me you were not talking about us. That you do not mean what you are asking me to forget."

Unable to lie, even to save a friendship, my eyes dart down to my shoes. I mutter, "Now you ask something I can't do."

The sound of footfalls is as loud as crackling thunder. My legs shake. I refuse to run from a fight. I lock my knees to keep myself upright. Szames's approach seems to take hours. When he speaks, his voice is right behind me, barely above a whisper. "Then I am forced to respond to what I now know."

Panic sets in. My heartbeat thunders in my ears. I am paralyzed beyond the ability to move.

"I am a prince, a man who has everything. Yet I have always felt there is something more out there. . . something more to life, something more to love. I seem to love more strongly than those I know. When I attempt to give that love to another, it overwhelms them. At first, I figured it meant I was to love more than just one, but that never worked. It left me unfulfilled."

A pair of massive hands cups my shoulders. "When you first looked up at me as you knelt, giving your pledge, I knew I found what was missing. A light flared to life in a corner of my heart, a part of my heart I thought long dead. Every minute I have spent in your presence has only made that flame stronger, brighter, and harder to ignore."

Gently Szames turns me to face him. With the crook of a finger, he lifts my chin so I have no choice but to look him in the eyes. "At first it might have been mostly lust, but, Reba, can you not perceive it?" In a husky whisper, he adds, "More than I can ever say."

My eyes open with surprise. I can feel him more clearly than I have ever felt anything. *He does care; he cares deeply. . . for me!* "Szames. . . I do sense you. . . But how?" I sputter.

"I did not know what to call it until you gave me a word for it. I have an empathetic gift. As a teen, I discovered I could sense intense emotions. With a touch, I could feel all emotion. I learned to shield early on. I usually do unless it is an intimate situation. Do you not see? I have known you from the first time you took my hand."

Looking deep into my eyes, Szames whispers, "I am sorry I have kept it from you for so long. I feared if I let on about my shielding, you would find out. . . *I love you.*"

Again I am shocked into stillness, mentally as well as physically. I heard his unspoken confession. Not only the words, but also the fire of the devotion behind them. The silence deepens. Realization dawns: he is waiting for a response.

With a mischievous twinkle in my eyes and a cocky smile, I slide my hands up his arms, lacing fingers behind his neck. Sharing his arousal makes my smile broaden as well as increasing my excitement.

"You know, I have always kind of known what a man was feeling, but I've never been with anyone who could feel what I'm feeling. Nor have I ever been able to substantially feel what a man does." *This could be quite interesting.*

Szames strokes my hair, easing the last bit of tension from me and heightening my arousal. "Interesting doesn't even begin to describe it. I expect it to be an experience like none other."

"If you'd shut up and kiss me, we could both find out." I pull him toward me with the seductive whisper. He chuckles internally at the mock impatience in my voice, my forwardness fueling his flame.

As expectant as if we have never kissed, we draw together. Lips touch, feather light. Slowly his part. I slide my tongue inside. I am unprepared for the intense reaction it causes as his heart beats faster and his temperature rises. A fire like none I've known envelopes me. Passion raging into an inferno sweeps through my senses, cascading in waves, tingling every nerve. My body is alive with a suddenness that is overpowering in intensity. I lose myself in emotions so alive a kaleidoscope of colors whirls about me, making our previous experience seem like a night's sky disappearing into the brilliance of the morning's sunrise.

When I begin to swoon, Szames brings me into his arms. Our bodies press together. Patience evaporates as desire multiplies exponentially. Quickly I find I have reached the limit of my control.

I barely manage enough restraint to end the kiss gracefully, not pulling out wet and sloppy. Panting, I reach for the tunic covering his mail. "This has got to come off. And I mean now." My growl is low and sultry.

"Could it be? Is it my turn to teach you something about magic?" Receiving a blank look, Szames adds, "This is going to be much more enjoyable if you do this. . ."

Threading my fingers through his, Szames closes his eyes. Reluctantly I close mine as well, concentrating on sharing his emotions.

I sense his lust raging as strong and as uncontrollable as my own, maybe even more so. Then with inhuman willpower, he grips the blazing desire. Szames restrains his passion without diminishing it. Binding it in shackles stronger than steel, he tames the beast.

Following his example, I embrace what I think of as overpowering. Through sheer force of will, I surround it, taming the raging lust. I can now form a coherent thought.

"I've known that you've wanted me for a while. Is this how you survived all these weeks?"

"I have pushed skills I have worked my entire life to master to the limit." Brushing my cheek gently, he adds, "You needed time."

In unspoken communication, we unsaddle our mounts and spread the saddle blankets on the meadow floor. Gliding across the carpet of grass, our eyes lock as we drink in the shared feelings. Slowly, hands moving inch by inch, we explore the bodies of our true mates, reveling in the sensations we invoke.

With exquisite slowness, clothes are shed, piece by excruciating piece. My skin becomes so attuned to his touch, the lightest caress sends shivers clear to my toes. When our lips come together once more, passion makes the embraces forceful, urgent.

United in body and spirit, we ascend to the pinnacle of ecstasy. The redoubled pleasure makes my palms tingle then turn numb. Then the world dims around the edges as Szames collapses on top of my limp form.

"Are you all right?" Worry colors Szames's voice.

"Oh yeah! More than all right." I send to him thoughts of my intense pleasure.

"I have never done that to a woman before, made her feel so much," he mumbles, moving me to rest on top of him.

"And no man has made me lose consciousness before." Sweaty, exhausted, and completely fulfilled, we doze, wrapped in each other's arms.

Almost a mark later, I move to retrieve my robe. Szames stirs as I pull it over us.

"My love, are you cold?" His hands tenderly caress my body. "Please tell me I am not dreaming, that you, my goddess, are here with me."

"Surreal like a dream, but real, I assure you."

Szames chuckles. "You continue to amaze me. . ." His sentence trails off as a blank look envelopes my countenance while my mind is redirected to my telepathic ability.

"Reba. . ." A rumbling echoes in the mind-voice like a gravelly chortle. *"I don't mean to interrupt but duty calls. The scouts are back. It's bad news. Alex is preparing the troops for immediate departure."*

"Trouble?" Sensing the abrupt change, Szames moves to retrieve our clothing.

"We are mobilizing."

We dress in a rush. When I enter his arms for a final embrace, a cold shiver works its way down my spine. "God, I wish we didn't have to go. I have a really bad feeling about this."

"You do, don't you?" Pushing me back, Szames gazes into my eyes. "Just promise me one thing?"

Waiting for my promising nod, he says the last thing I ever expected to pass his lips. "If anything should happen to me—if I do not make it through this war—marry Alex. Fulfill the prophecy."

"I will promise no such thing!" My anger dies as I sense the pain it caused him to ask. Discerning the dedication he has, the duty pushing him to make sure I comply, I sigh. "Fine, have it your way. You have my word. But I am not going to let you die!" As the words leave my mouth, a chill of premonition makes me shiver.

In a flash of white, the woods around me bend and change. An aerial view shows a group of soldiers surrounding a prostrate form. As I swoop downward, I recognize the blond hunk that I swore my allegiance to. Another flash brings me back to reality.

Fighting tears, I mount. *I lost Charles; I won't lose him too. I can't!* I wipe tears from my eyes, grateful that Szames is preoccupied with needs of the army. *I have the full premonition. I will change our destiny.* My jaw clenches in determination as I mount Jesse.

The camp is in a state of organized confusion. Szames dismounts. Striding to my side, he holds me tenderly, grazing my lips with a brief kiss before we hasten to the door to Alex's commandeered accommodations. Fear shadows us. Our tryst has ended with a foreboding haste.

Chapter Twenty-two

"You two finally decide to join us?" Alone in the room, Alex has no qualms about berating us.

"We came as quickly as we were able." Szames's defenses spring into place.

"Yes, I see that." Alex looks askance at our disheveled state. Walking past the general on the way to the table, he whispers, "Just remember, Brother, in the end she will wind up mine. They always do."

My acute hearing picks up every syllable. I place a restraining hand on my lover's arm as his hands clench into fists. *"Let me deal with this. I'm going to have to sooner or later,"* I send to him.

"You think so, do you?" I saunter toward Alex, my hips swaying. "You're so sure of that prophecy of yours?"

"Of that and myself. No woman has ever been able to resist me." Alex turns toward me, stopping when he is within arm's reach. "I always win."

As the words are whispered the crown prince exerts compulsion over me, making my head swim with unyielding passion. Using the technique Szames revealed, I clamp the force of my will around the pulsating desire he invokes. Like an iron band, I restrain the impulse to melt into his arms.

Moving closer to Alex, I halt when mere inches separate our noses. My voice is a fierce whisper. "If you ever touch me with your power, try to bend me to your will to do your bidding, I will put a curse on you so fast, your head will spin. I will curse your manhood so it will fail to rise in the presence of anyone your aura has ever touched."

Alex's eyes pop open. He takes an involuntary step back. "You dare to threaten the monarchy you have pledged to protect!"

"I am, indeed, upholding my word. I have promised to protect this kingdom and this monarchy. That includes protecting you from yourself, from morally corrupting the integrity of this sovereignty." I take a deep, steadying breath, leveling my gaze like a scolding mother. "And, Alex, it's not a threat; I have given you my solemn word, and I will keep it.

"To use a gift for personal gain which is purely self-gratification it's. . . it is an act so despicable it borders on evil. What kind of man are you to need such a thing to persuade women to your bed? You're lucky I don't spell that roaming cock of yours right now."

Releasing the resentment I have carried, the anger at his insincere flattery and his continued manipulation all these months, I growl, "If I catch you abusing it again, I just might, you spoiled brat of an excuse for a royal prince."

Into the shocked quietness of the room, the opening door is thunderous. Looking from me to Alex, Andrayia asks, "Is something amiss?"

I look pointedly at Alex, who gives a slight nod. "No, my love. Just finishing up some old business."

Szames wears a tight smile as he joins us at the table. "We are mobilizing. How far can we get in only half a day? What news could be so grave as to warrant this action?"

"The cavalry returned. The supply wagons were attacked with a force strong enough to shatter the shield stones they used. There was not enough left of the soldiers to identify the lost. I fear for the safety of the castle. We will return with all haste, departing as soon as you gather your things." Alex eyes never leave the map on the table in front of him.

"Is that advisable?" Szames questions. "The attack on the supply wagon could be a ploy to draw us into the open."

"Perhaps it is a ploy, but as it is, Reba is going to have to augment our supplies." Stubbornness born out of unaccustomed defeat colors his eyes when he brings them up. "My orders stand. We leave now."

I hold tight to Jesse as he leaps the stream. I dash into the mill. The minutes it takes to reassure myself that the Guard has taken care of all my things may be minutes Castle Eldrich doesn't have. By the time I am remounted, the army is ready to march.

"Reba and I should take point. Our scouts' advanced abilities will lessen the chances we will be surprised by ambush." Frost claws its way into my heart as Alex agrees to Szames's suggestion.

I shake off Fate's warning, determined to prevent the vision my intuition granted. My lover's lips curve in a goofy smile as we lope ahead. Fear vaporizes faster than dry ice in a boiling pot.

"Andrayia sends via Heather, 'What happened with Alex? He hasn't said three words since we broke camp?'" Jesse portrays frustration and confusion with the question.

"Hmm. Just tell her I'm sure that he will be crying on her shoulder about the evilness of the sorceress witch as soon as his wounded pride is healed." I evade disclosing any particulars, leaving it up to Alex to reveal what he will of the confrontation.

"News from the column?" The smile hasn't left Szames's face since our earlier rendezvous. "You don't feel upset by it."

"Andrayia is worried about Alex." I give him a devilish look. "I told her that he'll be complaining about me as soon as pride will allow."

"I am not so sure. Alex does not handle defeat well. If he confesses to her, it will be a good indication of his next move, whether he has decided he is beaten or whether he is considering this a temporary setback." Szames chuckles. "It has been a long time since he has been routed and never on his chosen ground: the field of love."

"I wouldn't call his pursuit 'love,' more like lust and vanity!" Looking across at the blond hunk, my lips twitch with anticipation.

His smile turns to a leer. "Now don't start thinking along those lines. If we pause long enough to embrace, I might not be able to stop." Tawny moves closer to Jesse. "But a quick one we might be able to get away with."

His promise of a quickie stirs passion in my loins.

"A quick kiss, that is," Szames amends. The world and its worries melt away as our flesh meets.

Jesse growls, tweaking his hindquarters to bounce me slightly. He launches into a mental lecture. *"We are scouting for a war that may decide the fate of both our species. . ."* He continues but I ignore the nagging, luxuriating in the feel of the heightening excitement of my lover. When our mounts carry us so far apart, we are in danger of falling out of our saddles, reluctantly we part.

"All right, all right already. We'll keep alert. Yes. We are in the middle of a war and we are scouting." I take the defeat almost a badly as Alex.

Looking around, I am shocked to see fog surrounding us.

"I told you so," from Jesse.

I whisper, "Sight." *Red tinged?*

"This weather isn't natural. It could be the trap you were worried about." No sooner are the words out of my mouth than a metallic ringing fills the air as Szames's sword clears the sheath.

"Tawny, send for half of the Royal Guard," Szames orders.

Both cats pause as the fog thickens until we can't see more than a few feet in any direction.

"Jesse, can you see?"

"Sight's not the problem. I could find my way with my eyes closed," Jesse replies to my inquiry. *"Tawny can't contact the others, even when I join with her, we can't get our thoughts to penetrate this unnatural fog."*

"But we can mind speak. Maybe if I join with you." It takes seconds to interlink our powers.

"It is no use." Irritation colors Jesse's tone. "We cannot penetrate this magical barrier. We must be able to communicate because there is no fog between us when we touch."

Let us turn back. We will find a way around it," Szames decrees, picking up on Jesse's broadcast.

Both mounts do a one-eighty, retreating out of the demon fog. Demons, concealed by the crimson fog, leap at me. A scream tears from my throat as Szames pitches forward in his saddle. Wielding my stave, I topple one beast with a blow to the head.

"Hold! Or the prince dies." The oily thoughts penetrate my mind with a sharp, stabbing pain. *"Follow the ones sent to you, or his life is forfeit."*

My lips twist into a snarl as I drop my staff. Realizing they will most likely kill him anyway, still, I'm unwilling to be responsible for the death of my soul mate. A scheme takes form in the seconds it takes to release the weapon.

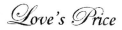

I send a thin tendril of thought to my partner as I slide slowly off his back. *"Jesse, I need you to put an illusion on my hair; make it look plain red."*

Another thought slices its way into my mind as Jesse's minor spell is cast. *"No magic. I am watching."*

"He was just releasin' me," I whine to no one in particular.

To my relief, the demon with the knife at Szames's throat follows, leaving the prince slumped in Tawny's saddle. I stumble along with the monsters that ambushed us. Losing myself in concentration, I try to reach through the mist to find Jerik. Bumbling to the ground after tripping over a root, I cuss loudly, compressing my lips into a grimace to hide a smile.

Sensing a malignity of gigantic proportions ahead, I begin recalling memories, shrouding myself in the past. A gate blazing bright crimson towers ahead. *No wonder we couldn't scry for the gate! This fog keeps all magic out, even telepathy.*

Men and demons part as I approach. More than a hundred soldiers and scores of demons ring the small clearing I am forced to enter. At the opposite edge of the meadow, a tree has fallen, leaning against a neighbor. An old, rotting log on the ground provides the third edge of a triangle, a permanent link for the dimensional doorway. Magic surrounds each piece of wood, forming a twenty-foot portal to the demons' world.

My feet stagger to a lumbering halt after crossing a little more than half the concealed glade. I stare ahead, transfixed by a sight so grotesque, it is all I can do to keep from pulling the blades from my boots and fighting my way free of this meadow. My legs tremble until my knees shake so badly I collapse to the ground.

The short, skinny man standing apart from the soldiers must be Gaakobah of Dunmore. He has thinning, blond hair and narrow shoulders, but more than that I can't make out. A haze surrounds him, and his head is swollen as if he has been through ten rounds with Mike Tyson. The eyes of the sorcerer glow a demonic crimson. A slimy, red tendril connects him to the sight keeping me on my knees.

Bulging against the constricting gate is the demon lord—mankind's true threat. It is the epitome of evil. Black hair bristles in patches on the slick hide. A cavernous mouth filled with fangs gapes in a silent laugh. The horned monstrosity fills every inch of the doorway. A white outline surrounds the luminous gate, intertwining with the demon's scarlet glow. The god of this land, Andskoti, uses his might to prevent his adversary from entering his domain.

"The feared Flame-haired One, groveling at my feet." The voice issuing from Gaaki has a booming, rumbling quality to it that no human throat is able to utter.

"But I'm not the arch-m-m-mage," I stutter in a high, wispy voice, giving in to my fear, letting emotion have full reign over me.

"Oh, that's good," the monstrosity bellows while a grating laugh tumbles from Gaaki's lips. "All right. I will play. If you are not Reba, then who are you?"

"I-I'm Becca, a twin sister that looks identical to her. . . nearly."

As the demon rolls with guffawing chortles, I slowly push back my hood, revealing Jesse's illusion.

The demon lord's laughter dies as I bend my red head in supplication. "Reba says being a mage allows her to tell when someone's lying to her. Can't you see? I am a twin."

"You look so similar. . . your aura. . . yet you commit no falsehood." The monster roars with fury. "You have magic, do you not? You ride her creature, use her staff. You dare to try and deceive me!"

I fall backward, scuttling on all fours as Gaaki's face turns molten.

"A-as you saw, t-the feline had to release me. That s-staff she gave to me, it wields itself. I do ha-ave magic, kind of." As the possessed man begins to listen, my voice gains strength. "But Reba's forbidden me to use it. She says it's dangerous."

"Forbidden magic?" Unable to conceal the demon's powerful emotions, lecherous cunning consumes the rogue sorcerer's countenance as he licks his lips as if anticipating a delectable treat. "Tell me of these powers, and perhaps I will let you live."

"I'm a performer. I entertain the men, keep the morale up." I shrug. "Reba made me stop. Sometimes. . . well." I look at my boots, shuffling like a scolded child. "I make men lose control. She said they might hurt me."

"Oh, now this." The possessed man giggles dementedly, his sanity hanging by a thread. "This is priceless. My grand trap sprung to catch. . . what? A thespian?"

"More than just a performer!" Petulantly I stomp a foot. "I can make any man desire me!" I chew the edge of my lower lip. "Any man attracted to women, that is."

"Well, perhaps we might get some use out of you yet, girl." The crimson light dies, and blue eyes can be seen. "You like girls, do you not, Gaaki?"

The released sorcerer nods with a vicious leer.

As scarlet dominates his eyes again, the demon wets his lips. "Feeling Gaaki's stimulation could be a worthwhile experience."

With a timid look at the gang of clamoring men who edge the clearing, my soprano voice trembles. "You won't let them h-hurt me?"

"You have my word." A sadistic grin appears.

A demon's word. Guess that's as good as I'm gonna get. My lips tremble as I whine. "I've gotta use my magic."

"I will watch your every move." In an instant the monster's mood oscillates. "You attempt anything but entertainment, and I will vaporize you where you stand."

"It is a harmless spell." I explain a portion of the enchantment I concocted on the stumbling trip there. "With your power, you can see, it will let the men hear and understand the music I use. It adds to their stimulation and changes my clothes."

As I flatter him, Gaaki's distorted face turns smug. "Proceed."

I choose the most obscure English words I could find. *I hope he understands as little English as Merithin.* In a measured beat, I begin the mantra.

"Powers surround and enthrall,
Sending out a true siren's call.
Words and concepts to understand,
Irresistible to any human man.

Proper clothes I'll also need,
Tight and sexy, alluring indeed.
And line the ground with linoleum
To be the center of the pendulum."

Feeling a hidden confusion from my captor, I release the necessary energy. A bright light flashes out from me, dazzling the eyes of men and beasts. *I hope the army has come within earshot! The partners should be if nothing else.*

The menacing growl coming from the demon lord dies as he finds me still positioned in the center of the meadow. "All that energy for recreation?"

A full quarter of my power has been drained. Smothering fear, I smile coyly. "It's what I do." With those words and a focusing of thought, music blares into the surrounding forest.

Men cringe at the sudden raucous noise, but as I drop my robe, I gain their complete attention. Tight-fitting jeans and low-cut shirt hug my body. The clothes are much more revealing than what this society is used to seeing. "Trouble" is spelled out in the song.

I smile, endeavoring to lose myself in the music as I once did while waitressing my way through college. The swiveling hips, shoulder shakes, and fancy footwork have men hooting and hollering before the song is half over. The gyrations that got me an offer to work at one of the hottest strip clubs in Phoenix have a universal effect on men. Feeling as if I have used a septic tank for a bathtub, I snap an empathy shield in place to block out the degrading lust broadcast from the soldiers. Perspiration glistens on my skin as quiet echoes throughout the meadow.

"Intriguing." Gaaki brings his hands together in a slow rhythm. "But hardly irresistible? Perhaps I will kill you. My nemesis may disappear with your destruction."

"Honey, did I say I was finished?" True fear emboldens my words as I arch an eyebrow. "I was just getting warmed up." Pausing as if unsure, I inquire, "You will protect me?"

The monstrosity gives a bored nod. The meadow blazes with magic once again as I chant. When the light returns to normal, my energy is down by a third. A chair sits in the center of the floor. Now I am wearing camouflage hose with garters, matching underwear, and an oversized army jacket. Nothing else. *Lord forgive me for what I do.*

Ivory legs folded under me, I sit on my knees, ignoring the chair that is nothing more than a prop. The subtle tone begins. I languish backward. The jacket separates a few inches when my back touches the ground, revealing the bare skin beneath.

Hands slink over my auburn tresses as faint organ music teases its way into the darkening meadows, proclaiming the opening of the song.

A rhythmic, pulsating subbeat entwines itself into the music like mounting, lusty desire. Slowly I move my hands up and down my body, revealing my breasts to the night. Wild jungle sounds, chanting grunts of native passions, begin as I spread my knees, raising my pelvis as if inviting a man inside.

Enigma continues the sultry song as I begin a slinky crawl toward the closest man, eyes aflame with desire. I pin the soldier in place with my gaze. Like a gymnast, my body is held inches from the ground while I ease my feet apart. My improved agility adds to the strip tease I preformed years ago for my husband. I arch my back, straightening my torso above open thighs, a look of ecstasy plastered on my face by sheer force of will. My slender hands thrust the jacket from my shoulders then continue to roam my body as I lose myself in memories of the past, seeing nothing but my husband standing before me.

"Loneliness. . . loneliness in my room."

A blast of red takes the soldier in front of me down as the man reaches for my breast.

Flinching, I step around the fallen body, pivoting on one foot. Swallowing the vomit rising up my throat, I lock my knees and bend over, presenting a firm rear end to the next group of men. Some of the faces are grotesquely distorted, signaling they are demon possessed, but it makes no difference. Despite the fate of their comrade, the soldiers are captivated as I run hands up the long length of my legs. By the time I release the hose and remove the first garter, several more men lay dead. *At this rate I won't need the rest of the army. . .*

The sarcastic thought helps me make it through the next stanza. As the beat picks up, I am back to shoulder shakes, this time bare breasted. Refusing to give up my undies, I peer into the crowd, desperation growing with each beat of the music. Finally, I spot what I have been waiting for: Men in Cuthburan blue and silver livery are sprinkled throughout the throng. The siren's call has brought every member of the Cuthburan army to me.

Under my breath, I chant the second spell I cast after entering this world with a slight modification.

"I'm calling a time-out as anyone would,
Using my magic, as you know I should.
Time will pass slowly for everyone but me.
Until I count, one two and three.

Like the guy with the watch in the movie I've seen,
I need some help from the rest of the team.
So with a quick touch, unfreeze them I will.
That way they can help me, this demon to kill."

My trap slams shut. All the demons, including the lord himself are so enthralled by the dance, they fail to notice the time spell until it has them suspended. In a few quick strides, I am able to touch the blond head standing inches above the rest.

"'Bout time you got here."

Szames's eyes open wide, looking me up and down. A few mumbled words call my robe and fighting clothes back.

"Y-you. . ." he stutters pushing his way out of the crowd. "You mean that was real? Jamison had just brought me around when I heard the music and saw. . . I thought I'd slipped back into the dream world."

"I could think of no other way to bring you to me." I retrieve my staff from his secure grasp. I stare at his chest, unable to meet his eyes. "Szames, will you ever forgive me?"

"Only if you promise to give me a private demonstration of that dance of yours." Szames leers.

Looking up into his twinkling eyes, I smile. "You've got yourself a deal!" My smile slips. "But what about the men? Will they ever respect me again?"

"Probably not." Szames picks up my chin with a finger. "Most likely they believe they have experienced a marvelous dream. Their hearts will be forever yours, as is mine."

The honesty of the spoken words provides the reassurance I need. "Looks like this little trick of mine is working out better than I planned. With their support, I have all the leverage I need against your brother and the council. Speaking of which, where's Alex? We need his help."

Szames's complexion reddens. "When the music sounded around us, the vision you spun was so engaging, I had no sense of my surroundings. My only thought was to follow and get to you."

We search the area, quickly locating the lost prince. When Alex joins us in the meadow, he turns beet red as his eyes meet mine. "Pleasant dreams?" I inquire.

Alex clears his throat, looking anywhere but at the siren who has called him. "I suppose you had something to do with that bewitching? If it had not been for Jerik's reassurance, I would have fought it tooth and nail."

"I'm glad you made it. I've used too much of my power getting you all here. I will not take power from you. It will drain your strength too quickly. Both my life and your brother's could very well be in your hands before this battle is done." I take a few minutes to sort my thoughts while the guys position themselves behind me.

"If you two are ready." The princes nod, one to either side of me. *"Szames, because of our close link, I don't have to touch you, but as I pull energy, you'll feel the effect."*

"Do not fret, my love. I will be careful." The mental caress he sends makes me want to melt into his strong embrace.

"One, two, and three," I declare. "Multiphase shield." Three layers of azure light surround the royal protectors and me.

The demon roars. A volley of ruby spheres smashes into the barrier seconds after it is erected.

Noting the shields are holding steady, I ignore his attack, concentrating on the incantation I have been preparing for weeks.

> "Imprisoned tightly in shackles of steel,
> Defying gravity through the atmosphere.
> With this spell I now weave,
> Into space you are heaved."

The spell rhymes as badly as some country songs, but still, magic surges from me. The gate expands as Andskoti releases gate that had held the demon lord captive The monstrosity bellows its confusion as magic winds about it. Unable to understand the modern litany, it is powerless to counteract the spell. Another bellow escapes the beast as it is lifted into the air, streaking away from the meadow.

"Rocket boosted by magic you'll fly,
Far from this place, up into the sky.
To the cornea of the sun you will go,
Streaking through the heavens to give us a show."

Only the technical knowledge of what NASA can do allows this mantra to take full effect. The idea behind the enchantment is too complex for the minds of this age to comprehend. With an outstretched arm, energy flows from my hand. The beast hurtles toward the flaming orb the planet circles. Power pours from me. *I have to get it past the atmosphere.*

The battle rages on around me as I drop the depleted staff. I sense the heat of the sun blistering the oily, black skin. I collapse to my knees adding more force to the spell. A flash of insight brings the earlier vision to the forefront of my mind. Szames's aura is dim, nearly drained of power. I break the connection, unwilling to endanger his life.

Giving one final blast of energy, I send the demon lord into the pulsing daystar. My hand falls limply into my lap. Blackness crowds my vision as a human throat utters a cry of despair. *Gaaki's connection to his lord has been severed. The demon lord is dead!*

The glowing energy surrounding the gate begins to shimmer then boil. With a cry of pain the rogue sorcerer collapses to one knee as the magical energy entwining the gate shatters.

"You deceiving witch!" Gaaki slides a knife from his sleeve. In one swift move, he hurls it toward my head.

Moving to evade the attack will take more energy than I possess. I watch helplessly, fighting to maintain consciousness.

The rogue sorcerer draws a second blade as I am knocked to the ground, a painful grunt sounding beside me. Through the fading light, from either dimming vision or the approaching night, I see Nemandi draw a knife of his own. His aim is true. Gaaki falls limply to the ground, the priest's blade buried to the hilt in his eye socket.

"May Andskoti forgive you for your sins," the thief-turned-clergyman's prayer is uttered into a profound silence. The invading army scatters in all directions. A few of the faces of the men return to normal: they throw down their weapons, sitting on the ground as if in a daze. With both their sorcerer and the demon lord destroyed, there is little reason for the enemy to continue the fight.

Unable to hold on to consciousness any longer, my eyes slide shut.

Chapter Twenty-three

"Cloak." The whisper activates the spell I based on Klingon technology. Everything on my person shimmers then disappears. Reassured I won't be interrupted, I wander into the blossoming garden under the light of two of the moons.

I can't believe it's been weeks since the gateway battle. Seems like it happened yesterday. Lost in the twisting paths of my mind, contemplating the moral dilemma I cannot find an answer to, the fragrant aroma of a purple rosebush with white bordering the petals draws me as a bee to honey. *Such vibrant colors. Szames was right; it's like being surrounded by jewels.* At the thought of the hunky prince, moisture gathers in my eyes.

"I will talk to Reba. Maybe she can talk to your father." The mention of my name causes me to swivel around.

"Jamison, this is not an issue that involves Cuthburan's arcane adviser." Tenderly Rose caresses the healer's face. "You knew as well as I that this day would come."

The silence expands between them. Jamison takes his love in his arms so she won't see the tears gathering in his eyes. *Doggone the royals' love of decorative rocks. If I move back to the path, they'll hear me.*

"I leave at the end of summer for Tuvarnava. Tell me, Jamie: Do you regret the decision we made?" Rose whispers, "Do you regret living each day for love, knowing I must marry another so soon?"

"I could never regret loving you, Rose, not for a single, solitary moment."

My eyes spill over with tears as the world flashes white around me. I blink rapidly to clear the spots as the crisp sun dazzles my vision. I hover over the group of travelers making their way through a pass so rugged, not even weeds dare to sprout. Senses reeling, I am drawn into my body, experiencing the vision with the fullness of my senses.

Jamison swings down off of Tawny's back as I dismount from Jesse. The cats spring up the mountain slope, sniffing about as they bound away.

"Don't get too comfortable; something isn't right about this place," Jesse sends as he disappears among the rocks.

I open my empathy wide, feeling for any malignant emotion.

Jerik lets out a huff, hunkering down on a rock to rummage through the massive pack he swings off his back. "Knew you'd count on poofing us up some grub, but there's nothing like a real hunk of bread and cheese from the cook."

"You can gnaw on that three-day-old bread if you like." Taking a small emerald from my pocket, I grab a nearby stone. "But I'll take some fresh from the oven, thanks very much." I mumble, "Basic lunch," under my breath as the rock sits atop the gem. The key word sets off a chain reaction. The stone melts and bends, turning into a stoneware platter. The air shimmers. Like a desert mirage come to life, the bread and cheese shimmer into being.

"I'll stick with magic any day of the week." Jamison snags a slice of the loaf and a hunk of cheese off the platter. Around a mouthful, he adds, "Not that I'm not grateful that you decided to come."

"You didn't think I'd let the two of you go exploring this so-called doomed pass without me, did you?" Jerik grumbles, glancing upward where some pebbles bounce from the heights. "I'm just surprised that husband of yours let you leave the youngster with him. He turned out to be a much better husband than I thought this world was capable of producing, especially being that he's a prince."

I look at the noonday sun, trying to gauge how much longer we'll have light in this pass. I sense curiosity from where the rocks shifted earlier. The feeling is strong but muted. "Not as surprised as I am. But when Rose requested both Jamison and me, I don't think he had much choice. She is his sister, after all. If she says she's in urgent need of a wizard and a healer, well. . ."

The rocky slope of the mountain begins to jostle like an avalanche without the snow. A shower of gravel sprays us as we spring away from the rock slide. We pull our sleeves over our mouths and eyes, trying to keep from suffocating on the dirt-filled air.

> "We must see; we must breathe.
> Air, clear immediately."

Brilliant blue tinges the world about us. The fresh air makes the sky visible once more. The feeling of curiosity intensifies. The pile of rubble three stories high shifts once more. A massive arm becomes distinguishable along with a head.

Metal sings into the day as my companions draw their weapons. Muted fear peaks sharply from the massive creature. "Stop!" The fright spikes higher with the shout. Calmly I continue. "Put your weapons down."

"What? You want us to do what?" Jamison glances over his shoulder at me. Noting the triangular shape my fingers have formed, knowing I can call a fireball with a single word, he eases his weapon back into its sheath. "I hope you know what you are doing."

"It's all right," I say to the creature. "We mean you no harm." The fear eases.

Grumbling, Jerik rests the head of the double-bladed ax on the ground. The face of the monster shifts. A low rumble sounds from the middle of the beast.

"Jerik, do that grumbling thing again."

The dwarf huffs. "Some adventure. A rock creature and we can't even kill it."

A higher-pitched rumble emanates from the monster. *Enough of this. We have a schedule to keep.* Quickly I chant the language gift spell.

"Do you understand me?"

I feel the creature's puzzlement as the words now make sense. "We wish you no harm, only to travel through this pass." Again I sense puzzlement. However, the creature backs away from the middle of the path. A weary sadness tinges the emotions.

"Are you alone?" I ask. "Nod like this for yes." I nod.

"Reba, do we have time to be playing twenty questions?" Jamison glances from the beast to me. "Rose—"

With the mention of his beloved, the world tinges white again. It takes a few minutes for my eyes to adjust to the dimness of the chamber. The warmth of an embrace causes my mind to reel. *I'm not supposed to feel things in a premonition.*

"Reba, I am pleased you could make the journey so soon after your son's birth." Rose brushes my cheek with hers before releasing me.

"He's getting big, almost a year old now. Besides, how could I not be there when my friend needs me?"

"Has it been that long?" Rose turns to the maid waiting patiently in the corner of the room for instructions. "I need nothing further, please wait in the reception chamber for the arrival of my last guest."

The muscular woman bobs her head and scurries to the next room. "I'm not sure Jerik knows he's expected. He said something about scrounging up a bite in this frozen palace."

"Then we will have some privacy. If you wouldn't mind securing my chamber?" Rose asks.

"Sight," I whisper. Though the entire castle is made of red granite, the royal chambers are bordered with deep crimson marmari-sterk around the top and the bottom. I nod, walking to the nearest wall. It takes a mere thought to direct the flow of energy to run along the sorcerer's abode as I chant the necessary lines. I sigh with contentment as I turn back to the couple.

"The room is now secure." No sooner do the words leave my mouth than Jamison's arm encircles the woman he loves.

"I have missed you so much," he whispers as he embraces the wife of the king of Tuvarnava.

I clear my throat. "You said it was a matter of pride for the sovereignty of Cuthburan?"

The couple parts slowly. A blush infuses the princess's cheeks as she glares at Jamison. The healer flushes too then looks away like a lovesick teen avoiding the eyes of the girl he's crushing on.

"Yes, it is. I have been unable to conceive a child. If I do not produce an heir by next summer, I will be put aside, returned home in disgrace."

Hope flares to life, shining like a beacon across Jamison's face. "Awesome! We can be married when you get back."

"My love, as much as my heart desires for that to be so, we cannot let that happen—I cannot." The heartbreak echoing from the pair causes me to put up my empathy shields as Rose expounds, "Much of our trade is based on the treaty written with my marriage. Should this marriage fail, the treaty and trade will fail as well. If the high priestess chooses to scourge me before returning me to my father, which is her right, the hard-won peace with Tuvarnava may be sacrificed too."

"Rose, I don't understand." Jamison mumbles, "You are as proficient a healer as I am. Why bring me all this way?"

Rose gestures for us to relax on the oversized furniture. "In the quiet hours of the night, when whispers reassure us we finally have privacy, I have convinced my husband, Palava, of the necessity of making this union last. My healing skills have been an unexpected boon for the monarch. They have been able to shift the power away from the church at last. Palava is willing to do whatever it takes to secure his family's new place of power."

"But I still don't see what I can do to help."

"Palava knows the fault lies in him. He tried to get his mistress with child for five years before I arrived. Even magical charms failed him. With Reba's security shield to guarantee our privacy, he may allow you to provide an heir."

"Whoa, babe! You want me to do what?"

"Jamison, my love, the child will have to come from somewhere." Tears gather in her eyes. "At least we may be together for another few seasons, and I will not have to take a stranger to my bed."

Silence falls between us as the door to the reception chamber opens. A mask of calmness slides into place as Rose rises to greet the newcomer.

"Prince Varpalava, I present to you Archmage Reba, Arcane Adviser to King Arturo, and Master Healer Jamison." We bow low to Tuvarnava's heir apparent.

"It seems this magic shield does exactly what you said, my wife. I was unable to see or hear you once the archmage finished chanting." The short, athletic prince eyes Jamison like a side of beef. "The hair color is a match. The height is excellent. And you say he has the same powers of healing that you do?"

"Yes, milord. With such a dominant trait from both contributing parties, our children will most likely be gifted, or grandchildren at the very least."

"He will do nicely." With a dip of his head in dismissal, Varpalava takes his leave.

I lock eyes with Jamison, wondering if his moral code will allow him to father a child he won't raise. The world flashes white again, a little less brightly this time.

I am reclined on a pillowed surface, my nose inches from Rose's. *What the. . .?* "The flowers are in bloom. I think it's time." Jamison whispers from my mouth. *Why am I inside him? I should be hovering above him.*

"We have until the beginning of summer, surely." Rose snuggles onto Jamison's broad chest. Her head pops up to look into my eyes—his eyes. "Jamie, this is the second time this octal you've suggested I should conceive. You tire of my company so soon?"

"No, my love. I could never tire of you."

"Then out with it. Why this urge to return to Cuthburan?"

A loud snore rumbles from the couch. My eyes dart to Palava's slumbering form. A soft hand gently grasps my chin, turning me to face her once again. "Jamie, you once said you could tell me anything. But lately I feel a wall between us. Please, don't do this to me. . . to us."

"Oh, my darling, I am so sorry if I've hurt you. That is one thing I never wanted to do." Jamison evades the question.

"Then share your heart with me again."

Staring at the tears in her eyes, Jamison relents. "This is much harder than I thought it would be; that's all." His eyes travel to her bosom, finding staring there is much more comfortable than into those deep pools that search the reaches of his soul.

"Has Palava done something, said something?" Rose demands.

"No." Bitterness tinges his normally jovial tone. "Nothing a husband shouldn't do."

"I. . . I don't understand," Rose stutters.

"Seeing him with you at dinner, seeing you on his arm, just seeing you next to him, knowing that he will be there when I'm gone. . ." A sigh shudders through him as he pushes the anger aside. "The things that have gone through my mind, things I could do with the power I wield, things I should never consider doing!" He brings his gaze to meet hers, willing her to understand. "I need to leave now, not later."

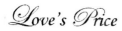

"Oh, Jamie! I am so, so sorry."

The anguish in her voice is too much. Pushing the crushing weight of pain into the corner of his heart, Jamison smiles as he cups her heart-shaped face in his hands. "Tonight, my dear, let's celebrate the love we've shared. Tomorrow we can mourn its loss."

Gratefully white tinges the world one last time. I blink my eyes rapidly. I stare dumbfounded into Jamison's eyes. Shaking my head to dislodge the vision, I blink my eyes some more. The sharp rock digging into my backside and the luminescent spheres above reassure me the premonition has ended.

"You can see me?" I ask.

"I see your aura and your blood flow. Was that one of your visions?"

"Cloak," I whisper. "So cloak is vulnerable to healer's sight and probably magesight too. Good to know. Why'd you have your sight active?"

"When Rose left, I heard someone fall. Seeing that smashed bush, it wasn't hard to figure out what was holding it down." Rubbing his chin, his mouth quirks into a half smile. "I feel like I'm in the Spanish Inquisition. Some thanks I get for picking those thorns out of your invisible hide."

"I think you missed one." Rolling over, I snag the thorn from my breeches. "You have my sincere gratitude for getting the rest out before I came to." *Must have been when Rose hugged me. The physical contact threw me off balance.*

Jamison grins. "So you always play Peeping Tom with that invisibility spell?"

"Look, I'm sorry about the third degree already. It is just so nice to not be looked at for once." I sigh. "Now I have to revise yet another spell."

Getting to my knees, I collapse on the nearby bench. Jamison joins me. "Did you help me lay down there?"

"I may not be a prince, but I can still rescue a maiden, even an invisible one."

"That's it! That must be why the vision took me inside you; the physical link or being touched with your powers linked us."

"Like, whoa, dude." Jamison sits up board straight, swiveling to face me. "You had a vision about me? Was it about me and Rose? You gotta tell me what's gonna happen."

"Look, seeing the future is a tricky thing," I hedge. "Even when you think you are doing something to prevent the premonition, it doesn't always work out."

"But not knowing is tearing me up. Reba, please, what could be worse than not knowing?"

"And that's why I was hiding in this darn garden all cloaked and shielded." I try to change the subject. "My intuition has gone into overdrive. It seems all I have to do is wonder intently about something and—boom—I'm drawn into the future instead of merely witnessing it. Then what do you do about what you've seen? It's like the worst kind of Peeping Tom!"

"That settles it. Now you must let me help. Maybe if we joined our powers and I observed the premonition, I could help you sort it all out."

I stare into his eyes. "Jamison, believe me, there are worse things than not knowing."

"Not for me." He gives a firm nod, acknowledging the danger. "I like to study the waves before I hop on one that really rolls me."

Wordlessly I extend my hand. Quietly I chant.

"The future is mine to see,
I share my vision with thee."

I center my perfect memory on the conversation I observed before I was overwhelmed by my gift of foresight. The world flashes white. As the fourth flash brings us back to reality, my empathy hammers me with pain so intense, I bring up my shields.

Jamison wipes his eyes. I turn to my friend. "I am so sorry. I tried to warn you. Lately I've been held captive by my visions. First Jerik, now you."

"Jerik? Is he in danger?" Jamison changes the subject.

"No, but someone he will come to love will die. But if I tell him, maybe love won't dawn for them. Should I tell him?"

"Reba, you get better at politics every day. You've really learned to talk in circles around a subject." Jamison shrugs. "I can't help you unless I know what you're talking about."

"You want to see this one too?"

"Can't be worse. Besides, I think I know what's wrong with intuition. Think of it like watching a play. You have gotten too

close to the stage. You are becoming one of the actors. Try
easing back, like you are watching something on TV."

"Humph, it's worth a try." Again I extend my hand.

I concentrate on the moment I saw Jerik talking to the maid
out by the stables. *I was wondering if he'd ever find love.* The
world flashes white.

I am striding down one of the dimly lit hallways in the
servants' quarters. Keeping Jamison's advice in mind, I draw
my mind back from the vision. *Whoa!* I steady my
consciousness as it hovers over my form. *Now that's better.*

The deep wailing of a child in distress grows louder with
each step as the minutes pass. In time the child's cries become
fainter. Unable to bear the sound of a baby in need, I spin
around. I ease the small, wooden door open.

On a tiny bed, no bigger than a cot, a rawboned servant
attempts to comfort the wailing babe while a two-year-old
plays at her feet. I duck into the doorway. The startled woman
looks up and attempts to kneel while holding the fussing child.

"May I?" I ask, reaching for the child.

"Milady, have we disturbed you?" The fear washing through
the woman isn't as great as it has been with some.

"I am always disturbed when there is a child in need." I
extend my somatic energy to the child's body. "He's hungry.
When was he fed last?" *Why does this woman seem so
familiar?*

"Milady, he drained me dry less than a mark ago." Tears
gather in the mother's eyes. "He's not seen his first solstice.
How can a child eat so much?"

"Perhaps having two so close in age was not a wise idea?"
A touch of magic eases the acid rolling in his middle. The child
quiets immediately.

"Milady, I means no disrespect." Her lip trembles in fear but
she continues. "I didn't have this un by choice. Me sis passed
givin' birth, so I took him. Me mums took care o' your
youngins as well as me and my sis. Babes in our family never
lack. I thought I could handle one more."

Memories, pale in comparison to the vision, appear: a
muscular woman, whose gender is only discernable by the
dress she wears, stands before my door, hefting a child whose
rugged features mark him as a boy. A small boy peeks out from
behind her skirts.

"Milady." Phedra ushers the trio to my desk. "This is Veallstor. She is available to be a wet nurse."

"Unless I miss my guess, your two children are still nursing?" *Her bosom looks ample, but three?*

"Yes, milady." Veallstor curtsies as she ruthlessly shoves her fear into a corner. "Me mums nursed four. Good milk runs in our teats. Me litt'l un's small, only eats half what she should, and the girls are quiet. They'll be no bother." *They are both girls?*

The memories fade into the background, and the vision sharpens again. "Dyrslegur, you have my deepest condolences. Ofriour was fortunate to have a sister like you. Do you have any idea who fathered the child?"

"No, milady." Dyrslegur wipes a tear. "Ofriour were an odd child. Too scrawny to haul the tubs of water for the laundry, she were assigned to help care for the animals." Recalling the chunky baby with the robust features, I'm forced to hide a smile. *Perhaps she was small comparatively?* "Mum never forgot how you blessed her for love that day. I'm sure love dawned for Ofriour. I hardly never saw her in the last years."

"Oh, you are such a precious baby. May love be forever yours." That was a blessing? "I see," I mumble, turning the infant to me. Robust features, wide shoulders, and a stocky body under a thick mop of dark hair. "Ofriour had black hair, if I recall?"

"Yes, milady. Blessed by Andskoti, the only one of us to have such."

The world flashes white. I'm hovering above the smithy. A dark-haired, robust woman blushes. She stares at her toes while Jerik hunkers down on a rough-hewn chair, tearing off a hunk of cheese. White blinds my vision once more.

I am once again holding the hefty babe in my arms. "I believe I know the father of this child. He left more than a cycle ago. I don't believe he knows he has a son. If you will allow it, I will take him as my charge until the father can be reached."

Brilliance dazzles my sight. I am surrounded by the night, the garden, and the Jewel of Cuthburan.

Jamison whistles long and low. "A premonition within a premonition."

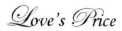

I clear my throat. "And it was a doozy. It seems their love will dawn slowly. Foreknowledge may destroy the fragile situation. So do we tell him?"

"In this case it seems we may be able to prevent most of the damage." The bitterness in the normally lighthearted voice brings tears to my eyes. "Since we are aware of the time frame by the birth line, we can keep Jerik around until the pregnancy is revealed; that is half the problem. My healing skills will take care of the delivery of his child."

"Now why didn't I think of that? The solution is so simple."

"You've had your hands full maneuvering those holy honors. With the common thread in the two, it's no wonder you couldn't focus on anything else."

"They will not force me to marry him, no matter how he's changed since the battle," I growl. Bells chime in the distance. "And my midnight rendezvous will help guarantee that."

Rising, the gloom surrounding my comrade causes me to blink rapidly to keep my composure. I lay a hand on his bicep. "Was telling you the right thing?"

Jamison takes a long breath. "I'll brace for the hard roll that his heading my direction."

"Knowing what you know, are you sure it's worth it?"

"I'd suffer through years of torture for one more day with the love of my heart." Tears gather in the healer's eyes. "Wouldn't you?"

"Years if necessary." I wipe the overflow from my face. "But right now duty calls."

Chapter Twenty-four

"Your Majesty, I see your point. I understand why a ceremony is required." I persist on the topic of the award proceedings that are rumored to be in the works. "However, I would feel much better if we could reduce the number of those attending. . . to fifty perhaps?"

"You are a strange woman, Reba." Arturo shakes his head, giving up hope of ever understanding his new adviser. "Any other female would want the entire kingdom to witness her achievements."

"As if all those horrid songs spreading over embellished tales aren't enough? I may seem strange to you, but I assure you, your ways are just as foreign to me." I sigh, looking at hands clasped together on my lap. "I suppose it is merely insecurity that motivates me, though. I am unaccustomed to being the center of attention. Frankly, I find it unnerving."

"So we have finally uncovered a weakness, eh?" The king pats my shoulder. "I suppose we could reduce the attendees to fourscore. I will stipulate two guests per invitation." The gray-bearded man chuckles. "It will be quite amusing to see the aristocracy choose between bringing a spouse or a firstborn."

"Thank you, Your Majesty." Shooting for less than a hundred witnesses, I am more than satisfied with eighty. Rising, I take my leave.

"Off so soon? It seems we never have time to sit and get to know one another." Arturo rises with me.

"We will have to put aside some time someday." I give a warm smile. "Unfortunately right now I have a dinner engagement."

"Occupying my son again, are you?" A grin steals across the monarch's face. "I would be a lot happier about the time you spend with my firstborn if new changes did not emerge from each of your rendezvous."

"Yes, well, Alex and I must learn to appreciate each other's strengths as well as tolerate the other's weaknesses if my arrival is going to benefit this kingdom as much as the prophecy states."

I take a deep breath. "Your Majesty, may I ask you something plainly?" My amber eyes beg for a break from the social maneuvering dominating my life for the past several weeks.

King Arturo appraises me for a moment. Finally his calculating thoughts lighten. "Only if you call me Arturo. If your question is something I can answer, I will."

"Is there any hope for Alex and Andrayia?" I voice what has plagued me since my miraculous recuperation.

"Reba, if I could, I would approve their joining. I would love nothing more than to give Alex the one thing I never had: the opportunity to follow his heart." The dignified elder sighs. "However, your presence here demands he take his duty into consideration. I am afraid the possibility of a rebellion exists if I do any less."

"I always thought being 'trapped by power and position' was total crap." I hold in laughter as Arturo's jaw drops at my unladylike language. "It seems I was naive in many of my assumptions."

"Give it time. You may yet see wisdom in the way this monarchy works." The fatherly feeling I sense touches my heart.

"Thank you, Arturo." I plant a chaste kiss on his cheek.

Unused to such honest displays of affection, it is Art's turn to flush. "Gratitude already? You have not yet received your complement of honors. Speaking of which, have you decided on your Choice Honor?"

Fluttering my lashes, I say, "How am I to decide what to ask before I know what will be bestowed upon me?" Bells toll in the night. "Doggone it! Now I am late." I curse under my breath then blush as I glance back to Arturo. "If you don't mind, a flight may reduce my tardiness to something approaching decorum."

Although the monarch's back stiffens, he gives a tight smile, inclining his head in dismissal.

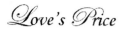

"Superman," is whisper into the night. My feet lift from the ground. Connie starts as I sweep in through the set of French doors leading to the balcony.

"Sorry, Connie. Didn't mean to scare you." I hurry across the room.

"I am sure, milady, I will come to expect surprises such as this in the days to come. Prince Alex awaits you in the reception chamber."

I suppress a smile at the elder's exasperation as I enter the adjoining room. "Alex, I am sorry to keep you waiting."

"I have only just arrived, milady." The raven-haired man smiles. "May I inquire how you fared with my father?"

"Not too bad." Leading the way into the dining room, I fail to keep the smugness from my voice. "Eighty will be in attendance at the ceremony."

"Eighty?" My dinner companion blanches. "Reba, are you sure fewer is better?"

"I'm afraid you are going to have to trust me on this. We want a controlled reaction, not a rebellion." I pause, taking my first bite while mulling over how much to reveal. "Alex, I made a vow to see that Andrayia winds up as your queen. I intend to do whatever it takes to fulfill that promise. All I ask from you is your indulgence for a few more days."

"You were ready to sacrifice your life for my country and would have if not for my brother's willingness to sacrifice his life for yours." The prince's eyes mist over as he recalls the pair of pallid faces lying on the brink of oblivion for two days. He shakes his head, dismissing the painful memories. "You have earned an eternity of faith."

"Thank you." I mumble, coloring at his show of gratitude. "Alex, about that final battle. . ." *There's no one else who was close enough to see, I have to ask him.* I test the bounds of our friendship carefully. "What happened after I passed out?"

"Surely you have heard the tales?" Alex says.

"Yes, from many different people. But I still don't know how. . ." I shake my head gently. "I need to know exactly what happened, to understand. . . why he did what he did."

Alex reaches across the table, silencing the plea as he places his hand over mine. "If that is what you need, read the thoughts from my mind. It is the least I can do."

I nod my head, pushing my plate from me. Grasping his hand in both of mine, I close my eyes. Boosted by empathy and telepathy and other accounts of the famous night, I relive the gateway battle from his perspective.

∿　　∿　　∿

I lay immobile, pale as death.

"No!" Rage echoes into the night as Szames cradles me, crushing me to him with his uninjured arm.

"Is she dead?" Alex demands as Jamison makes his way to the trio. "She cannot be! She is to be my bride."

"Are you sure she is to be your bride? That the entire prophecy was meant to be fulfilled in your lifetime?" Although Nemandi's lips move, the mild rebuke comes from the atmosphere around him: it is Andskoti who speaks.

A herd of footsteps echoes from the meadow as some of the demons make hasty getaways as Andskoti's presence is realized. Armor jingles as every man collapses to his knees. Alex's mouth hangs slack at the sight of the glowing priest.

"Szames. . . I must tell you." My eyes flutter but fail to open as unconsciousness loosens its death grip.

"Shh, my love, save your strength." Szames gently strokes the hair from my face.

"I was afraid. . . afraid it would end. That's why I didn't. . ." My strength fades. Seconds pass before I gain the energy to try and finish the thought. "I want you to know. . ." *I love you too.*

My strength gives out. I lay lifelessly in the arms of my lover.

"Andskoti!" The warrior prince demands Nemandi's attention. "I beg you, don't take her from me. I cannot live without her."

"What would you give for her life, Prince of Cuthburan?" the god questions.

"I will give all that I am, anything you ask. If a soul is demanded, take mine instead."

"Unfortunately her soul is not within my grasp. She is bound to a God of another world. I cannot touch her essence."

The small light of hope, which shone briefly in Szames's eyes, dies. "So what can you do? Why do you torment me with this?"

"Because I can offer you aid, if indirectly." His god adds, "Not only your life, but your soul may be forfeit. Furthermore, I cannot guarantee you will succeed in saving your beloved."

"What must I do?" Szames is steadfast as Jamison heals the gash in his shoulder.

"The life-cord holding us to our bodies is a derivative of our auras," Andskoti explains what has been only theory until now. "Reba's aura has been completely drained. Her soul lies between this life and the next, unable to find its way home. In time she may recover, or she will simply cross over."

"What must I do to guide her back?"

"A soul-link has already begun between you. I will speed the process. I can send you to the space between this life and the next, where you may call to her." Even though the prince agrees without hesitation, Andskoti continues, "By linking with a child of another God, you will forfeit all rights you have to the afterworld. You may be unable to find her. If you do not return before your aura is depleted, then you will die, even if she manages to recover and lives."

"I understand the risks. I accept." Alex's jaw hangs in disbelief at the sacrifice his sibling makes for a single woman, no matter how significant to our Cuthburan. "What must I do?"

Andskoti presides over the linking. Under his instruction, our hands are tied together so we will remain physically touching until one or both wakes or passes on to the next life.

"As you have wished, so it is done. Your souls are now joined as one," the words are uttered by Nemandi as Andskoti withdraws from the locale.

"Now what?" At a loss, Alex turns to the priest for answers. Without his god's direction, the young clergyman is unsure as to the best course of action.

Jamison speaks into the silence. "Reba's bedchamber at Castle Eldrich has an enchantment that might be beneficial. The sooner we get them there, the better. Until then, my pendant may help." Alex's jaw drops in astonishment as one by one, the healers traveling with the campaign bring their enchanted treasures to be placed on Reba's neck, fingers and even a wrist.

A stretcher is constructed. Alex assumes the lead position. The thought of losing his brother disturbs him; the worry is etched across his face. Jerik jogs back to the wagons. One is unloaded by the time Alex arrives. The dwarf stands waiting for the others to arrive. Each soldier sheds his cloak, placing it as padding in the bottom of the bed as they pass by.

Jesse's roar sounds into the night, demanding attention. At Alex's acknowledgment, he sends, *"Tawny and I will make the journey in less than a day."*

"I thank you for your offer, but even if you can travel faster than our horses, the wagon will never hold up under the stress," Alex replies.

"If we were mere mounts, that might be so. We will not be moving as you are accustomed; we will glide over the ground. Between the two of us, we will manage to lift the wagon as well."

"You have my deepest gratitude." Tilting his head, Alex asks a boon, "May I accompany you?"

"A ride on my back will be much more comfortable and not add further to their burden," a new mind-voice, deep and rich, echoes into the prince's thoughts. *"I am Guidro and will be your partner if you wish."*

Alex approaches the enormous alabaster feline, extending a hand. "I accept."

A partial binding is preformed while the wagon is readied. Straps are shortened as the horse's harnesses are modified to secure the wagon to the SpiritCats. With Jamison and half the Royal Guard, the odd party disappears into the night. By daybreak, startled sentries open the gates of Eldrich.

I slide my hands from Alex's. "He was more than willing to give not only his life, but his soul for you." His words echo my thoughts.

I clear the lump from my throat. Blinking rapidly, I endeavor to keep the moisture in check. Still getting used to the transformation the cocky aristocrat has undergone since my brush with death, not to mention his partnership with Guidro, I

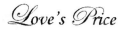

change the topic. Keeping my empathy wide, I test the honesty of his words. "So how did you do with the council?"

He gives a very unprincely grunt. "You would think that when Andskoti himself says now is not the time for magic to come for the throne, those stiff-necked, bullheaded—"

"So it went well, then?" Seeing the wry twist of my lips, the prince is helpless but to return it, letting his anger melt in the light of my humor.

The dinner passes as swiftly as the spring days flying past. All too soon, I find myself before the throne.

"Arise, Archmage Reba, Chief Adviser to the Kingdom of Cuthburan," Arturo's voice booms out, carrying to every corner of the room. "Archmage, we are now prepared to hear your Choice Honor."

I call to mind the formal request I composed. "Being a female warrior and foreign to this world, I find myself having difficulty relating to the women with whom it is proper for me to socialize. It is rather like you, Your Majesty, being forced to surround yourself with nothing but young men who have never been outside this castle and know little of the outside world."

As the snickering dies down, I continue. "I mean no disrespect to your wives or daughters, only to point out the difference between a battle-seasoned woman and a refined lady. I enjoy the company of your noble born, but I find myself lacking someone to whom I can truly relate."

"We see your point. Please state your desire," Arturo interjects.

"The policy has already been established with Sir Stezen's knighting." I gesture toward the doors, whispering, "Open says me." The massive, wooden barrier flies open. The startled guards regain their composure as the trio strides through the open portal. Yivgeni, head held high as only a master artist can in the presence of royalty, leads his two apprentices. The youths swivel the oiled masterpiece from side to side as they make a steady procession to the ruler of Cuthburan.

"Your Majesty, for her bravery in battle depicted by this portrait," I say and pause, giving everyone in the room a chance to absorb the painting.

Yivgeni, straightening from his bow, gestures toward his masterpiece: Andrayia, faced by three menacing demons, bravely stands her ground over the prone form of Prince Alexandros.

"For placing her own life in jeopardy to save the life of the crown prince, I ask that Royal Guard Andrayia be ennobled."

Arturo gives a slight inclination of his head. He doesn't seem to concede me even a partial victory as his eyes show swift calculation. "Gladly will we grant your Choice Honor. However, since she is a woman, the title will not be hereditary, serving only to make her suitable for noble union through which her lands will be passed." The king smiles. "This should not interfere with her acting as a companion for one of your status."

"Royal Guard Andrayia, please step forward." Arturo instructs the leader of his personal guard, which forms a half circle on both sides of the dais. "Kneel."

As the blonde warrior complies, the monarch touches one shoulder, her head, then the second shoulder with his scepter. "For bravery in defense of this kingdom, for honor and dedication to duty, I knight you, Andrayia of Northmark." Arturo names a small duchy not far from the lands he granted me in the first honor of eight.

"Thank you, Your Majesty. You are most gracious." I bow my head in acceptance of the gift as Andrayia resumes her position.

"We have one last honor to bestow upon you, Archmage Reba." King Arturo gestures to his right, where Alex stands.

"Milady Reba." The crown prince uses my personal title, which with the new grant of land, is now official. "Will you do me the honor of standing beside me as my wife, queen of Cuthburan?"

The buzzing of a fly would sound as loud as a rushing torrent in the stillness of the room as the nobility waits in expectation. Into the silence my voice rings clear and true. "Your Highness, before I answer, I must ask: Does your heart hold true love for me or does your heart belong to another?"

The murmuring following the question ceases as every person present strains to catch Alex's answer. "I know, Great Archmage, you are impossible to deceive, so I answer honestly: my heart belongs to another, but my duty lies with you."

I nod decisively. "I am afraid I must decline this honor. My religion dictates that my marriage must be one of intimate fidelity. Without love, the vows I will take at a joining will not be possible to keep." The clamoring of the well-dressed witnesses forces Arturo to pound his scepter on the armchair of his throne.

"We will have *order!*" the king demands. Bewildered, Alex reassumes his place beside his father. "Archmage Reba, it seems our attempt to distribute a Sacred Honor of Eight upon the fulfiller of our prophecy will be thwarted unless you reconsider my son's proposal."

"Your Majesty, I thank you for the offer to see to my companionship; however, my own spirituality will be in jeopardy if I were to be party to an unfaithful union." I pause to give both him and the crowd time to assimilate this new concept while racking my brain for a better answer.

"Perhaps I have a solution," the deep voice petitioning to be heard shocks the entire assembly into silence once again. Prince Szames steps forward from his position as commander of Cuthburan Forces on Arturo's left. The hush upon the crowd is deadly calm. Szames waits for his father to grant permission to speak further. With a cautious nod from his father, the fair-haired prince takes center court.

"Milady Reba, I find your position on marriage admirable. I would never be presumptuous enough as to ask for your hand so early in acquaintanceship." Prince Szames begins by apologizing for his family's transgression. "But I will ask your permission to court your favor so we may see if we are suitable for a lifelong union of monogamy." Having traveled down from the throne's dais, the shining blond head bows with dignified grace.

"Your Highness, what is 'courting' but an attempt by a man to woo a woman into a commitment, waiting to reveal his true self until a decision has been made? No, Prince Szames, I am afraid I must decline your offer of courting." The raising of an eyebrow is the only sign Szames gives of the shock I feel reverberating through our strengthened link. Pausing so Arturo may once again demand order, I frame my reply with care.

"However, I will accept what I believe is your genuine intent. If it is agreeable, we will take each other as companions in life, in love, and in intimacy, so we may see if we are indeed compatible for a joining." With two swift strides, Szames closes the gap between us so he can take my hand, delivering a kiss to seal the Eighth Honor. The unwavering sense of love and devotion coming through the link causes me to blush as the crowd cheers its approval.

"As Andskoti instructs, so have we done: the Holy Honor of Eight has been bestowed upon Archmage Reba. What we have given is small in comparison to what you have bestowed upon us. Milady Reba, We will forever remain in your debt." This time the dip of his head concedes me a victory without malice. His newest adviser has provided him with a graceful way out of the decisions the court has forced upon him.

"Jamison, long time no see!" I rub sleep out of my eyes, stumbling to the loveseat of my living quarters, as he releases me from a hug. "What brings you by this way?"

"Just thought I would drop in, see how you're doing. I've been so busy since you and Jerik added that new wing on to the Healers Consortium, I haven't poked my nose out to sniff the wind." Jamison smiles, taking a seat on the chair next to me.

"You're a terrible liar," I tease. "You should know better than to try and hide something from an empath."

"OK, so Connie asked me to come by." My eyebrows crinkle in annoyance, so the healer adds, "Don't be cross with her. She only mentioned that you've been exhausted since your return. She's a little worried."

"You'd think she could take my word on it. I already checked for disease and viruses, even checked my heart. I'm fine. Besides, it's not like I don't have plenty of reasons to be worn out! I've finished the Partners' Pabulum in mere weeks. Lord knows teleporting all that rock took mega amounts of energy."

"It's true, then. You've been napping every day since the gateway battle?" Jamison's worry increases, despite my reassurance.

"Sure, but with the duties I've assumed, is it any wonder I have been a little worn out?" I shrug off his concerns. "Now that Andrayia has taken charge of the new partners, I won't be draining my energy every day. I'm sure things will get back to normal."

"So you aren't going to even ask for a once-over, to confirm your diagnosis?" Jamison takes his abilities seriously, refraining from invading my privacy until invited.

I shake my head, stifling a yawn. "Go ahead and look. I'm fine."

"Hmm, seems those visions that plagued you after the battle have a deeper significance."

"Is there something wrong?" I sit up straight in my chair.

"Have you been hungrier than usual?" A ghost of a smile skitters across his face.

"Who knows? When I use my powers I devour everything in sight. Come on now, give. What did I miss? What's wrong?"

Jamison chuckles. "Nothing's wrong. Both you and the baby are perfectly healthy."

"Baby?" Unbidden, tears trace their way down my ivory cheeks. "No. I can't be. . . can I? The nobility is supposed to have a charm to prevent this!" *With the spell taking care of the flow I completely forgot to even check for other symptoms!*

"Let's see. . . you are nearly five months along, so I'd say sometime around the gateway battle would've been the time of conception." Jamison pats my knee reassuringly.

Pictures of Szames standing naked in the secluded meadow where we began our romance spring to life. With my photographic memory, I recall no presence of a charm. "I suppose neither of us were prepared that day."

"I'm sure Szames will do the honorable thing. The only question is do you want to break the bad news to him, or should I?" Jamison ribs me, getting a brief smile before the floodgates open again.

The healer wraps his arms around me as I sob hysterically. "Now, now, come on now. What could possibly be wrong?"

"Finally. . . I find the perfect man. . . we start a beautiful relationship. . . and he has to marry me!"

I've been acting like I am above all the laws, even the laws of nature and of God. My sobs, which have slowed, pick up speed again. "I don't even get a real proposal or a honeymoon or anything. I'm a knocked-up slut!" As my whine turns into a wail, the door to my private chamber slams open.

"Reba, are you all right?" Szames kneels by my side. "I felt waves of crushing emotions emanating from you before everything just stopped."

Seeing him down on his knees makes everything so much worse. Cascading tears wet my face.

Szames brings me into his arms. "Just let me in. I cannot know how to help if I do not know what is wrong."

Hearing the concern in his voice brings emotional calm within my grasp. After putting my thoughts into coherent order, I ease down the shield to explain. "Jamison has found the reason behind my fatigue. It seems I am pregnant."

"A baby? Us?"

Fears of forcing him into an unwanted marriage bubble up inside me.

Szames chuckles. Cupping my face between his hands, he waits until I meet his eyes. "I would have proposed to you that day in the meadow if I did not think I would scare you off."

Feeling the truth of his words, I melt into his arms. This time joy causes moisture to bring a shining light to my reddened cheeks

Laws of Sorcery

First Law
Portal Essence

The aura holds *umfang,* an essence in the aura that is necessary to open a portal between two worlds. For this reason, a portal spell may be cast only once by a sorcerer of the master status.

Second Law
Portal Travel

A sorcerer must be able to harness the forces of magic on the world to which he is traveling, else the spell will not be completed and the sorcerer will be suspended somewhere in between the dimensions.

Third Law
Measure of Life Force

Every individual is given an amount of energy necessary for a human lifespan. Attempting to increase this energy results in the untimely demise of the individual.

Fourth Law
Flight Restrictions

It is impossible to soar aloft into the heavens unless a sorcerer transforms himself into the likeness of an animal that has the ability of flight. Transformation into human form from an animal is impossible.

Fifth Law
Human Intellect

Certain herbs and a balanced diet from infancy have proven to increase intelligence in man and beast. Therefore, repetitive applications of an increased intelligence spell based on these findings is possible. However, direct transfer of knowledge only results in damage to both parties involved.

Sixth Law
Magic Resources

Each magical working removes a predetermined amount of corporeal energy from the environment. The corporeal energy field will take one year to recuperate from an apprentice-level spell, one and one half years for a journeyman, and two years for any master-level spell. Draining an area of all corporeal energy creates a magically dead zone that may never recover.

PROPHECY OF THE FLAME

HEARKEN TO MY WORDS: OUR SALVATION IS REVEALED BY OUR BELOVED ANDSKOTI. IN THE DARKEST HOUR, WHEN THE FATE OF MANKIND IS THREATENED BY A GREAT EVIL, OUR SAVIOR WILL COME WITH HAIR AFLAME, BY THAT YOU WILL KNOW HIM. CHANGE WILL SWEEP THE LAND LIKE FIRE ACROSS A SUMMER MEADOW. EMBRACE THAT WHICH IS BROUGHT, FOR IT WILL BE YOUR ONLY SALVATION. MAGIC WILL RISE AS THE ENTIRE FABRIC OF OUR KINGDOM IS REWOVEN. THROUGH THE BOND OF MARRIAGE, MAGIC WILL BE BROUGHT ONTO THE THRONE OF CUTHBURAN AT LAST. SO I HAVE BEEN SHOWN. SO LET IT BE KNOWN.

Glossary

Ap-bjan: Demonic invader with the body of a snake. The top portion is a two-headed ogre with three arms.

Aura: The field of energy that surrounds every human being. Magesight allows the aura to be seen in color patterns representing different affinities: blue for magic, green for healing, fuchsia for charisma, gold for empathy, burgundy for telepathy, etc.

AV: Aura virus

Consortium of Knowledge: University of Cuthburan

Corinth: A soft metal prevalent in Cuthburan. When mixed with other metals, it becomes malleable and prevents rust and tarnish.

Corporeal essence: The power in the aura that enables someone to change the physical properties of atoms. Aura coloration: shades of blue.

Eldrich, Castle: Home and ruling center for the royalty of Cuthburan, located in the city now known as Eldrich.

Ethereal Forest: Forbidden woods north of Castle Eldrich.

Great Waste: A dead zone rumored to be located somewhere in the northeast unexplored wilderness.

Healing potion: Silver liquid made from the breaking down of food.

Igildru: Demonic invader. Blacker than night, this monster is humanoid in appearance with the exception of the fused first and second finger of the left hand which are elongated, and can be use as a whip. Bones sprout from eyes sockets and the rear of the head as well. Usually carries a crossbow with tips that burst into flame upon contact.

Jarovegi: A long-limbed demon able to tunnel underground at remarkable speed. The bite of this creature infects the aura of the wounded, eventually killing the victim.

Kantri: Dark-haired girl who was given a guitar by Archmage Reba.

Kypros: Country bordering Cuthburan to the southwest.

Love's Dawning: The beginning of a romantic tryst.

Love's Day: A romantic relationship that has become sexual.

Love's Sunset: The end of a romance.

Marmari-sterk: A stone prized for building due to its light weight and denseness. Marbled marmari-sterk is also prized for its beauty. Secretly known as Sorcerer's Abode. Different shades of marmari-sterk have different enhancing properties: blue for corporeal, green for somatic energy, white absorbs all energy. The darker the color, the more energy it releases.

Northmark: Small providence in the northeast corner of the kingdom of Cuthburan.

Octal: A Cuthburan unit of measurement, eight consecutive days.

Partners' Pabulum: Square half mile area beside Castle Eldrich including the forest set aside since the castle's conception. The buildings house and train partner pairs.

Perinthess: Cuthburan metal alloy composed of brass and corinth.

Raloliks: Demon that jumps like a kangaroo. The fuzzy hindquarters shoot quills at the enemy. A scaly raptor torso with a vicious beak and fore claws complete this monster.

Ruff: An interchangeable ruffle at the neck of the dress line, starched or wired to stand out and away from the neck.

Scry: To trance, enabling out-of-body searching of large areas as well as other dimensions for a specific item or person or answer to a specific question.

Somatic essence: The power in the aura that enables someone to use magic to heal. Aura coloration: shades of green.

Tuvarnava: Kingdom to the northwest of Cuthburan.

Wyvern: Commonly known as a miniature dragon. A large, flying demon with wings like a bat and claws like a dragon. It has two arms that support the tops of its wings.

Character Glossary

Names beginning with Sz denote the European J, sounding like a cross between "ssh" and "j."

Alexandros, Crown Prince: Firstborn of King Arturo

Andertz: Bastard son of Andrayia and Prince Alexandros

Andrayia: Instructor in the arts of history, science, language, and mathematics to the nobility of Cuthburan; also the mistress of Prince Alexandros

Andskoti: Common name of the deity of Cuthburan

Anzin, Count: Ruler of Gandrus

Ansil: Veteran of the prophecy campaigns

Araine: A child assigned to collect stones for the archmage

Archbishop: see Prestur

Arturo, King: Ruling monarch of Cuthburan

Asdis, Marchioness: Wife to Vinfastur of Rhymon

Auricle: Member of the Royal Guard

Eldhress, Baron: Ruler of Brightport

Euon, SpiritCat: (Ew-on) Name means *little swift one* in the Forgotten Tongue; partner to Royal Guard Rucela

Baulyard, Count: Ruler of Mountview

Chazan: A child assigned to collect stones for the archmage

Cheryl: Elder sister to Rebecca

Constance: Also, Connie, Archmage Reba's personal chief of staff

Crystal: Head chambermaid, assigned to Archmage Reba upon her arrival

Cuthburan: The kingdom over which King Arturo rules

Edward: Master tailor

Erik: A child assigned to collect stones for the archmage

Frost, SpiritCat: partner to Villiblom

Gaakobah: Rogue sorcerer who has opened a permanent gateway to a realm that is demonic in nature. First and only master-level apprentice of Merithin. Gaakobah was dismissed while in apprenticeship for abuse of power.

Gabion, Duke: Ruler of Everand

Goran: Father of Gaakobah

Harold, Squire: Second son of Marquis Vinfastur, Ruler of Rhymon

Heather, SpiritCat: Partner to Andrayia

Hestur: MasterSteward of Cuthburan

Hrinia: Member of the Royal Guard

Jesse, SpiritCat: Partner to Reba

Keth: Brother to Phedra. Requested by Archmage Reba to be added to her staff when demons killed the rest of their family.

Kokkur: Camp cook on the gateway crusade

Laeknaen: Oldest living Healer.

Lani: Twin sister to Reba. (RaLain)

Yivgeni: MasterArtist of Cuthburan

Malegur: A healer whose gift is not activated at the first Awakening.

Maria: Stone collector for the Archmage, age seven.

Mik: StableMaster of Castle Eldrich

Mikaela: Member of the Royal Guard; fleeing an abusive husband

Miyana, SpiritCat: Name means *rebellion* in the Forgotten Tongue; partner to Mikaela

Nemir: Apprentice to Merithin.

Phedra: Sister to Keth. Request by Archmage Reba to be made part of her staff when her family and home were destroyed by the demons.

Phoenix: Nickname given to Archmage Reba by the musicians' guild

Prestur, Archbishop: Leader of the Church of Cuthburan.

Rokroa, Duke: Ruler of Kempmore

Royal Guard: Established by Archmage Reba during the siege of Cuthburan, an elite company of women who have been endowed with the ultimate abilities of Archmage Reba's comrades sworn to protect the archmage until the demon war is won

Rikard of Kempmore: Stonemason who created Castle Eldrich and surrounding city; known also a Master Stonemason Rik.

Rucela: Member of the Royal Guard

Scatiar, SpiritCat: Name means *good scout* in the Forgotten Tongue, partner of Hrinia

Sheldon: First of the Cuthburan line of rulers. Joined with Roseanne his first cousin then after her untimely demise, Monique, Princess of the Isles.

Sil: Short for Ansil

Stezen, Arms Master: Royal trainer of Prince Alexandros and Prince Szames; first peasant promoted to leadership during the Year of the Flame

Szeanne Rose, Princess: Third child of King Arturo, second born of Queen Szacquelyn, Princess of Cuthburan.

Szacquelyn, Queen: Second wife of King Arturo, Queen of Cuthburan.

Szames (Sha-mes), Prince: Second born of King Arturo, General of the Cuthburan Army.

Tawny, SpiritCat: Partner to Szames

Todd: Stone collector for the Archmage, age nine.

Tupper: MasterHealer

Varpalava: Prince of Tuvarnava, betrothed of Princess Szeanne Rose of Cuthburan.

Villiblom: Name means *flowering forest* in the Forgotten Tongue, member of the Royal Guard

Vinfastur, Marquis: Ruler of Rhymon

Vorkunn, SpiritCat: Name means *pity, compassion, and sympathy* in the Forgotten Tongue, partner of Auricle

William: Page to Crown Prince Alexandros; assigned to Archmage Reba upon her arrival.

Youngmen: Captain the Cuthburan army and Childhood friend of Prince Szames.

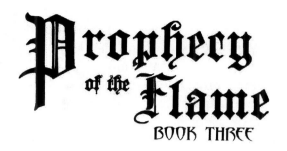

Prophecy of the Flame

BOOK THREE

Love's Journey

"Are you awake?"

Pain slices through my head. I send a tendril of healing power to ease it. *Maybe if I ignore her, she'll give up and go away.* I hold still as stone and limp as a wet dishrag, keeping my breathing even and slow.

"Please. . . please wake up." The teen's hand shakes me once more. Physical contact provides a clear channel for my empathy. Her desperation is reaching a breaking point.

"Janna," I sigh, opening my eyes. "What *is* your problem?" I glance around. We are surrounded by rounded, blue-black stone walls and high, narrow windows. *Looks like we made it to Merithin's tower.*

Janna's lower lip begins to quiver. "It's Misty. . . She's just laying so still, like she's. . ." Tears gather in her eyes. "Is she dead?"

I reach out a tentative hand to the near-frantic youth. "It's okay, Janna. We knew the trip here was going to be hard. I'm sure it's nothing. And please remember to call your sister Emily now that we are on this world."

"Yeah, but, the others are gone." Janna's whining protest comes to a standstill as the color drains from my face. My thin lips compress, disappearing completely.

With determined steps, I make a circuit of the room, chiding myself for not doing so earlier. Worry rises with each footfall as I pace. There are numerous incongruities. Using all my considerable tracking skills, I can find only two other impressions besides the ones for Janna, Emily, and myself. The winding, narrow staircase snaking around the edge of the room without so much as a guard rail marks this as the right time period, but something is greatly amiss.

"The others probably recovered faster than us; that's all." Schooling my expression, I try to ease the youngster's worry, though my own has shot through the roof. "Look over here, there's some platters with food, carafes of wine, and a pitcher of something warm."

"Then why did they leave us here," Janna's high-pitched voice nags, "just lying on the floor?"

The child's whining tone pricks my rising temper. "I told you, nothing's wrong."

"But they left Emily when she's so bad off."

My voice becomes calloused and hard. "I'll let you know when there's something to worry about."

Tears glisten in the teen's eyes. I expel a deep breath and shake my head. "While we wait for Emily to wake up, let's get something to eat."

With a barely perceptible nod, Janna squares her shoulders as she shores up her confidence. The girl takes a seat opposite me with her head high and back straight. Plucking a piece of fruit off the top, she bites without really seeing it. "Ooh, these are sweet."

The girl devourers the ripened delicacy before reaching for the piece of the dark loaf I cut for her. My fears continue to multiply as we spend the next couple of hours sampling the cuisine.

"It all tastes so weird." Giggling, Janna sips more of the spiced wine. "But in a good way."

I grunt then stand to stretch my back. I saunter over to my unconscious niece. With what little healing sight I can muster, I perform a more thorough examination to make sure the kid is still recuperating well. *Her vitals seem stable; her pulse is good.* I turn to Emily's sibling with sight still active. *She's drunk!*

"I told you to watch how much of that you drank."

"It's so good. It tastes a lot like the apple cider Mom made last—" Janna drops the cup on the table. Some of the contents slosh over the side. The depression plaguing the adolescent since her mother's death brings shadows back to the sunny disposition.

I've had all of this I can take. I reach out as if to comfort the girl while sending a tendril of power into the child. With lightning-quick reflexes embedded in my warrior woman form, I catch the collapsing adolescent. Placing the slumbering body beside her sister, where the imprint implies she materialized, I step back to consider the situation.

I retrace my earlier route, circling the room yet again. *Why are there only two other disturbances in the dust?* I examine the remains of a fractured emerald spread over one side of the room. *That gem was acting as a spell component. What the hell is going on here?*

The weight of the shield strapped to my back doesn't keep me from taking the stairs two at a time. A give a firm jerk of the metal handle. The door doesn't budge an inch. I begin to mutter, spitting each word from my mouth like a piece of liver.

"In this land where men reign,
An edge is needed in a female frame.
Triple their strength will lend to my fame."

I give a push from within. Tingling energy caresses my being as it streams from me. Light, the color of a summer sky, encompasses my form. An electric sensation seeps into my skin, settling into the bones. My head begins to pound. Expecting this, I use what is left of my somatic essence to relieve the migraine.

One calloused hand grasps the pommel of the sword strapped to my side. *This feels good—right. More natural than trying to take care of that whining brat.* The sound of ringing steel echoes into the circular chamber as I unsheathe the blade. "Open. . . this. . . door." Each word is punctuated by the sound of a metal pommel making contact with the very solid wooden door. "Or. . . I will. . . take it. . . from its. . . hinges!"

I relent, listening for any sound from the other side. Defining silence greets me. I begin again. Half an hour later, when frustration gives way to exhaustion, I resheathe the blade, breathing in gulps of air.

The stumbling footfalls sound loudly in my ears. I press my forehead to the wood. *No more sleeping pills; I'm out of healing energy.*

"Where are we?" Although pale, Emily appears unscathed by the transdimensional experience. "Did we make it to Cuthburan?"

"Why are you making so much noise?" A groggy Janna winces at the pain in her head as she is half-supported by her flaxen-haired sister.

"Yes, we're here. . ." I pivot about as the whoosh of the door swinging open behind me sings loudly into my ears.

"Aunt Becky!" My stiff arm cuts off Janna's mad dash. Emily, with uncharacteristic tenderness, helps her sister back to her feet.

"Reba?" My eyes narrow as I notice the blue in hers. *Our eyes are brown. . .*

"No, I'm Rhealyn, Reba's daughter." The woman smiles, but the light doesn't reach her eyes. "You must be my Aunt Lani, you and Mother are identical, except for the hair."

I understood her Cuthburish. Looks like the translation spell Ashley cast is still intact. "I'm Reba's twin, but here I'll be known as Anluanna." My lips curve as well, but inside anger seethes at the reception we've received. "Does my sister still reside in this city?" I gesture toward the girls. "We'd hoped to be reunited with her."

"She and Father are unavoidably detained. If you will follow me, I will show you to your rooms."

Lynn Hardy

Led by a series of dreams, encouraged by friends, Lynn Hardy began the journey to become an author. She stored her work in a computer file labeled "second job." Writing began as a passion she could not contain and has become much more than she ever expected.

Lynn has attended many science fiction conventions and has had the privilege of serving on panels about writing. Renaissance fairs are another favorite event for the author. Seeing others dressed in costume (as she always is during book signings) makes her feel right at home.

Lynn is now a stay-at-home mother of two. The road has been longer and more complicated than she would have ever guessed--not always smooth, but filled with wonderful surprises. Like most stories, Lynn is sure that her journey has only just begun.

"Each new book should take you to a brand new world – enjoy the journey."

Lynn Hardy

[i] "Strong Enough to Bend" as performed by Tanya Tucker
[ii] "I Will Always Love You" as performed by Whitney Houston
[iii] "The Star-Spangled Banner" written by Francis Scott Key
[iv] "Crazy" as preformed by Patsy Cline
[v] "A Boy Named Sue" as performed by Johnny Cash
[vi] "The Rose" as performed by Conway Twitty
[vii] "I'd Love to Lay You Down" as performed by Conway Twitty